ACROSS THE BRAZOS

BY

Ermal Walden Williamson

PRAISE FOR

ACROSS THE BRAZOS

by

Ermal Walden Williamson

"It is with great pleasure that I endorse Ermal Walden Williamson in the writing of this book, **Across the Brazos,** as a sequel to my book and screenplay, **The Cowboys.** As a man who shows that he knows a lot about the West, he gives authenticity to his story, and a credit to my book, **The Cowboys.**

I am pleased that he wrote this book. I think you will enjoy reading it. It's good. I should have written it myself1"
    ---William Dale Jennings, author of **The Cowboys.**

"**Across the Brazos** is the rare sequel, penned by another author who carries the blessing and support of the original author and maintains the character and dignity of the source novel ...

Across the Brazos follows Matt Anderson from a botched freight company robbery in Virginia City, Montana through post-civil war Texas and coming full circle to his roots on his family's ranch in Montana. Written with gusto, the story about greed and honor creates vivid characters and moves them with dispatch from adventure to adventure while painting a glorious picture of the Old West.

Fans of the Western novel won't be disappointed in this crackling story about a search for identity and personal honor, and should keep their eyes out for Mr. Williamson's next effort. He has taken Jennings' characters to another level and left this reviewer anxious to read more from this author."
    ---Doug Sanders, Wildest Westerns Magazine

"This book was written by a man who knows guns and the history of the Old West. **Across the Brazos** is an excellent mixture of the true West and the westerns of Zane Grey and Louis L'Amour."
    ---Judge Roy Bean, SASS #1

Across the Brazos

Copyright © 2022 by Ermal Walden Williamson

PB: ISBN: 978-1-63812-420-7
Ebook ISBN: 978-1-63812-421-4

All rights reserved. No part in this book may be produced and transmitted in any form or by any means, electronic, or mechanical, including photocopying, recording, or by any information storage and retrieval system, without permission in writing from the copyright owner.

The views expressed in this work are solely those of the author and do not necessarily reflect the views of the publisher hereby disclaims any responsibility for them. Published by Pen Culture Solutions 05/17/2022

Pen Culture Solutions
1-888-727-7204 (USA)
1-800-950-458 (Australia)
support@penculturesolutions.com

DEDICATED TO

William Dale Jennings, author of **The Cowboys** and to my wife Betty who has always shared my dreams

ACKNOWLEDGMENTS

Ever since I was a green horn in this wonderful world of entertainment, I have followed in the footsteps of my screen idol, John Wayne. Having grown up as a lad without a father, I had the Duke as my role model.

When I think about acknowledging people in the area of writing my novel, I really have to thank those who have supported me in my impersonation of John Wayne, because it is in the light of his giant shadow that this novel has come to be written.

Many thanks go to Pilar Wayne, John Wayne's widow for her acceptance and constant support of my role as a John Wayne impersonator, Hadley and Tulisha Wardlaw for sharing their Texas home with me while I was researching this novel, Barbara Teel for her thoroughness and excellence in editing, and Craig and Sandi Nelsen at Loveland Press for their guidance, support and effort in bringing this book to its final completion.

I would like to acknowledge my three wonderful kids who spent free time watching me perform on stage, who waited endless hours for me to come home from classes and rehearsals, and who supported me with their love; Liz, Bill and Daniel.

Last and most importantly, I want to acknowledge my wife, Betty, who has spent the better part of our lives supporting my career. May God bless her, and all the wonderful people who have richly been a blessing in my life.

Thank you.

PROLOGUE

THREE MEN - TWO GRAVES

Wil Andersen's last thoughts, as the rustlers beat him mercilessly with their fists and gun butts, were to protect his group of hired teenaged cowboys even though they only watched as if in pleasure. As he walked tall for the last time into the darkness, defying the lead rustler's commands to "halt!" his remorse for his failure was stolen by the wind.

As Wil lay dying, his mind raced back to his two sons, Matt and Lukas, and how he had failed them.

He was back at his Double-O Ranch in the northwestern section of America, 1858, the region which, six years later would become Montana Territory, south of the emigrant trail, near a small town just starting up called Alder Gulch so named for the alder tress lining the gulch.

His younger son Lukas was thin in face and long in body; yet not the height of his father. At twenty, he was determined to get away from his father and his ranch and strike out on his own. His determination was embedded deep in his soul. As a man, he would not be ruled by the strong hand of his father, nor would he die a broken rancher.

Matt was older by two years and had his father's good looks and height. He never crossed his father, no matter what. At the same time, he felt it was his duty and responsibility to see that Lukas learned the ways of an Andersen through and through.

The turning point came when Jeff Manning, a man of no morals, turned up at the Double-O Ranch looking for a job. He seemed to have no past, but he could ride, and proved himself an experienced ranch hand.

Wil Andersen took him on out of trust. It was one of the last times Wil would break his rules.

Wil's sons grew fond of Jeff Manning, his fancy stories about San Francisco, and his dreams of one day being wealthy enough to become a solid citizen of her streets.

At the time, however, he had no means of survival except for a sick horse and the clothes on his back.

Matt suited him up with clothes from his closet. Jeff was about the same size, and they fit him well.

Days turned into weeks, and Jeff seemed to fit in with the Andersens. He paid particular attention to Lukas who appeared enamored with the Bay stories.

Jeff fed Lukas' mind with dreams of grandeur and thoughts of leaving Montana. This could mean the easy way. Lukas envisioned a glamorous life as a wealthy man, and Jeff convinced him that to fulfill their dream, all they had to do was to rob a freight office in town.

"Freightin' is where the money is," Jeff told Lukas. "Big money and no one protectin' it. I know. I seen it when I rode through. A little bitty clerk is all there is in that freight office."

"What if we get caught?" Lukas asked.

"Hell, we get what we wants and clear out. We'd be gone before anyone knowed we were there."

There was only one freight office in the area. When rumors of gold in the Colorado Territory reached bordering territories, miners began working the rivers giving reason for freight companies to come in to supply miners and settlers. In most cases, the freight companies wound up making more money than the miners. They would pick up goods in Fort Benton on the Missouri and haul them down to the more populated regions of Bannack, Alder Gulch and the Ruby River.

It would take a hitch of eight mules or oxen coupled with three wagons to make the trek along the Whoop-Up Trail. The shipping charges were great for the haul, and miners and settlers paid with broken backs as they built sluices to mine the gold.

Jeff had been watching the freight company as it was starting up and figured the money being paid to the teller was worth more than the gold. He became obsessed with the idea of stealing it.

He picked a hot, dry day and was counting on most men being out of town working the sluices. Lukas and Matt were playing a few hands of poker at the Golden Eagle Saloon when Lukas finished his hand and folded. He uttered something about bad luck and left the table. He went outside and stood on the porch of the saloon and looked over at the freight office.

Matt remained inside finishing up the last deal. He figured his brother was itchin' to leave, so he would join him as soon as his hand was played.

The day was exceptionally hot for September in Montana, and this might have been what set Lukas off the most, because he was not thinking clearly the way his father had taught him. He spotted Jeff Manning leaning against a post in front of the freight office.

Jeff looked down the street and saw little activity. On one side a few people were walking in and out of stores and the saloon. On the other side was Townsend's freight office with its stables, wagons, and a small warehouse and office. When Jeff saw Lukas come out of the saloon, he made his move and went into the freight office. Once inside, he watched unnoticed until the last person left, then pulled his bandanna up over his nose and drew his .44. He pointed the barrel in the clerk's face and demanded the money.

When Lukas saw Jeff back out of the freight office, he untied his horse and Matt's and walked them across the street to meet Jeff.

Matt was coming out of the saloon when he saw Lukas across the street with their horses.

"Hey, brother," he yelled out, "where ya headed?"

Lukas ignored him as he nervously readied Matt's horse for Jeff to ride.

Jeff dashed out of the freight office with a saddlebag full of money and his pistol raised in the air. He whipped the saddlebag onto Matt's horse and started to climb into the saddle when Matt, realizing that a robbery was going on, ran up to him and pulled him down.

Jeff's gun discharged, sending a bullet through the plate glass window of McDougle's store across the street.

Reverend George Riordan, a middle-aged preacher, was driving his horse and buggy to visit a parishioner when the shots frightened his horse, which reared up and fell back onto the buggy.

Jeff's pistol repeated and a bullet tore through the preacher's back. Riordan's body slumped in the seat of his buggy as the horse frantically attempted to free itself from its harness.

The freight clerk threw open his door and yelled, "I've been robbed!" Seeing Jeff, he slammed the door and dropped to the floor.

Jeff fired at the clerk, hit the door and smashed it. The clerk froze in his prone position, feeling the echo of the gunshots like great blasts from howitzers.

What Jeff had not considered was that the temporary sheriff, Samuel "Whitey" Wiseman, in town with his ranch hand, Freddie Fenton, was buying supplies at McDougle's store.

The sheriff ran out of the store with his ranchhand when they heard the shots. It took the two men a few seconds to understand that a robbery was taking place. The sheriff's large voice boomed across the street. "Hold it, you men there! I'm the sheriff!" He quickly drew his revolver from its holster and aimed it at a stunned Lukas.

Freddie stepped to Whitey's side and aimed his shotgun at the confusion of horses and men.

Jeff climbed back onto Matt's horse and spurred him into a fast out of control gallop towards Whitey and his deputy. Jeff fired his .44 wildly at the two men but missed.

Freddie fired at short range, scattering shotgun pellets at the masked robber. Jeff's body fell backwards off the horse, and landed on the sidewalk at Whitey's feet.

Because he was Matt's size and wearing Matt's clothes, Whitey quickly identified the dead robber as Matt Andersen.

Lukas was back in the stirrups and mounted when another shot rang out from across the street. The sheriff shot him in the shoulder, jerking him off his horse and onto the ground. His horse careened into the preacher's buggy.

Matt quickly ran to Lukas' side, hidden from the sheriff's view by the buggy and Reverend Riordan's horse trying to free itself. Realizing that shots were ringing dirt all around him, he yelled, "In the saddle, Lukas!"

Matt picked Lukas up and put him on his horse, slapping the horse's backside to get him moving. Dodging bullets, Matt tried to climb into the saddle behind him, but the horse was already galloping. Matt's body fell against the preacher in the buggy. The preacher's glazed eyes were open, as if staring at death. Matt slid off the buggy out of fear and rolled under the walkway.

Other men came running out at the end of town. Halfway down the street, Lukas was met by a hail of bullets, bringing him and his horse hard to the ground. His head smashed against the roadway, shattering his cheeks. He lay motionless. All eyes were fixed on Lukas, which gave Matt a chance to further his own escape. His mind was filled with fright, but at the same time, remorse, for having seen his brother gunned down.

Matt rolled further under the walkway as people began to gather around Lukas. He looked out towards his brother and saw his still body.

A man with a shotgun in his hand stooped over Lukas to examine him. He motioned with his hand that Lukas was dead.

Some of the men assisted in freeing the horse from its entanglement while others went to the preacher. Frontier folk had seen enough death to know that he had joined his Maker.

Reverend Riordan was one of the most well-liked people in town and great consternation filled the minds of the crowd. He had just come to town to build the town's first church. Who would shoot a man of the cloth in the back?

Matt's horse was quickly captured and the money removed from the saddle. Several armed men stood over Lukas' still warm body and that of Jeff Manning. The shotgun blast had smashed the robber's face beyond recognition. Without a face, they all assumed it was Matt.

The people were certain that only two men were involved: Matt and Lukas Andersen, all except the town drunk, Zeb, who had seen a third man trying to escape.

Sheriff Wiseman identified the dead outlaw as Matt without hesitation.

His ranch hand, Freddie, who shot the robber agreed. He only had time to aim and fire his shotgun. In the chaos, the victim's face was a blur.

Jeff was an outsider; a man who had never been seen in town, but who had become friends with Lukas several weeks earlier when he sought employment at the Double-O Ranch. No one had known him.

Amidst the noise and confusion, Matt rolled out from under the sidewalk and, under cover of shadows, climbed the back steps of a vacant office up onto a roof. Sliding himself across the roof of the building, he lay still among a stack of wood pilings to stay out of sight. His ears could discern only a few words at a time, but he knew Lukas and Jeff were dead. He also heard a discussion about a missing robber. Apparently, no one actually saw him between the two horses, or if they had, he was thought to be another rancher trying to capture the robbers in all of the confusion. Several ranchers had shot at the men, as had the sheriff and Freddie.

Matt heard, "I tell you, I saw a third person."

"Hell, Zeb, what you saw was the Reverend Riordan. He musta tried to stop to help and was shot in the back." Whitey attempted to give the preacher a hero's send-off for dying in the streets the way he did.

Several women were hysterical, which only added to the commotion.

The clerk explained that only one man had come into his freight office.

Jim McDougle, the owner of the general store, said, "I almost got kilt. My window shattered and I ducked under the counter. My poor wife was in back, thank God. And thank God the sheriff came in to do his shopping today."

Another witness pointed to Jeff's body. "I saw that one there riding towards the sheriff and get blasted right off his horse. Never saw anything like it before."

"Just two of them," a woman sobbed. "Both young men."

The sheriff said, "One man had the money. The other was riding away. I saw two men, Freddie. What say you?" he asked while examining the retrieved money.

The ashen-faced Freddie, feeling sick to his stomach, said, "Hell, I was too damned scared, to tell you the truth, sir. I thought we were gonna get killed. And . . . and I fired with my eyes closed. I didn't know then, but when he fell from his horse, I saw . . . I suppose I had hit him right in his face. It was awful."

A man in black wearing a tall hat moved quickly through the crowd to examine the bodies. One of the ranchers pointed them out to him. "You'll find the preacher in the buggy. One man out there in the middle of the street. Another on the steps of the saloon."

"Fittin'," said another man.

The sheriff commanded, "Abel, you take a couple men and search the buildings south, while Freddie takes a couple of you up the street that-a-way. Just in case Zeb here is not drunk and there is a third man."

"Who were they, Sheriff?" came the cry from one of the women, brave enough to stand close to the scene.

"That one in the street is Lukas Andersen. Saw him in town with his brother Matt earlier. The one messing up the porch is Matt. If there's a third one, I don't know."

A rancher spoke up against the two dead men. "Two rowdy and no good young men. Wil thought he was bringin' them up right."

The sheriff agreed, saying, "Wil never spared the rod bringin' them up. Matt seemed to be levelheaded. Lukas, on the other hand, was wild most of the time."

A Swedish gambler by the name of Jan Olafsen sat alone at his table in the Golden Eagle Saloon, remaining quiet. He shuffled the cards in his hands over and over. He'd had a good glimpse of Matt and knew he was not involved in the shooting. But he said nothing, and no one paid a mind to ask him.

Anse Petersen was the saloon's bartender and Wil's best friend. Having known Wil for many years, he'd watched the wild antics of Matt and Lukas as they grew up and visited the saloon with Wil on occasion.

Anse had been tending bar when they were playing poker with Jan. If anyone had seen a third man, outside of Jan, he would have. His presence was large as he stood tall on the steps of the saloon watching the crowd in the street.

The sheriff's eyes caught him standing there and asked, "Anse, you see a third man?"

"No sir, Sheriff. Matt and Lukas were playing poker with this gentleman." He pointed to Jan who had come outside and stood beside him. "That's all."

Jan's mind recreated the scene that took place just before the robbery. He remembered asking for a drink, and Anse excusing himself as he went into the back room for more supplies. The two brothers had already been in the street when Anse returned.

The sheriff asked again, "You sure now, Anse?"

"Sure as rain. They were in here playing poker. Guess they quit and walked across the street. I jest came back inside from gettin' a drink for this gambler." He referred to Jan. "Only gone a minute. But there was no third man. I swear to it."

Noticing Jan's ostensible complacency toward the killings, the sheriff walked over to him and asked, "How about you. You see a third man?"

"I was playing cards with two men," knowing the Jeff's body was not Matt's, he had no intention of muddying up what seemed to be a simple case of mistaken identity. "Apparently," he continued, "they are now dead."

Again, the sheriff asked, "Did you see a third man?"

"No, sir." He had not but knew that a third man did exist, and that he was lying dead on the sidewalk.

Whitey was satisfied with his answer. He figured there was no reason for him to lie.

The sheriff ordered with his loud and husky voice, "Alright, folks, clear out. Unless you know something about a third man, I suggest you go home or back to your stores. If there is a third person involved, we'll find him. I promise you that."

Under his breath, he said, "Zeb, you shoulda been locked up. You're makin' my job too damn hard."

The gambler remained silent about the incident, not telling anyone what he actually saw. He had been in town just a few weeks and made some money. He figured he wasn't about to lose it by getting involved in something that belonged to the town and was none of his business.

One of the men searching the buildings climbed up the back of the building where Matt was hiding. He raised himself level with the roof and searched the area with his eyes but failed to notice Matt behind the wood pilings. Scared and shaking, the man left and went back down to search other buildings. His fear kept him from looking deeper in the shadows where he would have found Matt.

Whitey handed over the money to the freight office clerk while Freddie and others draped the "brothers" across their horses. After a meal, and while waiting for the final report from the searching parties, the sheriff anticipated a trip to the Double-O Ranch. "Two horses, two men. Freddie, that the way you see it?"

"Yes, sir."

"Anyone sure of a third person? Anyone?"

The searchers remained silent.

"Well, he ain't in town, and no one's left town, else we'd a seen him. Not that big of a town."

"I'll be takin' them back to the Double-O." Looking over to Freddie, he said, "Take care of the mess. I'll be back."

Anse yelled over, "I'll ride with ya."

He climbed on his horse and sidled next to Whitey. They rode out of town towards the Double-O.

Matt waited until he felt reasonably safe before climbing down from the roof. It was a long walk home, and the sun was down by the time he reached the ranch. Matt hid among the trees when he saw Sheriff Whitey and Anse riding toward him. He waited there an hour until he saw the sheriff ride out alone toward town.

Once home, Matt slipped into the brush outside, waiting to find out what was happening before he made a move toward the house.

Anse spotted him from his window and quickly walked out of the bunkhouse to meet him.

He came up behind Matt, putting a hand on his shoulder, which felt like lead to Matt. Matt turned around with his pistol cocked, aimed at him. Quivering, he whispered, "Anse! Thank God." Matt uncocked his pistol and holstered it.

Anse put his hand over Matt's mouth and shushed him. Any little sound could be heard on a quiet night. When Anse was sure no one heard them, he motioned Matt to come to his room, which was part of the bunkhouse made into a guest room especially for Anse. He had become part of the family and from time to time would visit the ranch, bringing Wil up to date with things happening in town.

Once inside, Matt stayed low to the floor and Anse turned the lantern's wick down, but not so low as to alert anyone. Anse spoke in a quiet voice as he set himself in his rocking chair for a view out the window. "Son, you're s'posed to be dead."

Matt wiped the perspiration from his forehead and swallowed hard. "Anse, what happened? What the hell happened?"

Anse poured a glass of whiskey and handed it to Matt. He poured one for himself. "Drink up, boy. I'll have one, too."

The two were alert to the sounds around them. Wil Andersen came out of the house and stood on the porch looking out at the hillside. He was hatless. Two horses stood tied to the rail just outside the house, Matt and Lukas', relieved of their owners' bodies.

It was a hot night. Wil spoke haltingly to his wife Annie through the open window behind him while his gaze was on the hillside. "I'll bury them in the mornin'. . . with two crosses. And I'll put a fence around the plot."

Anse looked at Matt as he sat with his eyes opened wide and watched the sweat beading across his brow. He whispered, "They think you and Lukas were killed trying to rob the freight office in town. And if you're here, then who the hell is in the living room?"

Matt answered slowly and softly, "My brother and that rotten son of a bitch, Jeff Manning. If they didn't kill him, I would have."

Anse was stunned. "His body looked like your'ns. His face was messed up somethin' awful. I think even your folks figured it was you."

Matt looked up at Anse and reasoned, "Two men, and our horses. 'Spec so. Lukas and I went into town for a game of cards and a drink. He left for a minute, and I played out my hand with this gambler fella. By the time I finished my drink and got outside, that bastard was comin' out of the freight office. And Lukas was takin' our horses to meet him." Matt paused and downed his drink. "He never told me anything about their plans."

"I suspected it was Jeff's body 'cause of his gunbelt," Anse said. "That weren't yours o the other fella. Didn't want to say nothin' at the time. Didn't know fer sure."

Anse watched Wil as he stepped off the porch and began walking toward the bunkhouse. Getting out of his rocking chair, Anse said to

Matt, "Stay here. Don't move," and left the room with the bottle of whiskey.

Anse stopped Wil just on the other side of his bunkhouse and said, "Been drinkin'. Want one, Wil?"

Wil took the bottle, drained it dry, and flung it as far as he could across the moonlit roadway.

The sound of the bottle breaking sent a chill up Matt's back. He wondered what his pa was thinking and how he could ease his pa's mind.

With his eyes narrowed, Wil gritted his teeth and looked at his friend, Anse. "Matt is out there somewhere, Anse."

Anse's jaw dropped as he watched Wil gaze out into the night air. Wide-eyed and startled, Anse listened for the next thing Wil said..

"You know that ain't Matt, Anse. Hell, I saw it in your eyes, as well as Annie's." He paused for a breather, took a chew of tobacco out of his pocket and broke off a piece with his teeth. "Sheriff Whitey knowed it, too. But he's keepin' quiet about it. Least while until we know what happened."

"What makes ya know that, Wil?"

"I know my son's body. One's Lukas. The other is that bastard, Jeff. That's his gunbelt, not Matt's. And Matt wore a leather bracelet on his wrist, the one I gave him on the day he became a man. And Matt never had a birthmark. That bastard has one on his arm." He paused for a moment, looked out into the darkness and continued, "He's out there."

"If you're right as rain, boss, whatcha aimin' ta do?"

"Damn right, I'm right as rain." He paused and fought back a tear. "Can't do nothin'. Yet. Matt's an Andersen. He'll be back."

"What if he don't?"

"He'll be back. If he's alive, he'll be back."

"Whatcha reckon happened out there, Wil?"

"Not for certain, but I know this much. Soon as somebody finds that extra horse in town, they're gonna put two and two together and be right back here. That you can bet on."

"Jeff's?"

"He had one. Broken-down mare, but rideable."

"No, sir."

"What d'ya mean, 'no, sir'?"

"Had to shoot her."

"When?"

"Yesterday. Ridin' out here from town, I caught Jeff walkin' in. His horse had stepped in a gopher hole and broke her leg. He couldn't kill her, so I did."

"Well, how'd they figure to get away on one horse?"

"Guess they figured to take Matt's horse and leave Matt in town." No sooner had the words got out of his mouth than he realized he was spilling the beans.

"What? Come around agin."

"I mean. Hell, Wil, I don't know what I meant."

"Dammit, Anse. You know something you're not tellin' me. What is it?"

Matt stepped out on the porch but stayed in the shadows. "He meant that I wasn't in on it, Pa."

"Matt? That you?"

"Yes, sir. And I didn't do nothin' either, Pa."

Matt approached Wil slowly and cautiously, fearing his pa's full anger. Unfortunately, he was not cautious enough, for Wil connected a fist hard to Matt's jaw, sending him tumbling backwards.

Matt picked himself up and stepped backwards away from his pa.

Anse stepped in, "Wil, go easy on the boy."

Wil stood straight and looked at Matt. "Come here. Let me get a good look at ya."

"Jeff planned it, Pa. He caused Lukas to side in with him. Don't know why or how. Alls I know is, it was them two and I couldn't stop 'em." He took in a deep breath as he whimpered. "Lukas is dead, Pa."

"Then the other body is Jeff's," Wil said emphatically. "That son of a bitch."

"Yes, sir."

Anse asked, "What now, Wil?"

"Gotta figure this damn thing out. Annie knows it's not Matt, too. I'm sure of it. Thank God she didn't say anything to Whitey, 'cause he said there was mention of a third man. I'm thinkin' he too 'spects Matt is still alive."

Grabbing Matt's arm tight, Wil said, "If word gets back that you're alive, he'll have to arrest you. And seein' how our preacher was killed in the robbery, the townsfolk ain't gonna be easy convincin' otherwise."

"Ma's gotta know that I'm okay, Pa. She's already suffered enough."

"Hold on, Matt. Maybe your pa's right."

"Damn! This is one time I'd give my ranch and everything I own, just to be wrong," Wil said. "Lukas was one hell of a son. Stubborn, but had a lot of good in him. And you say you didn't know nothin' goin' on? Hell. You musta knowed Jeff was in town and up to no good."

Once again Matt felt the pain of Wil's fist as it connected across his face, causing blood to spatter from his nose. His body hit the ground with full force, knocking the wind out of him. Lying on the ground, Matt turned over and said, "Pa, it ain't fair. I ain't done nothin' to cause you to hit me. I tried to protect my brother."

"You didn't try hard enough, damn it," Wil snapped back with his fist still clinched. "If you had, Lukas would still be alive."

Anse broke in, saying, "Hold on, Wil. It wasn't Matt's fault." He knelt down and wiped the blood from Matt's cut face.

Matt's voice showed pain, but he refused to whimper. "We were playin' poker. Both me and Lukas. Lukas lost and left the game. I stayed for one more hand, Pa. One hand. When I stepped out into the street, Lukas had both our horses and was headed across the street. When I went over to him, Jeff was comin' out of the freight office. Then is when I knew what was happenin'." Matt rose and finished wiping the blood from his nose and mouth. "I knocked Jeff away from my horse. But when I tried to get Lukas out of there, he was shot. And, Pa, there were shots ringin' out all over the place. And horses rearin', and people shoutin', and next thing I knew, I was rollin' under the sidewalk to escape."

"That's when someone thought they saw you?" Anse asked.

"They musta seen me, but the preacher was shot, and in all the confusion, I escaped."

"That's just the way Whitey told it, too." Wil said. "He kept it quiet about the third man. I'm a thinkin' he knowed it was you."

Matt rose and staggered over to Wil. "We got no right keepin' my bein' alive from Ma. None! Lukas was my responsibility, but I swear to God, I didn't know he was gonna rob anyone." His eyes swollen and red with tears, he fell at Wil's feet. "I gotta see Ma. It ain't fair, Pa."

Holding him, Wil said, "Wrong, son. Sometimes right don't seem right at all. Kinda feels like this is one of those times."

The door to the house opened wide, letting the light spill out into the roadway. Annie's figure could be seen as she came out on the porch. She had been crying and called out, "Wil?"

Wil's strong arms wrapped around Matt as he attempted to run to his ma. The darkness hid their bodies from Annie's view. He called back, "I'm out here thinkin'."

"Want me to join ya?"

"No, Annie. I'll be in d'rectly."

Turning back to Matt, Wil whispered, "What good would it do now, son?"

Annie turned and went back into the house, letting the light disappear back inside.

Wil kept ahold of Matt's arms.

Gritting his teeth, Matt said softly, "I gotta see her, Pa. I gotta."

"You let your ma see ya son, and she'll try to protect ya. She'll never let ya go. And ya can't stay here without no one knowin'. When Whitey comes by, he'll arrest ya. And knowin' the men like I do, they'll form a vigilante and hang ya. For sure, they'll hang ya."

Wil looked at his son, who was holding his head with his hands and sobbing, and realized he was taking a reason for living away from him. It went directly against Wil's own teaching. Loosening his grip on Matt, he said, "Damn it, son. Do what you have to."

Matt stood erect and looked over to the house. He could make out Annie's shadow through the window as she moved about. He moved closer to the house.

Wil and Anse stood motionless.

Matt continued walking toward the house until he came to the steps and stopped.

The wind seemed to stand still. No sound in the fields could be heard. Annie's silhouetted figure in the window sat down in her chair and began to rock.

Matt planted his boot on the first step to the porch. Quietly, he turned around and looked at his pa and Anse. He sensed his pa was right. He reasoned that if he walked in, his ma would do everything she could to protect him. She wouldn't be able to let him go.

If he stayed, he would ultimately become a prisoner on his own ranch. Eventually, he'd be caught. By leaving and starting a new life elsewhere under another name, he could possibly redeem his real name and that of his family, someday.

As he turned away from the house and started walking back toward his pa and Anse, the door opened again, and Annie stepped out into the darkness.

"Matt? Is that you, son?"

Matt turned quickly, meeting her open arms as she moved towards him. The embrace of his ma melted his resentment of his pa's fists.

Wil watched in silence as the wind whistled through the pines and carried its tune to the dark clouds that covered a new moon.

She said, "I knowed it was you out here."

Wil asked, "And the boy inside with Lukas?"

"I knowed it was that Jeff boy."

Silence fell upon her lips for a few moments as she gathered her thoughts. "You hurt any, son?"

"No, Ma."

"Your brother?"

Breaking from the embrace, he said, "I tried to stop him, Ma. I couldn't."

Anse said, "He's tellin' the truth, ma'am. What I saw of it, there was too much shootin'. And the good Lord jest saved his life."

She grabbed a hold of Matt's hand and reeled him back to her side. Looking into Matt's eyes, she asked Wil without moving, "What's to be done, now, Wil?"

"If he stays here, he's a dead man."

Annie drew in a deep breath.

"As it is right now," Wil continued, "Whitey has convinced the townsfolk that it's all over. If they learn Matt's alive and was in town during the holdup, they'll lynch him."

She looked at Anse for a response.

"Yes, ma'am. They were fierce mad when we left. The preacher was shot in the back. That's all the reason for them to hang anybody."

"They can't!" Annie retorted loudly. "They jest can't!"

Wil attempted to console Annie by holding her hand. "I told Matt he'd have to leave. For awhile. 'Til everything settles down. Then, maybe when all of this is forgotten and done away with, he can come home."

"When? My son's not a criminal. He has nowhere to go, Wil."

Matt walked away from them and gazed up into the dark sky. Dropping his head, he said, "If I go, I could never come back."

Annie looked at Wil and waited for a reply.

Wil kept silent.

Matt turned, walked back, and said, "I love ya, Ma."

She knew he had made his decision to leave.

Matt walked into the house for a last look at his brother's body laid out on the floor. The others followed him in. He knelt down and touched his brother's uncovered hand and asked, "Can I help bury my brother?"

Anse answered him. "Best not, Matt. Sooner you leave, no one will know."

Wil concurred, "He's right, son."

His mother sobbed.

Anse said, "Wish I hadn't shot that horse, now."

Wil asked, "Where's the carcass?"

"I pulled it off to the side and partially buried it with some weeds. Jeff said he'd finish it. Guess he never did."

"Damn. Can't take a chance. At light, backtrack, and make sure it's buried deep."

"Yes, sir."

"And you, son . . . you're gonna head out south."

Matt stood up and felt Annie's warm embrace again.

Annie looked over her son's shoulder towards Wil, and asked, "Are you sure he has to leave, Wil?"

Wil put one hand on Matt's shoulder and wrapped his other arm around Annie. "I love ya, Matt. That mean anythin' to you?" He turned towards Annie. "One son's dead. I don't want both my sons killed."

Annie watched in loving-kindness as tears fell from her cheeks.

Matt's tired body finally felt the pangs of weariness from running scared, the drink, and the beating from Wil's fists. Still sobbing, he collapsed in the arms of his pa as Anse kept him from falling.

Anse helped Wil carry Matt to the back of the house and lay him down on the bed where the night caressed him into a deep sleep.

Wil lingered over him awhile to ensure his safety before he left to return to Annie's arms. But sleep didn't come to either of them.

Anse sat on the porch and watched out into the night.

Daylight was slow to come to the ranch that day, but before she had peeked her head over the nearest rise, Wil was on the hill digging the graves.

Matt and Anse rode down the road that led to town as the sun had just broken the sheet of night.

Annie's fine figure of a woman clad in a plain housedress climbed the hill to join Wil. Looking out, she watched the shadowy figures of Matt and Anse ride away.

"He'll be back. Soon, Annie."

"I know." Annie looked at Wil, both sharing a moment of loneliness for the first time in their lives together. They were burying one son and watching another ride away.

"The cowhands shoulda gotten up by now. They can help you."

"I'd rather do it myself, Annie."

Annie stood there looking at Matt and Anse as they disappeared down the road. Wil stopped digging, grabbed her hand, and held it tight as they watched the two men ride away.

A tough rancher, Wil bred and raised cattle and horses and earned a decent living. His desire was for his sons to follow suit. He now felt that he had somehow failed his sons.

Annie never heard or saw Wil complain. Likewise, she was never one to complain, either.

The first of the wranglers crawled out of the bunkhouse. Seeing Wil and Annie on the hillside, they joined them. They had heard about the shooting the evening before while helping to bring the bodies into the front room, not aware of Matt's return or of his having left. They believed that the two bodies were those of Matt and Lukas.

Now, they drove the draped bodies in a buggy to the northern slope of the hill. The men helped with the digging, in spite of Wil's resistance. Once the holes were dug deep enough, the men gently lowered the bodies, one at a time, then returned to the bunkhouse to leave Wil and Annie alone.

Wil's mind wandered from the hillside as he thought about what had really happened with Matt. He thought, it's Sheriff Whitey's word against the town. They were shooting at Matt, too. If we tell the townsfolk it was Matt, they'd lynch him. This way, two graves. Two crosses. Matt and Lukas. No one will know the better. He paused on the hillside and looked down the road one last time. "He tried to stop Lukas. That's good enough for me."

With the last clump of dirt on the graves, he whispered to himself. "I wish he could have stayed." Then with an unconscious utterance, he cried loudly, "Hell!" and threw the shovel as far as he could.

Annie grasped Wil's hand and squeezed hard. She shared that strange look in his eyes, and cried inside with him, as a wife and a mother would at this moment of grieving. Then she asked, "Ready, Wil?"

Wil came back in his mind to this part of the ceremony. "Yeah." Taking off his hat, and bowing his head, he said slowly, "Lord, bless our children. And forgive them their deeds. Both are in your hands. Amen."

Annie knew what he meant by saying, "Both are in your hands." One son was at rest in the grave, and the other was riding away. Both sons were in God's hands.

Wil looked over at the house where Jebediah the cook was beginning to build his fire. Jebediah was an elderly man who was too old to sit a saddle, too skinny to be accused of eating too much of his own cooking, and too ugly to run away to a better job.

The couple walked down the hill to join him for a cup of coffee.

"Thought you'd be needin' sumthin', boss," Jebediah said. "Use a cup of coffee, ma'am?"

"Thanks, Jebediah," replied Annie, as she accepted the cup.

Wil looked back at the hill and at Annie by his side, then softly said, "They'll always be with us, Annie. Sharing a cup of coffee in the morning. We'll still see them ridin' the range. They'll always be with us."

Annie leaned against Wil's body, wiping her face with her apron, and looked into the sunlight. She said as only a mother could say, "I know that, Wil." She cried and wiped her tears with her handkerchief.

Wil caressed her gently for encouragement, "You can bet on it." Then he looked again at the hill where the two crosses stood, and thought, "If there was only another way."

Wil's memories drained as pain brought him back to the present. The young cowboys watched in agony as Wil's bloody hands gripped the sod one last time. The sound of the rustlers' horses riding away gave them a moment of relief and they ran to Wil's side. He heard his name called out by one of his young cowboys, "Mr. Andersen! Don't die on us."

Wil released the sod and felt his life leave his body.

PART ONE

TEXAS

CHAPTER 1

COWBOYS TO WACO, TEXAS

The Waco and Northwestern train eased to a stop at its destination, Waco, Texas, and three good-looking cowboys dressed in chaps got off.

Charlie Honeycutt, tall and gaunt, with auburn hair, was twenty and known as "Slim." Because of his age and height, he assumed the leadership role of the trio of cowboys. Attributing to this, also, was his patience in paying particular attention to things that were happening around him, which kind of made him a polite sort of person.

Dan Wrisley, once known as "Four Eyes" because he wore a pair of family heirloom glasses at an early age, was a few months younger than Slim. He lost those glasses when a rustler named Long Hair took and broke them. Dan carried a guitar, which he played expertly, and every once in awhile, when things were quiet, he would bring it out and play a tune.

At nineteen, Homer Bickerdyke was the youngest of the three. He was called "Shorty" because of his height, but he had broad shoulders and knew how to take care of himself.

The sun was just past high noon, and the day was unusually warm for three cowboys from Montana this time of year, summer, 1874. Looking around, they caught sight of the livery stable and ambled over to rent some horses. After they picked them out, they saddled up and rode into town.

Their hungry stomachs demanded they find a place to eat. Coming across a small restaurant, they tied up their horses, walked into the empty restaurant, and settled down at a gingham-covered table for a meal, and ate like three hungry wolves devouring a prairie dog. They cleaned up their plates with swabs of biscuits.

As the waitress picked up their plates, Dan asked, "Know of a Matthew Jorgensen in these parts, ma'am?"

Stopping for a moment with dishes in her hands, she replied that he was working the spread across the river. "I think he's the foreman or ramrod. Something or the other."

"We're from out of town, ma'am," Dan continued. "How do we get there?"

She put the dishes down on an empty table and pushed a ringlet of hair from her eyes, looking at the men in a flirtatious sort of way. "Gonna join 'im?"

Slim answered, "No, ma'am. Just need to talk."

"Wouldn't be staying?" She threw a look back at Dan as she picked up the dishes. She paused for a moment, then said, "No, guess not." She gave them directions and pointed out the window with her long fingers. "End of the road, there's a fork. The road to the left leads to the Brazos River. There's a bridge. Cross it, and follow the river. You'll find it." She disappeared into the kitchen, her voice trailing after her. "Or they'll find you."

"Well, let's go," Dan said, getting up from his chair.

Slim tossed a couple of golden eagles on the table and called out to her, "Gotta stop by the rangers' office."

She returned and picked up the eagles with a smile and said to Dan, "Few doors down on opposite side of the street. What's your hurry?"

Dan stopped and stared, but Slim and Shorty took him by his arms and dragged him out the door. Not too far down the street they found the rangers' office. The cowboys turned into the doorway and found two rangers and the captain behind his desk.

Captain Ralph Johnson was a gentle-looking man in his sixties and had a salt-and-peppered mustache. He was a little overweight for a man under six feet tall, but that was evidence of his wife Maggie's good cooking. He was reading the *Waco Gazette*.

Slim spoke for the three cowboys. "We're from the Double-O Ranch in Montana. Is any of you Capt'n Johnson?"

Captain Johnson answered, "You must be the three cowboys I heard about. Been waiting for you. Suspected it was you up at the stable. See you got some horses." He looked the three over and waited for someone to speak, but no one did. "Welcome to Waco, Texas. Just got in on the noon train, I take it? Well, come around and have some Texas-style coffee. It's free."

Dan spoke up, "No thanks, Capt'n."

Shorty took off his hat and sat down. "We want to get some riding hours in before the sun goes down."

The captain grinned and poured himself coffee. "Well, sit for a spell. At least you can stay a little while. Texas hospitality, you know." He sat back down himself.

The two rangers introduced themselves as Tom Elliott and Floyd Douglas. The former was at least six foot tall, trim, and in his mid-twenties. Douglas was shorter and a little older. He was rubbing down a rifle barrel with an oil-slick cloth.

The three cowboys examined the interior of the rangers' quarters with their eyes. Rifles and shotguns decorated a wall cabinet and pictures of numerous rangers hung on the wall. A flag of the Lone Star State covered most of the back wall and a sign, "Texas Rangers," hung just above it. A flagpole with the American flag stood to the right.

Slim spoke again, "Thanks, Capt'n. But we gotta get to this Brazos River Bar M Ranch where Matt Jorgensen is staying."

The younger Ranger Elliott answered, "The Brazos River Bar M Ranch? You fellas friends of Matt?"

Dan looked puzzled at the way the deputy addressed them. "No. Never met him. We just got a message to deliver to him, s'all." He smiled and looked over at the Texas flag. "Big flag. How come ya got only one star in it?"

Ranger Douglas replied, "Texas is the Lone Star State. We're now the twenty-eighth state of these here United States, and we be bigger than all you put together."

The captain smiled and looking at Slim, asked, "Why didn't ya just wire him or send a letter? Must be fire awful important to travel all this way to deliver a message."

Shorty answered, "He needs to come home, Capt'n. We tried the mail route, and we didn't hear from him. So we came to help him make up his mind."

Ranger Elliott set his tin cup down and looked at the three. "Matt Jorgensen? You really after Matt to take him back to Montana?" He let out a loud "heehaw," and continued, "If that don't get all."

Ranger Douglas stopped wiping the barrel and set his rifle down. "Doubt if he'll go with ya."

Slim looked Douglas sternly in the eye to show the seriousness of his question. "Why'd ya say that?"

Elliott laughed and said, "Matt? He's a hired gun. No one's gonna force him to do nothin' he don't wanna do."

The captain looked the boys over and continued, "You came all the way from Montana for Matt Jorgensen? The letter you sent me said his mother was dying."

Slim acknowledged by nodding his head.

"That's downright noble of you," said the captain.

Slim responded, eyeing the two rangers, "Thank you, sir."

Dan began to explain, "You see, his old man was killed up north on a drive. Me, Slim, Shorty, and some other cowboys were along as drovers. That was five years ago." He stopped when he noticed a note of disinterest in the eyes of the rangers. "Matt's ma ain't gonna last much longer."

Captain Johnson sat back down and began to analyze what the cowboys were saying. "How old are you, son? The three of you can't be more than twenty-two, twenty-three tops."

Shorty replied, "I'm almost twenty, sir."

Slim explained, "Shorty is nineteen, and Dan and I are two years older. In Montana, age don't count when a rancher has to get his herd to market and has no cowboys. Matt's pa took us out of school and made us cowboys for the drive. That's when he was killed."

Captain Johnson apologized for sizing them up wrongly because of their ages. "I drove cattle when I was fifteen. Know the feeling. Texas ain't no different." He got up and began to talk gentler. "Matt's been working for the Brazos River Bar M Ranch for a dozen years or more. That's a long time. Never figured him to be an outsider."

Slim answered, "Matt's dad and him, seem they had a disliking when Matt was young, and Matt left home. He probably thought Matt was dead, killed somewhere. Never heard from him."

The captain took a pipe off his desk, filled it with tobacco, and lit it. "He's never contacted anyone?"

Slim wirled on his feet and flicked at the hammer of his holstered gun as if getting a little irritated. The captain sensed his nervousness and eased up. "All right, none of my business, I suppose. Unless, of course, he's wanted by the law someplace."

Dan stepped in and answered directly, "He's wanted by us. That's it, plain and simple."

The captain smiled at Dan, puffed on his pipe and began talking to him as a man. "Dan? That your name?" Dan nodded, and the captain continued. "You're twenty-one years old. This Matt fella has ten or fifteen years on you and fast with the gun. How do you plan on getting him back to Montana if'n he don't want to go?"

Slim answered, "We won't push him, Capt'n. Matt's ma said she'd stay alive 'til Matt came home. The ranch is a needin' him. If he won't come back with us after we talk with him, then we'll jest leave and go home."

Ranger Elliott replied, "I'd go, if'n it was me. Don't care what. But I've never been out of Texas."

Ranger Douglas paused for a moment, then said, "No, that don't peel potatoes with me. You come all this way to ask him to go back to Montana and if he don't go, you just up and go back home. Gotta be more to it. I mean, what's in it for you?"

Slim stood up tall and looked out the window for a moment while the room grew quiet. He looked over at Floyd and then at the captain. He began to speak slowly and distinctly. "Matt is the only heir to the ranch. When his ma dies, it's goin' into probate, or somethin', and the state takes over. Us cowboys will be lookin' for jobs elsewhere. No big deal. We can handle it. But we have a ranch that has become more'n a job to us and we'd like to keep it."

The captain, looking more interested, asked, "Wouldn't she have willed it to you for that purpose?"

Shorty said quickly, "No. She put a condition in the will that only Matt gets the ranch. The condition is simple: we bring Matt home or the ranch goes to the state. We get nothing."

Ranger Douglas let out a slow whistle.

The captain stood. "Does that mean Matt has to take over the ranch and become a rancher?"

"All the way," Slim said, "or nothin' at all."

The captain smiled. "Boys, you might just as well take the train back in the morning 'cause there's no way in hell Matt is going to become a rancher."

Dan looked at the captain quizzically. "Why'd ya say that?"

The captain grinned. "Because he don't like cows, and he don't like ranching."

Ranger Douglas added, "He likes guns. And being a hired gun fits his pistol jest right."

Slim said, "Well, we're here. And we ain't goin' home 'til we ask him to go with us. If'n he don't, then we'll head back."

The captain answered. "Like I said in my letter to ya, Slim. Matt is a tough, fast gun paid to shoot first and ask questions later. He was hired to keep General Mitchell and his ranch safe from outlaws."

Slim nodded. "Know'd that. I've brought his ma's Bible for that reason. Figure if'n he sees it, he'll be more obligin'."

"Wish one of us could ride out with you, but it's a good jaunt. Don't know what else I can tell ya, except good luck."

Slim opened the door and said, "Thanks, Capt'n," and the three cowboys stepped outside.

The captain walked out with them and began giving them directions. "You stay the other side of the bridge and head south. Take the first fork and stay with the river. Day and a half, you'll find some longhorns. That'll be the beginning of his spread. Keep riding 'til ya see some cotton fields by the river. You'll see a trail heading east. Follow it 'til ya come to a large estate. That'll be General Mitchell's place, the Brazos River Bar M Ranch."

"We better get movin' then," Slim said, and the captain watched the three step into the street. He went back inside the office where the two rangers were talking.

Douglas said, "Captain, you didn't tell those cowpokes all we know about Matt, did ya?"

The captain looked out the window and watched the three walk down the street to their horses tied up in front of the cafe. With a look of concern, he answered, "You mean about him being a wanted outlaw? No. Don't see no reason to, either. First, I can't prove it." He turned and headed back to his desk. "Don't even want to try. Matt's one of the finest, most upright citizens we have in these here parts, and I have no reason to doubt his innocence."

Elliott looked at the captain with a puzzled expression. "Maybe I'm too green, but an outlaw is an outlaw. Ain't he, Captain?" The captain nodded and puffed on his pipe. "Well, is Matt an outlaw or not?" Elliott asked.

The captain looked up matter-of-factly. "Yes, Tom. An outlaw is an outlaw. But you go up against Matt and try to arrest him, and I'll be sending your ma a letter of apology for your sudden departure." Realizing he was being a little irate at the moment, he cooled his temper. "Look, Tom. Matt probably held up a bank or something. I'm not sure. I am sure of this though. He and Steve came to the general's aid after the war and I ain't never had any cause to suspect anything wrong with him."

Douglas interrupted, "Except for the times he gets drunk and disorderly. We had to lock him up once, that I remember, and that was because he and Steve clobbered too many of McDaniels' boys in a fistfight. That's when one of them called him a 'no good rotten son of a bitch.'"

The captain laughed. "That's all it took. We released them the next morning."

Elliott, being a little upset about the outlaw remark, put the question back to the captain, "What about your figurin' he robbed a bank or somethin'?"

The captin stood and looked down at Tom. "I got a gut feeling a few years back about something he said while drunk. I let it pass because it really didn't fit our Matt."

Captain Johnson looked back out the window and watched the cowboys swing themselves into their saddles. His eyes trained on them as their boots hit the stirrups direct and hard. Their steeds headed toward the bridge, passing his office on their way out of town.

"You wouldn't understand this, Tom, 'cause you were too young for the war. Matt and Steve fought under the general's command. Matt's a good man with a gun and cool in a crisis. He came up through the ranks. He saved the general's hide one day from one of your men's bayonets. Got that close to the general." The captain held his hands a few inches apart. "Matt took the bayonet through his jacket. Luckily, it didn't break the skin. He twisted the rifle from the soldier's hand and sent him to Saint Peter's. That's how Matt became a captain.

"Later, in a different part of the country, one of our own men accidentally shot the general in his right arm. That's how the general lost his arm. Before he was a great man with a gun; now he can't handle a weapon of any sort.

"After the war, the general returned to his ranch and needed help to get it back in order. Matt and Steve came to his aid when his estate had been run over by low-lying outlaws who didn't even fight in the war. Most of his cattle was run off or stolen. It's taken years to build up the spread the general has now, and much of that's because of Matt.

"Now Steve is the ramrod for the Brazos River Bar M Ranch and one hell of a rancher. Matt is their hired gun."

He looked at the two rangers and sat down. "You know, I think Matt might, just might, go back to Montana to see his mother once more. I figure he's that type of man if he does. But don't count on him staying there."

CHAPTER 2

THE BRIDGE

It was getting on into afternoon, and Slim, Shorty, and Dan knew they were burning daylight. The bridge they had to cross was situated some forty miles outside of town. It was long, a suspension bridge four hundred and seventy-five feet across, built twelve years earlier for ranchers to move their cattle to Kansas by way of the Chisholm Trail.

As they rode along, they took in the beauty of the countryside. This was Texas, Waco, Texas. It was vast and it was beautiful.

A few hours later, they confronted the largest bridge they had ever seen. It was a piece of art, a beauty to behold. Before they decided to cross, they dismounted and relaxed by the side of the road. The three looked intently toward the other side in a hypnotic gaze. They had arrived at their long-anticipated destination. On the eastern side of the bridge was the flatland of Texas, to the west were rolling hills. The view was a Texas picture far and wide as the eye could see. Nothing stirred to disrupt their attention.

In the distance, the cowboys watched the Brazos River some one hundred and fifty yards wide. Under the bridge, they could see the great river rolling south. This was the only spot for a hundred miles or so in either direction where cattle and horses could cross. The bridge made it easier for cattlemen to connect to the Chisholm Trail on their way to Kansas with their cattle.

Looking west, they saw the high bluffs of the riverbank, which made it difficult for man or beast to climb out of the water. The river was this way for miles.

"How we gonna know Matt Jorgensen is really Matt Andersen?" Dan asked, breaking the silence.

Slim replied, "Don't give it another thought."

"We gonna go or what?" Shorty asked, looking at the other two still in somewhat of a daze.

"Yeah," Slim answered, after a breath of fresh energy. He rose, grabbed his reins, and threw his leg over his saddle, pony-express style, motioning the others to ride.

The tollkeeper met them at the entrance to the bridge.

"What're you here for?" asked Shorty, as he reined up at the bar.

"Collecting a toll, mister," came the answer from the toll keeper. "If you wanna get across, it'll cost ya twenty-five cents."

While the three men dug into their vest pockets to come up with the change, he added, "That's for your horse. It costs a nickel for each of you."

Slim asked, "Everyone pay this kinda money?"

"Everyone goin' across. Costs money to build a bridge like this."

Dan said, "We got it. Jest never heard of payin' to go across a bridge before. Seems right, though."

The man collected the twenty-five cent per head fee along with the nickel for each of the cowboys and raised the bar so they could proceed. Two million, seven hundred thousand bricks paved the bridge. It was a sight for the cowboys to behold. A lot of sweat and toil had gone into building this majestic piece of art.

They hit the bricks of the bridge slowly to let their horses adjust and take their time to cross.

The toll keeper watched them, and shouted, "You can gallop across. It's no problem."

To which Dan replied, "At these rates, we want to take in the view and get our money's worth."

Several anxious minutes later they were across. It was a beautiful sight, both from the bridge itself and from the banks on the other side.

A quick dig with their spurs to the sides of their horses, and the cowboys began to lope on solid ground to their destination.

After a good long ride, they brought their horses to a walk for a few hours of slow and steady riding. As the sun began to set, they reined their horses into a group of oaks where they camped for the night.

Dan was good at making a fire, but Shorty showed his talent for cooking by whipping up a pan of beans with a slice of bacon, and a pot of coffee with eggshells inside. Dan brought out his guitar and played a gentle ditty while Slim wandered down to the bank of the Brazos River. He stood watching the ripples in the river play gently as the current headed downstream. He looked up and watched the myriad of stars dance through the night in rhythm to Dan's music.

The next day, after a night's camping, a bath in the Brazos, and a breakfast of biscuits in the saddle, the cowboys felt fresh again. The sky was clear and the sun was already showing that it would be a hot day.

By mid-afternoon they came across a small house and a ferry on the Brazos. A tall husky man was working on the shore with his lines when the trio waved at him.

Jerod was a stocky, blond Norwegian in his thirties who had made a ferry business a means by which to complement his duties as a ranger. From this spot on the Brazos, he could operate as a ranger, covering the south for a hundred or so miles, and stay in immediate contact with the rangers' headquarters in Waco.

He waved back and yelled out, "Howdy, men. Be right with ya." He tied up his lines carefully and walked up the bank to the cowboys.

His wife, a good woman with a stout figure, was in the house, a simple wood frame that sat on the hillside overlooking the Brazos. She saw the riders and came out quickly and waved. There was nothing pretentious about her.

As the cowboys neared the house, she said, "Howdy. You men look new to the area."

Slim spoke up first, saying, "Yes, ma'am. We're from Montana way."

"Well, light down and stay a while," Jerod said. "This here is my wife, Effie. I'm Jerod Torgeson, ranger and ferry master. Jest fixin' to break for lunch. Join us?"

"I'll fix a few more plates," Effie said. "Won't take but a few seconds, boys."

"Yes, ma'am," Shorty answered.

Effie went back inside while Jerod showed the trio where to wash up.

After a full meal, the three men were ready to hit the saddles and ride.

Dan was the last of the three to leave the house. While fumbling with his Stetson he said, "Mr. and Mrs. Torgeson, we certainly want to thank you for a great meal."

"Yeah," Shorty added, "beats any we've had since we left Montana."

The men rode away as easy as they had come, returning a goodbye wave to Jerod and Effie. They had just received their first good Texas feeling since starting their journey. It was to be short-lived.

When a longhorn came into view, Shorty was the first to spot it. "Look at that, will ya. My first longhorn. Dang, she's a beaut." Taking up his lariat, he spurred his horse gently, guiding it towards the animal. "I gotta see this up close. Dan, Slim, give me a hand."

The three, with loops in their ropes, rode toward the longhorn, its great horns extending some two feet on either side. They were determined to rope him. The great steer stood quietly, watching the three cowboys approach.

Shorty's lasso came down around the animal's neck while Slim looped his hind legs. The steer was down, but to be sure, Dan's rope came around the horns and pulled in the opposite direction, holding the rope taut. Shorty climbed down from his saddle and walked cautiously to the captured beast. Shorty's eyes were open wide like a kid at Christmas time. With his gloved hand, he felt the head, then stroked the horns for a good feel. He pulled off a glove and stroked the horn again for a better feel of the smooth, hard surface.

Dan saw two figures on the horizon. Then several more came into view. Shorty removed the rope from around the steer's horns and neck and climbed back into his saddle. Slim took the rope off the beast's hind legs and watched it get up and trot away. Up on their horses, the three cowboys gathered up their ropes, tying them off, and led their horses through the other longhorns.

While he watched the freed animal rejoin the herd, Dan said, "Sure wouldn't want him mad at me."

As they continued to ride, a whole herd of longhorns filled the plain. It was a sight to behold. The sound of hooves disturbed the air, not the hooves of the steers, but of approaching riders. The three cowboys reined to a halt and waited.

Ten riders pulled up close and blocked their exit. The leader was young and stocky. A clean bandanna hung from his neck, and his open denim shirt revealed a hairy chest. It was the clean bandanna that really struck Slim, an indication he had just left a ranch house. He was probably the owner. The rest of the riders weren't clean.

"Throw down your guns and get off your horses. Now!" the apparent leader said with impressive authority. "Drop 'em!"

The three obeyed and were on the ground immediately, holding the reins of their horses before another word came from his mouth.

"Back away from your horses. Let go, now!" The cowboys obeyed, hoping their rented horses were trained to be ground reined.

When shots from the wrangler's .45 filled the air, the horses spooked and ran off as the men hollered after them.

The leader turned to the three horseless cowboys and said, "Now get out of here!"

The three started to pick up their guns, but the leader spurred his horse in front of them. "You won't need them guns." Pushing his hat back, he leaned over the saddle. "You fellas can make it back across the river before the week's out if you start now. Just be thankful we didn't kill ya."

Finally, Slim broke the silence of the three. "We didn't come hundreds of miles to be chased home. We come to see Jorgensen; and I hope to hell he's your boss."

The leader leaned over the neck of his horse and looked down intently at Slim. "Matt Jorgensen? What makes you think he's one of us?"

Shorty stepped up to the leader quickly. "Cause we were told by the Texas Rangers in Waco he works this ranch. We're tired, and we're not goin' away until we see him."

The leader gave a short laugh, "Son, you're on the Brazos River Bar M Ranch, and it goes farther than your eyes can see. Now, you're trespassin' - and not only that, but you were caught ropin' one of our steers. You've got a choice. We can take you to the lieutenant and see that he hangs ya, or you can start walkin' back to Waco. What'll it be?"

By now, the other riders were getting their lariats in roping position and in one swift movement, the ropes hit their marks over the cowboys' heads. Slim, in a fast instant, had his knife in hand and started cutting the rope, but the leader spurred over and kicked the knife out of his hand. The wranglers yanked their ropes tighter and pulled all three to the ground.

"What'll it be?" the leader asked them again as they wrestled with the ropes. The riders tugged to keep them taut.

"Is any of you Matt?" Slim cried, spitting dirt out of his mouth as he rolled over.

The three cowboys lay still for a moment looking the group over while the riders eased up on the ropes. None of them could be Matt; not a one looked like his father, Wil.

Then from a distance, a rider cantered toward them as if to join in the fun. Without looking at the oncoming rider, the leader pulled his rope taut, knocking Slim back to the ground, and began dragging him "Okay, boys, let's show them some Texas hospitality." The others did likewise with Dan and Shorty.

The lone rider put his horse into a gallop and started whirling a lasso over his head. When he reached the leader, he dropped the lasso around him, jerking him out of the saddle to the ground. He rolled over a couple times before the rider slacked off the rope.

The leader began to cuss and spit out dirt as he untangled himself. "What the sam hill d'ya think you're doin'?"

Winding his rope in, the rider looked intently at the other two wranglers who still held onto their ropes, until they finally let the cowboys go. Then he looked beyond the ten to a group of horsemen in the distance. "We got company, Seth."

Seth, the unhorsed leader's name, pulled himself out of the rope in an angry rage. "The hell we do. These guys are trespassin', and we're chasin' 'em back across the Brazos."

"Not them three. Those men over there." He pointed to the rising cloud of dust.

Seth stopped short and looked. "McDaniels' group?"

The other riders wound up their lariats and waited for orders from the rider. "No time to figure it out. Get up, Seth, and go back to the ranch."

Seth picked up his hat and climbed back into his saddle. "These three roped one of our steers. We were just teachin' 'em a lesson and gettin' 'em on the road."

One of the riders added, "They asked about Matt."

The lone rider yelled, "I'll meet you all back at the ranch. Now, ride!"

He stayed behind while the others rode off. He looked down at the three cowboys who were recovering from the dragging and asked, "What d'ya plan on doin' with the steer? Eat it?"

The grateful cowboys began to pick up their guns, but the lone rider pulled his revolver and cocked it. None of the boys had ever seen a gun come out of its holster so fast. "Sorry, boys. You!" he said, pointing to Shorty. "What's your name?"

"Homer Bickerdyke."

"Homer, what? Why you smilin' like that? Never mind. Pick up your guns and hand 'em over, belts and all."

Shorty did what he was told. "Most people call me, Shorty." He tried to wipe his smile off with his freed hand. "It's just . . . well . . . I ain't never seen a longhorn before -- and I swore if I did, I'd rope it and just rub its horns for good luck."

"Yes, sir," chimed in Dan. "I put my rope on 'im to make sure he didn't get away. And so did Slim."

"Why ya lookin' for Matt?" the rider asked.

"We was hopin' you'd be him. Supposin' you're not. You don't look too much like his dad."

Steve smiled for the first time and replied, "Name's Steve Andrews. I'm the foreman. Seth is my ramrod. Good man. He has his orders to keep everyone off our 'stead. Sorry, boys, but that means anyone."

The cowboys began walking towards their horses a hundred yards away while Steve's horse kept pace. Shorty said, "They were ready to drag us to the river, had you not stopped 'em."

Steve answered, "Seth could have, had he a mind to. Be grateful he didn't. Where ya from?"

Dan answered for the three, "Up Montana way. Do we get to meet Matt, or do we have to go back across the river?"

Steve stopped his horse and eyed McDaniels' men. "You know any of that group yonder?"

Dan looked at the riders coming their way. "No. Who are they?"

Steve rode over to one of the horses and gave its reins to Dan. "For your sake, I hope they're not your friends." He spurred over to another horse and brought it to Slim who was running to meet him. "Hate to have to kill ya." Then he brought the third horse to Shorty.

"We've come all the way from Montana for Matt Jorgensen. We've got no beef with anyone down here," Dan said.

"We just got into Waco last night. You can ask the capt'n there," Shorty added.

Steve sat tall in the saddle and watched the approaching horsemen, trying to figure out what to do with the three cowboys. He cocked his .45 and got ready to fire. He returned their gun belts and said, "Ride for the river, boys. I can't waste time, and lead is cheap." He fired two rounds into the air and gave a rebel yell.

The trio headed out toward the McDaniels' group while Steve turned his gelding in the opposite direction and spurred into a gallop toward the ranch.

Cantering in a steady gait, they appeared to be somewhat at ease heading for the river, wondering why Steve had turned and gone the other way. They looked behind them and saw Steve still galloping away. Up ahead the group of men had stopped.

A few began to raise their rifles toward them. Instinctively, they turned and rode toward the river, away from the guns of the horsemen and the Brazos River Bar M Ranch.

CHAPTER 3

THE RANCH

The ranch house was a two-story Victorian with a picket fence completely surrounding it. To the back, and away from the river, was another house; smaller but of the same style. This belonged to Matt. Around the yard were the wranglers' shacks and a barn. The corrals stood in the midst of a large land mass with nothing around for miles except ranch land. The land was rich with good topsoil for grazing and farming, though few farmers were around. Cotton farming was gaining popularity, especially around the river. Still, rolling hills were mostly for cattle. A few clouds speckled the beautiful blue sky and oak trees dotted the prairie. The land was a perfect Western portrait. The Brazos River Bar M Ranch had thousands of head of longhorn roaming the hills with a couple dozen cowboys keeping them together.

The owner was Ted Mitchell, an ex-general in the Eighth Texas Cavalry of the Confederacy. He had been seeking the office of governor of Texas when he was severely wounded in the Civil War, losing his right arm. With his career path altered, he became a rancher. Not just any rancher; his dream was to own the largest spread in Texas. In order to do this, he needed the right people doing the right jobs.

He was still pretty good with a gun as a southpaw, but not nearly fast enough. Now he depended on the hands of another man to protect him: Matt Jorgensen.

Both men were volunteers in the Eighth Texas Cavalry. As cavalrymen, they furnished their own Colt revolver, carbine, and Bowie knife. The regiment furnished the horse.

Matt proved his prowess with the Colt, becoming the hired gun whose sole job was to protect Mitchell and his ranch.

Steve was good with both a pistol and a carbine but depended more on the latter. He was hired on as the foreman because his expertise with horses and cattle was second to none. Before the war, he'd worked as a foreman at another large ranch.

The Brazos River Bar M Ranch was all that General Mitchell had left. His only son, Seth, was his first born and rightful heir. But it was his daughter, Leisha, who in Mitchell's eyes would inherit it, along with his niece, Jaimie. Both she and Leisha knew as much about horses and cattle as any ranch hand.

Leisha was a beautiful lady in her late twenties, with a good figure and a full head of blond hair that hung down her back. She had a good sense of responsibility ingrained in her by both her parents, but mostly by her mother, a pioneer woman of the plains. During the war, her mother had held onto the plantation as well as she could without the general's presence. Her slaves stayed with her but were working less and less each day, hoping to see the Blue Coats some day soon. Just before the war ended, the general's seven-year-old niece, Jaimie, has come to live with them after her mother died of complications resulting from a vain attempt to give childbirth on her own. Her father, the general's brother, was killed in the war.

General Mitchell and his wife cared for Jaimie as their own daughter, and Leisha treated her as a sister.

A year later, the general's wife took a bad fall from her horse and passed away in her sleep.

Jaimie was now a striking young lady going on eighteen. On this day, General Mitchell sat on the porch cleaning his shotgun after a day of hunting. Jaimie sat with him, watching. She was always concerned about her uncle's safety. After all, he was in his mid-sixties and not as healthy as he once had been.

The ruckus of the riders coming in caused Mitchell to walk to the edge of the porch to see what was happening. Jaimie stood by him. They saw Seth, Mitchell's son, ordering the riders to grab their rifles and take cover.

"Wonder what's up?" Mitchell asked. The riders tied up their horses at the corral, and Seth walked towards the house. "Why are all the boys in? Why the rifles?" Mitchell asked. Pausing, he saw the look in Seth's eyes. "McDaniels?"

Seth nodded. "Steve saw 'em first. He told me to get back to the ranch right away. You know Steve can't order me around like the hired help. He wanted us to ride away like we didn't notice them."

Meanwhile, Steve whipped his horse around the main house and came to a halt at the front steps. The other riders were waiting for him.

Steve dismounted and stepped up on the porch to Mitchell and Jaimie. He confirmed Seth's report and ushered them into the house to prepare for the impending fight.

At the same time, back on the prairie, rifle shots rang out and puffs of dirt began to pop up, coming dangerously close to hitting the three cowboys from Montana. They were in full gallop towards the river when they saw a splinter of four riders peeling off after them. Slim led Shorty and Dan to a sharp left and headed south, parallel with the river.

Realizing their rented horses were not as fast as those of their pursuers, Slim yelled back at his two companions. "Soft spot comin' up. Feign a hit and fall."

The two acknowledged with a nod and as soon as another shot rang out, both of them fell off their horses. "*Not both of you. Damn!*" Slim said in disgust to himself. He continued riding.

Dan and Shorty's stiff bodies lay face down in the dirt, waiting for the other horses to pass. Sweat poured from their bodies as they awaited bullets to pierce their bodies or the hooves of horses to rip them apart. They lay perfectly still, not breathing. As the horses passed over and missed them, Dan and Shorty turned over, rose up and fired their .45s at the backs of the riders, bringing one of them down. Another rider reined up, turned, and started towards them at full gallop. Dan's gun jammed, but Shorty's fired and the bullet found the rider's chest. He fell to the ground, his horse barely missing the two.

The remaining pursuers saw what happened, veered off, and headed back to regroup with the others.

Slim wheeled his horse around and rode after Dan and Shorty's horses catching them at a nearby oak. He dismounted and walked all three horses to a big shade tree and sat down. Shorty and Dan joined him, throwing off dirt from their clothes.

"Soft spot," Dan said sarcastically, stepping over one of the dead men.

"This one's dead, too," Slim said, as he eyed the second dead man not too far away.

"My gun jammed," remarked Dan as he sidestepped the dead man.

"What the hell is that smell? You guys stink," Slim barked back at the two.

"Cow dung" Dan replied. "Gowd-awful cow shit. That's the soft spot we fell in."

Slim stood up and looked back at the group of riders heading towards the ranch.

Eyeing a water hole a far distance away, Shorty motioned towards it. "I'm for getting this crap off me -- right now." Slim and Dan joined him as he headed for the water hole

"We're lucky to be alive," Dan said.

"Yeah," Slim agreed. "So, this is Texas. You guys for stayin' or for leavin'?"

Shorty looked back at the group of riders and seeing no one following them, said, "Well, we've come this far, and we've been shot at before. Don't see any reason for leavin'. Besides, looks like Matt's gonna need our guns."

Reaching the water hole, Shorty and Dan removed their gun belts and boots and fell into the water. Slim looked down at their boots sitting on the edge. "Ya got dung on your boots, too."

Shorty dunked his head into the water and swished his hair. "Cow dung on my boots means I'm a cowboy. Cow dung on my clothes means I'm a jerk who don't know no better. Gonna join us?"

Slim sat with his leg crossed over his saddle and lit a freshly rolled cigarette. "I need a bath, too, but not right now."

Dan mused, "Ain't Saturday anyhows. Damn! My tobacco." He frantically brought out his soaking wet tobacco pouch from his shirt pocket. He watched Slim looking at the group of riders now almost out of their sight. "Whatcha thinkin', Slim?"

"Wonderin' whether we're gonna stay and fight for somethin' we didn't ask for? I'm sayin' we go back to Waco for a few days, maybe talk with the capt'n."

Dan agreed, "After all, we done killed two men."

Slim relaxed for a moment, enjoying his cigarette, and then replied, "Yeah. Tell ya what, Shorty. You ride back to Waco and tell the capt'n about this. Dan and I'll go to the ranch."

Quickly stepping out of the water hole, Shorty said, "You'll get killed!"

Dan joined him, putting his boots back on and strapping his irons to his hips. "You got as good a chance as we have, Shorty." He looked over at Slim. "Think we all three should stick together – kinda like, Slim?"

"Mind's made up," Slim said. "You go fetch Capt'n Johnson, Shorty. Dan and I'll ride to the ranch and create enough noise to make that bunch of bad men think all three of us are still here. If you're lucky, you should be back here in a few days with some reinforcements."

Slim and Dan hit their saddles, and Shorty began his ride toward the river. "I'll stay close to the river's edge so's no one will see me."

"Yeah," Slim responded quietly. "Good luck, pal."

Slim and Dan waited in the shadow of the tree while Shorty slipped away. He was far enough out of sight of the McDaniels' group to be noticed, but they waited for a margin of safety. Once Shorty had ridden over a couple of the rolling hills, Slim turned to Dan and motioned to ride back towards McDaniels' group. They rode slow and careful.

Once they were out of the shadows and in the clearing where the group could see them distinctly, they began to ride straight for the back of the ranch. They were quickly spotted by McDaniels' men, but no one went after them. Instead, they curiously stopped and dismounted.

The people at the ranch watched Slim and Dan ride up but were more concerned about the McDaniels' group that had dismounted just over the rise.

Seth stepped up to the porch and looked out towards McDaniels' men.

General Mitchell stood in the doorway with his shotgun in hand.

Jaimie walked on the porch to him. "They've dismounted. Just waiting."

Slim and Dan came to the back of the ranch at full gallop.

The general turned, and pointing his shotgun at them, yelled out, "Who the hell are you?"

Seth quickly stopped the general from raising the shotgun. "Those are three cowboys from up in Montana. They were trespassing, so we chased 'em off our land."

"You mean the young men you were having some fun with," Steve stepped in. "They shoulda been in Waco by now. 'Stead, we heard them being chased and shot at by some of the McDaniels' men. Looks to me like they did all right for themselves. No holes that I can see."

Seth added, "Just three guys lookin' for Matt. Said they came twelve hundred miles to find him."

"Matt?" Jaimie asked. "Our Matt?"

"Well, yeah," Seth continued. "Don't ask me why -- I don't know."

"There's only two," Mitchell said.

"One of them musta got shot," Steve answered, as he stepped off the porch. "Who got it?"

Slim and Dan dismounted quickly and tied up their horses to the corral. "Nobody got shot. Shorty's gone for Capt'n Johnson."

After tying up their horses, Slim walked up to Seth, and without stopping, let his right fist come across his face full force, knocking him over the hitching post. Seth recovered and reeled his fist into Slim, slamming him hard to the ground. Seeing his friend hurt, Dan stepped in and followed up with a swift and hard punch to Seth's stomach.

Steve ran to Seth's aid and grabbed a firm hold of Dan's arm, turning him in to him. "Two against one ain't good odds. Let 'em fight alone, mister!"

Meantime, the group of riders on the hill had remounted and was headed for the ranch.

As the men continued their fistfight, a band of riders from the ranch, led by Matt Jorgensen, rode up from the corral.

He yelled out while holding his excited horse back, "Turn him loose, Steve, and get the general and Jaimie in the house. Now!" He looked at the scuffed-up cowboys, tightened his jaw, then looked back at McDaniels' group riding in. "Seth, get the rifles on the roof and in the barn."

Seth obeyed immediately, getting the other wranglers situated with rifles.

Matt drew his gun, twirled and cocked it at the same time. He then pointed it at Slim and Dan.

Steve yelled out, "We can use 'em, Matt. They killed a couple of McDaniels' men out on the plains." Steve paused and looked at Matt, waiting to see if he would shoot them. "But it's your call."

Matt holstered his pistol. "Use 'em, then. But get 'em the hell out of my sight. I'm tempted to shoot 'em." Matt then whipped his horse around. "Fasten down the windows, General. Steve, take five of my best," he said as he motioned for one of the riders to check the barn. But he noticed Leisha was missing. "Seth, go look for your sister."

Seth ran as ordered, stopped by the corral, then headed for the barn.

Steve and the rest ushered the general and ladies into the house.

The young cowboys' feelings of awe at Matt's presence passed as Steve gave them orders. "Grab your rifles and take cover with the others behind the hay bales."

Dan blurted out, "You're Matt."

Matt reeled his horse around into Dan and looked at him angrily. Steve came down the steps. "Matt, same as last time?" He was referring to their last gun fight and how Matt used a special tactic.

"No. Little different," Matt returned, looking out at the motionless group. "McDaniels' men want me to come out now. We'll give them sometime to cool their heels. Kinda play according to our rules, not theirs. Keep an eye on 'em, Steve. Let me know if they stir any. And tell Seth I want him right away."

Matt climbed down off his horse and walked over to Dan and Slim, still looking angry. "Son, if you know something about me that I don't, spill it."

Slim answered, "We're from Montana, and we've been looking for ya. By your looks and all, you match your dad's."

Matt's angry look dropped from his dusty face, and he began to hang onto every word these strange cowboys were saying. His palms became sweaty, and he wiped them on his chaps. He couldn't stop the wetness swelling up in his eyes, so he looked away at the group in the distance.

He asked, "Where'd ya see my dad?"

Dan answered, "In Montana on his ranch. We worked for him."

Matt turned quickly as if to collar Dan, but instead kept his hands palm down on his chaps. Gritting his teeth, he said, "He's dead!"

Slim agreed, "Yes, S

ir. Been five years now. We were there when . . ." He stopped, looked at Matt and then finished. "We were there."

"When he got killed, why don't ya say it?" Matt snapped quickly. "You knowed I knew. Why'd 'ya come down?" Seeing a woman, dressed in men's clothes and carrying a rifle, coming out of the barn and walking towards him, he stopped his conversation with the cowboys and walked his horse over to her.

CHAPTER 4

SERGEANT MC TAVETT

"They got more riders this time, Leisha. We'll use you, but in the house with Mitch and Jaimie. Kinda . . ." Matt's words trailed off while Leisha passed him, briefly touching his arm.

Leisha was older than Jaimie by about ten years, and just about as beautiful. She had been raised on the ranch as an owner's daughter should be and had taken to being one of the boys. Her language, however, complemented her looks.

"Send a couple other guys inside, Matt. I'm standing outside with the rest." By that time, she had a foot on the steps, and she meant to stay there. Matt walked over to her and swished her up with one sweep of his strong arms.

"The hell you are." He took her into the house as Jaimie opened the door and set her inside. In a kidding manner, he said to Jaimie, "Shoot her if she even looks like she's coming out." Then to Leisha he said, "Damn it woman, I need your gun in the house in case anyone breaks through. I can depend on you. Some of those other idiots, all they think about is themselves, and they'd leave Mitch and Jaimie to get killed."

Seth had come upon the porch by this time. Matt looked at his beaten-up face. "I thought I told you . . ." He paused a moment and looked at Seth's face. "What'd ya run into? A bull?"

Dan had followed Matt to the porch and answered him, "No, sir. My fist."

Matt turned and looked at Dan and Slim with the same concern. "It'd take more than one fist." He looked over at Slim, who rubbed his chin and nodded.

Steve rode up to the porch and joined the conversation. "We're waiting."

Then Matt looked at Steve, at beaten-up Seth and Slim, back over to Steve, who shrugged his shoulders and replied, "Texas hospitality."

Matt faced Seth and said, "You're twice their size." Matt turned. "Oh, hell, get back to your wranglers and make sure they know what they're shooting at this time," he gestured towards the top of the barn. "I don't want any lead in my back 'cause I'm gonna be right out there in front. Don't anyone fire at anything unless you see them get past me. Understand?"

He then looked strongly at Seth as if he had no time to wait for a reply. "You keep your men here in the middle." He pointed at the area between the house, corral, and barn which had been fortified with hay bales for protection.

Continuing with his tactical plan, he grabbed some mane and gripping the reins, hit the stirrups straight and hard, swinging up into the saddle. He looked at Seth. "You've got the toughest job. But you've also got some of my men who can shoot straight. And ya got two extra guns with these cowboys." He looked at the two young men. "Hope ya can shoot as good as ya can fight." Sitting tall, he looked at the men around the ranch and commanding their attention, said, "I don't want one person to get within five hundred feet of this house. Ya hear?"

Steve and several other riders joined Matt in a gentle canter up to the front gate. Steve looked in the direction of the group in the distance still standing off their horses. "Think they've calmed down a little by now, Matt?"

Matt clinched his teeth and replied, "Gawd, I hope so."

Slim took a place among the bales of hay while Dan watched Matt ride out. Looking past Matt at the standing group of riders several hundred yards out, he began to see the unevenness of the numbers.

Dan whispered to Slim, "They got more than fifty men that I can count."

Slim nodded in agreement. "Matt has less than a dozen. Don't make sense."

Upon realizing their predicament, Dan continued to say a little louder, "Slim, dammit, we're gonna get killed. They get past Matt, they're gonna land right in our laps."

Seth looked over at the two whispering to one another as though no one else could hear them. He attempted to calm them down. "Worried?"

Slim looked over at Seth and realized they had been heard. "I know, 'Texas hospitality.' Well, how much of this Texas hospitality is there?" There was a pause between them for a brief moment that seemed to be a long time. Then Slim asked, "Do you figure?"

Seth rubbed his nose a little and grinned at the two cowboys. If anyone had a sixth sense, it would be these three sizing up the entire situation and agreeing there was no need in worrying at this point. Just be prepared to live, or die.

When Matt and the others reached the front gate, they rode a little further to set their horses high on the first hill, aiming to settle in a gorge about twenty or thirty yards in front of them when they came. Matt felt this would give them an edge. They stopped their horses and watched the group.

Finally, the leader motioned for his group to get mounted. There seemed to be no hurry. With a slight motion of his hand, he led them towards Matt's riders.

Steve leaned on his saddle while he watched the group approaching him. He said to Matt, "Why d'ya suppose they're taking their time?"

Matt took a couple of cigars out of his inside vest pocket and gave one to Steve. Lighting his, and then Steve's, he answered, "They know the rules by now. They come in and wait. We come to the gate and wait. They come galloping and shooting. We shoot back."

"That's what I mean. They're not galloping and shooting this time."

Matt exhaled a good puff of smoke. They waited.

It wasn't long before the group, more than four times the size of theirs, reached Matt and his men. The leader was Thatcher McTavett, a dark-skinned man with jet-black hair and a weather-beaten face. He looked like he would have some Waco Indian blood in him, but not good blood. He reined his horse sixty to seventy yards from Matt's and looked sternly into his face as if waiting for Matt to start something. He had over forty riders behind him.

Finally, he spoke. "Matt. I've come to kill you."

Matt adjusted himself to sit tall in his saddle, a shotgun resting in his arms. "McTavett, you ol' son of bitch. Didn't figure you had it in ya. Never did like ya much, and I like you even less now that I see you in the daylight."

Steve leveled his rifle in their direction and waited. He knew the game was being played. Otherwise, he figured, there would be no fun at all in the shootout. He eyed a man behind a shotgun. He said, "Last time I saw you, Sam, you lost a poke to Leisha. Lettin' a woman beat you out of a week's wages ain't smart."

Sam squeezed hard on the handle of his shotgun as he answered Steve. "Figurin' on gettin' that and more back today."

Matt took another drag on his cigar and let the smoke filter through the air. "You're not gun hands. Most of you never even fired a gun, and that's a fact. Right, Jasper?"

Jasper was a little man who fidgeted with his fingers when he was nervous. Today he was real nervous.

Matt started picking some of the men out of the group to size them down. "Jeremiah, I remember you always wanted to have an acre of cotton for yourself." Matt watched as Jeremiah, a thin, tall man in the back row, nodded his head. "And you, Phil, Nathan, and Bill. You don't want to get killed! Your parents taught you better. Hell, I don't want to have ta kill any of you."

McTavett started looking around. His calmness was beginning to build into anger as he watched what Matt and Steve were doing to his men with words. "No more talking, Matt."

Matt looked at the riders behind McTavett, not giving McTavett a glance. "Gentlemen, sounds like the widow McDaniels just wants to get a hold of the Brazos Bar Ranch, so's she can run the cattle empire all for her own little greedy self. You cowboys will be back doing what you were doing yesterday. Why get yourselves shot up and maybe killed?"

"Shut up, Matt," McTavett said, moving closer to Matt's horse.

Matt now kept his eyes steady on McTavett while he sensed his men were arming themselves. He motioned for his side companion to move in just a little behind him. He said loud enough for McTavett to hear, "Steve, looking at how close these men are gathered together, how many do you think we'll kill?"

Steve cocked his rifle while reviewing the situation. "You and I can get the first four or five from here, including McTavett. Most of the rest will either run or end up dead, the way I figure."

Matt pointed his shotgun at McTavett and cocked the trigger. "In that case, it's your call."

A few hundred yards behind them, Slim and Dan were witnessing the beginning of one of the best gunfights to take place. They were intent on gathering in all that was happening.

McTavett motioned for his second row of riders to come forward. Two in the row of ten men aimed their shotguns at Matt. The group spurred their horses, but the small gully had given Matt the edge he needed. McTavett yelled, "I call!" and fired.

Matt reared his horse, and McTavett's fire hit it, making it go down. The fall threw Matt's left leg out of the stirrups, and he landed on his back with his dead horse rolling over him before landing to Matt's side. Buckshot had hit the chaps of Matt's leg and drawn blood. Steve and the rest of his gunfighters fired, trying to bring down the loaded shotguns first.

A rider from McTavett's group rode down on Matt and started shooting at him.

With quick precision, Steve reeled in the man's direction, and brought him down with his .45.

Matt rolled over against his dead horse, using him for a prop, and drew his pistol just in time to fan it at two more riders coming at him. The men fell fast to the ground.

The bulk of the McDaniels' riders moved past the front line and galloped towards the ranch house, leaving Matt's crippled group. Matt saw Steve ride after them. "Stand clear, Steve. The wranglers will get 'em at the house."

But a stampede of longhorns had stirred up and moved in from the north, cutting off McTavett's attack on the ranch. A few men got through only to be met by the second group in the fortified hay bales. As the rest of McDaniels' group rode to the south flank of the ranch through the back, the Brazos River wranglers positioned in strategic points of the ranch, began firing, bringing down the riders fast and hard.

McTavett's men turned to retreat but were met by longhorns and still more Brazos River riders. Some were knocked off their horses by the horns and trampled, while others were shot by the riders. Many of McDaniels' riders, including McTavett, hightailed it back to the river. The group had been cut in size, but a remnant was still left.

Matt, Steve, and three others were left at the front. Matt reloaded his gun and said to Steve, "Be ready."

The remnant turned and rode back into their fire. They reined up to Steve and his men and surrendered, except for one rider. As he attempted to flee by jumping part of the fence, Steve brought him down with one shot.

The skirmish was over. Matt sat on his dead horse's carcass and, holding onto his pepper-shot leg, looked at the broken group of riders. "Well, you tried it again. Where's McTavett?" Someone pointed at his body lying not too far from Matt and his horse.

Steve walked over and kicked the gun from his hand. McTavett moved and raised himself up. Steve yelled out, "He's alive, Matt. What d'ya want me to do, shoot 'im?"

McTavett threw up his hands in surrender and pleaded mercy.

"No," Matt said, "but we oughta. He'll go back and tell that ol' McDaniels' widow." He looked at McTavett intently. "You tell Mrs.

McDaniels to keep on her own side of the river, or I'm gonna kick in her timbers. You tell her that, McTavett!"

McTavett lifted himself up and it became obvious that he was injured in the shoulder. He nodded, "I'll tell her." He paused for a moment then asked, "Do I get a horse?"

Matt tightened up again, and said, "Walk, damn you, McTavett. I hope you drown crossing the Brazos."

McTavett's riders faced Matt with their heads down, expecting to get shot. Matt continued, "We ain't gonna shoot 'ya. You can see the color of your leader, now. Get down from your nags and walk home."

They obeyed and walked haltingly towards their injured and dead companions.

Matt said, "Let 'em pick up their dead, Steve. You can take some buckboards to carry them. and then they can get themselves back across the Brazos. Leave the horses."

Steve and his men, making sure that McDaniels' men took no guns, motioned for them to pick up their dead.

McTavett limping, turned back to Matt, and asked, "What's gonna happen to our horses?"

"Spoils of war, McTavett. Spoils of war."

McTavett began to stutter in his nonsensical speech, only to get jabbed by Steve. "You heard him, McTavett. If I were you, I'd shut up and git while ya kin." He fired a round at McTavett's feet.

McTavett moved a little faster, then stopped. He turned to look at Matt's seemingly lifeless body. "Dead?"

Matt was slumped over his dead horse. Steve raised him up and saw that he had only passed out. Matt's limp body weighed down as if he were dead, and Steve gave all indications that he was dead. Angrily, he shot at McTavett's feet again. "Git movin'!"

McTavett obliged and hobbled off with the rest of his men. "We killed Matt. We killed Matt." None of the rest dared to look back.

Steve's words stopped the other group momentarily. "I've got a message for your Mrs. McDaniels. She's not brave enough to fight

Leisha herself, so she sends a gang of would-be gunslingers who ought to be pushin' a plow. You tell her to get outta the county, or Leisha'll come and get her. We're through playin' games." He turned back to Matt as the sound of buckboards rumbled in their direction.

Steve and his men looked up to see Leisha driving a team-up buckboard to haul their wounded and dead. She was still a distance away, but the noise distracted Steve and his men.

McTavett turned quickly as one of his men whipped out his gun and fired at Matt, hitting him in his left shoulder and causing him to roll backwards off his dead horse. With that bullet, McTavett chomped on his teeth because he was certain now that Matt was dead.

Steve returned with a volley of gunfire, hitting the would-be killer twice, ripping through his arm and hitting him in the head.

McTavett spun to the ground next to the dead man. He held his arms up and yelled, "Don't shoot! Don't shoot! He's dead." On his knees, McTavett motioned for his men to help him up. A buggy whipped by and the men dragged his body in before Steve could reload and shoot again.

McTavett was bleeding, and he appeared to be dying.

When McTavett's men were no longer a threat, Steve went to Matt's side and tore off his shirt, applying his bandanna firmly to his shoulder wound. Matt's face showed no sign of life. Working feverishly, he said, "Get up, you son of a-bitch. Don't die on me now."

Leisha brought her horses to a halt, jumped out with a rifle, and aimed it at McTavett. As McTavett's buckboard raced to the river, she heard Matt groan and rushed to his side. "Matt! You're still alive!"

Steve looked at the wound and saw that the bullet went clean through. He held the bandanna tighter.

"Barely." Steve answered. "Keep a hold on this neckerchief. It's okay. The hole is clean. Just keep the bleedin' stopped."

When a groan came from Matt's throat, she smiled. "He's a bloody mess, Steve. Where do we begin?"

Matt opened his eyes a little and whispered to Steve so only he could hear, "Make like I'm dead."

Steve nodded and continued working on the chaps. "I think you are, boss. Leisha has the bleeding under control in your shoulder though." As he set the chaps aside, he saw Matt's leg had been torn open by buckshot. "Not broken, but most of your leg is pepper shot."

Matt closed his eyes and grit his teeth as the pair continued to control the bleeding. Steve began to worry. "God, if the Doc don't get here fast, I -- I don't know, Leisha." Then he turned to the men around him. "Bob, Joe, ride hard for the Doc." No sooner was the command given than riders were in their saddles and riding fast to Waco.

Leisha helped Steve gently turn Matt's body face up. "Gotta get your chaps off, boss. Looks like ya lost too much blood." Steve felt a slight breath from Matt's lips.

He wrapped the leg wound with a bandanna, but needed another. Leisha shredded a piece of her blouse. "Use this."

After bandaging the leg, he stood up and looked at the McDaniels men now some distance away. Using Leisha's rifle, he fired another five shots at them, deliberately missing. He yelled, "You're a killer, McTavett."

McTavett, hearing the news, told his driver to get across the Brazos. Steve's voice was still ringing in his ears, echoing with gunshots from the other wranglers. "You're a killer, McTavett."

Matt regained consciousness, and realizing what was happening, painfully brought his hand to help the pair by wiping the blood away from his leg with his gloved hand. "Hell, I got hurt worse than this when I was gored by a bull. Remember?" Matt smiled at Leisha, then looked at his condition as he was being propped up against his horse. He grinned and gestured for her to sit next to him on his horse. "Ya . . . wanna sit a spell on my ass?"

She put her arm around him.

"They killed my horse."

"Hell with the horse," she said with clenched teeth. "They damn near killed you." She looked into his blue eyes and with a slight grin, said, "We've got some whiskey back at the ranch."

"Hell of a place for it." He groaned a little, and kidding her, continued, "Go get it." He paused a moment, then his eyes rolled back as he passed out, falling into her arms.

A nearby rider, having seen the incident from afar, turned his horse in their direction. Dismounting, he helped Steve and Leisha lift Matt into the buckboard.

Leisha climbed aboard and drove off with Matt.

Steve followed them back to the ranch.

McTavett's men had tried to see what was happening while they made their exodus. Having seen Matt lifted bodily into the buggy, they all concluded that he was truly dead.

In the field, the Brazos wranglers tended to their men, as the McDaniels' group hauled off their dead and wounded back across the Brazos.

The two cowboys from Montana were back at the ranch sizing up what had happened in the short span of time they had been in Texas. They wondered what their next move would be when they saw Matt being brought in.

The two walked to the buckboard as it pulled up in front of Matt's house and offered their assistance to help carry him inside.

Trying to ignore the two cowboys, Steve dismounted and helped Leisha down. Steve and the driver picked up Matt's limp body and carried it into the house.

Leisha cradled his shot-up leg, while Slim helped. Once inside, Matt was laid on a large four-poster bed.

Back on the plain, three of the wranglers who took off for a doctor observed the McDaniels' group heading back toward the river in buckboards. They rode up a hill parallel to the Brazos, keeping an eye on the group.

Within a short span of time, they met up with Captain Johnson and several Texas Rangers who were escorting Doc Wilson and his nurse, Maggie in a buggy. Maggie was also the captain's wife. Shorty was in the distance riding in their direction. The wranglers rode up alongside the group. After an exchange of words, they led the doctor to believe Matt was dead. "McDaniels' bunch met us head-on. We nailed them. And when Matt's back was turned, they shot and killed him."

The doctor was in his fifties and fit the bill as that of a country doctor. He was neatly dressed in dark conservative clothes and had his satchel sitting next to him. Maggie was in her late forties and smartly beautiful. She was riding along to help him, as she had done so many times in the past.

Captain Johnson looked at the wranglers, and said, "You're some of the Brazos' boys?"

A wrangler answered, "Better be."

The captain lowered his head and smiled through his mustache. He eyed Shorty and yelled out, "Did you ever find the man you were looking for, son?"

Shorty replied courteously, "Yes, sir."

Another wrangler replied, "Dead, sir. They were looking for Matt. He jest got himself kilt."

Shorty eyed the wrangler with his face reflecting disbelief and shock at hearing Matt was dead after they had just found him.

Eventually they came to the plain where McDaniels' group was heading toward the Brazos with their dead and wounded. Captain Johnson was hoping that by the time they got to the Brazos Ranch the fighting would be over. He got his wish.

He and Doc rode over and began questioning the men to find out what had taken place. To the captain, it looked worse than the last fight of a few months back, but then he was accustomed to their fighting.

Most of McDaniels' men had served in the Confederate Army. Ironically, some of their fellow soldiers were the ones they fought with today.

"This time," the captain said, "they were paid to fight for a piece of land. Why," he asked the doc, "when there's enough on both sides of the river?"

Doc was attending to a few of the wounded men when the captain spotted McTavett lying in the bed of a buckboard. He stopped to say a few words. "Thatcher McTavett. A better brawler than a gunman. A lousy man with cards. Always losing your temper. Not a night you wouldn't lose it. Only had a few teeth left, and you had more teeth than brains. But the ladies will all miss ya."

With that, McTavett sat up and said, "Capt'n, it'll never be a night that the ladies will be a-missin' Thatcher McTavett." He lay back down and groaned as the buckboard kept moving.

The captain sidled in next to the wagon. "You start this, McTavett?"

Without rising or opening his eyes, McTavett answered, "Can't say that I did. We were all a talkin', and no one was a doin', and the next thin' I know, someone shoots me-- twice." He gestured to his left shoulder and hand. "Had it not been for this nice young man pickin' me up, I'd a died. Probably won't ever be usin' me arm agin."

The captain received a nod from the team driver and continued. "What else happened?"

McTavett replied, "Don't rightly know, Capt'n. I was knocked off me horse, and me gun went off. Don't think I hit anybody. God help me if I did."

"God help ya if you did, you lyin' weasel. Who'd you kill?"

McTavett groaned a bit, opened one eye, and answered, "Don't think I hit anythin' but a big horse a-comin' down on top a me. Alls I remember. This big brown horse."

The driver turned back and affirmed what he said, answering, "He's right, Capt'n. I was behind him. Of course, there was a rider on the horse, and I think the horse squashed the hell out of him."

The captain motioned for the driver to stop the team. He addressed McTavett again. "Did you shoot him?"

The driver interrupted again, "The horse, sir. He shot the horse. It was self-defense."

McTavett closed his eyes and smiled, saying, "He shot me before he went down. He did."

The captain answered, "And the horse killed him? Who was it, McTavett?"

McTavett sat up, leaned against the inside of the buckboard, and answered the captain. "I was shot up, Capt'n. I fell off me horse. When the firin' was all over, me friend here picked me up and threw me in this buggy."

The team driver identified the victim. "It was Matt Jorgensen, Capt'n. His horse reared up, and his shotgun went off and hit McTavett. Next thing I saw was Matt on the ground and his big bay horse squashing him like a ladybug. Couldn't have survived no matter who he was, I'm a thinkin', it wasn't McTavett's fault. That horse fallin' like that."

McTavett groaned some more and the captain said, "The Brazos men identified him as Matt. I guess you finally got him this time, McTavett."

"Not me, sir. Someone else, maybe. I didn't cause any man to die."

"I'll be the judge of that. You're headed for the noose, McTavett." He motioned for the team driver to drive on, with a warning to McTavett that his friend had better not be lying.

He sat his horse still while he pondered what the driver had just said. "Matt Jorgenson, Capt'n." Then he began to wonder to himself whether Matt was the man the three cowboys were looking for, and if he was, it was too late to do anything about it now.

Before he could reason it out for himself, Shorty rode over to the captain's side and pointed down the road. "You'll find two more of their men down by that clump of oak trees along the trail." He pointed south.

The captain joined Shorty, suggesting he ride close. Looking down the road, he asked, "Just what happened here?"

"They chased us and shot at us," Shorty answered, trotting alongside the captain. "We shot back."

The captain examined the bodies and noticed the gunshots in their backs. "You shot back, or you shot them in the back?"

"I know it looks bad, Capt'n, but if you'll look at the road back here, you'll see where we fell off our horses."

"You fell off your horses?"

"Yes, sir," Shorty continued. "They shot at us and missed, but we pretended we got hit and we both fell."

"Same place? Same time?"

"Yes, sir. We fell face down in all that goo and laid still. We were expectin' to get shot or run over, but they never did. They kept ridin' to get Slim who was in front.

"Well, sir, when they passed us, we rose up and shot 'em."

The captain removed his Stetson and shook his head. "Sounds justifiable, son. I don't think you coulda made up a yarn like that. Let's pick up the Doc and Maggie and get to the ranch."

He then rode over and told the others in the McDaniels' group to resume their work and take the bodies with them. They continued their ride towards the McDaniels' ranch.

One wrangler attempted to convince Doc to leave the McDaniels' group to tend to their own for a while. Almost tripping on his tongue, he said, "Doc, ya gotta take a look at our boys first. Then you can go over and help the McDaniels' group."

Maggie looked at the wagons and riders heading to the river. Her gaze lasted for a moment, then she turned in the buggy to look around the ranch where more wranglers and riders lay on the ground. She and Doc agreed to take care of the Brazos' group, and then go across the river and tend to the needs of the rest, if necessary.

The doc whipped the horses to head on to the ranch. "Mor'n likely they can get Doc Brown to help. He lives in that direction, and I know he's been mighty welcome at their ranch. We'll help here first."

CHAPTER 5

THE EIGHTH TEXAS CAVALRY

When Maggie and Doc arrived at the ranch, Matt was stretched out face down on his own bed, sound asleep. His leg was well bandaged. Jaimie was leaving the room with a pan of water and a towel while Leisha finished putting on a clean blouse. She had washed the blood from herself, but her hair was still a bird's nest. She could care less. She had been working hard and long, but felt not one bit tired.

Maggie was tending to the needs of the wounded outside when the Doctor entered the house. He said to Leisha as he began opening his bag, "How bad is he, Leisha?"

Leisha looked up at the Doc and moved out of the way to let him take over. "Hole in his back, through his shoulder. Buckshot plumb through his chaps. Go figure, Doc. Good that ya come. We got most of the buckshot out of his leg, but there's still some left that we didn't want to go after."

The Doc began to tend to Matt's back. Matt started to move. Realizing he was coming around, the Doc called for some help. "Leisha, hold him! Jaimie, give her a hand." He examined the shoulder wound, cleaned it up, and bandaged it. Then he wrapped Matt's arm in a sling to keep him from using it. As Doc checked for broken bones, he said, "Leg is intact. Nothing broken, that I can see." He saw some buckshot lodged deep under the skin, and he began to probe for the pellets, one by one. He flipped each one out onto the floor. Matt flinched a little, gritting his teeth as he held back the pain.

"Damn," Matt groaned. "What're you using? My Bowie?" He tried to relax as much as he could to let Doc treat him.

Doc picked out a bandanna from his bag, rolled it up and placed it in Matt's mouth. "Here. Bite down on this."

Matt did as Doc suggested, settled down and suffered the pain, knowing he had no other alternative. "How many, Doc?" he mumbled.

"You only lost a couple, Matt." Doc answered. "Maybe a dozen wounded. One gut shot. Two got it in the butt. Couple leg injuries. Few broken bones from falling. And, you."

Matt asked point-blank, "Who, Doc? Who got it?"

Doc continued wrapping Matt's leg as he replied, "Steve's all right. Seth made out fine. The general never left his room."

"One lad from Mississippi," Leisha added. "And a boy from town who just started work for us. They got killed right behind you."

"Damn. Kids," Matt said angrily. "They shouldn't have been up front with me." Leisha turned her head away as she held back the tears.

Doc proceeded to pour whiskey on the wound.

"Thought you said it wasn't too serious, Doc? We lost two boys?"

"Seth buried them proper," Leisha said.

Doc finished the dressing and helped put Matt's leg back under the cover. "The other side lost at least a dozen, with twice that many wounded. Their guns were no match for yours."

"Hell, they knew that afore they came across the Brazos. But they came just the same. Let me ask ya, Doc, would you have?"

"No one in their right mind would."

"Right. And sure as fire, no one with a group of inexperienced fighters like these farmers."

Doc examined the rhythm of his heart with the heel of his hand, looked into his eyelid to examine his eyes, then said to the ladies present, "He'll live. Figure I got the last one out. Bandage it again, Leisha, tight, and let him sleep it out." He got up, walked towards the door, and stared out where he saw bodies being picked up and treated. "Looks like Maggie and I've got work to do."

Slim stepped up on the porch sidestepping the Doc as he left the house. He walked into Matt's room where Jaimie was walking out, talking to her briefly. "Is he dead?"

Jaimie stopped, smiled, and flirted a little with her eyes. She answered him politely but cutely, "Nah. Doc says he'll live."

He slipped past her and went into the room, meeting Leisha. "Is he asleep, then?" he asked.

Leisha finished the dressing and rose to meet Slim. "Anyone half his size would have been dead. Yes. He's sleeping."

Slim walked back out of the house to join his friends. He looked back to see if he could get another glimpse of Jaimie, as Steve bumped into him. Slim was appearing to be more in the way than being useful.

Steve reflected on the group. "Leisha tells me that you know Matt from Montana?"

Slim spoke for the three right away, saying, "Never met him. His Ma sent us down to fetch him. She's -- uh --" His words trailed off as his eyes caught Jaimie going back into Matt's room.

Shorty spoke up, saying, "She's dying. She wants to see him before she does. Which by now, she could be. I mean, who knows?"

Dan added, "She was in pretty bad shape when we left. But we promised her, and we're here."

There was a pause for a moment as if to change the subject. The boys were seeing their chances at getting Matt back to Montana went from next to impossible down to almost none. Slim asked, "How's his chances? I mean, of makin' it? Of comin' through?" He felt clumsy asking these questions.

Steve looked at the men, then back towards Matt's room. "We'll know in a while. He's just passed out. That's, all. It'll take more than a little buckshot to do him in."

Shorty picked up on it, and said, "Yeah, but look at all the blood. His leg could be gone."

Steve ushered them to a nearby tree where they could rest, away from the house. Things around them had pretty much settled down, but the smell of gunpowder still lingered in the air. The four sized up the situation as Steve remarked slowly, yet intensely. "I suppose we lost three or four good men. Half dozen or so have shots, cuts, or bruises. Doc will have his hands full for awhile. McDaniels' group lost a good dozen, and twice as many wounded, I guess. The War's never over."

One could see in Steve's eyes that this had happened before, and will for all intents and purposes happen again. Fighting in this country to take over someone's property was pretty much the run of the mill. It happened like clock work. Finding good men like Matt to defend one's ranch, not to mention one's honor, was rare. Steve knew it, and was thinking back to the times he had done this before. One time before, he was the one who was wounded, and Matt was tending to his wound. Maybe next time, one of them could bite the bullet for good.

Slim rested his hands on a high limb and eyed the distant figures of the McDaniels' bunch leaving. He asked Steve, "Why did all this happen? I mean, what is causing them to come here and fight you?"

Steve joined the cowboy's gaze towards where the McDaniels' group retreated, and to the men lying on the ground around them. Most of the wranglers were up and helping the wounded. Some were riding, making sure the McDaniels bunch took their wounded and dead without firing up the embers again.

He yelled out at the bunch, "Seth! Get a burial detail." Softening the tone of his voice, he said, "Make damn sure you mark their graves correctly." Then he turned and looked at the boys, and said, "I gotta notify their kinfolk. If'n there be any."

Slim observed Steve was not about to answer his question right away. It was all right with him. He backed away and asked in another way, "I guess you fought on the side of the South?"

Steve gave a nod as he moved next to Slim. "Damn right, boy. So was Matt." Then he took a wad of tobacco from his hip pocket and tore off a chaw with his teeth. After a few chews he continued. "Look around you, boy. We're all from the South. And you better be rememberin' where the hell you're at." He spit out into the dirt.

Shorty added, "You talk like an officer; giving all those orders, like."

Steve nodded, saying, "Lieutenant. The Eighth Texas Cavalry. Matt was my capt'n." Looking at the three, he asked, "You fight on the side of the North?"

Shorty replied, "Hell. We were too young. Matt's dad was too old, so he bred horses and cattle for the North."

The tallest among the three cowboys said, "'Bout time I interduced myself. I'm Charlie Honeycutt. You can call me Slim. We worked for Matt's Ma and Pa."

Dan inquired of Steve, "How long you know Matt?"

Steve replied, "Know him? No one ever knows him. Met him during the war. Had it not been for him, the general'd be in a grave somewhere and nowhere. One of your men had a bead on him with his bayonet while my back was turned. Matt busted him aside the head and saved him. Then, when I was standing there with my mouth wide open, too damn dumbfounded to realize we almost lost our general, he ups and shoots another right behind me. I guess I owe him for that. But then he never thought it that way."

Slim continued, "Then you both came to Texas and here?"

Steve replied smiling as he gestured, "Pretty much. We headed back for Houston. That's where we first hitched up and became part of Terry's Rangers."

He began walking away, taking in everything that was happening around him. He continued, "he told me he was from Montana, but couldn't go back. Found out why one night when we emptied a coupla bottles in a saloon.

"Then boss man had us looked up. He was our general and stayed up with Matt and me through the ranks. Liked the way we handled our guns, like 'nerves of steel', he said. Said he needed us on his ranch across the Brazos, and the pay was good. Then is when we came here."

Slim asked almost knowing that he wouldn't get an answer, or at best, the wrong answer. "Mind telling us what it was Matt told ya?"

Steve shrugged his shoulder in a nonchalant manner and answered him, "Up to him." He paused and then continued, "You asked a question about 'why all this took place'. Look around you. This is Texas, as far as your eye can see from the Rio Grande on the south to the plains of Oklahoma on the north. The largest state in the union. A lot of men fought for a mass of land as big as some of your other states. Men like Austin, Sam Houston, Jim Bowie, Davy Crockett; you name 'em. We are Texians first and Americans second. Our present governor was a general in the Confederate Army. So was the governor before him. We have fighting men all around us, and that's what Texians are all about."

He took a breath and pointed at the McDaniels group and continued. "See them. They are Texians, too. Many are ex-soldiers of the Confederate Army. Some fought alongside Matt and me. McTavett, the guy that shot up Matt, was a sergeant. Ninth Cavalry, I reckon. Was a good man. Damn, they were all good men."

Slim interrupted, hoping not to stop Steve from explaining, and said, "If they were fighting with you, why are they fighting agin' you now? I mean, hell, the war's been over some fifteen years now."

Steve took another look around to make sure the men were obeying his commands. "That's jest it, boy; the war is over, but they're still fightin' it." He pointed across the Brazos. "They came home to a new beginning. They enjoyed fightin'; and then they had to go back to farmin' or ranchin'. Hell, I guess they felt they're owed somethin' for their years away from home. Dammit. McTavett would settle for a few head and a small range, I suppose. And that's just what McDaniels is promising him, except it's our cattle, and our range that he wants to give him. And the rest all around us."

Dan broke a twig he had been playing with which caused him unconsciously to speak up. "Well, don't this McDaniels have enough land? Why's she want to take what's not hers?"

Slim pointed out around him like Steve was explaining. He said, "This is Texas, Dan. Too much land, and yet, I guess not enough."

Steve took his gun out of his holster, squatted where he was and rotated the cylinder to examine his spent bullets. While replacing the spent shells, he said, "Should have done this before." He paused and looked up at the cowboys, and added, "It's not just the land, kids. It's a whole bunch of things. Greed. Wanting what isn't theirs. Power. And just damned orneriness. Cussed everyone of them wanting to fight for the hell of it, knowing some will get killed. Sometimes it takes a lot of rotgut whiskey to get up the nerve."

Seeing the comedic side of Steve, Shorty allowed himself to burst out a laugh. He asked, "Where do you fit into this, Steve?"

Steve holstered his pistol and stood up. "Me? Hell, I don't know. Been with Matt too long, I suppose, and don't know where I'm headed. Boss man hired us for our guns but made me the foreman. Seth's his son, and he's my ramrod. Go figure."

Slim asked, "A moment ago you said Mitchell hired the both of you for your guns. How come you're the foreman and Matt's the hired gun?"

Steve laughed a bit and answered him, saying, "Matt don't like bein' foreman. Don't like ramroddin'. Hell, he won't even ride point. All in all, boys, Matt don't care for cattle. He tol' me that he had his fill of cattle when he was a young 'un, and would never want to ranch anymore."

Then he paused, got up and began walking again. He added, "Well, you done seen how Matt commanded the defense, and got right out there on the front line, knowing he was gonna get shot. But remember, he had this ranch protected. That's his job. And he does it well."

Seeing that he was getting a little excited, Steve calmed down a little, and said, "Notice how everyone took after Matt when he got shot? Matt is our savior, so to speak. He is Jim Bowie, and Davy Crockett wrapped up in one. There isn't anything anyone around here wouldn't do for him, and there isn't anything he wouldn't do for any one."

Shorty, good at interrupting, said, "Except tend cattle."

Slim looked over at the house as if to see someone moving about; especially Jaimie. He eyed the door carefully, then said, "This Matt is a valuable man."

Noticing Slim's gazing away from him, Steve continued, "Valuable? This ranch will be his some day, if'n he has a mind to hook up with Leisha."

Shorty broke in. "If'n he don't. What then?"

"Don't think that's an issue that's likely to come up. He'll marry her." Turning toward the house he stared at it as if into empty space and murmured softly as not to be heard, "Or else . . . ."

Slim heard that conditional phrase spoken a little shakily and turned to focus attention on Steve. "You got a likin' fer Leisha, too, don't ya?"

Steve turned and headed up on the porch, trailing his speech behind him. "Boy. You better watch your mouth. Gotta check on him."

The cowboys tightened their circle to discuss their next move. Shorty opened with, "Well, Matt's not fit for travel; that's fer sure."

Dan joined in. "Not saying that he would want to go with us if'n he was."

Slim nodded in agreement, scuffed the ground with his boot, and looked back at the ranch screen door. "He's not dead. That's a fact." Next, he directed his talk towards the sentiments of Matt's mother needing to see her only son before she died. "He'll want to go."

Dan and Shorty leaned in to listen closely, almost sensing what Slim was about to say.

Slim paused, looked at the other two, and asked, "When?"

CHAPTER 6

THE ROUNDUP

Nighttime on the prairie during this season was quiet and beautiful. It was summer, and the evening was warm. A halo circled the moon and the wind was beginning to pick up a little. The young cowboys from Montana were on the sheltered side of the barn asleep on their saddles. It hardly seemed like a battle was fought this day. Lightning fluttered through the sky. When large rain drops began to fall, the cowboys moved into the barn to keep dry. The hay was warm, cozy, and smelled of horses. The boys soon fell fast asleep again.

A hard rain continued to fall well into the morning, and the ground was once again clean, as if there were no battles; no wounded; no dead. The air smelled fresh. Up on a hillside, a few hundred yards away from the ranch, one could see the shades of wooden crosses as the rain ran off the newly planted graves.

The wranglers were up and tending to the horses early. The cook had food under a lean-to near one of the oak trees that decorated the ranch.

Steve was on his horse, riding tall and strong like the commander he was, shouting orders for the wranglers to start gathering the cattle. He turned his Stetson-covered head towards the Brazos River and stared. He knew the river would soon be rising, and the cattle would not be able to cross it; this would help drive them. It was time to get them over to the Chisholm Trail in Waco.

The town of Waco was a two day's ride days for lone horsemen up the bank of the Brazos. His main concern now was the McDaniels bunch having time to regroup and cut them off. "Damn," he thought to himself. "Wasn't thinking about the rain for another week." He knew it would be a hard rain, nothing small ever happened in Texas, and rounding up the cattle would take longer than he wanted.

The wranglers rode out to the edge of the ranch and began the arduous task of gathering the longhorns. They were harder to handle in a herd because of the length of their horns.

"Why," Steve wondered to himself, "did boss man decide on longhorns? Don't taste as good as Angus." Steve knew his cattle, being brought up on a ranch with good Angus breed.

Leisha and Jaimie walked out on the front porch of the main house. Jaimie looked over at Slim and the other two coming out of the barn with saddles in hand.

As the cowboys were walking to the corral, Slim kept looking over at Jaimie.

Jaimie yelled out, "Ya gotta have some breakfast. Wanna join us inside, cowboys?"

Slim was tempted. Not so much for the food, although that was a good enough reason. He simply wanted to be close to Jaimie. He looked ahead to the lean-to where some of the other wranglers were finishing up their breakfast. Putting on his rain gear, he answered her, "Can't. Like ta. Gotta help Steve." He continued walking. Turning to look back, he added, "Later?"

Jaimie motioned it would be okay. Leisha watched Steve as he rode out, grumbling a little at the wranglers who were still milling around the lean-to, eating. He was thinking, "They should be out on the range already."

Shorty yelled over to Jaimie, "How's Matt this morning?"

"Fine, Shorty. Coming along jest fine," she said almost straining her voice. She spotted Seth riding up to the corral at a fast clip.

He rode into the breakfast camp and over to the three cowboys finishing up their meal. He reined up, looked them over, and asked in a friendly manner, "You boys stayin' over?"

Slim answered for the three. "Figured on it."

Seth rolled back his hat and responded, "For how long?"

Shorty gulped down a swig of coffee and answered, "Just as soon as Matt's able to ride. Seeing that won't be any too soon, suppose we gotta do something around here to kinda earn our keep? Reckon?"

Seth, sitting tall in the saddle and looking around at the other drovers working said, "Kinda. We can use ya, I reckon. You wanna side in with the other drovers for a while and help round up the cattle? We've got a big drive coming up to head 'em for Kansas."

Slim tossed the balance of his coffee into the wind and agreed. "Tell us where to go and what to do, and it'll be done."

Seth addressed them now as a ramrod, "I like your style. Take your time finishin' up. Head out there," he pointed to the south of the ranch. "And bring in any strays you can find."

"How far do we ride?" Dan asked, downing his coffee.

Seth leaned down in the saddle to look Dan in the eye, motioned with his hand, and said, "As far as your eye can see. Take some grub with ya. You'll be gone a few days. See those wranglers south of here, they'll kinda guide you. Tell them I sent 'ya." He rode off.

The three young men cleaned up their plates and turned them over to the cook, a short and plump fellow who looked like he loved his own cooking -- a lot. He was dressed in jeans and a plaid shirt, with a well-worn hat, and muddy boots. A well-stained apron covered his front

He said to the three cowboys, "Get your gear, and stop by. I'll have some grub ready ta take with ya."

The three agreed and headed towards the barn. There, they picked up their saddles, then went over to the corral for their horses. As Slim finished tightening the cinch on his horse, he saw Jaimie as he looked over the cradle of his saddle.

She stepped off the porch and headed in his direction.

"She is a lovely picture to look at so early in the morning." He murmured to himself.

She was wearing a pair of dungarees, a shirt that accentuated her bosom, and a loose bandanna. Wearing no hat, she let the morning wind gently toss her hair. Without stopping, she approached him as he mounted his horse and said, "Good morning, handsome."

Slim adjusted himself in his saddle, checked the reins, and politely tipped his hat to her. "Morning, Jaimie."

Jaimie smiled back, "You look like you might be fixing to join the roundup? " She paused for a second, and then asked a little worriedly, "Or are ya leavin'?"

Realizing his buddies were eyeing him, on their horses and waiting,, he sheepishly answered. "Gonna stay awhile."

The cook served up the grub to put into their saddle bags. Packing his, he kept his face stern and avoided looking at Jaimie. He leaned forward in his saddle, holding his reins a little high, and urged his horse in to a walk. He tipped his hat again, grinned, and rode away, the other cowboys joining him.

Flirtatiously, Jaimie smiled, waved, and said, "See ya."

He responded, looking back at her, "Yeah," and rode on.

The three rode south up to the first hill where they encountered a couple of wranglers adjusting their ropes. Jaimie watched the quintet converse with one another, then ride slowly away. She stood watching for awhile.

Leisha stepped out onto the porch and eyed Jaimie. Leisha was wearing her blue denim riding skirt with long pockets, with a silver belt buckle. She wore a red blouse, and a blue denim vest. A hat neat and clean. Her blond hair hung loose under it.

"Kinda cute fella," she said with a grin.

Jaimie nodded in agreement and walked back to the porch with her head cocked back, and very kittishly up to the porch. She asked, "How's Matt?"

Looking out at the corral, Leisha caught a glance of Steve riding up to the chuck wagon to get his grub. She answered Jaimie without taking her eyes off Steve. "Matt will be fine. Some good nights' sleep, and he'll be back in the saddle in a week or two."

Jaimie smiled at Leisha, knowing the game she was playing. Every time Steve had to go away, she dressed handsomely just for him.

She looked over at Steve and how Leisha was eyeing him, and said, "How long they gonna be gone?"

"Couple of days. Maybe a week. I still like to look good for him. Let him know what he's got to look forward to when he gets back."

Jaimie matter-of-factly returned, "Matt doesn't even suspect?"

"He knows. Just doesn't let me know he knows," Leisha answered, while returning her gaze to Steve.

Meanwhile, Slim's silhouette rode far out on the rolling hills, traveling south. Jaimie watched until he disappeared.

The rain continued to come down softly kissing the porch where the two women were standing.

Steve grabbed his plate and walked over to the porch.

Jaimie excused herself as Leisha and Steve began to make light conversation about the rain. "Will probably rain for a couple days like this, I reckon." Leisha told Steve.

Steve looked at the mud building up in the ruts caused by the wagon wheels, and the hoof prints of the horses.

"Muddy," he answered.

Leisha looked around where most of the wranglers were too engaged in their work activities to be watching them. Then she slyly looked in the door and front room window to see if anyone else could be watching. Sensing the moment was hers, she slid her hand into Steve's and squeezed hard. He returned the grip, released it, and continued eating.

She whispered, "How soon you gonna be back?"

He answered, "Three or four days. Gotta round up all the cattle if'n we're gonna make the Chisholm Trail drive in a coupla weeks."

Sliding close to his side, rain dropped onto her freshly ironed clothes. She pressed hard into his side and slipped her hand around his waist feeling for an opening in his shirt. "Damn long johns," she said in mock frustration.

Steve looked behind her to see that no one was looking and kissed her hard on her lips. His hand came across her blouse for a moment, giving Leisha a little excitement in their kiss. They broke, and he walked away. "Keep that 'til I get back," he whispered as he jumped from the porch, heading back into the rain with his near-empty breakfast plate.

She looked out at him as his large figure strutted across the mud. She never knew him to be so big before. With all the rain and mud, and his chaps and rain gear, spurs and tall Stetson, he was now her hero. Not that Matt wasn't as good or better a man. She wanted Matt. But Matt had set his mind never to marry and settle down. Knowing this, she went after Steve.

She began to compare the two with more favorable reasoning for her now to love Steve. To her, Steve had a sort of down-home whimsical type of charm about him that Matt didn't have. Matt was too bossy, and didn't show enough concern for her as a lady. Steve was tender and more compassionate, and showed it by the little things he would do, like touching her breast lightly in passing off a hard kiss. He knew this was what she wanted, but could only taste a brief moment of it. It was enough to last until he returned. He was in love with her, and she with him. Although, if a word came from Matt's lips to change her mind, she would. She still believed that Matt claimed her as his girl, but with no serious intentions.

Her concern had been to find a way to break from Matt and become Steve's girl without hurting Matt. She reasoned with herself, "I'm in love with one man who cannot marry me, and I'll be damned if I'm gonna chance being a spinster all my life. I'm pretty, and I'm smart. I'll not waste my life on just anybody. And, if I can't have Matt, I'll take Steve. He's a better man, anyhow." Now, she figured, it would be only a matter of time and convenience before they could tell Matt of their committed love for each other.

CHAPTER 7

MATT'S RECOVERY

Matt turned in his bed and felt the pain. It wasn't so much from the buckshot-wounded leg, as it was from his chest where the horse rolled over the top of him. He had a busted shoulder and a side that no one treated. Hearing Jaimie working with the dishes in the kitchen, he yelled out, "Leisha!" He grimaced in pain, but called out again, "Leisha, honey."

Jaimie threw her towel on the back of a chair and came to his room. She saw this big, strapping, bare-chested man lying half off the bed towards the floor with his face down. Again, he called, "Leisha, honey? Can anyone hear me?"

Jaimie picked his body up tenderly and put him onto his back. His eyes were shut tight in pain. Once the pain subsided for a moment, he opened his eyes and saw one of the prettiest blonde ladies in all of Texas. Her hair was long and silken; her eyes were deep-water blue; her body was thin, but not skinny. He saw all of this in his nurse in just a few seconds. A grin spread over his rugged-looking face and the pain went away. His arm rose around her back, and the pain came shooting back. He reacted, closed his eyes again, and said in haltingly words, "Jaimie, I am one sorrowful human being."

As Jaimie bent close to his face, Matt smelled the freshness of the morning come from her body. All the pain in hell could not stop him from smiling again and wanting to hold her. She looked at his swollen-up shoulder and stroked her hand down his right side where the swelling seemed to run, at the same time turning him in towards the bed. "You're hurting still in your side, aren't you, Matt?" she tenderly asked as she held his frame with her small hands.

He helped hold himself up and answered her, "Yes, ma'am. It hurts like hell." He laughed a bit, and she gave him a puzzling look.

"Makes the pain in my leg go away, though."

Jaimie smiled and placed him on his back gently and straightened the covers around him. "I'll see if I can find Doc or Maggie. I'll be right back." She walked out the doorway just as Leisha walked in.

Leisha looked at Matt, a little astonished that he was suffering more than she knew. "Is your leg bothering you, Matt?"

Matt looked at her and reached out his hand to her.

"Miss Leisha. You seen Jaimie lately? She's growed up," he said.

Leisha did a double look at the empty doorway and back to Matt. "Yes, Matt. We all grow up, eventually." She made another subtle attempt to win his favor as his girl, knowing in her heart it was futile.

Matt got her message. His look at Leisha told him that he had as pretty a woman in front of him as went out the door. In fact, Leisha looked a little too pretty on such a rainy day, he surmised. "Must be the rain." He looked at Leisha eyeing the bedpan, ready to pick it up. He said, "It'll keep."

Leaving it beside the bed, she sat on the bed and uncovered his shoulders a bit.

"What about the rain, Matt?"

"You women have an uncanny way of looking real pretty and smelling real sweet on rainy days. Or else I ain't been paying too much attention." Matt pointed out the window while waving his left hand as he talked.

Leisha stroked his shoulder where he was showing pain and kissed it.

"You do that one more time, and I ain't gonna wanna get well at all."

Leisha kissed his bared chest, this time cradling his head with her hand.

He took her hand with his left hand and kissed it.

The kiss came across her hand and to her cheek as she turned in to face him directly. But she wouldn't let him kiss her on the lips. Now, that was Steve's privilege. But she gave her cheek to him in full surrender and laid her head on his chest.

His fingers found their way through her hair as she listened quietly to his heartbeat.

He whispered, "What a hell of a time to get me aroused. I gotta pee."

She laughed, and the voices of Maggie and Jaimie in the living room broke up their sacred moment together. Picking up the bedpan, she handed it to him, and commanded, "Use it! I'll hold them off 'til you call me."

She left the room and greeted Maggie in the front room where she was shaking the rain off her scarf.

Maggie was not new to this room. She had sat before that fireplace many years taking care of Jaimie and Leisha as children.

The room was very simple and manly looking. A large leather couch with three over-size chairs to match the adorned room. A huge fireplace with mantle of elegant stone was to the right of the door. A Confederate flag and the Lone Star flag draped the wall on both sides of the entrance leading to a hallway and other bedrooms; one of which was occupied by Matt. This was his house, his home.

Leisha cut off Maggie's entrance into the hallway. "The big man's answering nature's call."

Maggie, looking around the room said, "Big man, big room."

Jaimie cupped her mouth and laughed. She said in a childlike response, "You should have seen the big man half on the floor a while ago trying to find small pan."

The ladies eyed each other. Maggie was a sturdy strapping woman in her late forties, with graying black hair wrapped with a scarf she neatly tied in place after shaking off the rain. Her denim coat and pants belonged to Leisha, replacing hers which were stained with the blood of the wounded. Her boots were slightly soiled with mud; she had scraped most of it off before entering the house. Yet, this morning she looked as fresh and pretty as either Leisha or Jaimie. She knew her work was almost over, and she would be heading back home with Doc Wilson. She had had a good breakfast at the main ranch house with the young ladies earlier.

She looked over at Jaimie sitting on the arm of one of the chairs, and remarked, "It's been, what, fifteen years since the general's wife Emily took you in as a little girl? You were the prettiest thing I had ever seen. Ralph and I never had any children. Always wanted one. Suppose you were the closest thing."

Leisha sat down on the couch and sank into the leather. Speaking to Jaime, she said, "I was in school when you came here. I remember running home real fast knowing you were coming that day. Some people in a big buggy brought you and gave you to daddy. He told me you were my sister."

"Saucer blue eyes. Blonde curly hair." Maggie continued. "And you walked into anything and anywhere. You were completely wild."

"Was I really?" Jaimie asked.

"I remember daddy picking you up and walking outside with you," Leisha said. "He held you with his good hand, and sat on the porch swing." Leisha remembered, "I climbed up and sat down beside him, and began patting your head. I called you 'Sissy', until he taught me to call you Jaimie."

"Your name is Jaimie, but it was too hard for Leisha to say, so she'd call you 'Sissy Jane", Maggie added.

Jaimie smiled at Maggie. "You stayed here on the ranch with the general and took care of Leisha and me all these years. Even after you and the Capt'n got married."

Maggie walked over to the fireplace, turned and looked at the two young ladies, and said, "Then I met Ralph. I took you two into town one day, and Ralph was coming out of the Rangers' office. My, he looked handsome. I pulled my buggy up to the general store, got out, and he saw me. He came over and helped me with you two. I suppose I fell in love with him because of that Ranger star on his vest, and the two guns at his side; pearl-handled revolvers. God, he loves those," Maggie paused. "Almost more than me, I reckon."

Matt's voice rung out.

"Ladies. If Maggie is through reminiscing, there's a hurt man lying in bed here who kinda needs some attention."

Maggie smiled at the ladies, picked up her medicine bag, and headed for Matt's room. Entering, she saw Matt still lying on his back, with the covers pulled down to his waist. Maggie addressed him, "Good morning, Matt. Had any breakfast, yet?"

"Not hungry." Matt rubbed his left side and shoulder as if to point to the direction of the pain. He looked at her as she set her bag down, opened it, and then put her glasses to her nose. "You gotta do all that afore ya look at me?"

Maggie sat on the bed and began examining Matt in the tender areas of his left side. When she touched him, Matt bolted and let out a yell. He bit his lip and sighed. "Matt. Hate to tell you this, but you have a couple busted-up ribs." She poked around his shoulder dressing, and again smiled to pain's delight. "And a busted shoulder. Doc set you real good. You were in real pain when they brought you in."

Matt watched her rub ointment on his side and shoulder, readying the bandages she was about to apply. He answered, "All I remember is sitting on the ass of my dead horse and belting out commands. I don't remember for what or to who."

Leisha stepped into the doorway, and he saw her feminine frame. He said, "I remember seeing sort of an angel, and she came over and sat down beside me."

Leisha sensed his love for her, but still questioned its authenticity inside her. "Need the Doc, Maggie?" She smiled and stepped into the room.

"Nah. Just a busted rib or two -- and shoulder. Here, hold this for me." She pointed to a spot in the bandage as she began wrapping the bandage tight around his rib. She gently pulled his shoulder inside the bandage keeping his arm in place. "He'll pull through." She finished up, patted him on the head, and ordered him, "Pull your johns down. I want to change the dressing on your leg."

Doc Wilson was heard coming up on the porch and being addressed by Jaimie. "Good morning, Doc."

"Morning, Jaimie. Matt okay?"

Jaimie took his hat and showed him to the room. She followed him as he entered the bedroom.

"Morning, Matt."

"Morning, Doc. Just in time. Maggie almost had me undressed." Looking at the ladies, he said, "Ladies. If you please. I'd like some privacy."

Maggie stayed, but Leisha left the room. Matt pulled his johns down, and looked at the Doc. Doc examined Maggie's work. Taking her place on the bed, he resumed dressing Matt's leg.

The Doc finished the dressing and helped put Matt's leg back under the cover.

Captain Johnson's spurs could be heard as he stepped upon the porch. He bellowed out, "Doc. Maggie. You here?"

Jaimie opened the door for him and ushered him to Matt's bedroom where Doc and Maggie were packing up their equipment, getting ready to leave. As he entered the room, the captain said, "Good, I caught up with you. Just left the general."

"Mornin', Capt'n," Matt said. Always nice to know someone cares."

"Sorry, Matt. How ya feelin'?" asked the captain.

"I'm gettin' along better now that these bandages are finally in their proper place. Seems the Doc set me up temporarily, kinda, and Maggie, here . . . ."

The captain looked over at the couple again, and interrupted, "Kinda figured you'd be all right. He is, ain't he, Doc?"

"Good thing he's as strong as he is," Doc said. "Else a fall like he had would have been fatal."

"That's why I came over. Matt, you are going to be all right?" the captain asked.

"Listen to what the Doc says, Capt'n," Matt replied. "All I got is a busted shoulder, and a few ribs. The most hurt I got is from someone's shotgun."

"The general and I have agreed," the captain continued.

"On what, Capt'n?" Matt frowned.

"McTavett thinks you're dead. His men think you're dead. We want to leave it that way, if you don't mind."

Matt sat himself up a little higher in bed with the assistance of Leisha. "But I'm not dead. Why should anyone think otherwise?"

"I talked with McTavett yesterday as his men were hauling him away in a wagon," the captain explained. "He is ecstatic about the fact that he saw you die. He didn't say it, but from what I gathered from Steve and some others, he thinks he shot you full of holes, and your horse rolled over and finished you."

"Well, Capt'n, that's exactly what he did do," Matt smiled. "He shot me full of holes and killed my horse. My shotgun went off aimed at McTavett."

The captain, agreeing, added, "He got his left arm shot to hell. You hit him, all right."

"Good. Shoulda killed the son-of-bitch." Matt paused for a moment, and said, "Don't know for sure, but I think my leg shot out of my stirrup, and I fell on my left side. My horse rolled on top of my back."

The captain laughed a little, excused himself, and said, "Anyway, Matt, they think you're dead. With a capital 'D'. The general and I agree that with them thinkin' this way, as soon as McTavett is up and around, they'll attack again."

Matt looked around and asked Leisha, "Honey, I need another drink." He looked at the captain and said, "We already know that. This isn't the first time, and it won't be the last time he's come across the Brazos to fight us."

The captain took the glass of whiskey and drank it himself. Returning the glass to Leisha, he continued, "But with you out of the way, they will be careless in their next attack."

Matt gave the captain a look but smiled as Leisha poured another and took it to Matt herself. He agreed with the captain, saying, "Good point."

Steve entered the room and as usual stood in the background. Matt caught sight of him and said, "Steve. You hear any of this?"

Steve answered, "I was with the capt'n and the general when they discussed it. And I agree."

Maggie interrupted, saying, "Then we've got to make sure they still think that when we return to Waco, Doc."

"We can add a little to it by confirming your death." Doc volunteered. "To make it more official, I can fill out a death certificate at the city hall where it might be convenient for some of his friends to see."

"Good!" The captain shook Matt's hand and began to leave the room. "My Rangers will spread the word, too." Stopping at the doorway, he turned back to Matt and said, "Next time they attack, Matt. Get word to me first." He walked outside and towards his horse. His Rangers had been waiting for him.

Doc excused himself and left with Maggie. Both smiled at Jaimie as they left the house. Jaimie returned to Matt's bedroom where Leisha was quieting him down.

Matt looked at Steve and asked, "Where's Seth, Steve?"

Leisha stopped, looked at Jaimie, and back at Matt. She answered for him. "Seth and the boys are out rounding up strays for the cattle drive."

Matt lay down and, looking at the ceiling, said again to Steve, "When he returns, see that he reports to me."

His stare roamed the room and stopped on Jaimie.

"Is the general in his house?"

"Yes. He's been waiting to see you." Jaimie paused for a moment, and then asked, "You up to it, now?"

"Yeah. Go get him, please."

"You never say 'please' to me," Leisha said.

"She's a little lady." He caught himself and continued, "I said a 'little lady'. She needs to be treated with some tenderness."

"All women have a need for tenderness, some time. Haven't you noticed?" Her look at Steve suggested she was talking to him, rather than to Matt.

"I'll ride out to find Seth and bring him in," Steve said.

Gesturing with his hand, Matt tried to calm Leisha down as she closed in on him.

"Oh, Leisha, you know what I mean. Come here, kid." She fell gently on his chest away from his ribs, but he still grunted. Then, putting his left hand behind her head, he brought it down towards him where her lips met his.

After she allowed a warm feeling to come over her, a feeling she had been fighting because of Steve, she felt Matt's release of her.

"The general will be here in a minute. Better fix your hair," he said, pushing her away.

She sat up, tightened her lips, and gave Matt an Irish temper look that could kill. Standing up, she left the room without saying a word.

CHAPTER 8

A PLAN

It seemed forever to Matt until the general entered the room.

"Hello, Matt."

Matt returned the greeting. The general stood strong in the doorway, as if eyeing one of his wounded officers in a casualty tent.

"Leisha tells me you got a busted rib and a shot-up shoulder, but that you're going to live."

Matt smiled, rubbed his shoulder a bit, and patted his leg.

"Don't forget the leg, general. Got plenty of buckshot in it."

The general grinned a little. "Doc says the wounds aren't too serious. You just lost a lot of blood. Hell, I've seen you busted up worse than that."

Matt smiled and looked at the liquor cabinet against the wall. "How about it, General? I need another glass to make me feel like I'm gettin' better. Too early to join me?"

"Never was. Not now, and never will be." The general took a bottle of Kentucky bourbon from the cabinet and poured a drink for Matt and one for himself. They clinked glasses as the general made a toast. "To the Brazos River Bar M Ranch."

"The finest ranch this side of the Brazos. May she always be."

They gulped two more glasses of bourbon before the general set the bottle down. He looked out the doorway into the front room and watched Leisha and Jaimie talking, admiring their fine statuesque figures. The rain was coming down a little harder.

Without turning around, the general asked, "Why, Matt?"

"Dunno, General. Beats the hell out of me. Why?"

"Most of those men I didn't recognize. Some fought like army. Most fought like kids. Only one man knew what the hell he was up against."

"McTavett. Thatcher McTavett." Matt said through clenched teeth.

The general looked at Matt and felt his anger.

"One rotten bastard in the whole regiment, and he had to be in mine," Matt said.

"Your corporal," the general said. "And you were ready to make him an officer."

"He was a good man once. Until he got out of line with a coupla good men and beat the hell out of them. All because they took away a shot he wanted. Glory-huntin' bastard. I thought all his fightin' was for the Confederacy."

"The capt'n told you?"

"He told me."

"What do you think?"

"With me dead?" Matt asked. "I thought about it."

"With you out of the way, they would think some of our men would leave us?"

"Maybe."

"He could get more men knowing you were out of the way."

Matt agreed. "He could."

"The trap would be set, and we'd get him good." Then the general asked, "Where and when?"

Matt looked sternly at him. "The bridge."

"I've been thinking the same thing. Just wanted to hear you say it," the general replied.

"When our boys bring in the strays and get ready for the big drive along the Chisholm, they're going to have to cross that bridge with four thousand head of beef. Maybe five thousand."

"This rain will keep everyone back until it clears up. Maybe a coupla weeks or so. Another week or more before McTavett is well enough to ride. Our men can be at the bridge just about that time."

"We'll be there," Matt said. "By then, I'll be riding, too."

The general's excitement almost showed through his tough, rugged face, but he kept it under control. He was all military and knew better than to try a bluff, even among friends. "And I'll be there."

"I'll drink to that, General."

The general poured more bourbon. After making a toast, he glanced at Matt with a winning look and asked, "You got a plan?"

Matt licked his lips after finishing his drink. "I'm thinkin' of one."

The general walked to the doorway and turned. "Well, Matt. While you're thinking, put this one in your pipe. When we're ready for the drive, send Seth into town ahead of us and let him get good and drunk. Or let the McDaniels bunch think he is."

Matt tried to second-guess him. The general continued, "I want Seth to tell them you're still alive, and that you're coming after McTavett."

Matt smiled broadly. "I hear you loud and clear, General. It'll work. Just before they're ready to fight us at the bridge, his men will get cold feet and leave him to fight us by himself."

The general grinned. "That's what I'm hoping. Now get some sleep, and don't let anyone in on our plan until we're ready." He looked one more time at Matt, receiving his assurance. "I'm ready for some breakfast."

The general walked into the front room as Leisha and Jaimie were coming back in from the porch where they'd been watching the rain come down and walked through the front room to the kitchen. They rattled the pots and pans like they wanted to be heard, and Leisha asked the general, "I'm to suppose you're going to have breakfast in Matt's house this morning?"

He smiled and sat down in a slightly inebriated manner. "Yes, ma'am."

Matt looked outside his window at the pouring rain which continued into the night and through the next day. To Matt, it appeared as an omen to help clear his mind of battles fought long ago, and as recent as yesterday.

Three days of rain were beginning to turn the men's minds into wanting to go full gallop after a Texas tornado. Finally, into the fourth day, the rains let up and the sun began to shine. The cowboys returned to their rounded-up cattle from all points on the ranch. The cattle and horses were muddy, and their hoofs created a different trail wherever they moved.

Matt and Leisha were out on the porch watching, Matt standing, leaning on his crutch, and Leisha seated in a chair behind him.

The general walked up from his ranch house across the way and greeted the couple with a tip of his hat. He had a cigar in his mouth and offered one to Matt.

"Don't mind if I do. Can you hold it 'til I get myself seated in this swing?" Matt wobbled cautiously over to the swing and, with Leisha's help, set himself down. "Damn," he cussed as he looked at the general. "You with a no-good right hand, and me with a busted-up shoulder." He took the cigar from the general. "Kinda make a pair, don't we?"

The general laughed. "Yeah. Good thing we're not having visitors now. How're ya feeling, Matt?"

Leisha helped make Matt comfortable with a footstool for his injured leg and a pillow on which to lay his arm, which was still bandaged and in a sling. While the two men were talking, she put the cigar in Matt's mouth, lit it for him, then offered the general her chair before going inside the house.

Matt answered the general. "Swellin's gone down in both my leg and shoulder. Pain's gone, too. Doc says I should be able to ride in a few days. Hell, you were right. The buckshot only caused a lot of superficial damage. Thanks to my chaps, the bone was hardly even touched." He took a draw on his cigar, looked out on the trail, and watched some drovers bring the cattle onto nearby hills.

"How are our guests coming along?"

"Not back yet." They saw Seth coming up the trail with a group of wranglers, and Matt said, "There's Seth. Why not ask him." With a shrill whistle made with two of his fingers, he summoned Seth over to the porch.

Seth rode up, wet, muddy and unshaven. He was a man of few words. "Boss? Steve says you wanted to see me." He stayed in his saddle as he talked, and gave a quick salute to the general, which was his custom, even if he was his pa.

The general returned his salute and asked, "How are the young cowboys from Montana doing? Ain't seen them for a few days."

Seth shifted in the saddle to ease the pain of a long ride. He looked a little grumpy. "They're gettin' the hang of longhorns. Little slow, but they'll make it in for breakfast in the mornin'. Figure we'd camp out on the hill and give the land a little more time to dry out."

"Slide outta your saddle, Seth," Matt said. "We want to ask you about the battle the other day. Didn't get a chance to talk at 'ya."

Seth dismounted, wiped his mouth with his gloved hand, and tied his horse to the post. He removed his glove and took out the makings for a cigarette. While rolling it, he said, "Hell of a battle. Too bad we lost some."

"Don't talk much, do ya?" Matt returned. "Never did. Maybe what I like about 'ya."

Seth attempted to light his rolled-up cigarette with a match from his wet vest. "Last match." It didn't light.

Matt took a match from his pocket and offered it to him.

"Course, you'll have to come over here. I'm not walkin' well enough."

Seth walked over to the swing and picked up the match from Matt.

The general stepped further to the edge of the porch. "You know that the McDaniels think Matt got killed back there?"

Seth nodded and took a deep drag on his cigarette.

The general continued, "Can you tell the boys to keep it that way?"

Seth responded, "Steve already told us."

"We want them to think that some of our men will leave if there's another fight," Matt added. "Do you think you could get the men to talk it up a little?"

Seth relaxed more after puffing on his cigarette. "Are you gonna let them know you're alive?"

The general answered, "We've kept this a secret so far by keeping Matt out of sight. It's up to you and Steve to make sure the others think Matt was killed."

Seth frowned and looked back up the trail as if to see someone. "What about those three who came lookin' for ya?"

Matt smiled a little and hesitantly responded, "You think maybe they'll up and leave right away?"

Seth replied, "Don't think so. The older one has his eye on Jaimie. Real serious like."

"Damn silly infatuation. That's what it is," the general barked. "Bust it up. Convince them three Montana cowboys some way, don't make no matter to me, that Matt is dead, and get them the hell off the ranch."

Matt frowned and said, "Wait a minute, General. You can't just throw 'em off the ranch. Not after they fought for you. If they go on their own free will, well, all right."

The general started to say something, but Matt continued without interruption. "I know. I know. You've got your mind set on Seth marryin' up with Jaimie. Well, maybe so, but those are good kids. Well, General, dammit, I want to learn more about what's happening in Montana with my folks' ranch. I'm kinda leanin' towards goin' back." His eyes drifted out to the horizon. "I'd like to see Ma for sure."

The general looked at Matt more seriously, and then he looked out onto the plains of Texas as if searching for an answer. Matt realized for the first time in their relationship that he had planted a thought that was foreign to his commander, and that he had hurt him.

All of this time, the general had been planning who was going to marry his daughter and take over the ranch. Now he was hearing a different side of Matt, a side he never knew before. In the silence, he was thinking Matt would take Leisha and move to Montana. Now, in this moment, he was seeing Seth marrying Jaimie and taking over the ranch. Both possibilities were without his blessings.

He had treated Matt as his own son, more than Seth. His love for Seth was as a father for a son, but Seth was not quite the son that he had wanted. Matt was a strong and determined man, an ideal son to take over his ranch. Why would Matt even think about leaving? Why, he began to think rapidly, would Matt even want to entertain the thought of going back to Montana to a small ranch where he had no ties whatsoever, except that it was built by his father?

Seth realized with his whole being what the general was thinking. It was with this knowledge that he wanted to ride away forever. He felt his father did not accept him as a competent son, and in this moment of anger, he began to see for the first time how he could roll out from under Matt's shadow. He wanted to seize this moment with all the strength he could build up within himself. Throwing his cigarette down and looking at his father, he said, "I agree, Dad. You can't just throw the cowboys off the ranch after they fought for ya. And if Matt wants to go home to see his ma, let him."

The general saw his world falling apart all around him. It was Matt's weakest moment since the general had known him. It could be Matt's downfall. And he knew his son was taking this moment to destroy Matt. A rage was swelling up inside the general that he had never felt before, and he certainly didn't want to express it in any way.

He had felt the pangs of war. He knew what it was like to win *and* lose. He had lost his wife to war, and a brother, too. He had lost his plantation to war, and he had lost his arm. His son had come back from the war; not under his command, but still from battles, but it was his daughter who was the epitome of everything he lived for and believed in. He felt she lived for his life, and because of this, he would live forever. And he had won two good and loyal friends, Matt and Steve.

Now he felt that he had lost everything. His daughter would not be married to any man worthy of his name to carry on in his stead, and his son had not found a woman strong enough to bear him children to set his name proud.

His son was not a weakling, but at the same time, he was not a leader. He could take orders and carry them out, but he couldn't give them. He wasn't a mighty warrior, yet he was prepared to carry a warrior's shield. He would live, but he was prepared to die young. It wasn't his fault. He felt it was the life that was dealt him; therefore, he couldn't change it, nor should he try for fear of losing what he had. Seth wanted to be a knight but felt he would always be a pawn; and as a pawn, he resigned himself to be the very best.

The general waved him on. "Do what you can to make everyone think Matt is dead. We'll let the chips fall where they may."

Seth mounted up and rode back to the corral, where he continued to ride herd on the wranglers. A cow began to stray, and he chased it back into the herd.

Matt yelled out, "Where's Steve?"

Seth yelled back, "Up on the hill a mile or two back. Want me to fetch him?"

"Yeah. Tell him I wanna see him."

Seth showed compliance with a wave of his hand and rode off.

"Damn fine man, that Seth," Matt said.

The general looked out on the trail, and said, "He's a fine son." He paused for a moment. "Hope we haven't lost too many cattle. Price of beef on the hoof is still around fifteen cents. Pays out pretty good in Kansas." He relaxed a bit in the chair, and turned to face Matt. "You still trying to figure out the skirmish we had the other night, Matt?"

"Our plan has been gnawing at me for a few nights now."

"Get it out, Matt."

Matt pointed to the cattle coming in from different directions. "See those cattle? Six, seven thousand head, give or take. What's wrong with that picture, General?"

"From where I sit, nothing."

Matt agreed. "From where you sit, nothin'. Right. But I've been listenin' to them for the past few days, and nights." He bit on his cigar. "If you were going to take a ranch over, wouldn't you want to have the cattle right here?"

"Not necessarily so, Matt. They probably figured to get us out of the way and then take the cattle."

"That would be right, if they were fighting men, and if some were good wranglers. Sir, like you, I surmise there was not one wrangler in the bunch. And certainly not one good fighter, outside of McTavett."

"You're telling me they came in as amateurs and died for nothing. That's what I hear you saying."

Matt slowed down a bit to regroup his thoughts. "They might have been amateurs, men picked up from the streets in Waco. They were well paid. I'll bet a month's wages on that. But that's not what's important here. What I'm trying to say is this, they were not after your ranch. They were not after the cattle. They knew we were getting ready for the roundup as we do this time every year. They could have waited 'til we got the cattle ready for the Chisholm."

Steve rode up to the porch on the heels of hearing this conversation. His chaps, heavily mud-spattered, made him feel like an old man as he climbed out of his saddle. Jumping up on the porch, he set himself down hard on the swing next to Matt.

Matt's leg fell instantly from the stool, and he gave out a loud yell. He grimaced as he stared wildly at Steve and then settled himself back into the swing, propping his leg back up on the stool. "They were after me, Steve. They all aimed to kill me."

Steve tried to understand where Matt was going with this discussion.

"Had he been smart," the general said, "McTavett would have had the drovers take the cattle on the drive and let these birdbrains come in after the ranch." After saying this, he paused and looked at Matt as he began to dissect his own theory. "Wait a goddamn minute. This is what we were expectin'. And he knew we would be expectin' him to do that."

Steve shook the rain from his hat, and wiped his forehead, looking puzzled. "Just what the hell did he do back there?"

Matt thought for a moment. "McTavett brings in a group of horny toads wanting to make a fast buck. They're not fighters, and they're not wranglers. They just want to make some money. We agree on that."

Matt brought his cigar slowly to his mouth and dragged some more. Slowly he tried to draw the picture in his mind as plainly as he knew how, saying, "He made us believe that he was giving us everything he had, and being defeated, he goes back to the ranch, a whipped boy."

The general added, "Thinking Matt is out of the picture, and possibly you, too, Steve, McTavett will attack again where we're the weakest."

Steve picked up the conversation. "On the drive. He faked us out. That son of a bitch made us think he was licked."

Matt added, "That's what has been on my mind for the past few days. We're supposin' he thinks I'm dead."

Steve said, "We hope he *knows* you're dead."

"Let's look at it from his viewpoint," the general said. "Consider the man, McTavett. He's a glory seeker. We're settled on that. He wants the ranch and the cattle. He wants it all. He doesn't want to share his glory with any wranglers."

"McTavett wants it all: glory for himself, and the rest for McDaniels. How does he go about it? By throwin' us a decoy, General."

The general sided in, "The skirmish."

Matt sat back in the swing and said, "Right as rain. He has his wranglers take the cattle away from us."

"And," the general cut in, "knowing you are taken out of the picture, they can waltz in here later and take the ranch."

Matt threw his cigar into the street with his good hand and said, "Gettin' most of our drovers to quit. They did this to take me out. Then all we'd had left would be a handful of wranglers, and weary ones at that by the time they got back from rounding the cattle up in the rain. By damn, they almost succeeded. They even counted on the rain."

The general stood up and walked from one end of the porch to the other. "No, I don't figure them to be that smart. Now we have to outmaneuver them. Where will they strike at our cattle, Steve?"

"It would be wiser for them to wait 'til we get across the bridge."

The general began to walk away, but upon hearing Steve, stopped, threw his cigar into the street, and said, "The bridge! Matt, they'll attack before we get across the bridge."

Matt nodded, and asked, "And the ranch?"

The general summed it up, saying, "McTavett will put all his strength at the bridge."

Matt turned to Steve. "When will you be ready to move your cattle out?"

Steve looked at the clearing skies and at the cattle still coming in, and answered, "Give me two or three more days."

Matt turned to the general. "I'll be able to ride by then, and by God, I'll ride."

The general said to Steve, "Get some men into Waco ahead of schedule, and let the town know we're coming in."

Steve looked more puzzled than ever. "You gonna tell 'em we're comin?"

"They've got to really believe Matt died," the general said. "We're sending in Seth to convince them. Tell him the hotheaded kid got jealous over the new riders and took off for town to get drunk. Have Seth tell 'em we're fortifying the ranch and waiting for another skirmish. Meantime, Steve, you'll be bringing the cattle across the bridge with a bunch of so-called mangled-up drovers."

Steve began to see the plot and agreed. "This could work, General. Catch them out in the open with their pants down."

Matt said, "It'll work."

The general seemed to be in a distant world away from this one. He began to see his whole dream falling apart. As he started to leave the porch, he gazed over at Steve, then up the hill where Seth was riding. "We'll make it work," he said, leaving the porch for his house. Steve walked into the kitchen to get some vittles.

Matt kept his eyes on the general walking away, as if he were looking at a beaten man before the fight begins. He felt a calling from within that said he must go back to Montana. He was fighting this calling for the first time in his life since he left his parents' ranch. Earlier in his life, he sensed this would happen, but the war had put a damper on it. Now the war had been over for some time, and his world was the Brazos River Bar M Ranch. He knew the general was setting him up to take it over once he married Leisha. Now that the moment was closer at hand than ever, he was feeling strong, mixed emotions.

CHAPTER 9

TWO COWBOYS AND A LADY

Leisha had been watching through the curtain-drawn window all this time, her eyes on Steve. Once in a while she would check to make sure no one saw her.

However, Jaimie was also in the front room, and knew that Leisha had been eyeing Steve. She said nothing, but continued to notice. Her mind was on Slim. She leapt up as Steve yelled out, "You fellas light down and join me for some breakfast." Her eyes were eager to find Slim. When she looked, she found other drovers, but no Slim.

She quickly went to the corral and saddled her horse. Once mounted, she whipped her horse into a gallop, leaving the ranch behind. Her thoughts were on meeting the man who had been dominating her dreams ever since he entered her life. She knew he would be nearing the top of the hill leading into the ranch from the south. She had been pondering this moment of enchantment with enthusiasm but hesitated to show it in front of him. She fantasized about how to bring about the moment they could be together. In a few moments, she saw his stout figure astride a bay horse with rope in hand. His two buddies and several other drovers were close with him leading a herd of a few hundred cattle. She slowed her horse to a trot, then to a walk as she closed the gap between them.

As he saw her ride towards him, his thoughts meshed with hers. His body had the sweat and dirt of a cowboy mingled with the smell of cattle. He pretended for the moment not to notice her as he tended to the cattle, keeping them moving with his rope twirling in circles. His lips began to form a slight smile as he tried to hold back his grin. His eyes, though concentrating on the cattle, stayed fixed on her silhouette approaching him.

She stopped and waited for him to approach her. She sat tall and straight, clean with a new set of clothes, and pretty as a sunset on the desert. If ever the stars were with her, they were now. A dirty and tired cowboy, and a brisk and lovely young lady were about to meet for the first of a lifetime of experiences.

His newly acquired friends, along with his two buddies, watched as the two played kittenish games with one another.

Slim puckered up his lips into a dry whistle that never emerged as he closed in on their beautiful game.

She turned her head as if to look towards the river, expecting somehow to see it over a few rough hills.

He stopped his horse in front of hers and addressed her with, "Evening, Jaimie."

She turned and smiled. The cattle continued on their way with the other three wranglers as the couple became lost in their space and time. She threw her chin up and returned the address, saying, "It is, isn't it!"

Slim took off his Stetson and shook the dust by brushing it off on the saddle. He wiped his dry mouth with his sleeve and replaced his hat on his dirty matted hair. For the moment, he was oblivious of the drovers continuing their way, even though Shorty called out his name, "Slim!"

Jaimie motioned with her gloved fingers that someone was calling his attention.

He smiled and then returned Shorty's call. "Oh, Shorty. Bob. Joe. Allen. Eh . . . ." He lost his words. Regaining his composure, he motioned for them to keep going.

Dan returned, "We'll take them on in, Slim. See ya back at the ranch house." They gave out their cowboy yell and then spread themselves out to catch up with Slim's portion of the herd.

The couple remained silent for a while as if time didn't matter. Their eyes locked into each other, and their smiles turned into passionate desires to exchange a kiss. Neither one made the first move for fear of breaking the spell of the moment, until finally, Jaimie spoke up. "I thought I'd ride up here to watch the cattle come in. It's a beautiful sight, isn't it?"

Slim nodded his head in agreement, while looking around at the cattle coming towards them. Thousands of heads were being driven into the ranch to join up with those already there. For Slim, this was the biggest cattle drive he had ever seen; the longhorns stretched across the hillsides in a panoramic view that painted the landscape.

Seth had been watching the scene from nearby and rode towards them. As he neared them, Jaimie put up two fingers as if to stop him from saying anything. He reined up, and folded his leg across his saddle. He took out the makings of a cigarette and, once placed in his mouth, lit it. Letting a ring of smoke exit his lips, he looked over at the couple and asked Slim, "You got a problem?"

Awakened to Seth's stark and direct question, Slim, regaining his train of thought, answered, "Eh, no, Seth. Just chattin' with Jaimie."

Seth saw in Slim the innocence of youth which he had lost, even though he was still young. His own lifestyle had cost him his boyishness early in life, and now he yearned for a rest in town with a couple of women of the evening, and a bottle. In his own selfishness, he envied Slim for the gap in their ages and looks.

Jaimie was a radiant beauty in his eyes, and he wished she were not his cousin, as if that were excuse enough to stop him from loving her. However, his father's wishes and discipline would be enough to keep his hands off her. He would be lost without the aid and money he received from his father, even though he was a top-notch ramrod. To himself, he was just another cowboy; and without his family, he would be a drifter.

The general had taken a disinterest in his son, since Seth came out of the War unscathed. It's almost as if the general was calling him a coward for not having had the red badge of courage every soldier needed. The general suffered the loss of his right arm, though he could have been safe in the haven of a rear command. He was eager to get the battle over with, even if it meant going to the front lines on a charger. One error. One moment of hesitancy, when he looked over his shoulder to see that a command was obeyed, had cost him his arm.

Seth came from the War without a scratch. Matt's body was pierced by a Union bayonet, and Steve's by a musket ball. Seth had never felt the safe assurance of the general's love and affection since the War. Yet, he had stayed with the general and had been the ramrod of his outfit. Out of this, he expected to receive the ranch some day. He felt that the general owed this much to him.

The general also felt that a portion of his ranch would belong to Seth. Another portion would go to his daughter and the man she married. The last portion would go to Jaimie, and the man she married. Seth would have the largest of the three.

Maybe Seth saw in Slim a chance that Jaimie would elope with him and move north to Montana. In that case, she would receive a dowry, and the portion of the ranch that would have gone to her would be divided between the two siblings. Seth had no desire to do away with Slim, although he fought with him at first. He had come to admire the man in the past several days while rounding up the cattle together. Slim was an expert drover, who took orders well.

Now the two men were at war with each other in their own minds. Each one thought that the other did not want to give an inch when it came to Jaimie. A game had to be played out with each other, or else Jaimie's honor would be of no value. Seth realized that he must put up a fight for her safety and he must show concern.

Slim understood that he could lose her at this particular moment if he gave in and allowed her to ride away.

Both men were hoping that Jaimie's voice would provide a reason to speak. Seth inhaled deeply, looked around at the other drovers as if concerned about their working at that moment, and said, "We'll camp here for the night. Tell the others to bed 'em down."

Jaimie looked at Slim's deep and sorrowful frown as he knew he had to follow Seth's orders. He pulled his hat down over his forehead and spurred his horse up the hill towards some other drovers. Jaimie watched him ride, while Seth swung his leg back into the stirrup.

Looking sternly into Seth's eyes, she said, "You don't like Slim, do you?"

Seth crushed his cigarette out on his saddle horn, flicked the butt into the wind and watched it float harmlessly away.

"As a matter of fact, yeah. Yeah," Seth answered. "I like him a lot, now that I've come to know him."

"Then what seems to be the matter?" she retorted while focusing her attention again to Slim's ride.

"You, Jaimie," he answered.

"Me?"

"You're seventeen."

His answer was broken up by her interruption, "Eighteen in two weeks."

"Eighteen, then. Never gone with a guy."

She began to whip her horse into motion when he grabbed the reins and stopped her. "Whoa. You're quite the filly. Simmer down, a bit, sis."

"I ain't your sis, and if I want to ride, I can." She stammered as she tried in vain to recover control of the reins. "Leave the reins alone."

"Not until you hear me out." He loosened up on the reins as he saw she was acquiescing to his command. "I could care less, Jaimie, who you want to go with, so long as you go with your heart."

This phrase stunned Jaimie for the moment. She had never seen him this sensitive before. He had always been an overbearing braggart since they were kids together. Never once did he take her seriously; never once did he honor her wishes to be left alone. Now, all of a sudden, he was sounding like a gentleman she never knew.

Looking a little bewildered for the moment, she asked, "Do you mean that?"

"Jaimie, you're family," Seth assured her. Sure, I tried to get into your bloomers a few times. Never did, 'cause I knew I didn't earn the right. I respected you, honey."

Slim was far up hill and almost out of sight. Jaimie drew her attention more to what Seth was saying now as cattle and drovers moved all around them. He let go of the reins and walked his horse to the shelter of a tree, motioning for her to follow. Once the two were safe from the traffic of cattle and drovers, they dismounted. Seth put his hands on Jaimie's soft shoulders. This in itself almost caused Seth to change his mind as if to draw her into himself and kiss her. Instead, he disciplined himself and held a look at Jaimie as an older brother, and not as a cousin.

In a brotherly fashion, he talked to her, saying, "Honey, we grew up together. We fought, sure. We could have been great lovers, given the chance, I suppose." He smiled a smile of relief, so she could understand the seriousness of his intent. His smile broke out into a small laugh, causing her to smile.

She answered him, "Not even, Seth Mitchell. Not even."

He let her go and stood a foot further away with his hands on his hips, and said, "Not even, Jaimie? What's to stop me right now from kissing you? No one." He looked around at the emptiness between them and the cattle.

Putting her boot back into the stirrup, she answered, "The back of my quirt if you even try."

He tried to keep her from mounting and her quirt came across his face causing much pain, as blood flowed from his cheek. He was quick to grab the quirt away from her, causing her to fall to the ground and under her horse. He reached for her as she rolled further away from him. He stopped and raised himself up while taking his bandanna from around his neck to wipe away the blood.

She stood up and watched him for the moment, and saw a gentleness come across his face instead of anger. She hesitated, then walked over to him. Reaching to her canteen, she took it from the saddle, opened it, and poured water onto his bandanna. She soaked his face, as he looked into her eyes. A moment of sentiment was upon them. The bleeding had stopped, but the swelling was taking its shape.

He looked at the bandanna and examined the blood with his fingers. Polishing it between his two fingers as if grinding it to a sheen, a smile came to his lips.

She poured more water onto his cloth and held it to the wound. "I'm sorry, Seth."

Spreading out his arms, he showed her he was not going to harm her. He fell into a kneeling position and bowed his head at her feet. She followed him to the ground, still attempting to tend to his wound. Sounds came from his mouth only audible to her ear being close to his lips.

She began to think he was crying, then she ascertained his giddiness as a little kid. "Mister Seth Mitchell, what are you giggling about?"

He brought his head up to her eyes and replied with a grin, "I got my 'red badge of courage' from, of all places, my little cousin." He laughed a little, then cried in pain. "That hurts. Damn it!"

Apologizing, Jaimie cradled his face with her hands, and threw her quirt to the wind. "Stupid quirt. I didn't mean to hit you, Seth. Your face kinda got in the way."

Seth laughed, "My face kinda got in the way. If I knew I could get you down on your knees like this, I would have gladly let you hit me before." He laughed even harder, and she almost joined him, but stopped short of a small grin. "I apologize, honey. I -- I have just always loved you, I suppose, and never had the courage to tell ya."

She stood up and he followed her. She took the bandanna away for a moment and kissed his wound, getting blood on her lips. As he wiped the blood away from her lips, they stared at each other as if they were going to kiss. He said, "Not even?"

Jaimie finally broke into a little laughter, "Damn you, Seth Mitchell. You finally cause me to see something good, something decent in you, and, and . . . ." Her sentence trailed off as she dried a tear from her eye. "You are one hell of a prize catch, Seth. You better know that. Any woman would be proud to be your wife."

Seth looked at her with passion, wanting to hold her, and to kiss her, but realized his chance for romance with her was gone. The sound of Slim's horse was cause for them to finish their moment of passion with just a hug.

Jaimie put the bandanna back on Seth's cheek.

Slim reined up and dismounted with caution as he surmised what had been happening these last few minutes. He had witnessed a kiss on the cheek, a hug, and some laughter. Seeing Seth holding a bloody bandanna to his cheek, he asked, "What happened?"

Climbing into his saddle, Seth responded, "Fell off my damn horse."

Jaimie looked a little puzzled but went along with it. She added, "I applied some cold water to it."

Slim continued. "And the kiss on the cheek?"

"We're cousins, Slim," Jaimie answered with a smile.

"Fella, there's a few strays over by the river," Seth smiled and said to Slim. "Go get em, and bring 'em in." Seth sat himself back into his saddle and rode away, saying, "Might need some help from Jaimie. A fella can get lost out here." He spurred his horse into a trot and joined the rest of the drovers.

The couple needed no more an excuse than to agree, and they rode towards the Brazos. It's true that Slim could get lost. The ranch was so vast that anyone not familiar with the terrain could get lost. Especially with the sun beginning its descent behind them.

Jaimie whipped her horse to draw Slim into a race to the river.

His horse showed he was already tired from a day's work and slowed down to a walk.

She stopped her horse, turned and waited for him. Once together, they rode slowly towards the river in a syncopated rhythm.

At the river, they picked up four strays to bring back with them. A few more were walking along the river's edge. They started to ride over to them, but before they reached the place where the cows were, they stopped their horses. The moment of love was beginning to approach, as they looked down upon the Brazos River.

She reined up and dismounted from her horse, tying it to a nearby tree.

He did the same, but with less ease as he had been in the saddle for a few days, and the pain and stiffness appeared once his leg stretched over the saddle. He walked over to the river through the sandy silk and continued to walk down into it without removing his boots. When the water came over his boots, he sat down and splashed it on his body.

He leaned forward and dove headlong into the river, letting his hat float on top as if he could care less. The water felt cool and refreshing to every pore in his body. He gave out a loud yell.

Jaimie watched as she leaned up against the tree.

He turned and glanced up at her and said, "You think I'm silly, don't 'ya?"

Jaimie laughed and walked down to the edge as if to tempt both him and herself as to whether or not she should also walk into the water. She stopped and put her hands on her hips, and said, "Soak it up, cowboy. You've earned a good bath."

He pointed to his saddle bags and asked her, "Could ya get a bar of soap out of my saddle bags? Might just as well scrub up while I'm here."

She tossed the soap at him. For the next few minutes, that seemed to run swiftly like seconds, she watched him as he scrubbed himself without taking off his clothes. She sat with a locked smile on her face.

He looked up at her and laughingly asked, "What's wrong?"

Squatting down to sit on the grass, she answered him. "Sonny. I've been raised with one aunt and a hundred cowboys. Ain't never seen the sight of one like you before."

He looked at himself and back at her and mused, "What's wrong with me?"

Instantly she answered, "Take off your clothes. You'll get a whole lot cleaner."

He stood up and started unbuttoning his shirt. "Just figured I'd get the dirt out of my clothes at the same time." He stopped short, and, placing his hands on his hips, said, "What d'ya mean, a hunert cowboys. You watch them take a bath?"

Jaimie got up and motioned for him to continue, as she turned and walked towards her horse. "No. But I've caught a few without any clothes on. Go downstream a piece and get washed up." Adding a moment of frivolity, she said, "And quit being a sissy."

She watched the sun as it seemed to be setting faster. In a few moments, the sound of his wet body came out of the water completely dressed and dripping. She turned and saw him clean and sweet smelling from the soap. He stopped and asked, "Wanna kiss me?"

She looked at him and walked towards him, laughing. The two met on the shore, and stopped short of touching each other. Their eyes examined the seeming absurdity of the situation, he was completely wet and she was bone dry. She reached out to him and brought his body into hers. Their lips met passionately.

The delicacy of the moment continued with their embrace as they gazed into each other's eyes. His were brown while hers were blue. She added to the moment with her soft voice as she continued to look at every pore on his face. "The river Brazos," she murmured softly as she rubbed her fingers in his wet hair. "Los Brazos de Dios 'The arms of God'. That's what it means."

He kissed her forehead, her nose, and gently placed his lips on hers, while repeating what she said. "'The arms of God'. That's beautiful, almost as beautiful as you."

While he kissed her ears and down to her neck, she continued, "You know. They say that the spirit of a princess lives in the water. And if you see the churning of waters where you stand, then she is listening to you. Slim?"

He loosened her bandanna and kissed her neck just under her smooth chin while she pulled him in tighter to her body. He murmured, "Yeah?"

Feeling the warmth of his body against hers more fervent than ever, she told him, "I see the waters churning. You think she's watching us?"

He began to unbutton her blouse and continued to kiss her neck as he slid his lips down to her chest.

"If she is, she's gonna learn something," Slim said.

Her lips turned to meet his again as his arms reached gently around her waist. Then, in a moment, she purposely tripped him towards the water, and the two went under together as he heard her say, "Oh, what the hell!"

Coming up out of the water, they embraced each other with much warmth and love, and the sun continued to set.

In the same moment at the ranch, Matt stepped out on the porch of his house and watched the sun set, while he lit up a cigar.

Leisha followed him, putting her arm around him. The two seemed to be sharing a special moment with each other merely by holding hands.

Steve walked up to the porch and interrupted the moment by sitting on the swing.

Steve's little visit was a little too timely.

"Haven't you got anywhere else to roost?" Matt asked Steve.

Steve's smile broadened, showing his ivories with one missing in the back. He answered, "Could go to the bunkhouse, but nothin' to do 'til the others get in. Seth is doin' okay." Feeling ornery, he added, "Nah. This here swing makes my back feel real good after a long hard ride." Looking at the couple as if for the first time, he asked, "Am I interruptin' a good conversation, or sumpin?"

Matt lit his cigar and threw the match, still lit onto the ground.

Leisha stepped off the porch, stamped it out, and returned to the porch. She explained, "I had to put the flame out."

Matt added, "Yeah. So did Steve." He eyed the two, turned, took a puff on his cigar and then started to throw it away, too. Leisha made a motion for him to put it out. He crushed it in his hand in a speedy fashion as not to suffer much burn, winced, and walked into the house, leaving the couple on the porch.

Leisha stared at Steve as he tried unsuccessfully to hold back a laugh. She smiled, and said, "Well, aren't we the tricky one?"

"Me? What'd I do?" Steve shrugged his shoulders.

Picking up her skirt, she headed off the porch towards her house across the way.

"You know he's beginning to suspect you have a fondness for me. This doesn't help matters." With a wink of her eye, and a platonic kiss from her lips out of sight of Matt, she added, "See you at breakfast."

"Want me to walk ya home?" he whispered.

"You do, and I'll shoot ya," Matt yelled from the house.

CHAPTER 10

LOVERS AT BREAKFAST

The morning air was brisk, and Steve felt like a new man after taking a bath and shaving. He looked every bit the new man, dressed in clean clothes, as he walked up to the rear porch of Matt's house where Matt was having breakfast in the kitchen.

As he entered the screened door, Matt's husky voice commanded him, "Sit down, and have some grub."

Steve obliged Matt, as Leisha grabbed the coffee pot and poured him a cup of coffee. Leisha enjoyed her task at playing the rancher's wife, wearing a pretty dress adorned with a fancy white apron, and serving breakfast to the two gentlemen.

Matt was fresh, too, having had a good night's sleep, and a change of bandages.

Steve set himself in a straight-back wooden chair and took his first sip of coffee. He scooted the chair back a little and looked down at the floor, ready to tilt back and relax. Leisha's voice came quick and pretty, "You lean back and break my chair, and you'll make me another, Steve Brown, or wish you were never born."

Steve returned his chair to its original position and gave Leisha a raised-eyebrow look as if to say, "All right, mother." He looked over to Matt who returned a silly stare, and then looked around and asked, "Where's Jaimie?"

Matt swallowed another mouthful of coffee as Leisha put a plate of eggs and sausages in front of him. "We were just kinda wonderin' the same thing. Don't know."

Leisha returned to the stove to pick up the biscuits when she looked out the window and eyed the two cowboys from Montana, and no Slim. She looked to her left, further to her right as if expecting to catch him coming from the bunkhouse. Putting the biscuits down in the center of the table, she remarked, "Notice anything about Slim this morning?"

Steve picked at the biscuits, removed one, and tossed it in the air as it was too hot to handle. Then he gently picked it up from the table where it landed and began to eat it. He said matter-of-factly, "Didn't see him, either."

"You don't think those two might be together, now do ya, Leisha?" Matt asked.

Leisha poured Matt more coffee. "Looks like it," she said.

Footsteps came from the front of the house, and then the door opened and closed gently. Jaimie walked through the front room, around the side to the dining area, and back into the kitchen where she saw the three looking in amazement. She was neat looking, clean, and her hair hung loose around her shoulders. Aside from a few wrinkles in her blouse, one would say she just dressed herself.

Leisha took a quick look out the window, but did not see Slim.

Jaimie spoke, "If you're looking for Slim, Miss Leisha, he's tying up our horses in back, and I've asked him in for breakfast." She stared at the three of them still looking at her. She then took an apron from the hook and began to break eggs and fry up some sausages. "Thanks, Miss Leisha, for the biscuits and coffee. I'll give you a hand now."

Leisha stood back a little and watched Jaimie perform her chores with ease. She got two more plates and cups from the cupboard for their breakfast and placed them on the table along with silverware.

Jaimie continued, "We just got back from an early morning ride."

Steve returned, "How early?" He continued to feed himself with his second or third biscuit.

The screened door opened and closed, and Slim's spurs jingled as he tried to walk softly, not wanting to make too much noise.

Jaimie answered Steve. "Would twilight yesterday be too early."

Matt looked astonished at his seventeen-year-old cousin as Slim slipped his arm around her waist. He almost choked on his coffee and quickly put the cup down. He said, rather abruptly, "Jaimie, you're still a kid."

"That's not what you said a few days ago when I was bandaging you up."

"That was when I was out of my head. I'm pretty clear now and I can see you're still just a kid."

Steve cleared his throat and asked, "Anybody got any jelly?"

Matt continued, "What do you suppose the general's gonna say, you staying out all night with a man?"

Steve looked over at Leisha and asked, "Preserves?"

Leisha stood next to Jaimie to show the similarities. She asked, "Matt, you see anything strange?"

Matt looked at the two women, and for a good while he began to see a woman in Jaimie. The two ladies were almost the same size and measurements with Leisha being just a bit taller. He asked, "Well, what d'ya do?" He found himself asking stupid questions and tried unsuccessfully to right himself. "I mean, anything you can speak of?"

Steve slid his chair back and rose from the table. Walking over to the counter, he got himself a jar of preserves and returned to the table. Matt stared at him without saying anything. Jaimie had not answered, yet. Steve said, "You want something around here, you might just as well get up and get it yourself."

"Does that answer your question, Uncle Matt?" Jaimie agreed.

Slim politely asked, "May I sit down?"

Matt was still looking at Jaimie.

"What does that have to do with my question?" He looked at Slim and gave him his permission to sit down. "Oh, well, yeah. Sit down, Slim." Realizing that Slim had not said anything, he addressed him. "Slim, you got more sense than to keep my niece out all night without my permission. Why d'ya do it for?"

Slim sat himself down while Jaimie answered. "Would you have given it, Uncle Matt?"

"No," Matt answered angrily.

"Would daddy have given me permission?"

"No."

Jaimie took the pot off the stove and poured Slim a cup of coffee. She continued, saying, "So why should I ask you. Besides, nothing happened, and we had a wonderful time."

Matt's eyes opened wide.

"Just what did happen, Miss Prissy?" he asked.

Slim took a sip of coffee and put the cup down as he addressed Matt. "We gathered up some strays down by the river, and fell in."

Matt's ire rose as he threw his napkin down in his plate of eggs and sausages.

"You did what? You fell into the river? Together? How?"

Steve was enjoying his breakfast, and also the conversation. He watched Leisha as she tried to keep a straight face. Then, breaking the tension, he said, "This I'd like to hear." Then he held up his cup to Leisha and said, "More coffee. please."

Leisha accommodated him and filled his cup with coffee. She looked down at Steve and gave her girlish grin and said, "Me, too." She winked at Steve out of Matt's sight.

Jaimie began explaining while breaking her eggs and readying the sausages. "Well, I had ridden out to meet the drovers coming in, and Slim happened to come down the hill. Seth told Slim to go after some strays down by the river, and suggested I go with him to keep him from getting lost. We got four or five, then Slim, he . . . ."

Slim interrupted her as he began buttering his biscuit. "My turn. I was all dirty and smelly and she was all clean. I thought it only polite to freshen up a bit, so I took a bath."

Matt stood up and placed his good right hand on his hip ready to throw something towards Slim.

"Now, Matt. I had my clothes on," Slim added.

Jaimie interrupted him and said, "Until I told him to take them off."

Slim dropped his biscuit and rose out of his chair to put distance between him and Matt. In his defense, he said, "I went downstream, away from her. I swear, Uncle Matt. I mean Matt. I went down stream out of her sight."

Matt stood firm as he listened to Slim stutter his way out of this situation.

Steve got up, picked his hat off the wall, and left the house, saying, "Good time to check on the boys."

Leisha followed him to the door and watched him leave. Her heart told her that she wanted him to come back and stay. Her head was dizzy with the love story she was hearing. She shared a look with Steve's eyes as they parted. They wished that it had been them by the river together instead of Slim and Jaimie.

Matt yelled out, "Steve. Where d'ya think you're going? You're her uncle, too, ya know."

Steve answered looking back without stopping, "Yeah. I'm kinda in favor of it, Matt."

"Uncle Matt," Jaimie explained. "The sun fell so quickly, we decided to camp right there, and built ourselves a fire. Besides, we were wet and cold. And, yes, we kissed. But that's all we did."

Matt was still fuming but trying to reason out just what really happened. Softly he said, "I'll bet."

He remained standing when Jaimie asked Slim, "Want 'em up or over, Slim, honey?" She pretended not to have heard Matt.

Slim was quite uneasy at this point and was ready to exit with Steve; but he stayed. Edging himself back to the table where Jaimie was sliding the eggs out of the skillet, he said, "The shore was slippery, and we fell in. I built a fire, and Jaimie got dried off first while I rode a little to keep the strays from wandering away. I dried off later."

Jaimie put the skillet down, walked in front of Matt and pushed him into his chair. "That's all the 'splaining we need to do, Uncle Matt. You either believe us, or, or . . . . "

Matt looked up at Jaimie from his sitting position and asked, a little befuddled, "Or what?"

'Or, I don't want you for an uncle anymore. And, and, that's not true. I love you, Uncle Matt." She threw her arms around Matt and sat in his lap.

He winced a little in pain.

She rose quickly and said, "Oh, I'm sorry, Matt. I forgot about your ribs and shoulder."

"Not to mention my shot-up leg." He got himself up with the aid of his crutch, embraced her and kissed her on the forehead. "Oh, I believe ya, honey." He looked at Slim who was still holding onto a biscuit he had prepared to eat some time ago, and said, "And if I believe you, I have ta believe this young 'un, too. Hell, I guess you're a young lady, now."

She squeezed him gently around his sore ribs, kissed him on his cheek, and said, "I think you'll be pleased with Slim, Matt. He has some nice ideas about daddy's spread here."

Slim looked at Matt and took a bite out of his biscuit.

Matt pointed towards Slim's breakfast plate. "Continue. Ya got 'em sunnyside up. Like I like 'em." He excused himself, and left the couple alone in the kitchen. "I gotta go talk to the general."

Jaimie watched Matt as he limped out the back door with his crutch towards the general's house. She said in a loud feminine voice, "Don't get him riled up. I'll tell him later."

Stepping off the porch he said without turning, "He ain't gonna be so forgiving, I'm afraid. Join me Slim, when you finish. Like to hear what you got on your mind about this heah spread."

Slim answered, "Be there after a bite or two, Matt." He looked up at Jaimie as she walked over to the stove and put on some more eggs. She wanted him to stay a little while longer, and eating would be a good excuse. But he winked, and left the kitchen through the same door Matt did.

CHAPTER 11

THE TALK

Steve was on the other side of the door lighting his fixings when Slim approached him.

Watching Matt hobble back to his house, Slim addressed Steve, "Ain't nothing gonna slow that man down?"

"Like that in the War, son."

"How's that?"

"Got a minute?"

Slim watched Matt's slow gait, and motioned with his head that he had, but showed in his eyes that he was in a bit of a hurry.

"First of all, slow down. Give him time to think, give yourself time, too." Steve took a wad of tobacco out and tore a piece off with his teeth for a chew while he sat himself down on the steps, motioning Slim to do the same. "He won't tell ya, but I will. He earned this ranch, and now he's got to think about leaving it. All because of you and your pals."

"It's his choice. We're jest doin' what his ma asked us to. That's all."

"It goes deeper, son. You see, at the beginning of the War, I never really knew Matt. And that one battle I told you about, when he saved the general's life. Well, fact is, the general's never let him forget it.

"What the general saw was Matt giving his life for his. He gave him a field promotion equal to mine right then and there. The two of them became fighting fools. I saw their love and respect for each other grow with each skirmish. It was as if Matt was enjoying this War. And, he was now a Lieutenant."

Slim leaned in to listen more intently. "Was that where the general lost his right arm?"

"Nope. That was a different one. The Atlanta Campaign in sixty-four, where we had begun mixing it up with your General Sherman. The battle was near over, and General Mitchell was behind the lines on his stallion. Once he felt he was needed, he moved forward to where Matt was. Sort of a victory ride so to speak.

"That's when he drew attention from one of our own men. It was a hell of a battle, and we were all tense. Thinking he was the enemy creeping up on him, the man turned and fired. He hit the general in the arm.

"The general almost bled to death, and they had to have the arm removed. That was his last battle.

"Matt was now a capt'n, and made sure that the general got the best of treatment. As for the cavalryman, Matt kicked his ass, and told him to get out of his company as fast and as far away as possible. We never heard from him since. 'Spec he's still running.

"That's when ya came here?"

Steve replied, "Nah. In the spring of sixty-five, we fought at Bentonville. Tennessee. That's where we got our butts whipped. Some of our men, now under General Johnston, surrendered. Most of us, however, rode our mounts to safety and joined up with some other Confederates. Never fought again. That's when Matt and I skeedaddled to Houston."

Slim slid his Stetson upward, rose, and said, "Thanks for sharing that with me, Steve. Kinda makes me look at things a little differently."

"Come back when ya got more time. Got more stories to tell ya."

He ran swiftly after Matt across the road to the larger, two-storied house next door.

This was the general's house, which he had rebuilt from the ashes the war left behind. Matt's house was the new one; not so big, but still two-storied. It seemed that the general always had a love for only two-storied houses; it gave him a sense of power. His yearning was to become governor of Texas. He had everything going for him towards this goal. He was a hero in the war, having spurred his men into battle when others could have found excuses to retreat. He paid the price with the heavy loss of troops; and one arm. It was the loss of his one arm that kept him out of the race to become governor. The people were looking for a whole governor, and not one with only one arm.

"He had charisma, which made everyone want to vote for him. He had a charm about him that caused the ladies to smile deeply and sigh, sometimes wishing he were their mate. The men admired him for his manliness. He sported a beard in a gentlemanly fashion; cut to give him more dignity.

"When he entertained visitors, he dressed well for the occasion with an expensive suit and vest buttoned completely. His right sleeve was neatly folded upward and pinned to his coat to prevent it from dangling. In fact, one would have a hard time recognizing his loss had there been no reason to suspect it.

The general played his character of the one-armed hero to the ultimate limit, careful to not offend anyone, but charming the ladies who really were curious whether or not he had lost his arm.

His smile became that of a gentleman, and not of one seeking to remarry. He was quite conscious of who he was, and he refused to put on airs about his character. Once one was in his company, he or she could not help but admire his demeanor. He was totally a Texian, and it showed. He was born on this ranch, which belonged to his parents. They had moved from Virginia and settled here. He spent two years at William and Mary, and another four years at Annapolis.

It was in this fashion of a gentleman when he greeted Matt and Slim in his study. At one time, his visitors were greeted at the door by his manservant, and shown to the living room, now the War was over, and Jaimie and Leisha did the greeting.

Now, both ladies remained at Matt's house, in the kitchen, eating their own-cooked breakfast, and talking about the men.

Matt was accustomed to letting himself in once he announced his arrival.

Entering the general's house gave a person a feeling of being small, and the general big in stature. The stairs met the visitor once the door was opened. It was a large flight of stairs going straight up with a slight curve at the top. The banisters were each made of one tree, and polished brightly. A chandelier hung over a huge mirror on the top landing giving light so one could see with great magnitude his or her appearance. From the top, the stairs looked even to go further down as a perspective point of view. They were carpeted in red.

The general led the two gentlemen into his study; a room twice the size of Matt's kitchen, and filled with books. On one side of the room stood a huge fireplace, with a mantle, and footstool in front. Two pairs of overstuffed-leather chairs faced each other with a marble coffee table separating the pairs. A small settee was to the side of the room as to where the ladies would sit while the men discussed subjects.

Matt walked to the fireplace, where he leaned his crutch against the mantle. He was followed by Slim.

The general lifted the tails to his sporting jacket and sat in his favorite chair, while Slim and Matt remained standing.

Matt spoke first. "General, sir. This young lad has a thing or two to say to you."

"About what, young man?"

Slim looked bewildered at Matt as if he were betrayed into confessing his evening outing with Jaimie.

"Sir. I come from a country that has never seen longhorn cattle. What would you say to introducing the longhorns up north?"

Matt sputtered, looked at Slim, then at the general and laughed. His laugh was heard from outside, and clear to his own house where the ladies stopped their chores and looked west.

Slim continued to explain his quest for wanting longhorn cattle in Montana. The general listened, and Matt began to grow interested. The talk about Slim and Jaime would have to wait.

CHAPTER 12

MATT'S LONESOME RIDE

The ground was hard and rough, filled with rocks and sagebrush. Wild weeds and flowers decorated the terrain only minutely. Oak trees with their low lying branches, made riding difficult, and trails were hard to find after a rain.

Yet the ride for Matt was pleasant as he walked his new horse into the brush region as if to hide in nature's surroundings. It was the first time he had sat on a horse since the skirmish with McDaniels' bunch a week ago. He still felt the pain throughout his chest and shoulder, and his leg was still swollen and sore, but the saddle fit his frame and seemed to ease all else. He simply wanted to get off and be alone so he could think.

The cowboys from Montana had plagued him with the thought of his mother's dying and that she would be leaving the ranch to him. He knew in his heart he had an obligation to his parents to at least try to maintain what they had built up. It wasn't much, he thought, but to them, it was their life, a way of living. He thought about the Brazos River Bar M Ranch, and the future the general had in mind for him if he married Leisha. He knew he was not in love with Leisha, and never had been. It was a friendship started a long time ago that had blossomed into a warm feeling between them, but not true love.

Matt had never told her he loved her, and he never heard it from her lips. They sensed a distance between them, and it was time for him to face that truth. If he stayed on the ranch and married Leisha, it would only be out of loyalty and admiration for the general's wishes. It wouldn't be a bad marriage, just one without genuine love for each other. His task now was to face the reality for himself and bring it out in the open with Leisha.

He continued the argument with himself. "After all, I had never really slept with her as if we were married. She was no virgin when I met her, and certainly I've had many nights of great fun. It was not as if we had made a marriage commitment, 'cause we hadn't. We didn't even talk about kids. Hell, we simply didn't talk about it." They had both shared the general's ideas about marriage and went along as if to appease him. They never really sat down privately and talked about it. Why would they? They were really hiding the truth from each other.

"Oh, hell," he thought again, watching a rabbit cross his path and skitter into the bramble. "We believed we were going to get married. It was inevitable."

His thoughts led to commitment and morality. He looked at the sun, now about ten o'clock in the sky, and began to feel a little sweat run down his back. The day was beginning to warm up. He remembered his dad used to say, "Come on, kid. We're burnin' daylight." Why, he asked himself, was he thinking about his dad? He's been dead a few years now. It was his mother he should be thinking about.

Matt's thoughts strayed back to his mother always having a kind word and never raising her voice. It sort of atoned for Wil's brashness as a devil-may-care type of man and a law-laying-down type of father and, at the same time, balanced the family ties, so to speak. Wil liked his mother for her strength, but he loved her more for her quietness, although she wasn't always quiet around her boys. She voiced her opinions about what should be done and what should not be done. A lot of what went on around the ranch when Wil was gone was never revealed to him. Wil seemed to like it that way. Certainly, she liked keeping secrets from him. She was strong, yet soft.

The boys also seemed to know which side of the family to choose in case they had a need, and it appeared that Matt, being the older son, bailed Lukas out of scrapes now and then, even to the point of taking the blame for something he didn't do.

Now, after all these years, she kept the secret of his being alive and living in Texas from Wil, even through his death. He never knew the real story. Both Annie and Matt thought Wil never knew that Matt was still alive. But he knew. He was waiting for the time when Matt would ride back. But Matt never did.

A herd of deer skirted away from Matt's ride as he neared them, breaking his concentration for the moment. He reined up and sat quietly on his mount. He watched the deer and thought out loud, "You're a mother and you have your young-'uns. What do you do when your ol' man makes your young-'un leave home?" He stared at the doe as she paused and looked back at her fawns scampering around her. It was as if she were listening to him. He scooted up and sat tall in his saddle continuing his thoughts aloud. "Hell. Nothin'. Deer don't come back whining. They go on and become stags themselves."

He didn't care if Wil had known he was in Texas, or that he had never been in contact with him. What concerned him now was that his mother was dying, and he had to decide whether or not to go back. Knowing that he would light the embers when he arrived at the ranch, he sought the wind for an answer as to how he was going to fair out the situation. "The law could arrest me," he thought. "What good would it do for ma or me if I returned? Just to be arrested and hung?" Throwing his hat back on his head and looking towards the Brazos Ranch, he mused to himself, "They'd hang me, all right." His lips gripped tight, and his eyes squinted into the sun. His deep tanned face grimaced with wrinkles. "Dammit!" he yelled into the wind. There was only silence. A bead of sweat found its way down Matt's forehead, and he cried once more, "Damn!"

The sound of his voice was only strong from where he sat. The wind carried it only so far, and then it died out. There was no echo. Only quietness. Calmness. Not even a breeze stirred to cool his brow. He slumped in his saddle and sat there as a tired cowboy. His body was a stranger to him. However, his thoughts covered all pain as he wept alone.

He let the slack out of the reins, and with a slight movement of his right heel, his horse began to move, turning its head as if wanting to head back to the corral. Matt let him, but at the first sign of speed, he reined up, slowing him to a walk. Then, as if an afterthought, he neck-reined him towards a clearing where sand followed a dry creekbed, putting him into a canter. The horse began to tire as he felt the heavy weight of Matt's body pounding on his back. Several minutes passed by before Matt pulled the gelding into a slow, steady walk.

The sun rested high in the sky and looked down upon Matt as a lone figure on horseback trying to find his place in the desert.

Matt took out his canteen and let the water drip slowly into his mouth. He had taught himself and others to drink sparingly at all times. One never knew when they might need the last drop; and the last drop was the most precious. His lips had begun to show signs of dryness as he licked the water around them. He put the canteen back, removed his hat, and wiped his brow. The temperature would be in the nineties today, and the humidity was up there because of the heavy rain. His thoughts were for his horse, but he knew he could not dismount and remount without help, and the thought of being stranded in the desert with a bum leg made him rethink the idea of sharing water from his canteen with his horse. Instead, he loosened the reins once more, gently spurring the animal in the ribs to let him know it was time to go home.

His hands gripped the reins loosely as he held his horse under his command in a fast trot.

"Damn!" he said to himself, feeling the pain in his leg growing worse. "Go ahead, horse. I can take it if you can."

In the distance, on a hill, stood a silhouetted figure of a rider on a horse. The rider had been watching Matt for some time and now spurred her horse into a gallop in his direction. It was the fine figure of Leisha. She was looking for Matt. In a moment, she was siding him as he brought his horse to a halt.

Looking at him with a smirk on her lips, she said, "You've been out here for over four hours. I found you in the last few minutes. Been watching you from up there." She pointed to the hill from where she rode. "Hungry?" she asked. "I've got some jerky in my saddlebag."

Matt looked at her and smiled. "Hell, honey, I was about ready for my afternoon ceegar."

They both laughed as he reached into his vest pocket and came up empty. She dismounted, poured water from her canteen into her hat and gave it to his horse. It licked the water with great pleasure but was cut short because Leisha knew not to overdo it when a horse was hot. But Matt was quick to say, "Don't give 'im too much, horses need to cool down slowly."

Leisha gritted her teeth and answered, "Can't you let a person do something without correcting her, Matt?" She stopped talking and led her horse to the nearest shade tree a few feet away.

Matt rode his horse over to her. Leisha again took her canteen from her saddle horn, poured some water in her hand, and rubbed it on the noses of both horses. She looked up at Matt and smiled.

She sensed he was sorry and helped him with a little friendly body language he could understand. He smiled at her suggestive movements as she kept her back towards him. Then she bent forward and picked up her horse's leg to rub it down back to the ground.

She stopped for the moment, letting the leg ease itself. Looking over the saddle away from Matt, she said, "You were headed for the Brazos. Any reason?"

"The way the horse wanted to go; I reckon."

"It's real close by, if'n you want to cool off a bit." She waited for an answer she did not readily get. She turned and leaned her back against the horse, looking out in the direction of the Brazos River. "Feel up to some more riding? Or do you want to rest awhile?"

Matt leaned on his saddle horn, easing his back a little by twisting in the saddle as he answered her. "Figure it's only over the first hill. Say, thirty minutes." He saw her turn, and his eyes adjusted to her radiant appearance, like a gentle rainbow after the rain. "Kinda think I need a cold dunk right about now."

She slipped her boot into her stirrup, sat tall, and waited for his move.

Pulling his Stetson down on his forehead, he hit his horse with his spurs and began to ride away to the Brazos. Leisha followed. The ride seemed to be long for Matt as the pain wrung through his body.

He knew he shouldn't be riding this fast, but figured it was the manly thing to do.

The sun was bursting its rays onto the plains as the two riders sped towards the Brazos River in a crisscrossing fashion, playing with each other's thoughts as they rode. They seemingly couldn't wait to reach the river.

His thoughts were of easing his pains so he could enjoy this moment and forget about having to make a choice. Maybe a dip would make the pain go away, he reasoned with himself, although he knew deep inside that he had already made his decision. He bit down on his lip and rode on.

The minutes were painful for Matt, but the ride was worth every ache as they came upon the Brazos. In their mind's eyes, they saw Jaimie and Slim playful in the river, and up on the shore. Now they realized they were in the same setting.

Their horses were panting heavy as Leisha dismounted from her mare. Hanging her hat on the saddle horn and throwing her hair back, she asked, "You gonna stay in your saddle all day?"

Matt looked her over, and then rubbed his leg a bit. Unconsciously, he felt up around his shoulder. Taking off his hat, he wiped his dry mouth with his gloved hand.

"Doc says you should be exercising your arm and leg, and not just dangle on a horse. Get your ass down here where you belong, and I'll plant a big wet one on you." Her body began to stand taller as she prepared to ease him out of the saddle.

Matt obeyed her by slowly easing out of the saddle, while she helped by gently holding onto him to help keep his balance. His big arm slid around her petite waist and brought her to him ever so slowly. His steely blue eyes met her soft blue eyes.

Leisha's hands eased away from holding his frame to etch his cheek bones and wipe away the sweat. Her long thin fingers prepared a dry area around his lips as she brought her lips close to his.

The water was blue and cool looking with the sun looking at its reflection. A tall oak tree stood a few feet away, and the wind began to play with its leaves. Its shade covered the couple in artistic strokes of silhouettes.

The pair stood together until Matt's pain prevented him from standing any longer. He limped away from their embrace and placed himself down against the tree.

Leisha followed, lying next to him. Her voice sounded slight as she asked, "Wanna go in for a swim?"

"It's been a long time." Matt said, as he kissed her blonde hair, gritting his teeth while fighting the pain, not only in his shoulder, but along his leg from riding so long. He told Leisha nothing for fear of breaking the moment. He knew that in a few moments, he would relax and sleep awhile; the hour of ecstasy would have taken its victim.

"Matt, you've hurt your leg again?"

Matt returned, "It's just from the riding. Muscle cramps. Not from the buckshot, though the two make for a pair, let me tell ya." He sat up and laughed.

"Right now, you need some rest."

The sun slid down the sky until the shadow of the tree fell away from the pair. Leisha opened her eyes, to find Matt's eyes looking down at her. Matt had been the first to awake, watching her sleep. "How long?" she asked.

Matt brushed the hair from her eyes, and responded, "Couple of hours, at least. Leg feels better. So's the shoulder."

She sat up and folded her legs to her chest. Grabbing them with her arms and looking at the Brazos River, she said, "I wonder if this is what Jaimie and Slim did."

"What?"

"What we just did, silly. I wonder if they made love."

Matt smiled without answering her.

"Did you believe them, Matt?"

"About as much as I believe any Yankee could make a good soldier."

"That's the South talking in you, Matt. Talk straight."

Matt sat up, looking more intently into Leisha's eyes, and said, "I guess a Yankee could make a good soldier. Though I never met any -- good soldiers, that is." He saw her face turning from his, and continued to answer her. "No. No, I didn't believe either one of them."

"Why not?"

"Well, Miss Pretty. Let me see. First of all, it was all that giddiness they were trying to hide. The more they tried to hide it, the more giddier they got." He got a laugh out of Leisha, and he smiled back. "Then, the reality of them taking a swim together, and drying out their clothes, and not seeing one another. Them being there in the dark, alone together. No. There's no way in hell I could buy their story."

"Then why didn't you speak up? Why did you pretend you believed them?"

Matt took Leisha's hand and brought her back to his chest. "Because, missy, I saw in your eyes that you didn't believe them, too."

"Either." She corrected him. Rising, she brought him to his feet, and they caressed, bringing their lips against each other's. "The river does have a strange spell over lovers, I do believe."

CHAPTER 13

A KID IS KILLED

The ride back was uncomfortable for Matt—not that he was in much pain, for he had rested and had a charming Leisha to accompany him on the ride—but more because he was bottling up his real feelings inside now that he had made his decision to leave her and return to Montana. Looking at Leisha riding beside him, he breathed deeply and put on a pretense for her, hoping she wouldn't catch on.

"Wish I had a good ceegar right about now."

His hand felt around his vest pockets, but came up empty. Every so often a bolt of thunder would precede a deluge. But another type of bolt was about to hit Matt as Leisha asked, without turning to face him, "Wanna get married, Matt?"

Matt stared at her without saying anything. He examined her posture and good looks as she rode next to him. She looked good on a horse. She was everything he would want in a woman, but he didn't want her. He reached behind his saddle and began to open his saddlebags to search for a cigar. "Thought maybe I could find a ceegar in here."

A few moments later, he continued, "Nope. No ceegar. But got a little bit of whiskey." He brought out a bottle, uncorked it, and started to take a drink. He stopped himself, and gestured the bottle to Leisha. "Want some?"

Leisha looked at Matt, took the bottle from him, and drank all that was in it; which was not enough for two good-sized drinks. However, she swallowed all of it. Giving the bottle back to Matt, she said, "Thanks. Don't mind if I do."

Matt took the empty bottle, looked at it, and rubbed his finger around the rim to apply the remaining moisture to his lips as if to say he would have enjoyed a sip of it, too. He corked the bottle and threw it with his good arm into some bramble. Drawing his gun from his holster, he fired quickly at the bottle and broke it with a round before it hit the ground.

"You going to answer me, Mr. Jorgensen?" she asked.

Matt stopped his horse with Leisha following suit. He pointed to the busted glass that once was a bottle and said, "That's a good lesson. When a bottle is empty, you throw it away."

Leisha turned her face away from him in stern fashion and said, "I'm not a bottle."

Matt retorted with easy kindness, "No, you're not. But I am. I'm half-again your age, Leisha. I've never been married, and never intend to get married." Pointing to the bottle he continued, "Like that damn bottle, someone's got a bullet with my name on it. Not a good life for a woman to be hitched to."

"Hell, Matt, I've known your feelings for years. You're too damn afraid to get married."

"That's right, Leisha. That's right." He slowed down his dialogue with her as he regrouped his thoughts, trying to make sure he said all the right things.

Matt dismounted and walked over to the river leaving his horse ground tied. Leisha took her reins and his and tied them loosely to a bramble. She walked to his side.

"My ma is dying, Leisha. Old age, I reckon. I'm not there with her. Haven't seen her in over fifteen years. I wasn't there when my father got killed." He drew a breath slowly and let it out, as though he had just inhaled a good cigar. Looking out over the river, he continued. "But I remember the night he drove me away from the ranch. He knew I had nothin' to do with the robbery. That I was trying to save Lukas from it."

Leisha heard these words for the first time. She began experiencing a different side of him, because he was unburdening something that he had withheld deep inside himself for many years. She could sense that he was uncomfortable with this.

"I rode up to the ranch and asked for help," Matt continued. "And he told me to keep ridin', as if I was guilty. Wil Andersen could not see the gray line; it was either black or white with him. You either worked or you were lazy. You broke a horse his way or you were a baby." His voice began to quiver, and he grit his teeth harder. "But I was guilty because I had a run in with the law."

For fear of breaking this moment of confession, Leisha stood still and listened.

A shadow of a figure on the other side of the river watched the pair with great concern. A rifle hung from his hand as he moved closer to the bank.

Matt's eyes carefully scanned the other side of the river, and almost by sheer accident, he saw the figure take another bead on them. Instantly, he knocked Leisha down with his body, and the two rolled behind a giant oak tree. A shot rang out and echoed across the river, the bullet hitting the sand close to the pair.

Once he realized Leisha was out of danger, Matt rolled once more to the other side of the tree to see their stalker. He had brought his gun swiftly out of its holster. The figure across the river took another shot at Matt, which ricocheted off the bark of the tree. Realizing he had missed twice; the unknown assailant began to run. Matt emptied his gun quickly and accurately, hitting his target in the shoulder, bringing him down. The figure fell forward in pain, and then rose to escape any more bullets. Matt's gun was empty, allowing the figure on the other side time to escape. Matt stood while reloading and cussed the stranger for not staying and finishing the fight.

Leisha stood up straight, using the tree for a shield in case any more shooting took place.

As he holstered his gun, Matt watched the figure disappear.

"That does it."

Leisha's eyes were wide with fright as she looked at Matt. "Who was it?"

Without turning, Matt answered, "Whoever it was, our plan is shot to hell."

Leisha, not privy to the plan, began to question Matt. "We had a plan?"

"I was supposed to be dead. That way, we could flush them out and catch them in a surprise move, when they least suspected it."

"How would they know it was you, Matt?"

Matt grabbed his reins from the bramble and bitingly answered her, "They knew it was me. They wouldn't have chanced it on just anybody. I should have known better. Damn McDaniels."

Leisha took her reins and joined up with Matt at their horses. She looked into his face and saw the hardness in his eyes. She wondered if this was the man she really wanted to marry after all. Then, the realization of what he had said earlier struck her. "This could have been the bullet he was talking about."

Matt took her in his arms tightly and said, "Now you see why I can't marry you, or anyone? That bullet came that close from finishin' me. And you, too. That's why I'm scared of you gettin' hurt." Then his eyes looked tenderly into hers. "And, and leaving you a widow."

Leisha recoiled from his grip and looked into his eyes. "Damn you, Matt. Damn you." She mounted her horse and looked down at him. "Believe me, you won't have to worry about making me a widow." She spurred her horse hard. In a fast start, the mare took off in a run.

It appeared that Leisha could hardly control her, but Matt was assured by her expertise, and that she was in total control of the animal, so he left her to ride alone. He kicked at the dirt with his boot, held onto the reins of his horse, and looked out across the river as if to see his pursuer once again. He said to himself, "At least you're suffering, you son of a bitch. Maybe you'll die, and nobody'll know." However, saying this, he knew deep inside he was wishing almost for the impossible.

It was a long ride back to the ranch for Leisha. Soon she rounded the barn and rode her mare into the corral. Dismounting, she gave a wrangler order to take care of her horse as she headed to the main house.

Dan and Shorty had just ridden in as well and were about to dismount from their horses when they watched Leisha take the steps two at a time to the house, entering it and slamming the screen door behind her.

Dan asked, "Who put the burr in her bloomers?"

Steve watched the drovers as they settled the herd down for the evening. Seeing Leisha, he rode over to the house, staying mounted while looking through the screen door in an effort to see her inside, but by this time, she was already upstairs in her bedroom.

He stared up at the window when the sound of a quirt flew out and landed near his horse. He dismounted, picked it up, and stood, looking up at the window.

As they had been watching the scene take place, Dan and Shorty walked up behind him. Shorty said, "Kinda looks like she's had a lover's spat, don't it?"

Dan kicked him to shut him up, but not soon enough, for Steve had heard him. "No," Dan added. "Just looks like she had a hard ride and she's letting some steam off."

Steve was quick to agree with Shorty. "You don't throw a quirt out a window from having a hard ride."

Shorty added, "Nope. You throw the horse out the winder."

Dan kept the peace, knowing this could set off a man's temper. Not knowing how Steve would react to this triangle love affair, he wanted to leave. "You want us to go back up the hill, boss?"

Steve played with the quirt, and looked back up at the window, hoping that he might get a glimpse of Leisha or see her come back downstairs. Nothing happened either way. For a long moment, there was silence, except for the noise of the cows up on the nearby crest. Steve looked around the corral and over at Matt's house to see if he could see Matt's horse anywhere. He noticed earlier that it was gone. He tossed the quirt onto the porch and climbed back into his saddle.

"Yeah. Let's make sure we've got them bedded down for the night. Seth's bringing his in along about morning sometime."

Dan and Shorty, quick to comply with Steve's order, walked back to their horses. On the way, Dan hit Shorty in the shoulder and chided him. "Looks like a lover's fight! Whyn't ya jest shoot him and be done with it? Idjit."

Shorty took the punch, looked back at Steve riding up the hill, then said to Dan, "Do that mean Leisha has two boyfriends?"

"Ya want me to draw ya a map, dunderhead? Leisha is Matt's girl, but Steve is in love with her."

They climbed into their saddles and slowly rode to follow Steve, rather than to catch up with him. They could still see the look in his eyes as he stared back at the house.

Shorty asked, "If she's Matt's girl, then why does Steve like her?"

"'Cause she likes him. Sorta. I guess. Anyways, it looks now like she's in love with both of 'em."

Shorty took off his hat to scratch his head and said, "Wonder where Matt is."

Dan was fast to answer, "Don't know, and don't wanna be around when he shows up, either." He spurred his horse into a gallop, and Shorty followed suit. They passed Steve on the slope.

Steve yelled at them, "Take it easy, boys. You'll frighten the cows."

They obeyed and slowed their horses down to a walk to let Steve catch up to them. Dan apologized. "Sorry, boss. Wasn't thinkin'."

CHAPTER 14

TWO AND ONE MAKE THREE

It was evening by the time Matt returned, walking his horse to the corral. The moon gave a great light so that Leisha knew that it was Matt dismounting and getting ready to bed down his horse for the night.

A feminine figure of another person walked across the grounds and over to Matt. As she approached the opening in the barn, she picked up a pair of brushes. She laid them quickly on a sawhorse to help Matt with the saddle.

He left the chore to her as he grabbed his shoulder.

After she placed the saddle on the rail of the stall, she lit the lantern. Matt saw the gentle face of Jaimie smiling at him as the light embraced her.

"Thanks," was his gesture for her helping him with the saddle. He rubbed his shoulder and leaned up against the rail. He continued work as he mixed the barley and oats in the feedbag, and placed it onto the horses head for eating, as she took the brushes and began to brush down the animal. He waited for her to speak, but she remained silent.

Finally, he spoke again, saying, "Why ain't you in bed?"

"Too hot to sleep. 'Sides. Figured you needed some help. Leisha never came down to eat all evening. Could tell her horse was on a long ride. And Steve's been here all day branding. Now, he's out working with the wranglers up in the hills."

"So?"

"So, don't take much to add up that two and one makes three."

After leading the stallion into his corral, Matt closed the door on him, and then turned to Jaimie. "Young lady, you've got quite an imagination."

"Uh huh."

The two finished up and walked together out of the barn. The light was still on in Leisha's room.

"How's your leg and shoulder?"

"Hurts like hell. You know that."

"Just wanted to hear you say it." She kidded him with a small, childish laugh. "Better let me look at your shoulder. Might need a new dressing."

"What I might need, young lady, is some sleep. Shoulder will keep 'til mornin'." He turned towards his house, and with a backhand to Jaimie's buttocks, he smacked her, turning her in the direction of the general's house. "See ya, kid."

Jaimie stopped and rubbed her buttocks, and then with her hands on her hips and her legs separated and standing strong, she watched Matt hobble towards his house. Leisha had watched the whole incident. Jaimie sensed it. She looked up towards the window, just briefly, but long enough to cause Leisha to back away. Then she walked towards the house and stood on the porch while waiting to see that Matt had made it safely to his house. She heard Matt make the remark, "Women!" and the door slamming. She went inside with a smile on her lips.

The next morning was crisp and cool, as a Texas morning could be following a hot and humid day. Matt was already dressed and over to the general's house for breakfast. The general had been waiting for him on the porch.

After the usual morning greeting, the general added, "Leisha tells me you had an encounter with one of McDaniels people."

Matt made a seat for himself on the rail and faced the general. "Yeah. Came close." He said with a gruff tone. "I put a hole in him, or her, don't know which. Should have either killed him or slowed him down a bit. Hope it killed him."

"Can't be sure?"

"No."

"Damn! There go our plans."

"Yeah."

Jaimie came to the door and opened it, saying, "Breakfast is on."

The general rose and entered the house with Matt following him.

As Matt continued to the kitchen for breakfast, the general went to his room.

Tension started to build as Leisha turned from the stove and saw Matt. Matt stopped and wiped his hands on his legs as an act of cleansing himself from perspiring, as if he was afraid of the first words to come from her mouth.

He said, "Morning, Leisha."

Leisha returned, politely but coldly, "Matt." She poured the coffee in his cup at his setting. "Coffee?"

Matt nodded his head and sat down.

Jaimie brought the biscuits to the table, trying her best not to laugh at the two.

At that time, the sound of a cowboy's boots hit the porch, and the door to the kitchen flew open. Steve entered and removed his hat.

Jaimie dropped the pan of biscuits quickly on the table, being careful not to break anything. She burst into laughter and ran out the door.

Steve stopped and watched her and picked up the blank expressions on the faces of Matt and Leisha. "What's so funny?"

Matt responded, while sitting down at the table, "Beats hell out of me."

Leisha put the coffeepot on the table and ran out the kitchen to join Jaimie.

Steve settled down to the table with Matt, and began serving himself the coffee and biscuits. "Where's the eggs?"

"Behind ya, on the stove. Oh, christ, the bacon's smokin'."

Steve jumped up and removed the pan of bacon from the stove and threw them on his plate. He put the pan into the sink and went back to the stove. "Want some taters?"

"Ya sure you got room on your plate for them?"

While the two cowboys enjoyed their breakfast, Leisha had caught up with Jaimie by the corral. Jaimie turned and stood against the corral while Leisha settled next to her. Jaimie was still laughing.

Leisha asked, "You know, don't you?"

Jaimie attempted almost in futility to stop laughing while she answered Leisha. "You got them both fighting over you, and they've been friends most of their lives."

"I'm sure I'm not at all certain that I understand," Leisha lied.

"Oh, Leisha. Cut it. This is Jaimie. I know about you and Steve. Most of the ranch knows. Believe me they know."

"They do not."

"Leisha, you're the general's daughter. Every man here would love to make love to you, not just for the fun of it, but also because they know they'd get the ranch, too. And you think you've got them fooled?"

Leisha's face turned a bright red as if the truth were finally revealed, but she was ashamed to admit it. "The whole ranch?"

"Matt, included."

"Matt?" Leisha yelled, cupping her mouth quickly with her hand. She turned quickly towards the general's house and continued, "And we -- Matt and I -- we made love."

"First time?"

"No, of course not."

"The General suspected as much. Steve knew it, too."

"Steve? Oh my god. How did Steve find out?"

"Everyone kinda knows, Leisha. Question is not about you and Matt, but rather, you and Steve."

"Steve? Oh my god."

Jaimie climbed up on the top rail and continued, "you said that, already. My god, gal, you're older than me by ten years, and you act like a school kid. Do I have to spell it out for you?"

Leisha turned herself around to see if any of the ranch hands were looking.

Over at the chuck wagon, the cook was cleaning up his mess while most of the cowboys were headed to the corral for their horses.

"Can we walk away from here so as not to be heard?" Leisha motioned away from the cowboys.

Jaimie jumped down and the two of them walked away from the wranglers. The pair of them were dressed in tight jeans, and almost looked like twin sisters. Their shapes belied them as to who was who. Their walking only brought out the beast in the wranglers as they began to humorously and innocently whistle at them.

The general left the house with Matt and Steve joining him on the porch. Of course, Steve had a biscuit and a cup of coffee, while Matt held onto his cup. The general was all dressed up in a suit and tie.

The general looked over at the wranglers, took his gun from his holster and fired a shot at the ground in front of them. Putting the revolver back into its holster, he loudly barked, "You wanna whistle, whistle at me."

The wranglers opened the gate to the corral and started after their horses. The general looked at Matt and Steve and then towards the girls. "Fine pair of fillies. And two men like you fighting over them like a pair of mustangs."

Matt quickly jumped in, "Fighting? Who's fighting? Over who?"

Steve added, "Don't look at me. I ain't fightin' nobody."

The general looked sternly at the two men as if to admonish them publicly.

The wranglers were far from paying attention, but the girls were watching from a not-too-far a distance. They could make out a word of two if the wind was just right. The general asked directly, as if wanting an answer that very minute. "Matt. You gonna marry my daughter, or aren't you?"

Matt's answer was interrupted as Seth came riding over to the cook station from his station on the crest. He saw the general and the rest conversing on the porch, and politely waved, as to say "Good morning."

The general signaled for him to come over.

After dismounting, and tying up his horse, Seth walked over to the group.

He said, "Thought I'd still be in time for some vittles."

As the young ladies sauntered back to the house, Jaimie chimed in immediately with, "Forget the cook, he's already folding camp. Got some hot biscuits and gravy inside."

Steve added, "And some burnt bacon."

Matt chided, "Tasted mighty good to me."

Steve continued, "If'n ya like 'em that way. I like mine fresh and lookin' up at me."

Seth asked, "We talkin' about bacon or eggs? Makes no never mind with me. I'm so hungry I could eat a bear."

The general had other ideas for Seth. He told him, "Go mount Sidewinder for me. Then you can set a spell for breakfast."

Seth nodded, took off his hat, and wiping the inside with his bandanna, complied, "Yes sir. Usual ride?"

"Reckon."

Seth tipped his hat to the ladies on the porch, replaced it, and nodding to the general, he walked away.

Matt sized Seth up, saying, "Good man, Seth. Make a good foreman. Take your place some day, Steve."

"Some day. Still a little green behind the gills. But some day." This was all Steve could comment about. His mind was still thinking about Leisha, who had gone back into the house with Jaimie. He looked at Matt and scratched his chin, and then asked, "What next?"

Surmising he was going to ask that question, Matt thought to come up with a proper answer. Instead, he excused himself, saying, "Damned if I know," and sat down in the porch swing.

Steve began to mumble, "Can't fight ya, you being a crippled and all. Can't shoot ya, you'd outdraw me. Guess I'll go back up the hills and work the cattle down this way."

Matt looked at him, trying to understand him, but because of his down-in-the-dirt conversation, he couldn't. So, he asked, "Steve, what're ya mumbling about?"

Steve's silence infuriated Matt.

In the meantime, Seth had the general's horse saddled, and brought over.

Matt rose and walked off the porch with the general. The general mounted and looked splendid in his suit and tie. In Matt's eyes, he was truly a general.

CHAPTER 15

EYES FOR THE FOREMAN

Leisha walked out the door and watched her father ride away. "I'll catch up with you later, Pa." She waved and let a tear drop down her cheek. It is the general's time to ride the mile up western hillside to a small cemetery. On top of the hill, he would place flowers on the graves of his wife, his brother, and his brother's wife.

After watching him ride off, Leisha decided to join her father. She reined up near the graves and dismounted. She walked over to comfort her father.

"It's been a long time since your ma died, Leisha," the general said, without looking up but knowing it was Leisha who was standing beside him as he knelt at his wife's grave.

"Fifteen years since Jaimie's mom died, Daddy."

"Two motherless young ladies."

"And a wifeless young fella, too," Leisha added, as she put her arm around his shoulder.

"And Paul, my brother. You're in heaven with them, Paul." He wiped the tears from his eyes, and continued, "A musketball brought you here, Paul, to rest beside your lovely wife."

"Jaimie never got to know her mom. But she idolized her pappy, like I do mine," Leisha said, with warmth in her voice, and a tear in her eye. "He was a brave hero of the War. Like you, Pa; but you came back alive."

The general lifted his head, again without looking at Leisha, and said, "Barely."

"Mother would be proud of you, Pa. Had she survived the fall from her horse, she'd be right here to mend your spirit, like I try, Pa. I was in the house and didn't know anything about it for hours. When I went looking for her, I found her on a bank of the Brazos where a tree limb knocked her off her horse. An hour or two sooner, who knows? I don't. She was weak from the loss of blood when I got there. That night, she was gone. It was like the river took her spirit."

The general stood up and lengthening his body, looked towards the hills where the cattle were coming.

"Her spirit is in this whole ranch, Leisha. From the Brazos to here, up those hills, and across the valley towards Waco. This is her home."

The wind picked up and swirled dust around the grave markers as the two of them stood motionless. The clouds began to appear above as if from out of nowhere.

The soft hoofbeats of Jaimie's horse were heard climbing the hill. She stopped, dismounted, and walked slowly over to the general and Leisha. The two ladies put their arms around each other.

Jaimie spoke and said, "I brought these for Ma and Pa." She showed a bunch of wildflowers she had picked on the way up the hill. The general watched as the ladies placed them on the graves of Jaimie's mother and father.

The general asked, "Would you two join me in a word or two?"

Of course the nods were immediate, and gentle as the wind that played around the top of the hill like kittens playing with a ball of yarn. The moment was light. The general prayed, "Emily. Paul. Nancy. We miss you. I feel you are still with me every night, Emily. I could not make it otherwise."

Leisha added, "Me too, Ma. I love you."

With her eyes opened slightly, Jaimie tearfully said, "Me, too, Ma, and Pa. Me, too."

"I guess what we are trying to say, as we say each time we come here, is this. We are family. We are not apart. We will always be together. This is your home, now, and someday, Emily, I'll join you up here. And Paul, cuss your hide, maybe we can do some hunting, like we use to do. If Nancy will let you get away."

The three held hands together, and the general finished up, saying, "That's all we've got to say, I guess. We love you. And we'll stick together always."

The general had raised the two as daughters, though Leisha was ten years older than Jaimie.

As the three turned towards their horses they saw Steve riding up the hill away from them, and towards the cattle.

It was a slow steady trot, as if he was in no hurry to get there. His head turned to look at the three standing on the hill, and he waved to them. They waved back, then Jaimie and the general mounted up, and waited for Leisha.

"Go on back." Leisha stood holding her reins. "I've got some soul mending to do myself right about now."

"Okay" Jaimie said. "We'll see you at the ranch." She and the general rode back leaving Leisha there alone.

Leisha watched for awhile, then turned to look towards Steve, who was headed up towards the cattle. She knew the ride would take a good hour to get to the cattle, and she made her decision to join him. After seeing that the general and Jaimie were close to the ranch house, she mounted and rode fast to catch up with Steve.

Seeing her coming, he stopped his horse and waited for her to sidle next to him.

Once there, she looked deep into his hurt eyes, and whispered, "Hi."

He returned the greeting with a smile, and the two began to ride the slope together.

After a while, she asked, "Wanna talk?"

Without looking at her, keeping his eyes mostly to the front as if to eye the cattle, Steve answered her, "Suppose so. What about?"

"Well, for openers, about the way I've been treating you."

"How's that?"

"Like I'm trying to make you jealous, by not paying attention to you. Maybe."

"Don't make me no mind. I know you're Matt's girl, and you're gonna marry him."

"That's just what I mean, Steve. I'm not really Matt's girl." She stopped talking for awhile, waiting to catch her thoughts, and also to see how Steve would react to what she had just said. She was not too sure that what she said was really meant to be said. However, she had said it now, and she could not retract it.

All these years, she had been Matt's girl. Steve just had a small hand-patting acquaintance now and then, and nothing more serious than a kiss, if one would call a quick kiss in the dark inside a barn a real kiss. They did that one night when the moment was ripe, and no one was looking; so they thought. No one was looking, but at the time, they felt the whole world was watching them; so they made it quick. They wanted to see how each other would act towards their kiss.

It started a relationship between both for many months to follow. Because of her commitment to Matt, she let it go as nothing more than a flirt.

To Steve, his feelings became stronger each time she was around him. It was not that Matt was bigger or tougher than Steve that concerned him although this thought preyed heavily upon his mind whenever he yearned to have an affair with Leisha, but it was the idea of doing something behind his best friend's back that disturbed him. He had no rights to Leisha. She belonged to Matt and Matt belonged to her. That was how it was and that was how it would always be.

Steve also knew that Matt was never going to be hog-tied. When he was only twenty-two years old, his dad disowned him because he made a mistake; he tried to keep his brother in the straight of things. In this attempt of saving his brother, he lost both him and his own family the same night. To Matt, it was not fair.

Because of this, Matt swore he would not marry. He swore that he would never be a rancher. He developed an avid hate for cattle. In the War, he learned to use his gun and he learned to use it well. With his career cut out for him as a hired gun, he found his life again, and was holding on to it tenaciously. He would not let go of the gun; it had become his best companion.

Steve was thinking about all that Matt had told them these years they had spent together. Now, Steve was riding with the loveliest beauty he had ever laid eyes on, and he was becoming at ease with the situation for the first time since he had met her. His eyes turned towards her as he began to look at her seriously. Her horse was laid back of his horse a head's length which allowed him to get a full-frontal view of her.

She sat a horse like one who was born on one. She dressed the horse down with her beauty. Her posture was erect, and her hand held onto the reins like a true champion. Her jeans and blouse accentuated her body and complemented the picture of a rider and horse together. Her hair blew in the wind, she was truly a goddess in every sense of the word, and he could rightly see that Matt had had a golden nugget in the palm of his hand all these years.

But now the golden goddess was riding alongside him, talking with him. To them, no one was within a hundred miles of their voices. There were no witnesses to this scene of two riders riding up a slope together completely hypnotized by each other's presence. He felt his love for her so strongly that it was hard for him to stay in his saddle without wanting to jump off and roll in the grass with her.

He was in his early forties, never married, and no real girl friend that he could recall, and now he felt like a child again. His emotions were running to and fro with him at this moment, looking at her and yet still thinking of Matt.

Leisha's eyes were smiling at Steve, undressing him with every move he made as his horse gently stumbled and regained its gait again.

Sensing her feeling towards him, Steve threw his chin forward and rode on. Leisha followed. Some wranglers neared them with their cattle headed downhill. Steve knew the drive was almost ready as he rode around the wranglers, motioning for them to keep the herd moving.

Up ahead, the streams of cattle appeared like highways across the desert merging into one, and heading towards the ranch. Steve figured there had to be over three, maybe four thousand head. This is one drive he was looking forward to since he had been on the ranch. He would take them to the bridge, onto the Chisholm Trail, and drive them to Kansas. This would make the Brazos River Bar M Ranch just about the biggest in Texas. He figured the general might not become governor, but his estate would be like the rotunda, prestigious and grand.

For the first time in a long time, Steve was beginning to think of himself as someone important. After all these years being number two behind Matt, he felt that his worthiness was about to pay off. Leisha felt this sense of pride in him.

He stopped his horse with Leisha by his side and looked across the state of Texas from top of the hill. To him, there was nothing like Texas. He was born and raised a Texian.

Leisha looked intensely proud at Steve at this moment. "What do you see, Steve? Tell me."

"Texas."

"What about Texas, Steve?"

"I'm looking North towards Waco. And West towards the Alamo." He took his hat off and brushed his hair back as he looked West.

"Thirty-five year ago, we became the twenty-eighth state of these here United States. If the guys at the Alamo, and San Jacinto could see us now. Honey, this is what was meant to be. Texas." He let out a rebel yell and threw his hat up in the air. The air caught it as if in slow motion and brought it gently back down to the ground.

"You called me, honey."

"Honey, I'm in love with the greatest state of them all."

Leisha smiled with her lips and her eyes, and responded, "And, honey, I'm in love with the greatest man of them all."

Steve looked at her and paused for seemingly a long time without saying anything. He smiled.

Slim came up behind, moving his cattle towards them. He yelled out, "Boss. We should have them all down the hill before sundown."

Steve whipped his horse around and watched as Slim neared his cattle towards them. Slim asked, "Wanna take my place? I can go back up and help Dan and Shorty."

Steve spurred his horse forward and yelled back, "You take 'em on in, Slim. I wanna see the whole herd for myself from up there."

Leisha kicked her horse into a canter and joined Steve.

Meanwhile, the general had returned to the ranch. Matt walked out of the kitchen of the general's house as the general tied up his horse. "About the shooting, Matt."

"Yes, General?"

"Wanna tell me about it, now?"

"Not much to tell, sir. Leisha and I were down by the Brazos. Some one rifled me and missed. I took a few shots in his direction, and I hope I hit him. If he lives, then our plan to outsmart the McDaniels is out the window."

The general sat in the swing and took a long look at Matt. "I'd like to know who it was, and why the shooting."

"The shooting, sir, was to kill me. He recognized me. That I know," Matt responded, then taking a long deep breath, he continued. "What the McDaniels will do, I don't know."

The general replied, "I'm frettin' about this whole thing."

Jaimie came out on the porch wiping her hands on her apron as if she had been washing dishes or preparing food. She joined in the conversation, "Why, General?"

"'Cause." The general stood up, as Matt gave him a hand in getting out of the swing. He looked towards the Brazos and said, "'Cause, having a skirmish is one thing. We got them on the run, and that's what counts. But killing one person in an ambush, right or wrong, could be asking for trouble. And I'm thinking this might be what the McDaniels might need to get back at us."

Matt turned swiftly and motioned with a broad sweep of his arm and said, "It was self defense, General; he shot at me first."

"That's what I mean, Matt. Your word against theirs. If I were on that side, I'd make an issue of it, and I'm sure that might be what they'll need." He turned and went inside.

Jaimie focused on Slim bringing his cattle in. The wranglers rode out to meet him and helped him herd them into the corral. Jaimie also walked out to watch him. It took a while, but soon Slim caught sight of her climbing up on the rail and watching them.

He yelled over at her, "Got a minute?"

Jaimie nodded, "Any time. What'cha got in mind, handsome?"

He rode over to a calf and her mother nursing it; a black longhorn with a little bit of white to make it cute. The sight was pretty and quite passionate for a drover like Slim. He wanted to share the moment with Jaimie.

"Come on over here."

Jaimie complied quite readily and walked among the cattle to where Slim had walked his horse. He dismounted and dropped the reins to the ground. The horse was motionless while Slim walked over to the calf. Pointing to her, being careful not to touch her, he said, "Ain't she a beaut?"

Jaimie realized that she was out in the middle of the corral in her clean apron and watching some dirty cattle. She asked, "What's so beautiful about this?"

"Jaimie, this is mine. I helped give birth to it three or four days ago. Seth says I can keep her. Isn't she a pretty critter?"

Jaimie stared at the calf, and then at Slim, whose eyes were as wide as the calf's. She asked, "You gonna put that thing on the train with you when you go back to Montana?"

Slim stopped for a moment without taking his eyes off the calf and said, "Maybe not."

"What does that mean?"

"Just what I said." He picked up his reins and walked Jaimie back out of the corral. "A man does a lot of thinking up in those hills. I mean, alone, and all. And, Jaimie, when that mother gave birth to that calf, and I was there . . . . well, it meant something to me. Something special."

"You've seen heifers give birth before, ain't ya?"

"Some. But not like a longhorn. Honey, this is a longhorn."

Jaimie put her arm around Slim as they walked out the gate. She asked, "You said you did a lot of thinking up there in those hills. What about?"

After closing the gate, Slim stood there and looked at the cattle. "I like it here, Jaimie. I like you. And I like the cattle. And, the general. Dang it all, I like Texas. And if I can't take you out of Texas, I'm thinking maybe you can just take me out of Montana."

Matt walked up to them and interrupted them. "Slim. Let's talk."

Slim's eyes widened as Matt looked down on him, mean and big as ever. He saw Wil in Matt reprimanding him as Wil used to do. Slim's youthful playfulness changed dramatically to a man ready to take orders.

Matt asked, "Did I hear 'Montana' mentioned?"

"Yes, sir," Slim choked a reply. He was beginning to remember his mission; his reason was for coming to Texas in the first place.

Then he began to explain, "Sir, it's like this."

Before he could manage any more words, Matt interrupted. "Take a bath, kid, and clean up. Chow should be ready about then. We can talk over a drink afterwards. It's time for that." He turned to leave, turned again and asked, "Ya do drink, don't ya?"

Slim answered by nodding his head.

Matt walked on towards his house. Looking back over his shoulder, he said, "Good girl, Jaimie."

Jaimie showed a little blushing in her face while Slim dusted off his chaps and turned to go towards the other side of the bunkhouses where a tub was set up for taking baths.

"Good idea." Slim said. "I must smell as bad as I look."

Jaimie nodded in agreement, smiled, and waved a fond goodbye as she walked away towards her house. Slim returned the wave, and continued walking.

CHAPTER 16

A LADY'S HONOR

Steve and Leisha returned later that afternoon and ran into a cleaned-up Slim approaching the general's house. After reining up at the corral, Steve took the horses into the stable to bed them down for the night. Slim turned and followed him, while Leisha went into her house.

Looking at how clean Slim was, Steve said, "Reckon I should do the same. Get cleaned up. I forgot it was Saturday."

Slim helped bed down the two horses, and said, "Yes, sir." A pause, and the two men found themselves without words. Finally, Slim asked, "Isn't Leisha Matt's girl?"

Steve forked some hay into the stall of Leisha's horse and answered, "Yep."

"Matt know?" Slim continued brushing Steve's horse.

Steve kept forking the hay.

"That she's, his girl? Reckon." He answered.

Slim stopped the brushing and looked at Steve over the haunches of the horse and corrected his question, "I mean about you and Leisha?"

Steve finished with Leisha's horse's stall, and took his horse away from Slim. "Don't know," he said, leading the horse into his stall.

"You and Leisha serious?"

"You and Jaimie?" Steve retorted rather slowly.

"Yep." Slim mimicked Steve.

Behind them, a fist came through the air and connected with Slim's jaw, knocking him to the dung filled floor of the stable. Slim tumbled to the floor and landed under the hooves of Steve's horse.

Getting up, he prepared himself to fight, as he saw Seth standing over him.

Steve held Seth as Slim dove at him, missing wildly as Steve dragged Seth out of his path. Steve let Seth lose, and as Slim came up, Seth connected again across Slim's face, knocking him backwards and out into the corral.

Slim rose again, and as Seth approached him with another fist, Slim dodged it and landed a fist into Seth's midsection, sending him tumbling backward to the ground.

As Seth got up, he blocked another blow coming across his face, and followed through with his own fist connecting to Slim's stomach. Seth hit the buckled-over Slim with a follow-through uppercut, sending Slim across the corral and under a rail that kept the cattle separated from the main entrance.

Seth hurdled the rail and landed on top of Slim who attempted to get to his feet. Both men were bleeding from the nose and mouth, and a cut was laid across Slim's cheek bone. The weight of Seth coming on top of Slim knocked him back to the ground, and the two rolled over.

Slim took advantage of this roll over Seth, and pushed Seth's face into the mud and dung, causing Seth to sputter as Slim let loose. Slim rose and pulled Seth up with him by his long hair, and turning him around, landed his fist across his cheekbone and blood began to gush.

Seth sprawled out into the filth, desperately gasping for air.

Steve hurdled the rail and came to Seth's aid, picking him up and making sure he was breathing all right.

Slim backed away and into a cow. He stumbled backwards and fell to the ground where he sat for a breather.

Steve asked Seth, "Are you okay?"

Seth was breathing hard, he raised himself up on one knee, and looked over at Slim. Panting, he answered, "Yeah."

Slim was waiting for Seth to make the next move, scared that he didn't have the strength to defend himself again. The two eyed each other with wrath, but neither one moved. Slim exclaimed in fear, "You -- you come at me again, and I'll kick you in the balls."

Seth sat down and looked at Slim as he continued to pant for air.

Steve let go of Seth and stood between the pair of fighters. He asked them, "Had enough you two?"

Slim kept his gaze on Seth, and breathing hard, he answered, "Far as I'm concerned."

Seth rose slowly, and without warning started to jump on Slim, but was knocked out of the way by Steve tripping him. Seth went for his gun but found an empty holster.

Fearing this, Slim, too felt for his gun, but found his gunbelt was missing. He remembered he had left it in the bunkhouse when he changed clothes.

Seth's pistol lay several feet away from him, and the three of them stared at it.

Steve picked it up, cleaned it off on his pants, and put it into his belt. He looked at Seth eyeing the gun in his belt which gave Slim time to get to his feet and thrust his body into Seth's.

Knocking him back onto his face in the mire, Slim sat on Seth's back and pulled his head back with his hair. Through gritted teeth, he angrily said, "We can play this game all night." Panting, he continued, "What gives?"

Seth looked up at Steve who had climbed upon the rail to stay out of the fight. He asked, "You gonna sit there and let him do this to me?"

Steve looked down at Seth, and then at Slim still on top of him, and said, "Yep."

"My father will fire you for this."

Slim pushed his face back into the mud and brought it back up again. "I'm a patient man, usually. But Seth, you've been riding me something fierce. What the hell is eatin' you?"

There was no answer from Seth.

Seeing that Seth was breathing all right, Slim took Seth's arm and bent it back, while at the same time keeping a strong hold on his hair. "Damn it, Seth. Give it up. I don't want to hurt you any more."

"All right -- all right," Seth cried out.

Slim got off of him, raised himself on his knees, and kept his eyes on Seth, expecting him to make another move.

Seth rolled over and slowly sat up. He wiped the mud and dung off his face with his dirty sleeves and spat out the extra that wallowed inside his mouth.

"You're not good enough for her," he said.

Slim's eyes opened wide, and his face looked like it went through an eggbeater. He asked in amazement, "What? Are you talking about Jaimie?"

"You son-of-a-bitch. You took her and used her."

Slim stood up and, with his fists clenched, said, "No one talks like that to me, mister."

Steve intervened swiftly seeing Slim was ready to continue the fight. He lit from the rail and grabbed onto Slim. "Hold it, son."

Slim continued, "I never used her, Seth. That's the god-honest truth."

"The hell you say. Every man here knows you busted her."

Slim freed himself, turned around and kicked mounds of dung, and turned again swift and angrily. "We swam. We dried off. We came home." He walked over to Steve and attempted to plea his case. "Steve, that's all we did. I wouldn't have. And she made sure we didn't."

Seth yells out, "How?"

Slim turned and answered, "She told me we wouldn't." He looked up at Steve and said, "I respect her, Steve."

Steve replied, "I believe ya, son."

"So do I." A masculine voice boomed out twenty feet from the scene. It was Matt. He and the ladies were walking towards the corral.

"Get up, Seth." Matt picked Seth up and brushed him off a bit. "Now, I'm not taking sides, mind ya, but I believe the boy. And more than that, I believe Jaimie. And Jaimie heard every word you both said."

Jaimie ran over to Seth and put her arms around him. She looked at his face, and taking off her apron, she used it to wipe the blood and dirt off. Looking into his hurt eyes, she kissed him on both cheeks, and then on the lips. "You, boob." She held him up, as he put his arms around her.

Light sobs came from Seth as she pulled his face back to look into his eyes again. "Nothing happened, Seth. It could have, but it didn't. You see, I respect him, too."

Matt braced Seth for fear of him falling.

Steve picked up Slim and held him up. Slim's face was still bleeding, so Steve took his dirty bandanna from around his neck, and started wiping away the gore.

"Sorry it ain't no apron, son."

A smile came across Slim's face.

Seth cut his tears, and said to Jaimie, "You're my cousin, Jaimie. I couldn't love anyone more."

"And you're my cousin, Seth, and I couldn't love anyone more, either." And then, she looked over at Slim, and added, "Except, my husband-to-be."

A look of surprise came across Seth's face, as he looked into Jaimie's honest blue eyes staring over at Slim. "Can I go to him, now, Seth?"

Seth looked at the two, and a painful smile came across his face, too.

Jaimie lead him by the hand over to Slim. Letting his hand go, she grabbed Slim's hand, squeezed it, and said, "That is, if he asks me."

Slim let out a little yell as the pain shot through his hand, smarting from hitting Seth. She released it slightly, as he again squeezed hers, and folded her into his arms. His cheek began to swell, and his tongue felt thick, impeding his speech. All he could say, was, "Yes, Ma'am." And that he did, with a smile that hurt like hell.

Seth put his arm around Slim's neck, pulled it gently towards him with Jaimie in the middle, and said, "Hell, buddy. I'm sorry."

Matt looked at the two men, as Steve side-stepped around them. Matt suggested, "I thought I told you to take a bath."

Leisha had left the scene and now returned with towels and soap which she gave to the two men. She commanded, "Clean up, and then we'll tend to your cuts and bruises. Dinner's on the general tonight."

Steve smiled as the two men headed together for the far side of the bunkhouses with towels and soap in hand.

Matt looked over at Steve and asked, "What are you smiling about, Lieutenant?"

"Reminds me of us in the trenches that day you told me to take off my blouse," Steve replied, still looking at the men walking.

Matt did a double take at Steve, and added, "Hell, that was for insubordination. I shoulda had ya shot."

Steve returned his look at Matt, and replied, "Yeah. We fought over a girl we both wanted the night before. Found out later she was the wife of a soldier not on our side."

Matt turned his rugged face into a smile, and then into a laugh, as the two walked back to the ranch house with Jaimie and Leisha.

CHAPTER 17

MCTAVETT RECRUITS HIS ARMY

It was like most days in Waco; streets filled with drovers seeking jobs, derelicts sleeping between buildings, and other men of the evening at the mercy of some mighty fine women. The population was increasing with people coming to settle in this growing metropolis.

The new suspension bridge at the south end of town had given wranglers and drovers, hoping to get hired on a job going to Kansas on the Chisholm Trail, a reason to stop and settle in. The Green Slipper Hotel and Saloon was the most popular in town and catered to the wealthy. McTavett and his men were at the Red Garter Saloon, where the less wealthy gathered to play cards for the little money they had. McTavett had set up his field of operation earlier, recruiting men into his so-called army. His intent was to own the Brazos River Bar M Ranch. He drew from his experience serving under Matt and Steve in Terry's Texas Rangers during the war. Now it was his turn to play officer.

The core of his gang consisted of three men who had served under him when he was a corporal. Aaron was the ugliest of the three and the most ruthless. It never bothered him to kill a man. He stood beside McTavett at the table as a bodyguard. Frank was the heaviest and slowest and hated everyone, even his mother. He stood at the entrance to the saloon as a beacon, so the men they recruited would know where to come. Lem was the one who dropped out of school before he ever started. He was the idiot of the bunch who walked through town telling men about the roundup.

McTavett and his men had been out all day talking to men in the street that were hungry for jobs and food. They told them that a cattle drive was about to take place and offered them jobs as drovers and promised them a steady job on the ranch once the cattle were sold in Kansas. Most had never been on a cattle drive. But that was of no concern to McTavett. He wanted to hire their guns.

"You want a job or a handout, mister?" McTavett asked.

"A job," the man answered, curling his weather-beaten hat.

"Got a horse?" McTavett asked each of the men he talked with that day. But the next question was more important, "Got a gun?" When they told him what he wanted to hear, he hired them on the spot. The men ranged from street derelicts to old ranch hands from the surrounding area.

McTavett assembled them inside the saloon that afternoon where he had a spread of food on the back table. His gang stood guard.

McTavett fired a round from his .44 into the floor to get their attention while they drank his beer. "We've got eight thousand head of cattle to get to Kansas. Maybe more. The pay is fifteen dollars a month, paid at the end of the trail. Providin' you make it. Figure you'll be gone three, maybe four months."

"They all your cattle?" a voice asked from behind McTavett.

McTavett turned and walked over to the man who asked the question. He saw a grubby man in his thirties, wearing a dirty red beard and little hair. "Yeah!" McTavett returned, tightening his grip on his .44. "And some others. I aims to take as much beef to Kansas as I can get my hands on."

"Jest askin'."

"Well, I tolds ya. I ain't hirin' ya because you're the best drovers in town. I'm hirin' ya to get my job done. Texas was built on blood and there'll be more spilt along the way. If you can't handle it, git out."

A few men left, most stayed. McTavett was pleased with himself, for he felt he had picked the right men. "The rest of you can grab a plate of food. You'll continue to get hot meals every day along the way." He strutted around the saloon eyeing his new recruits.

"When you return," he continued, "you'll have a steady job on one of the biggest ranches in Texas, and you'll be paid well." The men muttered among themselves. Now McTavett knew he had their attention and that he could count on their guns.

"Fill your guts! And there's more beer. Tomorrow we'll meet and round up our stock."

It was dusk and the gaslights played tricks with the shadows in the street. McTavett sat at a table next to the window so he could more easily watch the people going and coming from the Green Slipper while he played cards. He had the ever-obsessive desire to be powerful and be able to walk into a saloon like the Green Slipper and watch heads turn. He fantasized to himself about being one of the silhouettes at the end of the street walking into the Slipper with a lady on his arm.

"We've signed up fifty drovers," McTavett said, throwing away a pair of cards in the pot. "Is that how you men figure it?"

"More like sixty," Aaron came back. "Ten men came in while you were down the street."

"Good. I'm gonna talk with the rangers in the mornin' and make damn sure they get Steve out of the way. Once I see him ride into town in handcuffs, we go into action."

"What if'n they don't catch Steve?" Frank asked arrogantly, dealing the cards left to right.

"Don't even think that way, mister! They'll bring him in." He rose to his feet and slammed his cards on the table.

"Didn't mean anythin', boss," Aaron came back. "Jest askin'."

McTavett drew his .44, spun the cylinder, and checked to make sure it was full. He holstered it and sat back down. "Tomorrow we gather our men and ride to the Brazos River Bar M Ranch and get ourselves some cattle. Our men are hungry enough for money and a steady job, they'll do whatever I tell 'em. And there won't be anyone on that ranch who can stop us this time."

Frank let out a loud "yahoo!" and slung his hat to the rafters. "It's about time!"

Lem followed him by letting out a rebel yell. Aaron just grunted and folded his hand.

"We gonna play cards tonight?"

The men sat down and continued their card game. After losing a few hands and feeling the labor of the day encompassing him, McTavett folded and cashed in his chips. He was through for the evening.

He paid his cordial goodnights and walked slowly across the street to the Green Slipper Saloon, imagining himself as the man who came to Waco and won her. He stopped along the sidewalk just before reaching the doors, took out the makings for a cigarette, and rolled it. He took a drag and slowly exhaled. He looked inside the saloon and, for a few minutes, watched and listened to the singing and laughing that came from within. He turned and bumped into a woman of the evening as she stepped up on the sidewalk to go inside.

She was a little taller than him, with her hair piled high on her head. She wore a low-cut red satin dress revealing the top half of her full breasts shoved together in a suggestive manner. Her hemline was short and cut to show a great deal of thigh. Even though the night air was cool, she wore no coat. Her lips were heavy with gloss and her cheeks were red with rouge. He could tell she was worth a man's day wages, and perhaps one of the costliest ladies of the Slipper. He stood and watched her as she brushed herself off, primped up her hair, and walked away from him into the saloon without saying a word, as if he wasn't even there.

"Well, excuse me," he said with a pretentious bow. He straightened up, threw his cigarette away in disgust, and yelled out, "One of these days I'll own this damn joint," and walked back to the Red Garter Saloon.

When morning broke, McTavett was dressed and walking down the stairwell of the hotel, an evil man determined to stomp all of Waco.

After a light breakfast at a nearby cafe, he left a sizable tip and headed for the office of the Texas Rangers.

Captain Ralph Johnson was sitting at his desk with a cup of coffee in hand, going over some warrants. His favorite pipe painted part of his facial expression as he puffed on it from time to time to keep it lit. He was hatless, and his thinning hair was neatly combed.

Two of his deputies were with him. One was inside cleaning his rifle, while the other was sitting on the porch with his chair tilted back against the front of the building.

Ranger Floyd Douglas greeted McTavett as he approached the office. "Good morning, sir."

"Good mornin'. Is the capt'n in?" McTavett asked.

"Yes, sir. Go right on in, sir."

"Thanks."

Seeing McTavett enter, Captain Johnson rose to greet him while Ranger Tom Elliott laid his rifle down to do the same. The Captain said, "Morning, McTavett."

"Mornin', Capt'n. Mornin', Ranger."

"Mornin'," Tom replied, and sat back down to continue cleaning his rifle.

The Captain sat on the edge of his desk and McTavett took a chair. "Cup of mud?" the captain asked. "Just made it."

"No, thanks, Capt'n. Just ate." McTavett sat and stared at the pair of pearl handled .44s in the Captain's holster. They glistened in the sun shining through the window, showing the delicate design of a steer's head carved into the handles of each one. "Any word?"

The reference was about the captain sending two of his deputies to arrest Steve for the murder of Billy. McTavett had brought in the bloodied shirt that Billy was wearing when he was shot. It showed three bullet holes in it; two from the back. Matt only hit Billy once in the chest. The other two were from McTavett's .44. He had shot two extra holes as insurance that Steve would be taken in for murder. His conversation this morning was a charade, as he didn't enjoy talking with the rangers. But he wanted to show he was concerned about justice, his type of justice.

"Nope," the captain answered. "Ain't been time for them to return yet. Just left a couple days ago."

"When you bring him in, I want to see him face to face. Any man who would shoot a kid in the back deserves to be hung upside down and twice on Sunday."

"I agree with you," the captain answered. "Just can't see Steve doing anything like this."

"Well, he did, Capt'n. Billy pointed him out jest before he died."

"I see you've been busy these past few days."

"Oh, yeah," McTavett returned a little nervously. "Hirin' some men to help us drive our cattle to Kansas. Got a couple thousand head."

"How many men you got, you figure?"

"Oh, maybe thirty or so," McTavett said cautiously. "We got more'n we can use, figurin' on some of them bellyin' out."

"We looked and counted over fifty."

"Fifty? Nah. Don't think so."

McTavett walked to the door, bade the captain and Tom goodbye with a flip of his hat and went out on the porch. "Gotta get back to my men." Without saying anything to Ranger Douglas, who was still leaning against the building, he stepped to the right of him and walked down the sidewalk.

Seeing McTavett, the three men from his gang crossed over from the other side of the street to meet him.

The four joined up, talked a minute and walked in the direction of the Red Garter Saloon down the street. Aaron asked, "Gettin' close, boss? The men are ready to ride."

McTavett returned, "Gettin' damn close. Those deputies should be at the Brazos Ranch by noon. I wanna see them bring Steve in. Then I'll know it's time."

"Anythin' wrong?" Frank asked.

"With Capt'n Johnson? Askin' too damn many questions. Tell the men to meet us at the grove tomorrow and be ready to ride all the way to Kansas."

They arrived at the saloon. McTavett took a table at the back of the room where it was less noisy and grabbed a bottle of whiskey before looking around at his new recruits. He felt victory was within his reach. He had taken over the McDaniel's Ranch as his own. He knew he had killed Matt, and now the rangers were arresting Steve, the second fastest gun in Waco. He was already a powerful man by his own standards. He had nothing but the rangers standing in his way, and with a powerful band of men behind him, he knew he had nothing to fear.

He was now prepared to take over the Brazos River Bar M Ranch and, with the McDaniels' count, he figured he would own the largest herd of cattle in all of Texas. With his army many times bigger than that of the Texas Rangers, he also knew no man or organization could stop him. His whole intent was to own all of Waco.

He leaned back in his chair, lit a cigar, and watched as more men came in to get hired. He poured himself a glass of whiskey from the bottle on the table and saluted his partners who were talking with their new hands about the opportunity to make money.

Suddenly, a sense of fear came over him like the bristly hair of an animal when an enemy approaches. Rising from his chair, he stomped outside the saloon and looked down the street. It appeared quiet and he couldn't put his finger on the reason why.

He looked south towards the bridge and then north to the rangers' office. Nothing was moving. No one had attempted to trip his hand, and he was concerned. He feared the rangers were plotting against him, and yet he felt he had no reason to suspect anything was going wrong. Only a strong gut feeling, like he had at times during the war when he could smell the enemy nearby.

He took another puff on his cigar, bit down on it with his teeth, and walked back into the saloon. He returned to his table and sat down. His palms were sweaty, and he rubbed them on his pants.

His men sensed he was uneasy. "What's the matter, boss?" Aaron asked as he got up and walked over to his table.

"Nothin'!" McTavett barked back at him. "Everythin's all right." He poured himself another drink as he watched Aaron return to his table. He was allowing fear to take over his whole body, even though he knew that the worst thing he could show his men was fear. "Damn!" he said to himself as he downed his drink.

He looked out the window from where he sat and saw only a few stragglers walking past the saloon. He saw no rangers.

CHAPTER 18

THE MEETING AT THE GENERAL'S HOUSE

The general was sitting in his front room puffing on his pipe, waiting for the others to come in.

The sun was setting on the prairies of southwest Texas, and the ladies had made a dinner that was enough for twice the company. Leisha and Jaimie picked up the bowls of green beans they had prepared earlier in the day and set them aside for the evening meal.

Matt was the first one to come through the door, followed by Steve. The general greeted them and offered each a seat as he sat in his large leather chair near the fireplace.

As the other men entered the house, they each greeted the general with hat in hand, then slung them on the rack next to the door. The general had made sure that Slim's friends from Montana were among the invitees, too.

Matt sat opposite the general in a huge chair in the big room and Steve stood by the fireplace.

The remaining four men picked up wooden, straight-back chairs from the dining room and carried them to the front room so they could sit down.

While it was not a formal meeting, the men waited patiently for the general to address them.

Slim and Seth sat opposite each other, with Dan and Shorty in the middle of the room. All attention was focused on the general.

"Gentlemen, what I have to say isn't easy." Accepting a cigar from Matt, he took a stick from the fire and lit it.

He looked sternly into the eyes of the men as he proceeded to speak. "We're in a range war. Have been ever since '65. Oh, we've had fights here and there, but nothing like what's waiting for us out there on the prairie. What I have to say is mostly for the benefit of these boys from Montana."

He stood and faced the men from in front of the fireplace mantle. "The rest of you can listen as I reminisce. My ranch was a big spread once. It was destroyed by the war. Thanks to some of you, we built her back up. Now we're being threatened by scum who want to take it away from us. The man of whom I speak was part of my regiment. He learned well from me. Too well. Now he's gathering up men to destroy me, but I'm not going to let him."

Slim asked, "You mean McTavett?"

"We have some twelve thousand head, give or take, right Steve?"

"Right, sir. Give or take."

"We have to drive them to Kansas. This is our first drive since the war, and we're ready. But before we get started, we have to storm past a son of a bitch who's waiting out there to take them away from us. He's got the McDaniels ranch and some thirty or forty hands strong, ready to drive."

"None of them's worth the dirt that fills their cuffs," Matt interrupted. "They ain't good drovers, just guns. And I'm not too sure about that."

"Nonetheless, he's got men, and he's got cattle. He'll try and take ours somewhere between here and the bridge. I'm bettin' it'll be at the bridge where we have to slow down."

"My bet, too, General," Matt said, rising and standing next to Steve at the fireplace.

"How they plan to go up against us seems as crazy as he is," the general continued. "We drove them back the other day, but as I see it, that was just a test to see our strength."

"Well, he found out," Matt added. "And it almost cost him his life."

"Now they think Matt's dead," the general went on, "he'll come in full force."

"Can't we get more men?" Seth asked.

"No time," Matt answered. "I'll use some of Steve's drovers as defense when the time comes. They can fight."

"We're going to do all right." The general took a good puff on his cigar. "We have the best."

He looked at the three cowboys from Montana and frowned.

"They're good wranglers," Steve said to the general. "With Matt being out of his head most of the time, and almost dead at other times, I put 'em to work 'til he got on his feet. Had to give them time until they could talk to ya. Well, Seth had them work up in the hills bringing the cattle down for our drive to Kansas."

"You done chased off one group," Shorty added. "They won't be a botherin' us again. Will they?"

"McTavett and his gang of cutthroats want this ranch really bad. He'll be back," Matt answered.

Steve agreed. "He's done it before. He'll do it again. As for the beef, we'll still have a thousand head or more on the ranch that are not ready for the drive. He'll come for them, too."

Slim asked, "I'll ask again, jest who the hell is this guy, McTavett? I mean, I know he was a sergeant in the same unit as Matt and Steve."

The general stepped in between the men in the center of the room and militarily gave his answer. "Yes, he was a sergeant once in my regiment. And he knows military tactics. Survived some of the biggest battles we had without a scratch. Murfreesboro. Chickamauga. You all saw how he survived our skirmish. Probably got a part in the hair and lived to laugh about it."

He relit his pipe and kept their attention as he continued, "He's a glory seeker. He wants this ranch only because it's a battle to win. If he got it, and I say 'if', because he's just crazy enough to be able to take it. He'd lose it."

"He's like Matt, in a way," Steve added, "only with an evil twisted mind."

"He's yearnin' to conquer you, Matt, the general continued, "and I suspect now that he thinks you're dead, he's like a toreador; he's got the sword in hand, ready for the kill."

Matt stood beside the general, lit a cigarette, and said, "That, boys, is why I can't leave."

"You've got 'til some time in November to prove your worth," Slim said. "After that, the ranch goes to the state for a park, or somethin'."

"This is the end of summer," Matt reminded them.

"You don't want to go back," Slim remarked brashly.

Standing up, Matt gritted his teeth hard, looked at Slim and answered him, "Son, I have nothin' left to go back for. Matt looked sternly at Slim. He knew he hadn't given them a satisfactory answer. "Sounds to me like you had some good years with my ma and pa. Those years were taken away from me. My pa's dead. My brother's dead. I can't change any of that." He paused a moment, then continued, "I want to see Ma. I'd like to take off right now and see her, but I can't. I'm chancin' she'll still be alive if I leave later, and not right away."

"That's an awful chance for any man to take," the general spoke up. He took another drag on his cigar. "A man must make choices. I need you here, there's no denying that. But I don't want you holding it over my head that because of this you didn't see your mother before she died."

"Well, General," Matt said straight away. "We've got a showdown, and I ain't leavin' you until Steve gets his cattle safe across the bridge."

"How soon, Steve?" the general asked.

"Seein' how we've got a good start, we should have the cattle movin' in a coupla days. Get to the bridge by the end of the week."

"Matt?" The general looked at Matt and waited for an answer.

"McTavett will be at our front door any moment, as I see it," Matt replied with his hand tightly holding onto the butt of his .45. "We'll be ready for him."

"If all goes well, boys," the general addressed the three at the far end of the room, "will that work for you?"

"General," Slim answered, "that's all we came down here for."

"We'll help in any way you want us to, General," Dan joined in.

Matt walked to the door. He looked out at the stillness of the night and took a long drag on his cigar, letting the smoke drift out into the cool air. He turned and walked over to the three cowboys. "I'll go with you once the cattle are across the bridge." He looked around the room. "But I'm comin' back after we get your damn cattle to Belle Fourche. You can have your damn ranch. This is my home."

"Bullshit!" Slim blurted out. "That damn pistol is your home.

"Son, keep it up, and you'll get a whuppin' the likes you'll never forget." His hand went to the handle of his pistol.

"Whatever you might think, Matt, I kinda imagine the kid is right." The general looked at Matt's hand holding the grip on his pistol tightly.

Matt stopped and looked at the general. Realizing where his hand was, he released his grip.

"I'll sign over this ranch to you right now, Matt, in front of every witness in this room, to take effect upon my demise, if you will do me one favor." The general leaned forward in his chair.

Matt looked at the general, paused for a moment, then walked over to the fireplace. He took a log and added it to the fire. Then with the stoker, he began to poke at the fire to stir up the embers.

It was Matt's hour, his time for confession, denial, rejection, defeat, or admission. He was not sure how to say what was on his mind. Then he broke the silence: "I don't want a ranch, either in Montana or here. I can't handle one."

The general looked at Matt and decided to get him off the subject.

"Matt. I think maybe you've got a couple of moves left," the general answered. "Like a good soldier, why don't you reconnoiter and let me know your next move." Then he looked at the ladies and said, "I'm hungry, people. Let's eat."

As he straddled the chair, Matt looked at the food already set out on the table and then said, "The hands of two women in the kitchen toiling an entire day brings forth a meal, Texas style."

"Now that's worth fightin' for," Steve added sliding his big body into a chair next to him.

The general sat at the head of the table. "Let's not sit on ceremonies, gentlemen, as some would say. Dig in and let's eat."

The rest of the men took their chairs back to the table with them, and without anymore coaxing, dug in.

"And you gentlemen think I'm goin' to leave this?" Matt asked, slicing the beef.

"Got beef in Montana," Danny answered, leaving a white ring around his mouth from gulping a tall glass of buttermilk.

"Since you're in an all-fire hurry to get me back there, you best be sure you stay alive. What you saw the other day will be nothing compared to what's in store for us in the next few days."

Shorty looked up from gnawing on some buttered corn and smiled with his eyes. Then the truth hit him hard, and he dropped the ear of corn.

"What's the matter, son?" the general asked. "Corn burn your fingers?"

"I'm all for getting our cattle on the Chisholm and turnin' you loose," Steve added, tossing a steak on his plate. "Kinda anxious to see what Kansas is like."

Leisha and Jaimie stood in the doorway of the kitchen listening. Because of the myriad thoughts running through their minds, neither said a word to the other.

CHAPTER 19

A SURPRISE VISIT BY A WIDOW

The morning was crisp, dew hugged the ground, and a chill filled the quiet air.

A buggy and two riders appeared on the horizon of the Brazos River Bar M Ranch, breaking the silence. The cook rang the breakfast bell as wranglers, who had been watching the buggy, moved about the cooking area. Steve ran over to get Matt, who was coming out of his house carrying his boots and pulling his galluses up over his shoulders.

"I see it," he said, walking fast.

"Want me to ride with ya?" Steve asked.

"Let 'em come in. If I don't miss my guess, that's widow McDaniels." Matt continued to get dressed while on the run. Once dressed, he went up to the porch of the main house and joined the general who was already dressed and ready.

After Leisha and Jaimie peered out of the upstairs windows, they recognized the widow and hurriedly got dressed so they could join the men on the porch.

Alva, Nellie's ranch hand, drove the team of horses down the long road leading to the Brazos River Bar M Ranch, past the corral, and pulled them to a halt in front of the house. Alva was a thin man in his fifties, about five-foot-ten with a good posture, which showed in the way he was sitting up in the buggy.

The two ranch hands riding alongside pulled up their reins and brought their horses next to the buggy. One was young, tall and lanky, and the other was in his sixties; too old to ride to Waco with the rest of the other ranch hands and wranglers. Both men were armed.

Alva was seated next to the widow. He rose and started to step down from the buggy.

Matt saw he wasn't wearing a gun. However, he wasn't sure if he had a rifle on the buggy floor. "Step out, or I'll hafta kill ya." As his hand rested on the handle of his .45, Matt's eyes told Alva that he meant what he said.

Alva looked at Matt, then at the widow as she rose. She began to exit the buggy, waiting for someone to assist her.

The young ranch hand dismounted his horse, and Matt fired a warning shot at his boots. Defying Matt's threat, he staunchly walked to the buggy and offered his hand to the widow.

Everyone's eyes were on Matt's trigger finger.

"Son, if you drop your gun belt, I'd feel a lot easier about all this." He looked up at the older ranch hand. "You in the saddle. Your gun belt, too."

Matt had a reputation as being a man of his word which Clarence felt since Matt's pistol was pointed at him. But his loyalty lay with the widow, and he waited for her to tell him what to do.

With a stern look in her eyes, the widow motioned him to obey Matt. Clarence dropped his gun belt. The older man did the same and dismounted.

Matt kept his finger on the trigger as he watched the widow take Clarence's hand and gracefully step out of the carriage. The widow stood looking at the men and two ladies. There was tension in the air as they all waited for someone to speak.

Matt's teeth clenched tight, and his steely eyes kept a steady watch on Clarence and Alva. There had never been any love between the Brazos River Bar M Ranch and the McDaniels since the war. It was after the war when the general and McDaniels came home to find their ranches devastated. The general's ranch was the larger of the two many times over and had less damage, so he had a better opportunity for reconstruction. McDaniels had little competent help. When the general offered to lend him a hand, however, McDaniels refused. He felt it was too late by that time. His pride had turned into jealousy, and his jealousy into hate.

The widow blamed her husband's hate for his early death. Some nine years had gone by, and the past had been blotted out by the feud.

The widow was now a pretty woman in her early sixties, her face slightly rough, but tanned gracefully by the Texas sun. Her eyes were a grayish blue, but one could tell the spark of youth had left her many years hence. She wore her auburn hair, touched with a little gray, tied up under her Stetson. She was dressed meagerly but neatly, not a hole or a wrinkle in her clothes. One could readily tell she was a proud woman. But for the past several months, she had left her pride behind and obeyed the greedy wishes of another -- McTavett.

She planted her feet on Brazos River Bar M Ranch soil, straightening her shawl as she threw her shoulders back to show everyone she thought herself a great lady. She smiled at Clarence as he escorted her to the porch. She stopped when she recognized her enemy, the general.

She looked sternly at him before she resigned to be the first to speak. "Hello, General. Matt. Steve."

Her Scottish brogue was prevalent even in her wisp of a smile. She looked at and recognized Leisha, too. But she pretended not to remember the young Jaimie. "You're new here. Whatever happened to the little girl?" She hoped her teasing would cause a smile to break across Jaimie's face. She succeeded, and it brought one to Leisha as well.

"I'm that little girl, Widow McDaniels. I'm Jaimie."

"I knew ye were, young 'un. I just wanted to see a smile from someone."

The widow stood still for what seemed the longest time in the history of Texas as she looked into the faces of each of the men. No one smiled, and Matt's gun was still aimed at Clarence. "Ya gonna shoot that thing again?" she asked. "'Cause if you're not, I'd be obliged if you'd holster it and offer me your hand."

Matt knew the widow had put him in his place. He was also impressed by how Clarence handled himself. Matt holstered his pistol and offered his hand to the widow.

As he brought her up to the porch, the ladies went to her side and took her arms to keep her from falling.

The general extended his hand as a courtesy, and she accepted. The two looked at each other like two school kids meeting on the playground for the first time. He simply said, "Widow McDaniels, welcome to the Brazos River Bar M Ranch."

The widow returned the gesture with a slight curtsy and replied, "Thank you, Mitch."

"And what, may I ask, brings you to our beautiful land from across the river?"

"Mitch, you can just cut the Southern hospitality nonsense. We've never been friends since after the war, and I ain't gonna cotton up to you now. Jest wanted to let ye all know what's been goin' on." Her voice sent a chill as well as a lilt of humor to those standing around. "Well, we gonna stand all day, or do you have a chair to offer a tired lady?"

The general opened the screen door and gestured for her to enter. "Of course, we do." The general whispered, "Do I call you Mrs. McDaniels? Or Widow McDaniels? Or may I call you, Nellie?"

"I enjoy being called Nellie, Mitch."

"Well, then, Nellie. Come on in." He turned to the ladies and said, "Ladies, if you will, please make Nellie McDaniels feel at home."

She cut her way past the general to one of the porch chairs and settled herself in it. "This chair will do. That's Alva tendin' the buckboard. His helper, Henry. Clarence is the young man. Good 'un."

The general sat in a chair next to the widow. Matt kept his eyes on the men while Leisha entered the house.

"I was told ye was dead, Matt. Surprised me to see you up and active."

Matt replied without looking at her, "Wishful thinking."

A smile came across her face to match the general's. He was very impressed with her confident manner. She reminded him of his wife. She, too, had spunk, but then, she had to in this time and place.

"It's been a long time since we've met like this, Mitch." She allowed a moment to pass between their opening remarks before she continued to speak. She wanted to say the right thing but at the same time, she had to let him know she wasn't a weak person. Finally, she said, "Ye don't know how much better your smile makes me feel."

"Thank you, Nellie. Yes, it has been a long time. Too long, I imagine."

Steve picked up the two gun belts and took them into the house.

Alva stood close to Matt on the porch. He wasn't wearing a gun.

"Want it back when we leave," Clarence said.

"You'll get it," Matt replied as he holstered his pistol. "You gonna come up out of the sun?"

"I'll stay."

Matt asked Alva, "Notice you ain't totin'. Any reason?"

Alva answered matter-of-factly. "I told him not ta. Figured I couldn't use one iffin I had ta. Not a gunfighter."

The general offered his hand to the widow. "Widow McDaniels, let's go inside."

"And let the men be men? Oh, hell. Forget the tea, ladies. I'll take whatcha got in good strong liquor. Think this is a call for something stronger than tea," the widow said.

Jaimie opened the door as the two entered the house.

As Steve returned, Matt said, "I'm going inside. You keep Clarence company." He motioned for Alva and the older gent to enter first.

Inside, the ladies served brandy to Widow McDaniels and the general in front of the fireplace. Matt stood by the mantle and offered Alva a seat.

The general asked, "Everything all right, Matt?"

"Yeah, the kid just wanted to show us how fast he was." He gave a sigh of relief and added, "Pretty fast for bein' a kid."

"His brother was just killed by one of your men," the widow said.

Leisha's eyes widened as she looked at Matt.

"Oh?" Matt said.

Jaimie stared into Matt's eyes, realizing something was wrong.

"That's one of the reasons we came over here." Widow McDaniels continued. "I realize it was in self-defense. Billy told us. Clarence knows, too. It's just hard for him to get it out of his craw."

"How'd he get killed?" the general asked.

Matt interrupted. "If it was on their side of the Brazos a few days back, I killed him."

Widow McDaniels looked at Matt, astonished. "Billy didn't see your face. He thought it mighta been Steve. He thought you were dead."

"Sorry."

The general gave a command to Matt, "At ease, Captain." He looked over at the widow. "I'm sorry. Is this why you came?"

"Partly."

"Partly?"

"My foreman thinks Matt's dead. We all did."

Matt looked over at the widow. "Coulda been."

The widow continued. "With Matt dead and Steve put away for shootin' Billy, he figured it to be a good time to start puttin' together his army."

"His army? McTavett has an army?" the general asked.

"He's a fool. He's gone to Waco."

Matt asked, "What's he hope to find in Waco?"

"Men who haven't eaten for a long time to ride with him. He wants your ranch *real* bad."

The general nodded and stood up. "And you? What about you?" he asked.

"Oh, hell, General. I don't want your ranch. Never did." She stood up to even the stand against the general.

"But they're your men," the general said.

"They're McTavett's men. Never were mine. Oh, maybe a handful here and there who started with us years ago, but their loyalty vanished when McTavett promised them better jobs if he took over your ranch. They're planning to take the Wilcox to the south and the Berrys to the north, and who knows where else."

"Why're you tellin' us this?" Matt asked.

"For heaven's sake, think about it for a minute, man. I have a ranch. Had a good husband. That was all I needed. When he up and died, my world went with him. That's when McTavett came in. He found out about Ned and came promisin' to take care of things."

"You believed him?" the general asked.

"What wasn't to believe? He was handsome and a smooth talker. Like I said, I had a few men. But none could run the ranch like Ned. He came in at the right time and helped me. It was almost a year 'til I realized what he was up to."

"He's been with you a lot longer than a year, ma'am," Matt returned.

The widow sat back down and said, "I know it looks bad. When I found out his intentions, then heard about his raids on your ranch, I was mortified. He told me ye stole the cattle from us, and that he went to see ya time after time to get them back. After the last raid, a few of my more faithful men left him. They figured he was going to die, being shot up and all. That's when they told me about his plans, and I decided to pay you this visit."

The general took out his pipe and lit it. "That's been several weeks now."

"Yes, and I had no way to make my move until a few days ago when they left for Waco."

"Then all we have to do is stop 'em," Matt said.

"There's more to it than that."

"Like what?"

"They think Steve murdered Billy. They want the Texas Rangers to arrest him."

"But Billy told you it was in self-defense."

"McTavett thinks Billy died without talkin'. But he came out of the coma after McTavett left. There are other ranch hands who believe we came here to settle with Steve. They're expectin' us to return."

"How many are there?"

"No more than ten or so."

"Ma'am, with your permission, a few of my men can ride over and chase them out."

Nellie stared at Matt for a moment then looked at the general. Finally, she said, "Let Clarence go along, too. He'll help make sure they don't shoot at your men."

The general took a drag from his pipe and said, "It'll take you a couple days to get back. Best you not be here when the rangers show up, anyway."

"I'm going?" Matt asked.

"Looks like," the general answered.

Just then Steve entered.

"You know what, Matt? Clarence came over here to call me out. Something about shootin' his younger brother."

"It's me he's after," Matt said. Then he looked at Widow McDaniels and asked, "What do you expect out of all this, ma'am?"

Nellie looked at Matt. "I want my ranch back, Matt. Maybe a few good men to run it," she said seriously.

The general knocked the ashes from his pipe and put it in his pocket. He sat down and addressed the widow. "Any good men at the ranch, now?"

"Yes, but I don't know rightly who is for me or who's agin me." She looked at Alva and the other ranch hand. "Alva, out of all the wranglers left at the ranch, who could work under you?"

"Ma'am?" Alva looked at Widow McDaniels.

"I said, who could work under you? You're the boss now, Alva."

"I don't expect favors for what I do, ma'am."

"Ain't no favor, Alva. You've been with me. You've stuck with me. Ye and Henry over there are the only two who have, outside of young Clarence. And I treat him like he's me own son."

"Thank you, ma'am." Henry was older, thinner, and a little more bald than Alva when he had his hat off; but he was strong and a good ranch hand.

"Who we got back at the ranch that'll work under us?" Alva asked Henry.

Henry removed his hat and scratched his head. Putting his hat back on, as if this action would give him pause for thinking, he rubbed his hands on his pants, spit his wad of tobacco in his pocket hankerchief and wiped his lips with his sleeve.

"Excuse me, ma'am. Didn't know I was gonna be called up to speak. Can't talk with tabacky in my mouth."

The widow waited for his reply.

"None of 'em," he said. "They stayed behind because that's what the boss, eh McTavett, wanted. He wanted them to watch over the ranch while he was away, to make sure it was there when he got back."

The general had different plans. "Now you see why you're going?" he asked Matt. "Take a few men and make sure what Henry is saying is true."

Matt put his hands in his back pockets and turned away from the general. But then turned back to ask, "And what if McTavett's men come here while I'm gone?"

"If he's in Waco building his army, that's going to take time. The rangers are on their way here to arrest Steve for murder. And we've been told ten or twelve men are waiting at the McDaniels' ranch. This is the opportunity we've been waiting for. We can take the ranch back for the widow and run out some no-good wranglers doing it."

Matt looked at the widow with wondering eyes. "This what you want, ma'am?"

"It's what has to be done, Matt. I'm not asking you. It's not my right. I don't deserve your help."

"It's our responsibility," the general said, "if we're ever going to live in peace in this God-loving country of ours. I'm just happy to see you here today."

"Mitch," she said, "we've lost men on both sides. Some of mine were good. Billy was the last. I don't want to see any more dead."

Steve walked over to her and said, "If Matt goes, there's a good chance blood will be spilled on both sides."

"If we don't go, the widow's lost her ranch," the general answered.

"What are you going to do, ma'am?" Matt asked again.

The widow stood. "Well, for openers, I'll go back with ye, or without ye."

The general looked at the widow. He put his good arm around her shoulders and escorted her to Leisha, who walked with her down the hallway. "Be ready to ride at daybreak, Matt. Right now, she's got some resting up to do."

CHAPTER 20

THE RIDE TO THE SANDY BAR M RANCH

The next morning came swiftly to the Brazos River Bar M Ranch. Almost no one slept. The logs in the fireplace were still smoldering from the night before.

Twenty riders were in their saddles, ready to ride.

The ladies walked Widow McDaniels to her carriage. The air was cool and the widow wore a heavier shawl, one that belonged to the late Mrs. Mitchell.

The general followed the ladies and helped Widow McDaniels into the carriage where Alva was already seated with the lines in his hands.

Matt, putting on gloves, walked out of his house swiftly. "Make sure you keep the reins, Alva." He put his foot into the stirrup of the sorrel saddled up for him to ride. Lifting himself up, he swung his strong right leg over the saddle. There was no appearance of weakness from his gunshot wound. He was back to being Matt the gunfighter.

He bade the general farewell. "We'll be back in a coupla days, General."

"Steve assures me that the cattle will be ready for the Chisholm when you get back. We'll have a hoedown waiting for you and your men."

"Hear that, men? A hoedown!" Matt spurred his horse, brought his arm down, and yelled, "Let's ride!" With a rebel yell he led his men out. They joined him in the yell as they headed off to the Brazos. Matt and old Henry rode beside the carriage as Alva whipped the horses into a fast gait. Mrs. McDaniels held on tightly to the grips on the side of the carriage.

By the middle of the next day, they saw the ranch in the distance. Matt had his men regroup. The sun was high and the day was warming up. Matt left Alva and Henry in charge of Nellie and ordered them to wait until the fighting was over.

"Not too much activity as I see it," Matt said leaning forward into his saddle. "Maybe there won't be a fight."

"Oh, there'll be a fight," Nellie spoke out, taking off her bonnet. "They're meaner than hornets, Matt. Watch yourself."

"Thanks." Matt looked around at all of his men. "Alva, you and Henry keep Mrs. McDaniels here under these trees. When it's safe, we'll send someone back to fetch ya. If we get ambushed, well -- hell. I don't know what to say."

"We'll be all right, Matt," Widow McDaniels replied.

Clarence sidled up to Matt without saying a word. Matt told him, "You're not coming."

"You gave me back my gun. That means you trust me." He slipped it out of his holster and rotated the cylinder. "It's loaded, and I'm ridin' with ya."

"You gonna shoot at them or at me?"

"Billy was my brother. You killed him."

Matt squirmed at Clarence's words. They were harsh, yet true. He asked, "What's your point?"

"Point is, he died on this ranch. You might die here, too. If you do, I want to see it happen."

Matt's teeth tightened in his jaw, and his eyes grew steely. "And if I don't?"

Clarence didn't answer.

Matt looked at his men who were waiting for him to give the order to ride. He was conscious of his apprehension about Clarence but he wouldn't allow himself to be scared. He was facing a kid who had lost a younger brother. He knew what was going through Clarence's mind but wouldn't give him a chance to keep his vendetta.

Matt said, "Son, I'm giving you an edge. When the time is right, you better use it."

Clarence positioned himself to ride in front with Matt as they rode to the ranch. Looking over his shoulder at Matt, he said, "You have an edge on me, too. I've never killed anyone before."

The rest of the men lined up for a charge. Matt spurred his horse to the front of the line, passing Clarence.

The widow was watching what was happening, and knew it was all because of her. She felt a pang of guilt.

She watched Matt raise his arm and bring it down again in a command to charge the ranch.

The men rode hard down the slope. At the first sight of Matt's riders, the McDaniels group ran for their horses. Matt's men began firing to keep them on foot. One, two, three men were hit.

When he had the opportunity to use his gun, Matt's finger froze. A vision of the young kid he had killed running away from him by the river flashed in front of him. He tried again but his finger froze, and he never fired. He hoped no one noticed. Maybe the commotion had been too great for anyone to have paid attention.

It was a short fight. Only three wranglers were wounded in McDaniels' group. The rest of them picked up their horses and rode towards Waco.

As Matt turned his horse and saw the retreating men, he reined up. "No need chasin' 'em. Let 'em go." He dismounted and walked over to inspect the three wounded ranch hands.

"This one here just got grazed by a bullet across his head," came the report from one of Matt's riders. "He'll be all right."

"How about the other two?" Matt asked, as he walked past the slightly wounded man.

"This one here's gut shot," reported another rider.

A third man rose from examining the wound of another.

"This one won't sit for a while. But he'll be all right," he said.

"Walk then, mister." Matt ordered him. "And you with the scalp wound. See what you can do for your other partner there."

Matt's rider, attending to the wounded man, yelled out, "No need, Matt. He's bought it." The wrangler laid him down.

"Why'd ya shoot us? Ya killed Butch. My best friend. Ya killed him!" one of the hands shouted at Matt and his men.

"You shot at us," Matt yelled back. "Ya shouldn't rustle cows and ya shouldn't keep a fine lady hostage. Any more reasons, and I might shootcha just for bein' too smart for your britches. Well, you two can pick him up and bury him off the ranch." Then he began a tour of the rest of the ranch.

Walking over to the corral, he climbed up and sat on the rail. Pushing his hat back on his head, he looked out over the range.

The ranch spread wide. There was a modest single-story ranch house, bunkhouses, and a corral. But it was nothing compared to the size of the Brazos River Bar M Ranch. Matt took this all in and said to himself, "Bet she could make a good living here. Nothin' wrong with this place. Wonder how many head of beef she's got?"

He jumped down from the rail and walked through the cattle. He examined a few head to find the Circle Sandy Banks Bar M Ranch brand on them. The letter "M" stood for the McDaniels' name. It was difficult to tell whether there was any cover-up, but he was certain there was. The Circle SB - M brand could swirl around another brand underneath, making it almost impossible to detect. Even the Brazos River Bar M would take some detecting.

"BR - M"

Matt found some sloppy branding that proved his suspicions. He was certain this happened many times, as the McDaniels had no reason to have such a great herd of cattle with McTavett's lack of expertise in the field. He was more the military man-turned-gunslinger. Matt could find out from Alva and Henry, if they were willing to talk about it. At the moment, though, this was not his concern. He had won back the ranch as the general had ordered. To ferret out any rustled cows, Steve could examine the herd later.

The two wounded hands rode out with the dead one strung over the third horse. Matt watched them ride saddle-less, noting that two of his own men were riding with them.

"Where're you fellas goin'?" he barked.

"Figured we'd ride with them for a spell, then bring the horses back," answered one of the riders. "Don't worry. They'll be all right." As they rode off, the rider said to the two wounded hands, "If'n you be nice fellas, that is."

Matt called, "Join us on the road back," then he walked over to the ranch house and peeked inside the door. His curiosity satisfied, he strolled over past the barn. He continued walking up the hill, stopped, and viewed the scenery from the back of the ranch.

Clarence rode up slowly behind him.

Matt turned and pulled his gun cocked out of his holster. Clarence fell quickly from his horse, face down in the dirt in full surrender, his arms extended above his head. In that split-second, Matt could have killed Clarence, but his finger refused to pull the trigger. He had frozen up again, although it wasn't evident to Clarence that he couldn't pull the trigger. He only knew that Matt didn't kill him when he felt he could have.

Matt walked over to him, stuck his boot under his stomach and turned him over. His voice spilled out in anger. "You were dead, mister! Good thing you fell when you did!"

With the fear of God in his eyes, and his cheeks turned ashen, Clarence cried for Matt not to shoot him. "My gun belt."

Matt asked, "What?"

Clarence pointed to his gun belt wrapped around the saddle horn on his horse.

It took Matt a moment to understand what Clarence was saying. When he did, he walked over to the horse, removed the gun belt, then looked down at Clarence and saw no gun on him. Matt's hand quivered as he holstered his gun, and his mind again raced back to the day on the Brazos when he had shot Billy. Now he had almost shot the older brother, unarmed and afraid.

He put his arm on the horse and rested his forehead against the saddle as his mind wandered back to the day his own brother was shot and killed in a robbery. Matt took the gun belt off the saddle horn, removed the gun, and tossed it as far away as he could. Then he threw the gun belt down at Clarence's side, looking at him for a time without saying anything.

When Clarence didn't move, Matt bent down, picked him up by his arm, and hit him across the mouth with a sweep of his hand, drawing blood. He expected him to fall, but Clarence remained standing. With his fist, Matt knocked him backwards, to the ground. Clarence picked himself up slowly and wiped the blood from his face and mouth. He smiled, as if he were enjoying the beating.

Matt raised his voice in anger, "Dammit, mister. Fight!"

Clarence stood there. Finally, his voice cracking, he said, "I couldn't shoot ya."

The riders had gathered around the two men. No man ever went against Matt's wishes, and this was no time to change the rule.

"You almost got yourself killed. Jest like your brother, dammit! You kids don't play guns."

He walked away to his horse, lifted himself into the saddle and looked at the riders. "Joe, help the kid get fixed up." He raised himself up on the haunch of the saddle and saw the widow's buggy approaching. Knowing she had seen the confrontation from afar, he waited for her.

She pulled the team to a halt, jumped out of the buggy and walked over to Clarence. She looked at Matt. "I'll tend to him." Taking Clarence's bandanna from his neck, she poured water from a canteen she had taken off the side of Matt's horse and wiped the blood away. "Ye killed his brother. Now ye want to kill him, too?"

Clarence took her arm and walked her over to Matt. Looking up at him, he said, "Widow McDaniels. It's all my fault. I told Matt I was gonna kill him."

"He's bigger and tougher than ye, boy." She looked up at Matt and said, "But ye drew on him."

"Yes, ma'am."

Clarence looked at her, and said, "He thought I was gonna kill him. I rode up on him." He looked at Matt.

Matt glanced down at the boy, then at the widow, and over to the men standing around watching.

"What are you men lookin' at? We've got ridin' to do," he said.

"Not 'til I have my say, mister," the widow interrupted.

The men, half turned and ready to resume their formation to ride, stopped and looked at the gravel-voiced widow.

"We've got another killin'. God knows how many more. I believe Clarence when he says he could have killed ya. I've seen him draw and shoot rabbits and things." She walked up to Matt and put her hand on his boot that was firm in the stirrup. "It hurt me when Billy was killed. He was a mite wild, but he would have turned out all right. God bless his soul." She took her shawl and wiped her tears. She looked at the men. "Clarence took it harder. After we buried Billy, Clarence went out for days. We couldn't find him. He came back late one night. He was out of bullets. I asked him where he'd been, and he told me he had to get even for his brother's death."

Matt's teeth were set on edge as he listened to words he didn't want to hear.

The men waited for the rest. Clarence stood motionless.

"I've seen hurt in my time. I've seen hate. I saw them both in the boy's eyes. We didn't give him any more bullets. He got them from the other hands. Started to ride out again when I stopped him. It was my tears that brought him out of the saddle, Matt. And he promised me, then and there, that he would not go seeking revenge. And I believed him."

Then the mud hit the barn. It was about to happen sometime and now was the time. There was no way that Matt could restrain from what he was going to say. He just had to say it. "Ma'am, I lost my younger brother in a gunfight, too. Revenge is not easy to give away. My pa told me to keep ridin'.'" His voice began to trail off as he tried to regain his composure, thinking deeply about that time many years ago. He looked at Clarence and then at Nellie, and said, "That's the difference."

"I did not know," she said.

The widow took her hand from Matt's boot and put her arm around Clarence.

The men prepared to leave with Matt. "With your permission, ma'am," Matt said.

She answered, "I wanna thank ye for gettin' my ranch back for me."

"McTavett's not through, yet."

"No," she said. "Don't 'spect he is."

"What if he comes back?"

"Don't know, Matt." She took Clarence with her and walked to her house.

Alva met her and they entered the house together.

Henry tended to the buggy.

Matt watched as the men began to ride into position to leave.

"You thinkin' what I'm thinkin, boss?" one of the riders asked.

"That the widow McDaniels should ride back with us? Yeah. You ready to spend the night here?" Looking north, he saw the two wranglers finishing up on the grave. "Hell, those two are still diggin'. Go help 'em and send 'em on their way."

Two riders rode to help them while the rest rode over to join the widow.

When the grave was finished and the two no-good wranglers started their walk to town, the rest of Matt's riders rode back and regrouped.

Another hand said, "Well, Matt, if'n you need us for company, we'd be comin' with ya. But I'm a thinkin' that there might be somethin' we can do to help the widow along. Bein' a long trip, she just might need us for protection."

Before he could finish his tirade, Matt wrinkled up his face, threw his hands to the air, and said, "Oh, hell. I'd do the same, if'n I didn't have ta get back and report to the general right away. Go ahead. Stay the night. For me, I'm gonna camp up in the holler just over the hill a few hours from now, light a fire, and cook up whatever's in my saddlebag, or I might shoot me a rabbit."

Before he could finish his sentence, the men spurred their mounts and rode back to the widow's ranch.

He yelled out after them, "Tell her she's got a dance to go to. I'll ride on ahead. Hit the trail at daybreak." Then he said to himself, "Hell. What am I sayin' that for? They're gonna have a hard time keepin' up with her."

It didn't take too much coaching on the men's part to convince the widow to go back to the Brazos Ranch for the big dance. And, by the same token, it didn't take her long to talk them into staying for dinner.

Matt pulled his hat down on his brow and whispered to himself, "What a woman." His spurs put his horse into a gentle trot, and he headed back to the Brazos Ranch, alone.

CHAPTER 21

THE DANCE AT THE BRAZOS RANCH

It was just after noon the next day when Matt rode his horse up to the Brazos River Bar M Ranch. Most of the wranglers and drovers were in and around the corral getting the cattle ready for the following day's drive.

Steve was branding a steer when he saw Matt approach. He finished what he was doing and threw the hot iron into the trough. It hissed when it hit the water. Taking off his gloves, he walked over to greet Matt.

"Good to see you back. Everything go all right?" Steve took hold of the horse's halter so Matt could dismount easier, then led the animal to the corral where he tied him up.

Matt stood for a moment feeling tired. Every joint in his body ached. He walked over to the well and drew the bucket, taking a ladle to drink the water. He turned to Steve. "Killed one. Wounded two others. The rest ran."

Steve looked at Matt's face and sensed something beyond his words. He seemed to have the sixth sense for hidden meanings in a person's demeanor or talk. Matt was hiding something, he thought.

He asked, "Wanna talk about it?"

"No. No, I don't. Jest wanna wash up and . . ." His words trailed off as he looked up and saw men laying out a dance floor

and stringing lights in the courtyard. Some of the neighboring ladies were milling about the kitchen, preparing vittles. Then it hit him. There was a drive tomorrow, and tonight was the hoedown. "Holy Jehosophat. I done forgot all about the dance tonight."

Steve looked over Matt's shoulder and saw the widow's buggy heading their way, with the rest of the men riding alongside her. He said, "They didn't."

"Holy Je . . ."

"I know. Jehosophat."

"I rested and rode easy. They must 'av left early."

"Apparently they couldn't wait." Steve left Matt standing there and walked over to the buggy.

Matt went to his house and dressed down. His intent was to rest up that afternoon so he could be ready for the hoedown. He slung his gunbelt over the back of a wooden chair and plopped his weary body on the bed. He tried closing his eyes, but he kept staring instead at his .45 in its holster. He remembered the first time he fired a carbine as an eight-year-old. He also remembered watching his pa shoot at Indians coming down the hill after their cattle. Mostly though, his pa knew the hunger the Indians suffered throughout the winter, so he made sure they picked off a few cows just to leave his family alone, although he had to shoot some in defense.

Inadvertently, he had practiced early to be a fast draw, it seemed to come naturally to him. He worked for hours and days oiling and shaving his holster just right so that his hand could slide in and around the gun butt easily to draw it out. It never occurred to him that he was honing his craft to become a fast draw. But the more he worked with his pistol, the better he became. Eventually, he saw its importance when he traveled through Kansas and lost everything he had to a gang of robbers. He came back later and claimed his belongings at the cost of the life of a thief.

He also thought about the young boy he recently killed, and how, because of his guilt, he froze when confronted to use his gun again. Now, as he stared intently at it, checking every inch of it with his eyes, he thought of the impending gunfight that lay ahead with McTavett.

He longed for sleep, but for some time, it never came. He heard the pounding of nails and the laughter of the ladies outside, but he knew he wouldn't be up for a good time. In fact, he set his mind to it.

His thoughts filled the room with McTavett's laughter and disgusting face leering down at him. "He thinks he killed me," Matt's mind began to contemplate. He imagined seeing McTavett's face swallow up fear as he looked down on Matt's illusory corpse. "He'll find courage, now," he thought, "because he figures I'm dead. And I'm the only thing between him and his taking over this ranch." Sweat beaded up on his forehead as his eyes narrowed in on the trigger of his .45. It wasn't his fast draw he was concerned with now; it was whether or not he could pull the trigger when aiming his gun at another person.

He rose from his bed, walked over to his Colt, and removed it from its holster. Pulling back on the hammer, he spun the freed chambers, seeing that all six were filled. He shucked the cartridges into his left hand, twirled the pistol, cocked it, and aimed it as if to fire at a distant mirror on his bank of drawers. He pulled the trigger and watched his steadiness in holding the Colt, then twirled it once more. He eyed himself in the mirror and said, "Easy. Real smooth and easy." He replaced the cartridges and holstered the pistol.

He turned towards the window. Seeing people outside, he began to tremble slightly. He caught hold of a post and regained his balance. "Their lives depend on my gun," he thought again. "What if . . .?" He stared down at his now steady hand and then out the window. He watched the people working feverishly to prepare for the dance, a dance he had no real interest in this night, but he watched until he could stare no longer. He eventually turned and flopped back on the bed. He fought sleep, but his eyelids finally grew heavy, and sleep became his master.

A few hours were all he needed, and when the sun lowered itself, his body felt rested. He looked out the window and saw lanterns lit in the yard, preparing the way for the dance that was soon to begin. For the moment at least, he forgot about his fear, strapped on his .45, and went outside to enjoy the festivities.

That night proved that a hard day in the saddle or branding in the corral could be forgotten really fast when music played, a feast was to be had, and pretty ladies lined up in a row for a dance.

The widow stepped out of the house dressed in her finest going-to-meeting clothes, with her hair let down and flowing across her shoulders. The general was decked out in his finest suit and polished boots, for his eye was on the widow.

She wanted to have fun. Then she began to notice some of the people staring at her and talking. She sensed their animosity. She was the owner of the ranch that had been coming across the Brazos killing their loved ones and running off their cattle. She was the vicious Widow McDaniels whom everyone knew as hateful and vengeful for how her husband died without any help from fellow ranchers.

What they never found out was how her husband died because of his pride in refusing help from other ranchers. To them, he was the one who had set himself against the world. She had asked him to seek help. She thought all along that the ranch was bigger than one man could put back into shape.

Sure, Ned McDaniels had thought, some of the men who had come back with him would stay with his ranch. Some did. Others went on to different ranches or home to a loved one. They saw no salvation in a small ranch with few cattle.

All the time her husband was away at war, her solitude was spent visiting wives whose husbands were also in the war. When their husbands returned, the wives spent the days and nights with them, and she was left to deal with her own.

The months turned into years, and Ned lowered his esteem and became a drunken rancher who cared little for her and even less about his ranch. She suffered this, but no one else ever knew. Now, for the first time since his return, she had ventured out on her own to rejoin the rest of the world. Tonight, could make the difference. In her heart, she prayed that the people would accept her.

The three cowboys from Montana seemed to be waiting the longest for the hoedown to start. They had even helped some with the cooking.

Slim's eyes brightened when he saw Jaimie walk through the door onto the porch, with the light shining behind her, accentuating her radiant beauty. His calluses from the month's work felt no pain. He was in paradise with the girl of his dreams as he saw her walk towards him to take his arm as her escort for the evening.

Shorty and Dan looked around for other girls from outlying ranches and farms to appear. They were not disappointed.

The buggies began to arrive; one, two, four, and then seven wound up on the lawn, with more coming down the road. Riders had escorted them to the hoedown from as far away as a morning's ride. However tired one might have felt from the long trek, the joy of the festivities erased all pain.

Leisha stepped into view and caught Steve's arm where he had been waiting at the entrance for her arrival. If there was a contest between Leisha and Jaimie as to who was the fairest at the dance, it would have ended in a tie. They had spent hours helping one another with their attire, hair, and make-up. Having lived together for such a long time, they had almost become twins in dress and thought.

Matt left his house and stood on the porch to view the event. He was impressed. This was a great day for everyone. The cattle were in; the wranglers had finished their jobs, and the drovers were rested for the evening's festivities. Some of his riders joined up with him to walk to the courtyard.

The men were hungry enough to eat a bear, but at the sight of the single girls from the other ranches, their thoughts turned to merriment. It was the "Midsummer Night's Dream" for the young people. The older folks watched with glee, and yet most of them knew how to do the Texas Waltz, or the Kentucky Reel. The plates were filled and the people began to eat. It was only a matter of time before the dancing would start, and everyone was ready.

The general stood on the porch and watched Widow McDaniels throughout the evening to see how she was taking the women and their gossip. He knew she was hurting and watched as she wrenched her dress with her hands and scuffled her feet on her way to the door, as if wanting to disappear into the night. He motioned to Matt to fire off his revolver so that he could make a speech. Matt obeyed and lifted his .45 above his shoulders and fired. The noise momentarily deafened several ladies close by and startled others. But he got their attention.

The general began the gala with his speech. "Ladies and gentlemen. We're here tonight to eat, drink, dance and have a wonderful time. Our cattle are in. This is a big night. We'll be driving them to Kansas in the morning, so get your fun in early."

Walking over to Nellie, he took her by the hand and waltzed her out into the courtyard for the center of attention. "I know what you're thinking. And you're right. This here is Widow McDaniels. The meanest bitch the other side of the Brazos."

Laughter began to ease the tension for most, but a few still held onto their stern look of resentment.

He continued, "But no more. This lovely lady is our guest. She has become the victim of Texas society under no fault of her own. Her husband died, God bless him, several years back. A proud man, he wanted no help from any of us. Worked himself to death. He left Nellie with a ranch, cattle, and no one to care for them."

He looked into the eyes of many of the people gathered, as all ears listened to his every word, even the biddies who kept their distance at first because of who she was.

"A soldier from the war, a good man in my regiment, stopped by and offered his services to Mrs. McDaniels. She had no other recourse but to accept his kind and gracious offer of help."

He heard the name "McTavett" and "that son of a bitch" rumble through the crowd. "Yes, that was Corporal McTavett. As Matt and Steve can bear me out, he was a fine soldier. Later, he became glory bound and wanted to kill more for his own satisfaction. The war ended, and he came here. He sought me out, and I turned him down because of who he had become in the last part of the war. A good man turned bad. Nothing I could do about it then."

"He's a son-of-a thieving, killing, raping hyena and oughta be shot dead on sight," came words out of the crowd from an older gentleman in the back, shaking his fist into the wind.

"You're right, Ezra. Right as rain. Well, he's in Waco right now getting together an army to come against our ranch. You ranchers aren't involved yet. But you could be. We'll be prepared for him. But the main thing, so as not to spoil the evening, is that Nellie finally got away and came over to tell us what was going on. It was he who was fighting to get control of my ranch. Not Nellie. She was told a pack of lies about us."

Nellie stepped back into the light and straightened her chin up to show her pride was still there.

"Now, ladies and gentlemen. We got her ranch back for her. And all of us here, well, we're going to help her build it back up the way it should be. A good old-fashioned barn- raising. Forget about McTavett; his day is coming. So, for tonight, let's all eat, drink, and dance 'til the cows come in. And, Steve, let's get some life into this here party."

Steve took his arm from around Leisha's waist, grabbed his pistol, and shot it in the air. As he gave a rebel yell, he was joined by the rest of the crowd. The tenseness of the night had been broken. Nellie was surrounded by the other ladies, and the men headed for the punch bowl.

Sometimes, Texians can be the most forgiving people in the world. Sometimes.

A few of the cowboys found their mates and danced off the floor into the shadows. Most of the married folk tapped their feet, clapped their hands, and smiled with their eyes at all that was happening. Nothing was sacred on this night. Some marriages would be performed when the men returned. Children under their teens ran through the festivities, laughing and eating. The ranches would someday be filled with more children for them to play and go to school with.

Matt was not shy when it came to filling his plate before he went to one of the tables to join the other men.

Leisha flipped a pat on the back of Matt's head while she walked by him with Steve. She said in passing, "Save me a dance!"

Matt returned with, "If it's okay with Steve."

Steve winked at Matt and took Leisha to wait in the food line.

203

The night of merriment really started when the caller yelled out for the square dancing to start. Everyone was beginning to feel their fill, while some were still feeding themselves with second and third helpings. A Texas barbecue can't be beat by any stretch of the imagination. The whole cow had been buried in hot coals and cooked all day. All of the delicacies derived from this animal were intermingled with other tasty foods that only came a few times a year.

As the evening wore on, Matt soon found himself in the arms of Leisha, dancing a slow waltz. Her lips were next to his ear as she whispered, "I'm glad we've had some good times."

"Yes, ma'am," Matt returned.

"Is that all you can say, Mister Jorgensen?"

"Well, you belong to another man now. What can I say?"

"You can tell me that you're happy for me."

"You ain't married yet."

"Not yet. But we will be. He's asked me."

"And . . . ."

"I've accepted."

He turned her as they danced, waltzing her side by side. He brought her back into his arms and said, "Then you know I'm happy."

"What are you going to do?"

Glancing over her shoulder, he saw two Texas Rangers slowly riding up to the ranch. He continued to watch them as they dismounted. "Right now, I guess my services are wanted elsewhere. If you'll excuse me."

He took her arm and escorted her back to Steve.

Leisha sat in a chair while Steve sidled up to Matt. He had been watching the Texas Rangers, too. They walked over to greet them.

"Gentlemen. You've come a long way. Anything wrong?" Matt asked.

The rangers exchanged handshakes with them, and then one asked, "You're Matt Jorgensen, aren't you?"

"Yes. And you're Richie. Or rather, Richard, something or other." Pointing to the other Ranger, he added, "And you're John."

Both rangers accepted Matt's introductions since they had not been strangers all these years in the territory. Richard said, rather startled, "We've been told that you're dead."

"Nope. Who told ya? McTavett?"

"Yes sir."

John commented, "He said you were killed in a range war. And the capt'n sorta verified it."

"And how is our Captain Johnson?"

Richard answered, "Fine, sir."

"And Maggie? Mrs. Johnson?"

"Fine, sir."

"Now that we're all fine, I'll ask again. Why are you a long way from home?"

Richard answered, saying, "Well, sir. We were told to arrest Steve for murder."

Matt looked at Steve, and Steve returned a bewildering look. "Steve, you kill somebody?"

"Recently?"

Matt looked at the rangers and repeated, "Recently?"

"Yes, sir," John answered.

"Who'd ya kill?" Matt asked Steve.

"Since the range war last month?" Steve shrugged his shoulders.

"Yes sir. Last week. A man named Billy," Richard answered.

The name hit Matt real hard, and his teeth clenched while his eyes looked out beyond the night to relive Billy's killing.

"He didn't kill him," Matt said.

The rangers eyed Matt as Steve took ahold of Matt's arm.

"I did," Matt said.

"Beg to pardon, sir, but our orders strictly state that Steve murdered -- or killed Billy, and we're here to bring him in," Richard argued.

"Who said so? McTavett?" Matt stared at Richard.

"Yes, sir."

"Seems McTavett's responsible for saying lots of things. How did he state it?"

"He said that Billy told him so on his death bed."

"His dying statement, sir," John reiterated.

"Why would Billy say something like that, Matt?" Steve looked at him.

"Maybe because Billy didn't say that, Steve," Matt answered. "Remember, McTavett said that I was dead. Billy didn't say who killed him. But our old buddy McTavett wants you out of the way, so he puts the blame on you. With you arrested, and me dead, he's got an open field for taking over this ranch."

The rangers looked at each other, and then at Matt and Steve.

"Capt'n said we have to bring Steve in, sir," Richard said.

"Why? If I said I killed him. What are you going to do with me?" Matt asked.

"I don't rightly know, sir," Richard answered.

"When I shot and killed Billy, it was in self-defense. Steve here was up in the hills rounding up cattle." Matt continued, "He was nowhere around." He turned and pointed to the wranglers who were standing behind them listening. "Ask anyone here who rode that day."

Many of the wranglers agreed with Matt. Matt reached around Steve to where Leisha was standing, and brought her forward. "And this little lady will substantiate my story."

Richard looked at Leisha and asked, "How?"

"Because I was with Matt when Matt fired his gun and killed Billy. When we came home, Steve was just coming from the hills with some cattle."

John asked, "How did you come about killing Billy, sir?"

Matt looked into Leisha's eyes, then into Steve's, and turned slowly to the rangers to explain what happened. "Leisha and I were riding together. We had stopped by the Brazos and were talking. After a while, a bullet from a rifle broke a branch near where we were standing. I saw the flash from across the river and turned and emptied my gun in that direction. I found out later that I had hit Billy."

"He was shot twice in the back, and once in the front, sir," Richard reported.

"Not in the back, Ranger. I saw his face when I fired," Matt grimaced.

The widow walked up to the rangers and stood between the men. "Gentlemen, whoever told you that he was shot in the back is lying. I treated Billy when he came home."

"Who are you, ma'am?" John asked her.

"I'm the owner of the Sandy Banks Bar M Ranch across the Brazos."

"You're the Widow McDaniels?" Richard asked almost unbelievingly.

"Yes, son. I'm that widow," she answered politely.

"You heard the lady, son," Matt retorted. "Who told you Billy was shot in the back?"

"McTavett!" Steve interrupted.

"Yes sir. He showed us Billy's shirt. It has three holes in it. Two in the back," John agreed.

"Well, son," Matt said, "I fired three rounds at him. He faced me. I hit him at least once, maybe twice. None of my shots hit him in the back. He fell, got up, and ran. I had no more bullets. Even if I had, I wouldn't have used them. I never fire on a running man if I can help it."

"I found one bullet in his chest," the widow continued. "I removed it, but he had lost too much blood and there was no savin' him."

"What do we do now, Richard?" John asked his fellow ranger.

"Our orders are to bring Steve in," Richard said. "We can't go against our orders, sir. But we'd be obligin' if you came, too, Mr. Jorgensen."

"Well, son. You can't go against your orders." Matt turned and saw that the festivities had stopped. "Tell you what. We'll let you take us both in, providin' . . ."

"Yes, sir?" Richard asked.

"Providin' you spend the rest of the evening filling yourself up and enjoying the dancing. Now, you're hungry and tired, right?"

The rangers turned to each other, shrugging their shoulders in an agreeable manner. John said, "Can't say anything against that." He turned to Richard and asked, "Well, can we?"

"We've got your word?" Richard asked.

"You've got our word," Matt agreed.

"Boys, let's grub down," the widow said, taking them by the arm.

"All right. But first thing in the morning, we head back for Waco," Richard said.

"With both of you. Right or wrong. Let the capt'n decide, or the judge. Whichever. Right, Richard?" John looked to Richard.

"Let's eat," Richard agreed, eyeing one of the pretty ladies standing nearby.

Steve looked at Matt, then at the rangers, and remarked, "Yeah. First thing in the morning." Then he asked Matt, "How are the cattle going to get to Kansas?"

Matt hunched up his shoulders and said, "First things first. Right now, let's keep this party alive."

After the music resumed and everyone was back to dancing and eating, the general walked up to the widow. "Mighty pretty waltz they're playing, Mrs. McDaniels."

Being slightly startled by his sudden approach, she almost spilled the plate of food she had been holding almost since she arrived.

"Why, yes. Yes, it is," she said coquettishly.

"Care to twirl around with a one-armed old man?"

"Oh, my. I haven't danced in ages. Don't think I remember how."

"That gives me a little edge. Come on. I'll refresh your memory."

She accepted his offer, set her plate down, and accompanied him to the dance floor. She picked up the hem of her dress, and after a few clumsy movements, they began to glide across the floor, much to the amazement of the others who paused in their dancing and eating to look their way. They looked pretty good together.

"I haven't seen that sparkle in the general's eye for many years," Leisha said to Jaimie.

"You're mighty pretty tonight, Nellie," the general whispered.

"Why, thank you. Oh, that does bring back memories, Mitch. I haven't heard my name mentioned in years. Certainly not like that."

"Then, Nellie, may I add that you are the prettiest woman on this dance floor tonight."

She looked around a bit, and replied, "I seem to be the only woman on this dance floor at the present. Shucks, everyone's lookin' at us, Mitch."

"Let 'em."

"I think they're not likin' me."

"Just a few biddies enjoying gossipin' about someone. They've picked you for the night."

"You know, Mitch, a month ago, I never would have dreamed of ever being in your arms like this."

"Tell me about it, Nellie."

The music swelled in certain places, and they parted a dance step for a moment, then came back together again. She refused to answer him by keeping quiet for the moment and simply enjoying the dance.

"One thing I like about a waltz, Nellie, always coming back to your partner."

"If I weren't so old, I'd say you were making me blush."

"You're only as old as you feel, Nellie. And I feel like a teenager right about now."

"Ye know, I have a strange feeling about this night."

"Like what?"

"Like, I shouldn't be here in the first place. Dancin' like this. And me havin' a smile on me face," she said in her Scottish brogue. "I don't deserve this. No, no I don't." She sensed several of the women eyeing her with a vengeful glare.

"You seem to be enjoying the night, Nellie. I hadn't heard a brogue in a long time. It sounds good."

"I thank ye, but no. I should be a leavin'. I done ye wrong. I let McTavett and his cutthroats fight ye. And I had no sense in me head to stop him."

They stopped dancing, but the music played on. She walked away, leaving the general standing alone. He walked slowly to the punch bowl, where he was met by Jaimie and Leisha.

Jaimie, with her hands on her hips, said in a mocking brogue, "And what be ye standin' on the dance floor alone for, and be lettin' your lady walk away from ye?"

"She's right, Jaimie. I'm not good for her."

"That be not what I'm a hearing, me fine man. I be hearin' that she didn't think she was good enough for ye," Jaimie continued in her mocking brogue.

"Come on, Jaimie. Let's go talk with her." Leisha said, trying to pull Jaimie along with her.

But Steve came over and, taking Leisha by the hand, waltzed her out on the dance floor, leaving Jaimie behind.

Taking her hand in his, the general said, "No, Jaimie. Let me talk with her. You've got a dance coming up, if I don't miss my guess."

Slim and his two friends from Montana walked up to Jaimie. As the two friends proceeded on to the punch bowl to fill up their cups, Slim stopped to escort Jaimie out onto the dance floor.

The general went to meet Nellie on the verandah as she entered the door. He stopped her and turned her around to face him.

"The night is beautiful, Nellie. Let's not spoil it by thinking of the past."

They walked out to the edge of the verandah, away from the lights. Looking up at the sky he said, "See those stars, Nellie? They're the same stars that were shining when your men came over and shot up my ranch."

"I thought you said we weren't thinking of the past."

"Just want you to see them from my perspective. A lot of people here lost some loved ones in those skirmishes with your men. Some can't forgive you. Maybe they never will. But you know something? They're people, Texians. And given time, I think they'll get to know you."

"Not very likely, I'm a thinkin'. If it was me wearin' their shoes, I would have a hard time forgivin'."

"Like the stars, Nellie. I don't see one of them any different than I did that night. They sparkle. They shine. They look down upon us as if they could see into our hearts. The people dancing out there think they know you. It's all an appearance. Give them time, and they'll be looking at you like I am, right now."

"And what do the stars be seeing now, General Mitchell?"

"They see the wonderful world we live in, Nellie. A great state called 'Texas'. A beautiful ranch. Cattle on the hillside. In the corral. People dancing and having fun. And a lovely lady on the verandah."

"And two old people trying to talk with each other."

He laughed as he repeated her words. "And two old people trying to talk with each other. No, I don't see two old people at all. I do, however, see two people who have never gotten to really know one another in all the years we've been neighbors."

"And never will, I'm a thinkin'." She turned and walked back to the party. As he followed her, she placed her hand in the cradle of his arm, letting him escort her back to the dance floor, where she could hear a few of the women standing nearby resume their whispering, supposedly about her because of the way they would lower their eyes when she glanced their way.

A rancher, who had been standing off the dance floor by himself, cut in for a dance with Nellie. Bowing, the general excused himself, leaving Nellie to dance with a man she recalled meeting when she had first met her Ned. "My," she said with embarrassment, trying to remember, "but I know your face. You're . . . Oh, hell, mister, tell me your name, please."

"Ike McGuire, Nellie. I stood up for you at your wedding thirty some years ago."

They danced together and talked. "Ike. You made it back, too, I see."

"Came back all in one piece. No family. Never had a family."

"So, whatcha doin' these days?"

"Plowin'. Sowin' and a plowin'. Got a cotton spread down by the river. Not much. But it's paid fer."

"You were married?"

"Yep. Up and left me. Found a better man, I'm supposin'."

"Ah. There's no better man than ye be, Ike. I knowed ye for years now. I remember how you built your house, and ye helped Ned and me."

"Yes, ma'am."

As they sashayed and formed a line with the rest, they continued to talk as they drew into one another. "Got a girl?"

"She's the one who's been doing the most talking about ya."

"Oh, that bippy, I mean. Oh, no." She momentarily stopped, regained her composure, and then resumed dancing. "I'm sorry, Ike. I didn't mean to sound crazy like that."

"No, ma'am. You're not the crazy one, she is. And I told her so. I told her if she didn't stop all that talkin' about ya, I'd take her home right then and there."

"Oh, ye didn't? She must hate ye, right now."

"She's still here isn't she? Got a smile on her face, yet?"

After looking over at his girlfriend, she turned back and said, "I donna think she knows how to smile, Ike."

"She will. She's a lovely girl. Else I wouldn't be marryin' her. Wanna meet her?"

"I'd love to. Do you think it be safe? I mean, I don't wanna be causin' a disturbance, or anythin'."

They stopped, and with her hand in the cradle of his arm, he escorted her from the floor to meet his girlfriend standing on the sidelines. She was plain looking, but almost pretty. Both she and Ike were in their late fifties. Like Nellie, she too was a widow. She had two grown and married daughters who had taken to Ike, and were at the party with their husbands, all now on the dance floor.

"Martha. May I introduce you to Nellie McDaniels. You remember me talking about her and her husband, Ned. They helped me build my 'stead many years ago. Years before we knew about any trouble with the North."

"Pleased to meet you, Nellie," Martha said, her voice low and with a pretentious smile.

"Thank you, Martha. I know it's hard on all of us, with my appearance here and all. But I hope to assure you that I am contrite in my feelings and want to help in any way I can to make amends for the awful past."

"I'm glad." Martha turned to Ike as if expecting him to take her away from the meeting. Ike turned her back to face Nellie, saying, "You two have a lot in common."

Having introduced Martha's daughters and their husbands when they joined them from the dance floor, Ike now said, "Well, we're going to go out with the rest of the men for a ceegar and let you women talk awhile." That said, the three men left the women to fend for themselves, which they were well accustomed to doing.

Before long, Ike and the rest of the party heard laughter coming from the women as they began to warm up to one another. A smile came across Ike's face as he joined the circle of men who had been watching the fiasco.

"You're quite the sage, Ike," the general said while offering him a glass of punch.

"It'll take time, general. It'll take time. But after all, time is all any of us really has, isn't it?" Ike said, drinking his punch and perking a smile.

His two stepsons-to-be joined him and toasted to the event. The older of the two said, "Seems to be quite a lady."

"Most definitely," the other agreed.

The general held back his smile and lit his pipe as he stared over at the widow.

She felt his attention, but due to her absorption in the moment, dared not return it.

CHAPTER 22

TERROR AT THE FERRY

It was now two days since the two rangers had left Waco. Looking out across the floor and through the saloon doors of the Red Garter, McTavett saw the captain and Ranger Tom riding south. He finished his drink and rose to walk out of the saloon.

Aaron and Frank walked out with him, sensing something was happening that might involve them. The trio walked over to the livery stable and saddled their horses.

McTavett told the men, "Ride slow and not together. Take a back street to avoid attention. I don't want anyone becoming suspicious. I'll wait awhile and ride north and double back. We'll meet outside of town in the groves."

When the captain and Tom reached the ferry, they were greeted by Ranger Jerod Torgeson, owner and operator. The ferry was on the east side of the Brazos, and upon seeing the rangers ride up, Jerod pulled the ferry over to meet them. Once on the other side, he helped the rangers board their horses for the trip across.

The Brazos was about seventy yards wide and deep in the middle. At times, during a cloudburst, its waters could be dangerous. It was a calm night at this point, so the ride across was pleasant. The clouds, however, were beginning to suggest a storm was in the making.

On the other side of the Brazos sat Jerod's house. In the cool evening, smoke rose slowly from its chimney. Jerod's wife, Effie, was inside the house. As soon as she saw the men exiting the ferry, she left her household duties and came outside. Wiping her hands on her apron, she welcomed the rangers.

"Hello, Captain Ralph. Tom. Saw you comin', so's I put some biscuits in the oven."

"Thanks, Effie," Ralph responded. "We'll take you up on it."

"Rich and John passed here yesterday," Jerod said. "Talked about arrestin' Steve. They should be comin' by again soon."

They entered the house where Effie offered them dinner and a place to stay.

"Biscuits will only take a minute. Sit yourselves down."

"Doesn't sound like Steve'd do a thing like that, Ralph," Jerod remarked.

"I know, Jerod. But Tom here has evidence to the contrary. At least in theory."

"What kind of evidence?" Jerod asked.

"A shirt," Tom said.

"A shirt?" asked Effie.

"It's, well, evidence that goes contrary to fact, ma'am," answered Tom.

"Hope so. But if Steve didn't kill this boy, who could have?" Effie asked.

Ralph answered, "Effie, that's why we're meetin' the rangers. I want them to take a look at the body and see if the evidence fits the crime."

As the night began to move fast upon the little house, the kerosene lanterns quickly brightened the room. A sound across the river caused Jerod to stir and go to the porch. McTavett and his two men had ridden up to the ferry. They dismounted and rang the bell to let Jerod know they were there.

"Ahoy the house!" McTavett yelled out when he saw Jerod open the door. "Is the ferry still running?"

"Yep. Be right there," Jerod yelled over, slipping his coat back on. "This late night. I can't understand it."

Effie walked down with him to the ferry and untied it once he got aboard. She watched him take it across with strong hands against the Brazos as the winds began to stir. This time of night was no time to be riding the ferry, but Jerod felt it was his duty to keep it going until the sun went down. The sun was low to the horizon and about to set. Effie continued watching as Jerod expertly landed the ferry on the other side.

His hands were huge, and his muscles were taut as he drew the cable in and tied the ferry to the wharf. As they loaded the horses on board, the men experienced a difficult time with them. The waters were getting stronger because a storm was brewing.

McTavett was not a patient man. The more he saw the animals act up, the more he pulled on their bridles. At one point, he slapped his horse much to the consternation of Jerod.

"No need in doin' that, mister," Jerod cautioned him. "He's jittery 'cause of the storm."

"You tend to the ferry," McTavett threw back at him against the wind. "I'll take care of my animal."

Once on board with the horses tied, it was even more difficult to bring them all back across. Although McTavett still seemed to be raising his voice about something, Effie couldn't make out what he was saying because the wind took his words and scattered them.

The captain and Tom stepped out onto the porch to watch. They knew McTavett quite well, and they were accustomed to his senseless tirades. They went down to the landing and gave Effie a hand in helping pull the ferry into position.

After a safe crossing, McTavett noticed the rangers, and his disposition changed. He began to act like a gentleman and smiled as the ferry landed.

"Thanks. Where ya headed, Capt'n?" McTavett asked.

"No where." Ralph answered. "Jest waitin' for some of my rangers to return."

"You fellas are welcome to some food," Jerod said. "Effie and I will tend to your horses while you put the feedbag on."

"Thanks."

Jerod and Effie were expert wranglers with handling horses on and off their ferry, regardless of the weather, and it showed as they walked them to the corral and turned them loose.

Once inside, the conversation changed among the men as they began to discuss the killing of Billy. "Kinda about time for the rangers to be comin' back, don'tcha reckon?" McTavett asked, as he dished up a plate full of stew from the pot.

"Maybe," Ralph answered. "Kinda figured they'd be here by now. Of course, they'd have to find Steve to arrest him. Maybe he's not there."

"Why are you meetin' 'em here and not in town?"

"Just checking on a theory. That's all."

"Theory? What kinda theory?"

"Well," Tom said, "I've got a theory that says Steve might not have shot Billy."

"Oh, and what's this theory ya have, young 'un?"

"I kinda figure that he coulda done it. But evidence tends to tell me that someone is tryin' to make it look more like he did it, plain and simple. Don't make sense."

"How d'ya mean?" Aaron asked.

"Well, we've got more evidence saying it was Steve, without being sold a bill of goods. Then I go to suspectin' that someone wants us to think it is Steve so much, that we arrest him right away to a lynchin' party. The evidence kinda makes Steve look like a mean villain, if ya know what I mean."

"I don't folla ya. I'm the one here that said Steve shot him. Me and my two men heard the boy tell me. You tryin' to call me a liar?"

"No, McTavett," the captain said. "But it appears that someone, for some reason, has tampered with the evidence. And with tampered evidence, we have to be sure that the crime happened as it is told to have happened. Do ya understand?"

"Tampered evidence? What tampered evidence?"

"You brought in a shirt, McTavett," the captain said. "you say you took it off Billy's body before burying him. That's the evidence we have, and the only evidence we have right now."

"And you're sayin' it's been tampered with? By who?"

Tom answered, "Well. It kinda looks like you might have done it, McTavett."

"I tampered with the evidence? Hell, I haven't got any reason to be tamperin' with any evidence. It's murder. And Billy told us who did it."

"Maybe he did," the captain said. "And your word is good. And Steve did kill Billy."

"But I've got my suspicions, McTavett," Tom said.

"Like what?"

"First of all, was it Billy told you Steve shot him? With three holes in him?"

"He told us it was Steve. No one else was there. Jest him and Billy."

Tom took the shirt from the saddlebag and showed it to the three men. "The position of the holes kinda tells me that Billy was in no position to tell anyone anything. Hell, I'm not blind. Those shots would have blown his insides right out."

The men looked at one another and said nothing.

Ralph added, "And Billy defended himself when Steve opened fire on him for no reason?"

"That's right, Capt'n. Don't make sense. I know." McTavett took the makings from his pocket and rolled a cigarette. Sticking it in his mouth to light, he showed he was at a loss for matches.

Tom accommodated him with a light.

"Thanks, son."

"Two things' got me puzzled, McTavett," said the young ranger.

"What's that, son?"

"First of all, sir. Please don't call me son. 'Cause I ain't."

"All right, so . . . Ranger." McTavett let the smoke out slowly. By this, he was again attempting to show that he was in control of his emotions and not afraid of anything. "What's botherin' you?"

"How a man with three bullets in him, in these particular areas of his body, could talk at all. And then, the shirt.

"I'm not a lawyer. Jest a ranger. But me and the capt'n were talkin'. Ya see the holes?" The ranger held the shirt up and pointed to the varying sizes of the holes.

"What about 'em?"

"Well, if you look at them carefully, there's a lot of difference in them."

McTavett knew that because he caused the extra bullet holes. At this point, he wanted to sound sure of his story. "I don't see any difference in them."

Effie discovered she needed more water and excused herself from the house.

"Well, sir," Ranger Tom continued, "the one in front, where it hit his chest, is the smallest."

"Capt'n, what is your man here saying?" Frank asked, nervously.

The captain, who was smoking his pipe in cadence with McTavett's cigarette puffing, let out a stream of smoke before answering. "See for yourself, McTavett."

The ranger said, "Sir, I have not done anything with this shirt. I put it in the cabinet for safekeepin and locked it up. The other day when I examined it, I brought this to the capt'n's attention. It was dry enough then to take a good look at it. You brought it in wet and dirty."

"That's the way it was. Blood is wet."

"Yes, sir." Ranger Tom gently put his finger into the hole he was describing. The hole was smaller than the other two. "See how this is smaller than the ones in back?"

"Don't mean nothin'. Could have been the way the bullet hit the shirt. Who knows."

Jerod opened the door and entered after watching from outside. He stood to McTavett's side, slid his hat back on his head, and listened closely to the ranger's argument.

Ranger Tom continued. "Two different sizes of holes fired from the same gun?" He looked at McTavett but saw that he showed little interest. "Two holes. Now, look at the hole in the front of the shirt."

McTavett took the shirt and examined it. "Maybe he was only shot twice, then. One of the bullets comin' out the back instead of goin' into the back. Reckon?"

"Could be. Now if the bullet came out the back, it would explain the larger hole. I agree with you."

A sigh of relief came across McTavett's face, only to fall when the ranger continued.

"But it didn't go out the back. It went in the back." He took the shirt from McTavett and showed the threads on the holes where they differed. "I think it happened this way, because the hole is the same size as this one on the lower right side here in back, and the threads are torn in different directions as if going in from both sides, not comin' out."

"I don't agree with you. Anyway, what does that prove?" McTavett asked, showing discomfort in his voice.

"Don't know fer sure, yet. Jest have some questions in my mind."

"Go on, Tom," the captain said. "Tell him your theory, about how you think someone shot the shirt full of holes after Billy was shot, after the shirt was taken from his body."

McTavett's face began to twitch. The ranger continued, "Oh, yeah. First of all, I think someone is trying to make it look bigger than it is." He realized what he had just said, in almost an accusatory fashion, and began to help his story along by apologizing. "I don't mean by you, sir."

"Oh, yes, I see. But no. No. I didn't put it there. Maybe it was put there. But I didn't put it there. And I don't like the idea of you accusin' me, Ranger." McTavett was standing and threw his cigarette on the floor.

Jerod walked over and stomped it out. "Effie makes me keep it clean in here, sir."

McTavett felt pressured from three sides now, with the hint of sarcasm coming from this ranger. "What's your point, Ranger?"

"The point is that if Billy was shot and killed with one bullet, why was it necessary for anyone to add two additional bullet holes? Don't make sense, now do it sir?"

McTavett retorted angrily, "He said Steve did it."

Ranger Tom continued with his theory. "Sir, if I can be permitted to continue, I think I can show you the absurdity of this whole thing." He took the shirt and held it close to McTavett for him to see. "Do you see anything else that is different about the shirt, sir?"

McTavett was allowed to reexamine the shirt but came up with no answer. Just as well, because he felt that anything he said would only incriminate him further.

Ranger Tom took the shirt and held it by the light from the lantern. "Maybe the lantern will help you, sir."

"Cup of coffee, McTavett?" the captain asked. "I'm gonna have one." He went to the potbelly stove and removed the coffeepot from the top and started to pour himself a cup of coffee but found there wasn't any.

McTavett showed that he wasn't interested.

Ranger Tom went on with his theory. "See the edge of the holes, sir? There is no blood on these two holes in the back."

McTavett began to fidget with his holster, as his heart started to beat faster.

The captain interrupted. "Tom here showed me that the blood was only around the one hole." He took a puff on his pipe, keeping his eyes on the trio of men.

"We're not accusing you, McTavett. You certainly wouldn't take a dead boy's shirt off and shoot it full of holes. Don't make sense. And then bring it in to my office to swear out a warrant on someone who is innocent. Especially since you didn't kill the boy in the first place. Why would you do such a thing?"

The rangers looked at McTavett skeptically, waiting for his explanation. "Can you see how it doesn't make sense, sir?" Ranger Tom asked.

Great beads of sweat trickled down across McTavett's face. "Billy stayed alive long enough to tell us Steve did it. That's all I know. Nobody fiddled with his damn vest, like you say," McTavett protested.

The ranger continued. "I see a shirt as being evidence that someone tampered with it to convict someone of a crime; in this case, murder. The question is, why, if he didn't kill him in the first place?"

"Why ask me?"

"Because you're the only person that we know of who has been in control of this shirt. Now, sir," and the captain said 'sir' with sarcasm, "did you put the extra holes in the shirt? And if you did, why did you, sir?"

"Stupid. You are idiots. All you Texas Rangers are idiots. Somebody shot a friend of mine in the back and killed him. I bring the shirt because I buried his body. The bloody body of a friend of mine lies in a grave. And you stupid sons of bitches are accusing me."

Almost expecting him to erupt with violence, the captain put down his pipe and answered McTavett in a calm voice. "McTavett. We haven't said you killed anyone. Just that it looks like you, or someone with you, tampered with the evidence. That in itself is not a crime punishable by death. However, it would lead one to believe you had a motive behind this, and if you are attempting to put a man on the gallows, then, sir, that is a crime punishable by death." Taking a breath, the captain stopped for a moment to watch McTavett's reaction.

"However, at this point," he continued, "we just might have enough evidence to hold you over for the circuit judge to investigate this whole matter. You're a strong suspect in this killing. Why would you want to add incriminating evidence to a case that needs none, if Billy did indeed tell you that Steve shot him? And you have other witnesses to back up his story? No, we're not going to arrest you. Just yet. But stick around town, and hope that when the rangers bring Steve in, you have nothing to worry about."

"If you don't have anything to arrest me for, then I suggest you leave me alone."

Although McTavett had said nothing, Ranger Tom added, "We're goin' to examine Billy's body. Something we shoulda told the other rangers to do."

"What does that mean?"

"That, sir, means that we will dig up Billy's body, which you say is buried, and examine it for wounds. That, sir, will be our next move. And, sir, if the capt'n, I mean, when the capt'n gives me the word to arrest you, I'm gonna do it with pleasure. 'Cause I'm gonna enjoy watching you hang for killing Billy."

Almost as if the timing was right, Effie entered the front door with a bucket of water. She saw the three men sensing the danger that hovered over the room.

McTavett watched the eyes of the rangers go to the door. Using this to his advantage, he drew and fired his gun at Ranger Tom, killing him. He turned and emptied his gun into the captain who had his two guns drawn and cocked. The captain was killed instantly.

Jerod had his gun out and fired but missed McTavett. Before he had time to fire again, he was hit by a bullet fired by one of the three men. His wife, screaming in torment, fell on her husband's bloodied body in agony over what had happened.

McTavett struck her head with the butt of his pistol, satisfied that he had killed her.

The three men stood for a moment, startled by what just happened. The sight was unbelievable to them.

Aaron asked, "What in holy hell did we do?"

McTavett went over to the body of the captain and took his pearl-handled revolvers. He then examined each of the rangers to make sure they were dead. "Bust your ass, men. We're dead if somebody connects us with this." He headed to the front door, making sure the other two men left ahead of him. He gave the house a look over to assure himself that everyone was dead and then ran out, giving a rebel yell.

After climbing on their horses, they looked back at their crime.

"What do we do now?" Aaron asked.

"Well, stupid. The other rangers are on their way back. They'll find these bodies and hightail it to town. Then all the rangers in Texas will be after our asses."

"We split?" Frank asked.

"Hell, no. We stick to our plan. I'll go to Waco. After I make sure no one suspects us, I'll prepare our men to meet us at the grove. Next day, we haul ass for the Brazos Ranch. We take the cattle to Kansas where we'll be rich."

They boarded their horses on the ferry and hauled it across the Brazos. It was beginning to rain, and it appeared that the Brazos, as if seeking revenge for their killings, slapped at the ferry with her waves, making it harder for the men to pull it across. But she failed to stop them.

Once on the other side, the three spurred their horses towards Waco in a full gallop against the rain. Except for the light from the window, the dark enclosed the house and the ferry and all the surroundings as the three figures on horses rode away. What was once a quiet home and business for a man and his wife had turned into a graveyard.

CHAPTER 23

NO HONOR AMONG KILLERS

The ride made for a long night for the trio. By morning, the storm had subsided, and the men brought their tired horses to rest in a grove. A fire was waiting for them, tended by Lem.

Frank quickly dismounted and pulled McTavett from his horse with a force that knocked the wind out of him. "Who the hell do you think you are, gettin' us in this mess?"

McTavett sprung back and his fist connected squarely on Frank's nose, breaking it. Frank reeled around and hit his face against a boulder. The blood flowed and several of his teeth were broken. McTavett pulled him up by his hair and planted his fist hard into his belly.

Frank doubled over, spun around, and kicked McTavett in the groin.

McTavett fell against the horses in excruciating pain.

Frank grabbed a huge stone and was about to smash McTavett's head when Lem grabbed his hand. Lem hit Frank across the cheek and sent him tumbling to the ground.

Aaron walked over and kicked Frank in the face, then turned and thumped McTavett in the seat of his pants, making him fall on his face. He brought his heavy boot up against McTavett's neck and held him down.

Lem jumped and sat on Frank.

Gasping for breath, Aaron said, "Stop it before we all kill each other."

Recovering from their fight, the four men began tending to their wounds. McTavett and Frank sat up and stared at each other. Aaron stood up while Lem brought them water.

"Jest what the hell did you shoot those rangers fer?" Aaron asked.

"I got two. Somebody else got the other," McTavett said.

"Me," Frank said. "I got 'em. Didn't want ya to get shot, an' he was ready to shoot ya."

McTavett said with a sigh of relief, "Yeah. He would have, too."

"What happened? What about some rangers?" Lem asked, rubbing his head.

"We got into a bind and shot it out with some rangers. We're alive and they're not."

"That don't look too good, does it?" Lem said sarcastically.

"No, Lem. That don't. But it's done, and we've got to put it behind us."

McTavett doused the fire with dirt for fear of being spotted. They sat together and continued to talk.

"What was the reasoning behind it all?" Aaron asked again.

McTavett rubbed his neck to ease the pain where Aaron had held him down. "They confused the hell out of me. They were thinking I killed Billy. They saw right through me. How the hell did that blond sissy-ass kid see right through me? Damn. Alls I did was to fire a couple holes in Billy's shirt sos the rangers would go after Steve. Nobody, and I mean nobody, could be that smart. What was he? Some kinda genius or somethin'?"

"You blew our plans?" Aaron blurted.

"Hell! We've got men in Waco waitin' to move with us. Got at least a hunnert. Give or take."

Aaron said, "I've been with ya, and I've seen most of 'em. How you gonna get to 'em now. The rangers will be combing the area, you can bet on that."

"We goin' back to Waco?" Frank asked, standing up.

"I gotta go back. Nobody knows we're involved. Hell, it's easier now than ever. We have the rangers riding all over the countryside looking for killers. They'll probably ask for our help, and we'll all go to the Brazos Ranch. Alls we gotta do is stay calm and work our plan."

"The rangers will get together and find out it was us," Aaron said. "We're here. They're there. When we go ridin' back into town, they'll stop us. They'll ask questions. You got his guns, too. I saw you take 'em."

"They're in his saddlebags. They'll hang us with them," Frank added.

"No one's gonna hang nobody. Damn. I made a mistake. A lousy stupid mistake. Everyone makes mistakes now and then."

"You go into town wearing them, they'll shoot ya," Aaron warned.

"I'm not gonna wear 'em. Not 'til we get to Kansas, anyways."

"You're so sure about this thing. Why?" Aaron asked.

McTavett took the guns from his saddlebags and rubbed them across his pant legs. He was infatuated with the weapons.

"'Cause I can feel it," he said. "A general can feel victory. And I feel it. Steve is our only threat and the rangers have him. We'll go to the Brazos Ranch and take it. Your concern is getting the cattle to the bridge. We'll have a hunnert men. They'll do what I want them to because they're starving. We take the cattle like they were our own. Once we're across the bridge, we head 'em north for Kansas." McTavett began laughing.

Aaron asked, "What the hell is so damn funny?"

"Aaron, me lad. They had me believin' I actually killed Billy." Then he stopped as if he had another thought. "Hell. I had a perfect way to get what I wanted, and I screwed it up. Damn! Damn! Damn!"

CHAPTER 24

A WOMAN SURVIVED

The evening rains brought a mist with the dawn of the next day upon the banks of the Brazos. A female figure limped slowly out of the ferry house.

Effie had survived the pistol beating and with her head wrapped in torn pieces of cloth as a bandage she made it to the barn. Finding her horse, she saddled it. In great pain, she climbed aboard and rode slowly toward the Brazos Ranch.

When the sun reached its zenith, she found an oak tree and settled down beneath the shade of its large branches. She drank from her canteen and fell asleep. The sun changed positions and began to shine its heat upon her face.

Ultimately, her face began to burn from the sun. She awoke when a shadow passed over her. To her, it seemed only moments had passed. Looking up, she could barely make out the shadowy figures of a few men. Startled, she yelled and recoiled.

"We're rangers, Effie. We're here to help you," Ranger Rich said calmly so as not to rile her into shock.

"She's got a bad bump on her head, Matt. The skin is broke and she bled a lot. Good thing. Else she'd probably be dead," Steve said after examining her.

She looked closer at the men and half smiled.

"Hello, Steve. Matt."

"Well, she knows who we are," Matt said. "Guess you're gonna be all right, Effie."

The men tended to her wound and brought her food and water from their saddlebags. There was no doubt that her life was saved by their timely help.

When she gained enough strength, she began to explain to them in broken sentences what had happened.

The rangers prepared a litter and fastened it to her horse. Steve volunteered to take her to the Brazos Ranch while Matt and the two rangers rode back to the ferry crossing.

It was evening when they reached the ferry. Matt took his time going up to the house. He knew what to expect, and he wasn't eager to see it. These were his friends, good friends. "Any of you wanna stay outside?"

"Hell, no!" was the resounding reply from both rangers.

They went up to the house and Matt entered first. The rangers followed. The sight was gruesome, even for an ex-soldier like Matt. The sweet smell of fresh biscuits, eggs, and coffee that once filled the air was stolen by the stench of blood and death. They examined the bodies to see if any spark of life remained. There was none.

"Nothing more we can do here," Ranger John said. "Let's get those bastards, Matt."

"Well, Matt," Ranger Rich said, "kinda looks like you were tellin' the truth. Question now is, where are they?"

"Figure, since we didn't see them on our way, they had to go into town. We'll head towards Waco, then one of you will have to bring back a wagon for the bodies," Matt said, biting his lip.

"I'll get the wagon," Ranger Rich said. "You and John find those bastards. And shoot 'em. I'll ask questions later."

The three pulled the ferry back to their side of the Brazos. They tied their steeds to the ferry and rode it across. Once on the other side, they spurred their horses toward Waco.

Effie had lost a lot of blood but her spirit was strong. She would make the ride back to the Brazos Ranch on the litter.

In a short while, she and Steve met up with Seth and the herd headed for Waco. Steve dismounted and tied Effie's horse to a nearby tree, then rode toward the cook's wagon.

"Let me have the wagon to take her back to the ranch," Steve told the driver as he hopped aboard and took over the reins.

As they transferred Effie to the wagon, Seth asked Steve, "What happened?"

"McTavett killed Jerod, the capt'n, and a couple other rangers. Jerod's wife is in bad shape."

"What d'ya need from me and my men?"

"Right now get Effie to the ranch, and get Doc out here right away. Keep the cattle movin'. I'll ride and get Matt's men."

"I'll go," a young lad with a swift horse replied, and he spurred his horse into a fast run to town to get Doc Wilson.

"Get going, Johnny and don't stop. Not even for McTavett," Steve cried out after the young rider.

"How is she?" Seth asked.

"She's alive, Seth. She's a tough woman; she'll make it."

Steve turned to one of the riders and said, "Jeremiah, you've had some training with wounds in the army. Tend to her."

Jeremiah jumped down from his horse and climbed into the wagon. Steve followed.

After a while, Jeremiah said, "She's got a concussion, Steve. She's gotta have a doctor right away."

"He's comin'. Anythin' ya can do for her, Jeremiah?"

"I'll do the best I can, Steve."

"Good. The ride gets a little easier up the way, Effie. Think you can manage?" Steve asked, bending over to look at her in the wagon.

"I'll make it, Steve. Jest you get them killers for me."

"We'll do that, Effie." With a clenched jaw, he repeated to himself, "We'll do jest that."

"He was too good a man to have had this happen to him."

"Yes, ma'am." He looked at her one more time with a tear about to fall from his eye, and then jumped out of the wagon onto his horse and spurred him into a gallop towards the ranch at breakneck speed.

Reining up, Steve explained what had happened to some of the men who rode out to meet him. "McTavett and his men killed the capt'n and young Tom. Jerod, too. His wife is hurt bad. They're bringing her in, but we've got work to do. Need some riders, fast."

"Take a fresh horse, Steve," one of the men said. "Mike, loan him yours."

Exchanging horses, Steve said, "Go tell the other men to catch up to us." He then turned to the men that had gathered with their steeds. "Men, we've got some riding to do. Let's go!"

Their horses caught up to Seth and his cowboys moving cattle and, with the fury of a whirlwind, they rode through them, causing some of the herd to spook and run. "They're your damn cows now, Seth," Steve yelled out without stopping. "We're comin' through."

"Come on through, Steve. We'll catch up to ya' in Waco," Seth yelled after them.

They rode hard again, knowing that Effie was determined to make it. All they wanted to do was make the men who did this to her pay with their lives.

Rain began to fall on Matt and the two rangers as they rode toward Waco. The ride carried them to the grove where hoof prints indicated there were now four men to hunt down. They found Lem's fire still smoldering.

After they carefully inspected the area for trouble, they tied their horses and took off the saddles. They made a camp for themselves for the night with a lean-to to keep off the rain, built a fire and brought out pans for cooking. Beans and bacon were the order for the night.

It was going to be a few hours before they would be ready to ride into town. With the darkness and rain, no food, and little rest for the men or their horses, they knew they would be useless if they ran into trouble. It was something they learned in the war and this was no different.

"What if they're still close by?" Ranger John asked.

"Thought about that," Matt said. "This grove of trees makes a damn good place to hide out."

"Yeah. Thought about that, too," Ranger John said, looking around.

"The fire's been smoldering for at least two hours. Maybe longer. Figured they're close to bein' in Waco by now, else no need leavin' a good fire," Matt said.

Matt picked up a log and was placing it on the fire when a shot rang out. It barely missed him. He hit the ground and rolled away from the fire.

Ranger John reeled at the sound of the gunshot and saw the flash. "Well, you were wrong," Ranger John yelled as he drew and fired his six shooter.

Another shot rang out and ricocheted off the ground near Matt. He moved away from his position and hid behind a tree as three more bullets passed close by.

Ranger John fired again at the flash and heard a bullet hit its mark.

Lem's rifle fell to the ground, and he tumbled down the hill following it.

Rangers John and Rich ran to the bushwhacker and held their guns to his head, ready to pull the trigger.

Lem's eyes were opened wide as he gasped for air.

"Don't shoot, mister."

"Who are you?"

"I'm Lem. I was told to watch for anyone comin' by."

"Why? Who told ya?"

"Hold it, Ranger." Matt ordered as he came up out of his position. "How badly is he hurt?"

After examining him, Ranger John answered, "Damn. Just busted his hand."

"Good shootin'"

"Aimed for his damn head."

Matt grabbed Lem and stood him up. With his pistol placed precariously under Lem's chin, Matt said, "Now, Lem, let's you and me hope this thing don't go off. So, you better make every word you say count."

"I didn't do nothin'. It was them three. They's always getting' me in trouble. I don't want trouble, Mr. Jorgensen."

"So, you know who I am? Who was it, Lem?"

"They told me, sir, to watch the groves and make sure nobody got by. I just tried to scare ya. I coulda gotcha. Real easy. I'm a good shot, I am."

"I believe ya, Lem. Now, who is 'they'?"

"You gonna get me in trouble, Mr. Jorgensen, if I tell ya?"

"They're bad men, Lem. They killed some Rangers. That's real bad."

"Yes, sir. They told me that. They even fought with each other. I tried to get them to stop, but they didn't. They're crazy, Mr. Jorgensen."

"Was it McTavett?"

"Him and two others."

"Who, Lem? Who are these two men?" Ranger Rich asked.

"A fella called Aaron. He's mean. He's got a real temper. The other's a big man. Real crazy, like."

"Who?" Steve asked.

"Frank. He's called Frank."

"Where'd they go?" Matt asked, as he put his gun back into his holster.

"Waco. You gonna fix up my hand you done busted?"

Matt took Lem by his arm, pulled him to the river, and threw him in. "Ya can swim, can't ya?"

Lem didn't answer as he struggled back to shore.

"Pack some mud on it. And stay outa my sight, if ya wanna live."

"You're not turnin' me in?"

Ranger John took Lem's rifle and threw it into the river. "You're useless as a tit on a bull without your gun."

"What are we gonna do with him, Matt?" Ranger John asked.

"Like you said, he's useless." Matt looked at Lem and said, "Get outta here."

Lem climbed the bank and walked back to his horse, only to be stopped by Matt, who turned around and hit him as he neared him. "Not on your horse."

"It's a long walk. I might bleed to death." When he saw the stern look on Matt's face, he started walking toward Waco.

"Not that way, fella." Ranger Rich stopped him and headed him in the opposite direction. "This way. Back to the McDaniels' ranch. Someone there might take care of ya, one way or t'other."

The men watched Lem as he waddled away, defeated and broke.

"I'll take the first watch," Matt said, removing his rifle from its boot. "Someone might decide to double back."

"You think?" Ranger Rich asked, putting on his slicker. "What fer? Lem?"

"They ain't got no passion for anyone," Ranger John joined in, pulling his slicker over him as he lay down by his saddle. "No reason to come back, I figure."

"Get some sleep," Matt ordered, throwing his slicker around him. He looked out into the empty darkness of the night as the rain trickled down, and he cocked his rifle.

The wet drizzle made sleeping difficult for the rangers as it slipped off the overhead leaves and branches. The thought of cold-blooded killers on the loose and Lem waddling around in the night kept their minds open to all sorts of sounds. Sleep was hard to come by for Rich and John. A few hours of sleep seems to give a man all the rest he needs. It finally came with these men.

The sound of horses woke them as riders rode close to the camp. Matt and the rangers were ready for them with cocked rifles and the riders came to a halt.

"Saw your horses tied up, figured you were bedded down," Steve yelled out.

"We heard you comin'," Matt replied. "Get down and rest yourselves. We'll be goin' into Waco shortly."

Looking at the warm fire and the pans sitting on the ground, Steve said, "I see you've got some coffee made." He dismounted, walked over to the fire, and poured himself a cup. "Nothin' better'n hot coffee to warm a cowboy up on a rainy night like this." He took a long sip, swished it around, but then spit it out quickly. "This ain't nothin' but hot water."

The Rangers laughed as Matt threw his arm around Steve. "Someone forgot to bring the coffee."

"I've got some in my saddlebags," one of the Rangers piped up as he dismounted. "Never go anywhere without m'coffee."

The rest of the men dismounted, tied their mounts, joined the others around the lean-to, and watched as the Ranger poured the grounds into the pot. Someone once said, "An army travels best with food in its belly" or something to that effect. These men knew the rule and sat down together. As tired and sleepy as they were, they ate first and slept afterwards. Matt kept first watch as he concentrated on the hatred in his soul for McTavett.

At the sound of rustled sage, in one swift move, Matt turned and drew his .45, aiming it in the direction of the sound. A lone figured stumbled and fell to the ground.

"Don't shoot," the man gasped as he looked up into the mean eyes of Matt Jorgensen.

"Lem! What the hell?" Matt holstered his .45,

"Take me in. Please." Lem pleaded in broken words, weeping into the palms of his dirty and bloodied hands, stained from his gunshot wound.

Steve stepped out of the shadows behind Matt with his .45 drawn. "Want I should shoot him?"

"You walk real soft, friend," Matt said to Steve, startled that he was behind him.

"Learned it from an ol' friend," Steve answered, meaning Matt.

"Yeah," Matt returned, then added, "No. No. He's no good out there, but he might have more to tell us in town. We'll take him with us."

Steve knew Matt for a soft heart for an orphaned calf. He figured the same for a wounded man, regardless how mean or how much a coward he was. He grined and picked Lem up under his arms. "Git up, you stinkin' polecat. Bed down out there away from the fire. But if I see you movin' towards any of us, I'm goin' ta think you're gonna try to kill us, and I'll jest shoot cha. Git my drift?"

Lem nodded quickly, stumbled over by a bramble and fell down. He had no intention of moving the rest of the night. But he did feel comfortable, knowing he was accepted in the company of Rangers. He had seen the inside of the jail sometimes before. He was just going home.

CHAPTER 25

THE BATTLE ON THE BRIDGE

The next morning, the air was clean and dry. It was a beautiful day in Waco, a growing city that was alive and active. Business began as usual in the hundred or so buildings, planing and flour mills, and foundries.

Several rangers rode slowly down the main street. They passed an icehouse and a carriage factory, and a well-equipped fire department. Several churches dotted the way. There were no signs of murderers on the street.

Doc Wilson drove his buggy, following the young rider out of town. Maggie Johnson, the captain's widow, was seated beside him.

Matt, Steve, the two rangers, and the Brazos riders rode into town and up to the buggy.

With his whip in hand, Doc greeted Matt and stopped the buggy.

Matt rode closer and dismounted. Walking up, he said, "I'm sorry, Maggie." He looked at the pain in her eyes. "Wish it was me instead."

"I told her to stay here," Doc said. "No place for her out there, but she wouldn't have it."

"Thank you, Matt," Maggie said. "It must have been his time." She wiped her face with a handkerchief. "How's Effie?"

"Our young-un here probably told ya. State of shock, I reckon. Told us who did it. You better hurry out to her, Doc."

"We'll bring Capt'n Johnson back."

"Yeah."

"Who's that fella you got hogtied on his horse?" Doc asked.

"That's Lem, Doc. He didn't have anything to do with the killing but he's one of their men. He's gonna show us where McTavett's hiding."

"It was McTavett?"

"Yeah. That much we learned from Lem."

"Get him for the Capt'n, Matt. Get him good," Maggie said, putting her face to the wind.

Doc whipped his team of fine horses and headed south. Maggie looked straight ahead as if she could envision what she was going to see but didn't want to.

The riders rode over to the Rangers' headquarters, where they were met by three men on duty. Rangers Rich and John informed them of what had happened at the ferry landing.

Matt turned Lem over to the rangers.

"Lock him up. And have someone tend to his hand. It's busted a might," Matt said, staying on his horse.

They took Lem into custody.

Ranger John left with a team and wagon back to the ferry landing to join Doc and Maggie. Other rangers had left the headquarters, riding in separate directions to round up more Rangers.

By the time the riders were ready to move out, at least two dozen of the best Rangers had gathered at the headquarters for the search. Ranger Rich was in full command now. Rifles were taken from the rack and distributed to the men.

"Got any ideas, Matt?" Ranger Rich asked.

"Lem said McTavett and two others did the killing. They were headed to Waco and are supposed to have an army of men. McTavett hired some wranglers, but I didn't know about an army."

"That's the army, Rich," Steve answered. "Wranglers. Every busted cowpoke down and out on his luck and living in the gutter or fired off a ranch for being lazy. Lem said McTavett hired them to take over the Brazos Bar M Ranch."

"What's your thinkin', Matt?" Ranger Rich asked.

"We've got a lunatic on our hands."

"Which way you headed?"

"Back to the ranch. Along the east bank."

"McTavett is mine. He killed my Capt'n and he'll be wearin' his guns," Rich said. "All I ask is that, if you find him, leave him to me." The men mounted their horses. Pointing to the surrounding streets, he assured them, "My thinking is that he's hiding somewhere in the city. We'll comb the streets until we find 'im."

Matt watched a small group of a half dozen Rangers ride into Waco. Matt and Steve took off with the Brazos riders in the direction of the ranch.

"Why the ranch, Matt?"

"'Cause we didn't see any signs of them here. An army of no do-gooders and no sign of them anywhere. That's why." He gritted his teeth as he put his spurs to the horse's flesh. "Nobody's there but the girls."

They rode hell bent for leather.

"Oh, my gawd!" Steve yelled. "We've gotta get to the ranch before they do."

Doc and Maggie were on the opposite side, heading for Waco and were coming up to the grove. Matt waved, but they failed to see them.

Six rangers rode hard towards Doc and Maggie to join up with and help Matt and Steve.

When the horses started panting, Matt ordered the men to dismount. "Walk your horses, men. We'll water them ahead."

The sky had darkened. It looked like more rain, a harder rain, was heading their way.

While kneeling down to help himself to water, Matt heard a gunshot in the distance. He rose and waited. More shots rang out.

Steve mounted his horse and rode over to Matt.

"I heard it, Steve."

"Maggie? The Doc?" Steve shouted in short breaths.

"God, I hope not." Matt mounted and spurred his horse north.

The other riders mounted and followed Matt. They saw Doc's buggy kicking up dust as it hurriedly headed toward them.

Doc yelled out, "It's McTavett, Matt! They pulled out of the grove with his men just after we passed him and ambushed some rangers."

Matt signaled that he had heard and directed his riders to run ahead of the buggy. Soon they saw the small group of rangers behind them, fighting fiercely with McTavett and his men. The rangers were notoriously accurate with their rifles, but they were outnumbered by McTavett's army. Coming to their aid, Matt's riders removed the rifles from their boots and began to fire across the river to draw McTavett's fire away from Ranger John and his party.

Matt and his riders rode to the riverbank and rode their horses down its slopes, digging them with their spurs to get them to swim. The river was swift and difficult to cross, especially when a storm was brewing but Matt kept moving with the river, hoping McTavett wouldn't kill him before he got to the other side.

McTavett looked up and saw the riders on their horses swimming in his direction with Matt out front. He was amazed. "Matt? Matt Jorgensen? Is that ye?"

"It's me, McTavett!" Matt's voice carried in the wind.

"You're supposed to be dead! What'd ye do? Come back from the grave, did ya?"

"I'm alive, McTavett! No thanks to you. Your shotgun killed my horse, tho'. Good horse. Hated to see him go. Promised him something before he died."

"What's that?"

"That I'd kill you for killin' him."

McTavett said to himself, "How in Mary's name did he get alive?" He fired again and again but missed. Rearing his horse, he saw the futility of riding into Matt's men while fighting the rangers. He pulled his horse north and commanded his men to follow.

Matt brought his horse up the bank followed by Steve and the other riders. They began firing as they rode up the slope to the aid of the rangers. They only stopped firing when McTavett was out of range.

"Thanks, Matt," one of the rangers yelled out. "We almost bought it."

"How many men you lose?"

"Two. Another shot up real bad." The ranger looked around and ordered, "Pete, take Sam in the buckboard and catch up to Doc."

Looking south, Steve saw the dust from the herd of cattle heading their way. "Cattle being driven across Texas is about as pretty a sight a man would want to see," Steve gestured, wiping the sweat from the inside rim of his hat. "Next to a pretty woman, that is."

Matt nodded in agreement as he stared in pride at seeing a thunderous herd of over five thousand head of cattle being driven to Waco by Seth, the three cowboys from Montana, and the Brazos River Bar M drovers. One could see their joy by the way the drovers waved their arms and yelled into the wind at the riders waving back. The feeling inside their bones echoed the pounding sound of the hooves, the dry sod filling the air with clouds of dust and dirt.

The dust was also heavy along the banks where McTavett and his men were riding. Matt and his riders rode their horses hard, hoping to catch up to them before they got to the bridge. But his hopes vanished when they caught sight of them in the distance, starting across the bridge.

Recognizing an impending battle, the toll keeper fled, soon disappearing from sight.

Looking south, Steve kept Seth and the drovers in his sight as they moved the cattle slowly in their direction. He thought to himself, "I'm being paid to get them to market. Instead, I'm riding lieutenant with Matt, again."

Lightning flashed out of the east. Thunder roared across the Waco skies. It began to rain. It didn't trickle but came suddenly and grew. The hard-trodden trail filled up with water.

Once at the bridge, McTavett and his men rode across the Brazos to Waco to prepare for their onslaught with Matt and the Brazos River Bar M Ranch drovers. McTavett turned his mount and sat his horse ready for battle. He had built up confidence that his army would, once and for all, defeat General Mitchell, a man he had served under during the war. McTavett figured that the years he rode with a glory-seeking officer as an obedient soldier were now paying off in dividends because now, *he* was the glory-seeking officer.

"I've learned from you, you bastard!" he yelled through the hard-falling rain. "Now all the hell I suffered through the war is giving me my glory. Come and get me, you cowards of the sword. I'll show you how a real man fights and I'll live to tell about it to me grandkids."

While McTavett's men numbered under a hundred, he still had more than Matt. But because of their undisciplined form of riding, many never bothered to slow their horses and slid dangerously to the sides of the bridge, injuring not only themselves but their horses, too.

They commandeered wagons with horses from innocent Texians to use in their fight. Their intent was to show strength in numbers and make lots of noise. It was a maneuver McTavett learned in the war.

Having just ridden across the bridge in the rain, the more expert riders had a feel for it and knew their horses would outperform Matt's.

Aaron rode alongside McTavett. "What are we going to do?"

"Wait until they get on the bridge and they we'll pour hell down their throats. Listen for my command. Then, full charge."

Rain rolled down his Stetson, and across McTavett's face. "Some of you men lie down in those wagons. Use your rifles. When I give the order, you fire. When I order 'charge,' you riders better damn well ride for hell. Else I'll put ye there." They waited for Matt and his men.

The wait wasn't long, as Matt's riders rode fast to catch up to McTavett's men. He stopped his riders at the other end of the bridge. Matt rode up to the gate with Steve to size up the situation. The Brazos riders numbered less than thirty but were all sure shots.

McTavett's men were inexperienced hired guns, just bodies, nothing more.

McTavett yelled across the bridge, "I be askin' ye agin. Be ye the ghost of Matt Jorgensen?"

"And I'll tell you again. I'm gonna kill ya."

"Not good enough, Matt. And Steve. That ye, too?"

"Ye got a good eye, McTavett," Steve said. "Take a good look, 'cause it's gonna be your last."

"Whacha talkin' about? I ain't done nothin'."

Frank and Aaron had ridden on either side of McTavett. With his men surrounding him, McTavett said, "Keep together, men. They're pullin' a bluff. When we get through this, we're gonna have ourselves a ranch. All of us. We'll be rich men."

"You went too far," Matt said. "Ya killed some rangers."

"Not me, Matt. I wouldn't do that. Ye knows me. I ain't a killer." McTavett turned to Aaron. "How the hell did they find out? God bless me poor sainted sister, I ain't got any luck at all."

"It's all or nothin' now," Aaron replied. "If they know it was you, they know we were in on it, too."

Matt watched them move into position. With Steve's help, he readied his men on the bridge.

Matt rode slowly, just a little way onto the bridge, then he stopped, holding his right hand up, grasping the reins loosely in his other. "Why don't we settle this once and for all, McTavett? Jest you and me. Leave our men out of it." Matt felt uneasy. He still lacked the nerve to draw and shoot. Not since he killed Billy had he fired his gun. Though he took it out of its boot, the rifle hadn't been fired. He knew now that this would be a test of his courage. Could he draw and fire at a human being again?

"Sounds sportin' enough, Matt." McTavett began riding a slow ride toward Matt. "Who told ye?"

"Effie."

"She lived?" McTavett stopped his horse, took his hat off, and threw it on the ground showing his wild crop of black wavy hair. "Damn it! If that don't beat all." He looked at Matt, then at the rest of the riders positioning for battle. His mind was thinking that his army could handle all of them, but Matt was still a man to contend with and Steve a close second. And now he had to fight both of them. He thought, "If Matt was on the ground, my men could ride the rest down."

"All right with me, Matt. Let's dismount and go at it."

Aaron noticed that McTavett wasn't moving to dismount. "You, too, McTavett! This time it's going to be a fair fight. I don't want any more murders on my conscience. You kill him fair and square. If it ain't fair then, we'll kill ya and leave your carcass to rot."

"You jest do that!" McTavett said. He watched Matt dismount and sensed the uneasiness of his army. He rode his horse back to Frank and Aaron and dismounted. Filled with fear and trepidation, he tried not to show it. McTavett had never known fear, but now he had good reason. He was boxed in with a raging river below. "Stop the rains!" he yelled, looking up into the sky. "I hate rain." He handed his reins to Frank.

Matt looked down at the far end of the bridge and watched McTavett walk toward him. It would be a long walk on the wet, slippery bridge. As McTavett attempted to take his rifle from its boot, Aaron stopped him with a heavy kick, throwing McTavett forward.

The two men walked closer to one another while Matt's riders brought up the rear. Neither side was going to surrender because of the fall of their leader. They knew the battle would begin when either man went down.

Matt looked closer at McTavett's gun belt and saw Captain Johnson's pearl-handled revolvers. "You even have the damn nerve to wear the capt'n's guns."

Aaron was uneasy and rubbed his chin. Regardless of the fight, he knew he would be marked a murderer, one who had killed the rangers. Nothing in Texas was as bad as killing a ranger. The world would catch up to him. He knew he was marked to hang.

But Frank reveled in this infamy. A devilish smile settled on his face as he saw the two men closing in on each other.

The rest of McTavett's men stayed put. They knew they would feel the sting of his venom if they tried to leave. Most were still willing to fight.

Rich and his rangers from Waco rode toward the bridge behind McTavett. At the same time, John moved in behind Matt with his rangers. In the distance, they could see the two groups warring with each other.

McTavett saw the rangers closing in on him. He ran back and climbed onto his horse, spurring it toward Matt.

Matt mounted up quickly.

At the top of his lungs, McTavett yelled "Charge!" and released his hell with his two guns blazing. His army moved forward as devils from hell and fired their guns in all directions. Horses slipped and lost their footing when the men spurred them to run. Some reared when shots fired out and men fell.

"Charge!" McTavett yelled again. His horse reared and ran forward.

McTavett's men brought up the wagons in the rear, moving fast and furious across the bricks. Some horses started to cross the bridge but became confused in the melee of warring men and gunfire. It was the chaos and noise of battle — experienced by many of the men during the war — all over again. Both sides began to suffer casualties immediately. It was a gory picture.

The remnant of rangers from Waco reached the bridge and boxed in McTavett's men between themselves and Matt's men. Ranger John and his rangers joined Matt's men, firing at McTavett's army, and helped cause havoc among the drifters and outlaws.

In their confusion about how to fight, many of McTavett's men simply gave up without a fight.

"Ride, you bastards, ride!" McTavett yelled as he rode his horse across the rain-slicked bridge. The rain came down harder, almost blinding him.

Those of McTavett's men who were still on their horses rode with their crazed leader. Others ran on foot alongside. The wagons rolled across the bricks and the clatter added to the noise and confusion as riders inside them fired into Matt's men.

Matt heard the sound of cattle coming up behind him. As he and the other cowboys approached the bridge. Seth called out through the pouring rain, "Get out of the way, Matt! We're comin' through."

Matt and his men turned their horses around and rode out of the way, letting the cattle stampede through. The wranglers fired their guns into the air and waved their blankets across the cattle's eyes, stampeding them across the bridge. They caught McTavett and his men from one end of the bridge while the rangers rode on the other end from the Waco side.

One of McTavett's hired guns spotted Steve and fired, hitting him in the thigh. Steve's leg sprung out of his left stirrup. Another bullet entered the side of his horse. Steve was thrown from the saddle and rolled down the riverbank, stopping at the base of a tree. He looked back at the bridge and caught a glimpse of Frank riding toward him. Leveling his Colt, he fired a hail of bullets, knocking Frank out of his saddle and under the hooves of oncoming cattle.

Rangers, riders, and McTavett's goons dove from the bridge or were pushed into the river.

Confusion reigned among McTavetts' men, causing many to drop their weapons and flee. Several men were trampled, and some even jumped into the river to escape only to drown or be killed by the sudden impact.

As McTavett's men were boxed in on both sides with cattle chasing them back to Waco, most of the men turned and gave themselves up to the rangers. Others fell off their horses and lay still. Many were shot; some died. Some fled, never to be heard from again.

Matt was poised and ready in case McTavett tried to escape the stampede.

Shorty was across the bridge, behind the first hundred head of cattle, when Aaron's gun sounded out and brought him down.

McTavett's gelding was stopped by the cattle, reared up and was pushed into a slide off the bridge. The horse and rider hit the river with bone-jarring force and went under. McTavett bobbed up; his horse's body had spared him the fatal impact.

When Matt saw him, he yelled, "Oh, no! You won't cheat us again." He rode to the rail of the bridge and dove into the water after him, positioning himself behind McTavett in the water.

The rains poured harder, and the waters raged around him. He lost sight of McTavett and could barely see his horse treading water. McTavett was gone. Matt gasped for air, his arms swinging wildly to stay afloat. He almost passed out. As his head barely floated above water level, he scanned the river for signs of McTavett.

McTavett's horse feverishly climbed the bank when Matt got a glimpse of McTavett swimming downstream and began to swim after him. He was determined that McTavett would not escape this time. He swam faster, and with the swift flow of the river, finally caught up to him. Matt grabbed and caught his arm. The two began to fight, but the strong tow of the river took them under and downstream.

McTavett felt the air leaving his body as he sank under pressure of Matt's arm. When they came up, he was gasping for air.

Rangers Rich and John turned their mounts on the riverbank and rode downstream to where the two were fighting. A couple hundred yards away they saw McTavett digging his nails into Matt's face, making Matt release his hold.

McTavett swam away, only to have Matt catch him again.

Blinded by the blood in his eyes, Matt weakened his hold on McTavett.

As they washed ashore, McTavett got the better of Matt. He picked up a tree branch and swung, barely missing Matt as he rolled away from its blow. McTavett brought the branch down again. A shot rang out and the branch flew out of his hand.

Matt looked up and saw Rich and John running along the bank toward them. McTavett raised both hands in surrender and waited to be arrested at the river's edge. Rich slid down the bank and John followed. Neither had fired their guns.

As if in surrender, McTavett turned his back to the rangers and waited for their approach. Matt stumbled out of the water. As Ranger Rich reached for his raised hands, McTavett turned and caught him with his forearm, grabbing his throat and using him as a shield. He removed the pistol from Rich's grasp and fired at the other ranger, wounding him. McTavett twisted his hand over Rich's shoulder and pointed the gun at Matt, pushing Rich to the ground.

"I've got no time to find out who's faster, Matt. Sorry it had to be this way."

A rifle shot echoed across the river, and a bullet tore through McTavett's body. He jerked backward and hit the bank.

Matt pulled him up, slamming his fist into his jaw, knocking him back down.

McTavett still held the pistol tight, knowing that losing the gun would mean his finish. He rose and cocked the gun to fire at Matt. A shot was fired and McTavett froze. Another shot was fired and the bullet burst through McTavett's body, killing him. He crashed into the river and started floating downstream.

Ranger Rich scurried back up the bank. When he saw that Ranger John was only grazed, he mounted and rode away after McTavett's body.

Ranger John mounted and followed him.

Matt stood in the river and looked across the Brazos to where the rifle shots had come from.

Nellie was standing next to her carriage, still holding the smoking Winchester.

Alva stood beside her, controlling the horse.

The general was on his horse next to the carriage. He was holding a rifle, but Nellie had pulled the trigger all three times.

Matt's gun was still in its holster.

The general called out, "You okay, Matt?"

"Yes, General." He looked down the river at the two rangers riding after McTavett's body as it floated away.

"Nellie saved your life, Matt. Couldn't cock my rifle in time." He patted his armless shoulder.

Matt waved to her. Rangers on the bridge led many of McTavett's men away. Dead bodies and wounded men were lying across the length of the bridge. Rangers led their horses carefully around the bodies as they rode across the bridge. Once on the eastern side, they rode down the bank to the river.

The general dismounted and helped Nellie back into her carriage.

"I can get in myself," she said. "Alva, take my horse."

She looked at the general, turning the lines and whip over to him. "Do you mind?"

The general took the lines and headed the team for the ranch.

The battle on the bridge had subsided, and the cattle had calmed down to a meandering walk across the bridge.

Steve was up and hobbling to his horse. The rain began to come down harder.

In the buggy, the general asked Nellie, "You got the branch with the first shot before I had a chance to draw my pistol. Why didn't you just kill him then?"

"Couldn't kill him, Mitch." She drew her rain-soaked collar tightly around her neck "Saw too much good in him. He turned bad all of a sudden-like."

"No, Nellie," he talked loudly through the rain. "Men like him don't turn bad all of a sudden."

"You didn't really know him, Mitch. He worked as my foreman for over a year. He worked damn hard."

"He was a good soldier under me. I knew him. Something went wrong during the war. Not after. For some strange reason, he wanted our ranches, Nellie. Yours and mine."

"When I hit him, I felt like I hit myself. I thought I'd killed him. I was hoping he wasn't dead. Then . . . then, when he turned that gun on that boy and shot him, I grabbed my rifle again and was gonna shoot him."

"Then he drew against Matt. One second more and Matt would have been dead."

"I know. That's what scared me more than anything." The general threw the lines across the horses' backs and yelled out, "Yo!" Looking at Nellie, he smiled and said, "Let's go home, Nellie."

Slim broke away from the crowd, running up the ramp of the bridge. He called out, "Dan! Shorty! Seth!"

Seth rode up to him from across the bridge. "Follow me, Slim." He turned and went back on the bridge, leading him to Dan, who was sitting on the side of the bridge, crying, and holding Shorty's lifeless body in his arms.

"I'm sorry, Slim," Seth said, as he climbed off his horse.

Shorty had been shot with one bullet in the chest. His gun was in its holster. He was still clutching a blanket tightly in his hands from his efforts to stampede the cattle. After all, his expertise was cattle, not fighting—he had always left that to those around him who knew more about the skill of using a gun.

Slim removed his drenched hat and knelt in the mud next to Dan. With his bandanna, he wiped the mud from Shorty's face. The blood was still seeping out of his body, lightly.

"Put his body in the buggy, men," the general ordered. "We'll take him back to the ranch."

"Thanks, General," Slim said, lifting Shorty's body and covering it loosely with a blanket. "He loved Texas. He seemed to love the longhorn more than anything else. But I think he would want to go home now. I think we should bury him in the Montana sod." He threw himself into the buggy alongside Shorty's body and prepared himself for the ride back. Because it was raining, no one saw his tears mix with the rain.

The buggy moved away, rolling along the east bank to the Brazos River Bar M Ranch, leaving the dead and the wounded behind.

CHAPTER 26

ONE MORE LOOK AT TEXAS

Matt stood looking out the window of the general's front room at the vast expanse of land across the Texas countryside, his home for many years. He was preparing to depart from this land to head north to his boyhood country, a place he thought he would never see again.

The general stepped up behind him, his figure reflected in the window next to Matt's. "Any regrets?"

"Been thinkin', General."

"What about?"

"How to tell ya."

Steve rounded the front room from the kitchen on a crutch. "You fellas get your goodbyes all said?" He walked over to Matt and without a warning, planted a haymaker on his chin, sending him sprawling to the floor.

Matt pushed himself up on to his elbows. "What the hell was that for?"

"You boys want a last drink together?" the general asked as he picked up a bottle from the cabinet.

Steve got three glasses and held them while the general poured. "Your best bourbon, General?"

"Yeah."

Steve took a glass and offered Matt a hand off the floor. Matt rubbed his jaw. Without a word of explanation, they toasted one another. After a couple of swallows, Matt looked steely at the two men.

"You gonna tell me?" Steve asked.

The general looked at Matt. "Son, you've been trying to tell us something ever since we returned."

"Don't bother, Matt," Steve interrupted.

"What?"

"The general pointed it out to me. I saw it at the bridge."

The general added, "Son, you almost got yourself killed when you let McTavett draw down on you on the bridge. The widow was able to do somethin' a hundred yards away what you couldn't do ten feet away."

Matt said nothing but stared at the floor.

"Call it 'guilt'. Call it whatever. I suspect that your killing that fifteen-year old youngun' set a cold chill inside you and caused you to think some." The general looked at Matt's hand as it quivered. "How many boys have we seen do the same thing when they saw their first kill? It was our job to get them back into action before they got themselves killed. Think about it, son."

"This was different. This wasn't war."

Steve put his hand on Matt's shoulder. "Compadre. It was war all over again when those bullets whizzed by your head. Your instinct should have been to protect yourself. And some of your friends. Namely me."

"To kill!"

"When necessary." Steve walked away and chose his words carefully. "A bullet doesn't ask the age."

"Then why did I freeze on the bridge?"

"Damn if I figured it out yet. I wouldn't be on a crutch today, and I'd still own the best damn horse in the county."

The general responded. "Perhaps you didn't freeze, Matt. What I suspect is, like any natural man, you stopped to think. And in war, or in self-defense, that's not what you want to do. It gives the other man the edge."

"When McTavett was going to shoot a ranger and had the drop on me? Why couldn't I draw and fire my gun?"

"Same answer, son."

"Will it go away? I mean, the fear? The guilt?"

"No one knows, Matt," the general answered.

"Had I not been shot, I would have knocked some sense into that thick brain of yours right then and there," Steve added.

Matt looked at Steve and eyed his helplessness on a crutch. "Sorry, Steve. You can have Skeeter as a gift from me."

"Was kinda lookin' toward it anyway, Matt. Doesn't make up for me almost gettin' kilt, though."

Matt broke a little smile and watched a grin come over the faces of the general and Steve. "Calls for a ceegar." He pulled three cigars out of his inside vest pocket. "Maybe my luck will change in Montana?"

Steve said, "I damn well hope so."

PART TWO

MONTANA

A NEW BEGINNING

CHAPTER 27

MONTANA SOIL

Several days later, the train pulled into Virginia City, Montana because Bozeman had not yet got its rail siding. Disembarking the train, they were met by Russell, a wrangler for the Double-O who had been wired of their coming. He was a stout man, and appropriately chosen for the task of helping with Shorty's coffin. Russell was a Norwegian with muscles that bulged out of his shirt sleeves. He was one man that Matt sized up real quick and decided that he wouldn't want to pick a fight with him. On the other hand, Russell was also a tame man of a gentle nature, with blue eyes and blond hair.

"I'm Russell, sir," he said, in a strong voice which impressed Matt. "Most jest call me Russ."

"You'll do."

"He means, he thinks you're okay," Dan said.

"That your wagon, Russ?"

"Yes, sir."

They set to work getting Shorty's coffin out of the baggage car. Once the coffin was loaded aboard with their other gear, Dan climbed in back with the coffin. Russ took the reins.

Once aboard, Matt took over the lines.

"Just show me where to go, Russ, and we'll be all right."

Russ was a little put off at first, but relinquished the reins and settled back for a long ride, as the three men headed towards the Double-O Ranch with Shorty's body.

"Take a turn at the end of the road, and it'll head us out into the country. We've a long way to go."

"Just let me know which way to go," Matt answered, "It's been too long a spell for me to remember much of this country, as pretty as it is." Matt paused. "Tell me something."

"Yes, sir."

"You say 'yes, sir' one more time, and I'm liable to dump you out."

"Yes - uh. Sir, I'm not comfortable at calling you anything. Can I just call you, Matt?"

"Fits." Flipping the reins loosely across the backside of the team of horses taught them to keep the gait and follow their new leader's commands. "Get up, there." Then, looking straight ahead, he asked Russ, "How's my ma?"

There was a long pause as Russell stared into the Montana horizon.

"She's dead, Matt. I'm - I'm sorry."

There was a quietness like the wind had quit, and the sound of the horses' hooves and the turning of the wheels was oblivious to the moment. The shock took seconds to sink in, and when it did, Matt was slow to say anything.

"When?"

"Yesterday morning. Had no way of tellin' ya. She tried to stay with us. Poor soul. Her heart couldn't keep beatin'."

The wagon kept going, as thoughts spun around inside Matt's mind. "Why am I coming back? What good can I do her, now? Why don't I just turn this horse around and get on the next train for Waco?"

The wagon kept going, and he received no answers to his silent questions. It was a while before any one spoke.

"Can I say something, Matt?" Russ asked.

"Go ahead. Free country. Isn't it, Dan?"

"As far as the eye can see," Dan answered.

"You really Wil's son?" Russ asked.

"Yep."

"Then, how's come you left, and now you're coming back, all of a sudden?"

"Didn't anyone tell him, Dan?"

"Nope. Thought it best to keep it among just a few of us. The ones who were raised by Wil, to speak."

"Well, Russ. Let's just say, I got homesick and decided to come home."

"Most of us figure you came back to take the ranch. And we don't rightly know what will become of us?"

"First things first. If I take the ranch, and I say 'if', cause there's a lot of attachments to that idea; then you'll have a job there. If you're good enough to earn your keep, that is."

"I'm good, Matt. I can throw a rope around a horse further than any of them. And I have strength of three men when it comes to dogging. And I can shoe faster than any of them."

"Then, my good friend Russ, I don't think we have anything to worry about."

"He's good, Matt. One of the best hands we got. One of the reasons they sent him by his self, I'm supposin'."

"Another thing, Russ. Does anyone know I'm Wil's son?"

"That's what they said, sir, eh, Matt. But we were told not to talk it up. You're supposed to be buried next to the house. And, now you're supposed to be buyin' the ranch. Too many supposin's."

Matt whipped the reins over the horses' rumps and yelled, "Yo. Get up there." Then without looking at Russ, he asked, "Who's they?"

"Your ma and your ma's lawyer lady."

"A lawyer, eh? A lady? I never thought they had lady lawyers. Not in Montana, anyway."

"Yes sir. Just recent like. And she's all lady, Matt. Real nice lady."

The trip across Montana's land was long and hard; nothing like the flat prairies of Texas. The road was narrower, and filled with ruts from the constant rains and winter snows. Matt kept the team at an even trot, sometimes just letting the reins go, and sliding himself back against his seat to close his eyes. At other times he would whip the horses for a fast walk, and even a faster trot. Then, when appropriate, the riders would get out and walk the horses; something he learned while in the cavalry. The other two had no qualms about how he drove the team of horses. He seemed to know better than the rest about how to get along with horses.

Along the roadside, every once in a while, he would eye a cow and give it a blank stare. His thoughts were still not favorable towards ranching. His thought returned, "Why the hell have I come this far?"

Finally, they approached the hill which would give him a glimpse of the Double-O Ranch. The same house was sitting slightly on the hill and away from any gully where the rains and snow would gather. It had changed though, it was larger, with an expansion for two more bedrooms, and a larger den. When he was alive, Wil was not accustomed to too many rooms. He never acquired the taste for a den.

Where there was one barn, now there were two, with storage for more hay and fodder, and more stalls for the horses. The corral was much larger than the one Matt had ridden in before. In fact, there were three. The other two were smaller than the main one. However large it seemed to him now, over what he remembered, it was still no Brazos River Bar M Ranch. He would perhaps occupy one of the bedrooms in the main house. However, he was curious to know who would acquire any of the others.

He asked, "Who sleeps in the main house?"

"You will, now, Matt," Dan answered. Your father had two more bedrooms added in case you returned and got married. Your mother had a den added. She knew you would want to read, being an officer and such."

"You an officer, Matt?" Russ asked quite inquisitively.

"Capt'n," responded Dan.

"The South?"

"Any problems with that?"

"No, sir - uh, none."

"Good."

Matt pulled the team into the ranch and stopped in front of the ranch house.

Russ leaped out and tied them to the hitching post.

All of the wranglers were outside to meet them.

Matt's eyes scanned the lot of them as if he were trying to recognize any, but they were all strangers to him.

They were at a loss as to how to react to the new boss. The stories about him were many and strange. Mostly, they had heard that he and his brother, Lukas were wild boys who drank, shacked up with prostitutes, and gambled. When they lost their money, they went on a robbing spree. The story about the freight office was blown out of proportion. They came in with a gang and shot up the town. It was the brave sheriff that gunned down most of them, including Matt and Lukas.

Now that Matt returned, the mystery had spun an even wider web. No one had been told the truth. They only speculated that, somehow, Matt escaped the guns of the sheriff, or was only wounded and came back to life, broke jail, and ran north to Canada. The tales were almost messianic in nature.

Some heard that he fought on the side of the Confederacy. Knowing Wil's allegiance to the North, this rumor was quickly played down by most.

Now, looking around at these men, he saw that a few were older than him, but most were younger.

They were looking for a strong boss. They knew they had found him in Matt. No one dared to walk up to him and ask him about the truth. They continued with their work.

As his eyes caught theirs, he saluted them with the two fingers on his right hand as if to say, "everything was okay". He, too, wondered how many of them fought on the side of the North.

"We'll take the team now, Matt," Dan said, adding, "Russ, you and some others take care of the coffin. Put it in the front room. We'll be burying him in the morning, first thing."

Matt turned quickly and asked, "Where?"

"Up on the hill, Matt?" It was more of a question. "If it's all right with you." His words trailed off.

Matt looked up to the hillside where he knew his mother would be lying. He also remembered Wil had marked two graves with crosses there. One was his.

He walked up the hillside to the top. Her grave was fresh. He opened the gate to the yard and entered. Taking his hat in hand, he knelt beside her grave and looked at her marker as he stopped a tear's attempt to roll down his cheek. The marker read,

"ANNIE ANDERSEN
1817 - 1882
WIFE - MOTHER
THE COWBOYS' MA"

Slowly, he drawled inwardly to himself. "Ma. I missed ya something terrible. I've kept most of your letters. They kept me going through the War. Made me feel good on the porch, down in Texas, when I'd look up in the sky and knew you were under the same sky, just further north. I tried, Ma. I tried to get back before . . . . Ma. I love you."

He turned his eyes briefly to the marker next to hers, and recognized it belonging to Wil. It was not the same marker the boys put in the field, and his body was not in the grave. But just the same, a marker stood next to Annie's because they never located Wil's hastily dug grave that they made somewhere on the plains between Bozeman and Belle Fourche.

"He was a good man, Ma. Good father. His sons jest disappointed him. Wish I coulda come home and done him proud. He wouldn't have it. Had I stayed here, he would still be alive."

He stood up and looked at the other markers. The two crosses were still there. They were old and weather-beaten, but he could make out the markings.

"LUKAS ANDERSEN
1838 - 1858"
"MATT ANDERSEN
1836 - 1858"

His thoughts quickly raced back to that morning he left with Anse. He looked back and saw Wil digging the graves with Annie by his side. He never dreamed he would be back again, standing by the graves of his parents, Wil and Annie Andersen.

A short distance away was a marker of one Charlie Nightlinger, they used to call "Black Charlie". He got his name from being black, and older than the night. He was their cook on the trail, and boss, after Wil was murdered. Now he was with Annie on the hill.

Matt's eyes returned to his parents' graves. He looked upwards, closed his eyes, and whispered a prayer.

He stayed there for hours, just sitting, while the rest of the men continued their work. Dan and Russ left him alone.

Suddenly, the figure of a woman climbed the hill to be beside him. She stood in silence, watching him. Afterwards, when she felt it appropriate, her gentle, womanly voice broke the silence and startled him. "I'm truly sorry about your mother."

His gun whipped out of its holster, cocked and pointed in the direction of a young lady dressed in riding clothes. Her hair was swept up under her Stetson, and she wore a light jacket to keep out the Montana chill.

"I suppose I deserved that, Mister Andersen."

Matt was convinced that what he saw was the loveliest woman he had ever laid eyes on. It was Leisha and Jaime rolled into one. The voice was not exactly angelic, as it had a slight roughness to her tone.

"I'm sorry. I didn't hear you walk up," Matt apologized.

"You were concentrating. I apologize for disturbing your time of mourning. My name is Miss Paterson. I'm the attorney for your mother's estate."

"Then you know who I am."

"Yes. I've been expecting you for some time, now. They told me you'd be in today. I live in Virginia City."

"You rode all the way from Virginia City? That's three days drive. I know. I just came from there."

"No. I was staying with a friend close by, Mrs. Wrisley, Dans' mother. She brought me here."

Matt looked down the hill at a tiny woman embracing Dan. "She must be one happy woman."

"Quite."

"Who's this Charlie Nightlinger?"

"He was your father's trail cook. I guess they called him, 'the old mother'. He was a Negro."

"A Nigger? Buried next to my parents?" A Negro would never share a plot with white folks in Texas. Here in Montana though, the culture was different, and he found that he had to readjust.

"You may have the right to have him removed, Mister Andersen. It will be your choice."

"Damn right, it will. I'll have it done right now." He turned to leave, but Beth's words interrupted him.

"Once the estate is cleared up, Mister Andersen. First things first."

He looked towards her as if he could bite lead. But he restrained himself.

"Mister Andersen, is it all right if we discuss some matters once you've got settled?"

"Kinda rushing things a bit, ain't ya? I just got home."

"I realize that, but time is of the utmost importance. You only have a few weeks in which to comply with your mother's request. And I'm afraid you are going to need every minute you can spare. We can talk when you come to the ranch house."

"I see. Then why don't we get to it, Mrs. Paterson?"

"Miss, Mister Andersen. I'm not married."

"Oh. What happened to your husband?"

"Mr. Andersen, I am not married. Never been married. And I have never discussed such matters with a total stranger in the shortest time on record. If this matter were not of a quite serious and important nature, and out of my love for your mother, I would bid you good day."

She turned and walked down the hill ahead of Matt. Matt followed, with a look of wonderment on his face, coupled with ecstasy in his heart for this girl he had barely met; and in that short period of time, he had already alienated her.

"Do I follow you?" Matt asked.

"If you like, Mister Andersen. If not, I am sure Mrs. Wrisley is quite capable of telling you what I was about to tell you when you became so rude."

"I don't see how I became rude. And you keep using that word, 'quite'. You're certainly not from around here."

"I have no intention of discussing my private life with you, Mister Andersen. It is your life that matters to me at this point." She stopped and turned towards Matt, almost causing Matt to collide with her on the hillside. "That is, if you will allow me."

"Cold," Matt said, rubbing his hands together. She caught the jest of his remark and looked towards the gravesite to avoid the pun.

"Could you tell me where I am to stay?" Matt asked.

"The ranch house, Mr. Andersen, is yours on a temporary basis. You may stay there for the time being." She continued downhill with Matt at her heels. "Where you will be staying once you're on the trail, is not the least of my concerns."

"Trail? Did you say, 'trail'?"

Reaching inside her jacket, she pulled out a letter and handed it to him.

His eyes were affixed to the smoothness of her face, and her sparkling blue eyes. Taking the letter from her, he began to read it, almost stumbling down the hill after her like a kid as she continued her upright walk.

"It's from your mother. I drafted it. It simply states that you have until Thanksgiving this year to fulfill your serious intent and responsibility to become a rancher and owner of the Double-O Ranch." She paused, then said, "As proclaimed by President Lincoln, that date is the last Thursday in November."

"We celebrate Thanksgiving in the South, too, Miss Paterson," Matt interrupted.

Miss Paterson continued. "If you had not been found, or if you had been found, but refused to return to the Double-O, or if you did return, but failed in that space of time to live up to her expectations, then . . . ."

"Then, what? Miss Paterson?"

"Then the ranch will revert to the state as their property to do with as they deem necessary."

"Whoa! She is sultry and has a temper to match." He began to read the letter while she looked on. "I can read, Miss Paterson. Or do I call you Lawyer Paterson?"

"As you choose, Mr. Andersen."

"How does this all relate to my riding some trail, may I ask?"

"The letter states that you are to perform the duties of a rancher, and you will take a herd of a thousand or more cattle to Belle Fourche and sell them."

"Belle Fourche? That's in South Dakota."

Matt's voice sliced through the air like a hungry bear coming down out of the woods for breakfast. "That's at least sixty days. We'll never make it, lady."

"Miss Paterson," she barked back at him.

"Miss Paterson. If we left today, we wouldn't be back 'til the end of November. That's cuttin' it pretty close."

"Mister Andersen. Your deadline is Thanksgiving Day. That, in my books, adds up to seven weeks. Surely you can make it in that length of time."

"Yes, ma'am. If it doesn't snow, and if outlaws and Indians don't get us."

"It doesn't usually snow up here until after Thanksgiving, Mister Andersen. Sometimes before. But you'll be on the way back, when you have no cattle, and you can make better time, I'm sure."

He stopped and stared at Miss Paterson as she neared the ranch house where Mrs. Wrisley and Dan were standing. Seeing them, she addressed them in that order.

Then to Dan she said, "I'm Miss Paterson. Mrs. Andersen's lawyer for her estate." Then in a teasing manner so as Matt could get her jest, she added, "You may call me, Beth."

Matt caught the jest and raised his eyebrows to let her know.

"Nice to see you made it back home in one piece, Dan," she said. Then, looking over at the house where Shorty's body lay in the front room, she said in a more somber beat, "I'm sorry about Shorty. I understand he was one of your best friends."

"Yes, ma'am. Thank you. You met Mr. Jorgensen?"

"I have."

"He's a little mixed up. I mean, having lost his parents and all. And now, after fighting a war, and living in Texas, he comes home to all this. Ya gotta be gentle with him, if you know what I mean."

Beth turned to Matt as he stepped up to them, and said, "Matt, this is Mrs. Wrisley. Dan's mother."

"Howdy, ma'am."

"Matt. Pleased to meet you. I've heard a lot about you. Mostly through Dan's letters."

"Yes, ma'am."

"I'd be pleased if you'd call me, Jean."

Matt acknowledged her with a tip of his hat, "Jean."

"I want to thank you for taking good care of him. He's my only son, and his father passed away," Jean said.

"It's more like he took care of me," Matt replied.

"You've got a big job on your shoulders, Matt, and Dan will be your best man."

"I think so, ma'am."

Matt felt some feelings for Mrs. Wrisley and could see where Dan received his determination. She was a stout woman, and very determined. It was her determination that caused Wil to put Dan in the saddle for the cattle drive, in spite of the fact that he wore glasses back then merely for sport, and not out of necessity.

Jean addressed Matt and Beth, saying, "Shorty's folks are on their way over."

"Yes. Thank you," Beth answered. Then to Matt, she informed him, "Jean is spending a few days here to help with your mother's things until you take over. If it's all right with you."

"I want you to know, Jean," Matt said, "how much I appreciate your son traveling all the way to Texas to bring me back. It took. . . ." he hesitated. "Well, it took some doing, let me tell ya."

"And he did it, too. Right?"

"Yes, ma'am," Matt agreed. Nervously, he wiped his hands along the seam of his trousers, then asked, "Dan, who's the ramrod of this outfit?"

Dan looked at the men and pointed out Slick, a tall, lanky man in his thirties, with dark wavy hair. He wore chaps most of the time, and a dirty black hat. "Slick. Come meet the new owner."

To Slick he asked, "How many head?"

"Twenty-nine hundred, three thousand at last count."

"How many you got cut out for the drive?"

"Bout that many."

"How many are too young?"

"We'll cut out about five hundred."

"Let's cut out fifteen hundred. I only need half again as much for security that we'll have a thousand when we reach Belle Fourche."

Slick replied, "That's a lot of beef to leave for another winter."

"Then you bring the rest with you, if they're ready for market. Tell you what. I'll take Russ and half your best hands, and you take the rest and follow me two- or three-day's journey behind. Got that?"

"Four days at the fastest. Yes, sir. But I don't see why we have to split up the herd. We got enough men."

"Time, my good man. Time. The quicker we get there, the quicker we get back. If you got enough for three thousand, then you'll only need enough for a thousand. Leaves nine-hundred to restock the herd."

Seeing Slick for the first time, he was impressed that he appeared to be serious about his job.

Russ was standing nearby when Matt called him. "Russ. You ride with my herd."

"Huh?"

"We'll explain as we go."

Slick knew he had met his boss. There was no arguing with him. He watched Matt as he turned and walked briskly away. He said to Russ, "Stick with him, Russ. He looks like a mean one."

"I already done found that out for myself."

"Get someone to take my bags inside, Russ. I'll find my bed when I'm tired." Looking past Beth and Jean, Matt yelled out, "Dan!"

Dan came running to his side in quick obedience. "Yeah, Matt."

"Slick, you and Dan here need to pick out some of the best of the lot, and tell 'em to volunteer. I want most of these men riding with me, and the rest riding with you, Slick. We're riding four days apart. I'm taking fifteen hundred head into Belle Fourche."

Dan asked, "Want me to go with you?"

"What d'ya think? Where's the cook? I'm hungry enough to eat a horse. Speakin' of which, get me the best one around."

Most of the cows had already been branded, but the roundup was far from being over. Now Matt's drive was getting set and ready to move out when he would give the word.

"I have a roan," Slick said. "Fifteen hands. You probably want a sorrel, maybe sixteen hands, or more. That one over in the corral. Ain't been broke, yet. Want me to have one of the men break her, sir?"

"My name's Matt. No sirs around here. I'll check him out. Stallion?"

"Yes, sir, eh, Matt."

"I'll do it in the afternoon after Shorty's burial. The morning's for the funeral, and a damn fine funeral it'll be. Tell the boys to finish what they've got goin' and be at the graveside in the mornin'. Shorty's folks are due any time, let me know when they get here."

In the meantime, Dan had summoned the cook, a Chinese man by the name of Fong.

"Matt, this is Fong. He's our cook and damn good trail cook, too."

"Well, Fong. How about rustling up some grub for me, Dan, and Russ over there."

Dan added, "Chop, chop, Fong. He don't speak English too good, Matt. A few words, like 'grub', and 'wash hands', like that."

Obediently, Fong turned immediately, and went into the house.

Matt looked towards the house thinking about where he was going to be sleeping.

Beth told him, "There's your old bedroom, Matt. Yours and Lukas'."

"Of course."

Beth said softly, watching Matt begin to walk away, "Before our talk, I'd like to address your men one more time. This will be my last time here for awhile, since I'm staying in town."

"You can sleep with me, Beth," Jean said. "No sense in trying to drive all the way back to town in this weather. Can't you see a storm settlin' in?" She said it just like a take-charge lady; it was the pioneer spirit in her.

She was right, the clouds had gathered and were turning the clear sky into a Montana gray. Beth agreed to stay.

Matt shrugged his shoulders as if to say he had no say so in the matter and stood there with a silly grin on his face.

"In that case, I'd still like to talk to them after you have your say," Beth said.

Before she could object, he took his gun from his holster, and rapidly fired off three rounds, shaking up the two ladies. "Excuse me lady. This is how we do it in Texas."

"We do it that way in Montana, too," Jean smiled.

Beth showed less appreciation, grumped, and taking Jean's hand, led her to the corral.

Dan rode up to Matt with a horse all saddled for him to climb up on for the impressive ride everyone was waiting to see. This was not the one he would be riding before the cowboys in the arena tomorrow. Yet, a cowboy is only a cowboy when he's in his saddle, and for the moment, he needed to be on a horse. It has a way of showing strength and power. The dignity comes with the way a cowboy sits and rides.

Matt hit the stirrups and swung himself into position as the horse lunged forward into a nice easy canter towards the corral. They saw Matt in his truest form. Beth saw him too, and was impressed by the way he commanded every man's attention. He was a true Texian.

Looking around at the cowboys, Matt addressed them in his easy style, showing no signs of being nervous. He was a leader.

"Howdy, ya'll. I'm, Matt. Matt Andersen. Annie and Wil's son."

A voice boomed from the opera seat, the top rail. "You fanned that gun of your'n pretty neat."

"Practice."

Another voice added, "Are we gonna keep the ranch?"

Beth walked over and lifted herself up on the rail. "First of all, Matt has come to tell you his side of the story."

Russ added, "He told me on the way up, and I believe him."

Dan stared at the group of cowboys, and said, "I know Matt pretty good now. What he says is the God-honest truth, as far as I'm concerned."

Matt sat back on his saddle, looked the men over, and began telling his story. After he had finished, he asked for questions.

The same voice as before from the opera seat yelled out again, "Just wanted to hear it from you, Matt."

"I speak for the rest, Matt." Russ said. "We're behind you. Not because we need the jobs, but because we believe your mother, and what you said kinda tells it like she did."

Matt nodded a note of thanks, and added, "Gentlemen, Miss Paterson here has something to say to us all. So, listen up."

Beth said in a soft voice, "Gentlemen. We do have a problem. In fact we have many problems. A couple of which are: First of all, I can be aiding and abetting a criminal. Matt is not technically wanted by the law, yet, simply because he is supposed to be dead. However, now I know otherwise, and so do you.

"When the sheriff finds out, he'll be wanting to arrest Matt. There's no statute of limitations on murder. Matt will be wanted for murder.

"Second, the sheriff might want to arrest all of us, because we'll be in this together. Do you understand the risks?"

She watched as they nodded their heads in unison. She continued. "And then there's the will. Matt's got to prove he's capable of being a rancher by Thanksgiving, or else the ranch goes to the state. That means you men will either have jobs, or be unemployed."

Another voice asked, "What if he's arrested? He won't be able to take the cattle anywhere."

Russ commented. "We're gonna make sure no one knows he's here."

Dan commented, "We've gotta get these cattle to Belle Fourche, sold, and the money in Lawyer Paterson's hand the day before Thanksgiving."

Beth assured them. "I'll help settle the debts, and turn the deed over to Matt. Then you men will have a permanent ranch to work on." She looked over at Matt, and added succinctly, "If Matt has a mind to keep the ranch."

Matt took off his hat, waved it, and said, "Gentlemen. Show me where the chow line begins." Then he rode out of the corral.

He stopped by Beth and Jean, standing near the gate.

"She's a widow, Matt."

"I heard. Remember?"

Jean added, "Been taking care of myself for many years, too."

"I'm sure you have."

Beth replied, "She comes around once in a while and helps Fong with the grub. He learns English from her, and she learns Chinese from him. They have a culture thing going."

"I'm sure."

"Today's one of the days, and she's here to welcome you with a meal fit for a king. She's already shown me the pies she made before coming over."

"Well, Miss Paterson, Jean, it do seem I reckon I need not worry about eatin' around here."

"And cantankerous, too." Jean interrupted. "You need to eat, like any grown man. Take care of what it is you have to do, and in a while, you'll be ready. I'm certain."

"Yes ma'am." That was all Matt could muster for the moment, feeling impaired by two females determined to care for him before he bedded down. For the moment he felt like he was back on the Brazos with Leisha and Jaimie; except these ladies were a little older, and Jean had no eyes for a younger man.

No sooner had he said this, than a buckboard with Shorty's parents drove up. Shorty's father was a man in his sixties, short and stout, and dressed proper as a gentleman.

Shorty's mother was about the same age, but smaller in stature. She was a lady of fashion and sporting an umbrella.

They pulled up to the hitching post, got out, and walked over to the crowd which was beginning to disperse.

He asked, "Am I addressing Miss Paterson?"

Beth stepped forward and greeted them. "I'm Miss Paterson. You're Mr. and Mrs. Bickerdyke?"

"That be us." He answered.

"Welcome to the Double-O, Mr. and Mrs. Bickerdyke. We want to express our deepest sympathy for the loss of your son."

"Thank you," replied Mrs. Bickerdyke. She looked around at the men, and lazily around the ranch. It is the first time she had been here since before Shorty left for Texas.

"Your son is laid out in the front room. He's dressed proper for you." Beth added.

Matt and the rest watched as Beth and Jean led the parents to the house.

Without looking back, Beth motioned with her right arm for Matt to join them.

Matt looked embarrassingly at the gesture, then grabbed Dan by the arm. The two of them followed.

Beth was right. The meal was fit for a king. All the wranglers and ranch hands filled their bellies and turned in early.

Matt sat on the porch where he had sat many years before as a youngster.

Dan dropped by to say goodnight to his mother and headed for the bunkhouse for the night. "I'll be up early, Matt."

"Sunup, Dan."

Beth stood in the doorway with the light flickering behind her. Her figure was full and inviting for a man who had been without a woman for some time. Matt sensed the easiness with which Beth was portraying herself. She was displaying her emotions as an actress would for an audition. Her every move was calculated to mean something very positive.

Matt turned and looked at her silhouetted figure draping the doorway. He could not make out the expression on her face, and she knew it. She liked it that way. It was her way of being coy with him without him knowing it.

"I've made my bed inside with Jean. I figured you'd want it that way," she said, looking at his eyes as they searched her body.

"I'll sleep over in Anse's bunkhouse. Checked it out when I came in."

"Nice of you to give up your room to the Bickerdyke's."

Closing the door, she slipped back into the house leaving Matt to his thoughts. She poised herself on the other side of the door and held onto her thoughts of wanting to make love to him.

Matt rubbed his leg and slid his Stetson back on his head. He took out the cigarette makings and relaxed into the evening.

The next morning, the sun rose on his face as he sat slumped asleep in a chair outside the bunkhouse.

Together, with the noise from the breakfast camp, wranglers and ranch hands getting themselves ready for the morning, the brightness of day woke him. He had a good night's sleep. In fact, he had not anticipated such a long sleep; and no one bothered to wake him.

He jumped to his feet and moved toward the well where he stopped for water.

Dan had been up and waiting for him.

Beth was still asleep.

After breakfast, he met with the Bickerdykes at their buckboard. Shorty's coffin had been laid in the back and draped. They were ready to head out.

The wranglers were on their horses preparing to ride with them. Russ had the buckboard out for Jean and Beth to ride.

Slick brought out the roan all saddled for Matt.

Matt said, "I'm glad to have known Shorty. I have said words over many a man on the battlefield. May I add here that Shorty was one more hero I have had the pleasure of serving with. And more than that, I owe him a debt of gratitude for bringing me back home."

He mounted the roan and sidled the buckboard for the funeral. He looked at the draped coffin and added, "Shorty. We're both home, now."

In moments, the Bickerdyke's buggy with the Double-O cowboys was out of sight. They were taking Shorty home.

CHAPTER 28

A HORSE NAMED "CRAZY ALICE"

That afternoon, Matt kept his promise. The tall sorrel was waiting for him in the center of the breaking ring, bare as the day he was born. Good looking, strong, and stout, any man would be proud to own a horse like this. Though few could ride him, Matt was sure he could.

The cowboys sat on the opera seat waiting for the moment. The ones who rode with Wil remembered how he had challenged each and every one of them to be able to ride Crazy Alice. Then, when they did, they had to break in at least six horses for their trail ride. Now it was their turn to see Wil's son ride "Crazy Alice". This time it was a stallion.

Matt strode into the arena, knowing that eyes were on him. He had been told the story about "Crazy Alice" the night before. As he ate a light breakfast earlier, this ride was gnawing on his mind. Now he wished he hadn't eaten. His stomach filled with a strong determination to get this over with, and his forehead was sweaty. He had been trained for this when he served in the Texas Eighth Cavalry. There he rode with cannons going off. What could a little rousing from the stands do to him here in a controlled environment?

Taking his lariat in hand, he approached the stallion. He moved the knot back a little and let out the rope a little at a time. Letting the loop fly, he lassoed the head of the sorrel and felt him pull hard against his hold. Letting the horse feel the unfamiliar thing around its neck growing tighter with each jolt, Matt carried his weight with the angered horse around the corral.

The sorrel, thrusting his legs, flew high into the air, and back onto his hooves, but he found he could not get rid of the rope.

Matt wrapped the other end of the rope around the center post and eyed the horse as it came towards him. Matt jumped away and watched for the moment when the horse would realize his situation and sense the futility of fighting.

Slick came out and helped saddle the big horse. Matt began breaking patter with the stallion while he placed the harness over his head. Soon the stallion felt another piece of unfamiliarity, a saddle on his back. Slick held on tightly to the rope, biting the ear of the stallion to keep it in tow. Somehow it made the stallion forget about a weight on his back.

"Ready, Matt?" Slick asked while still biting its ear.

Matt's foot slipped into the stirrup, and his leg swung over the back of the horse. His boot found the other stirrup, and grabbing the reins, he yelled, "Let 'er loose, Slick."

Slick let go and hit the railing as the horse jolted.

For the moment, Matt was regretting having agreed to break his own horse. His thought was of betrayal by one of the men, or at least a mean trick. That thought lasted less than a tenth of a second, as his hand gripped the reins tightly and he dug his spurs into the shank of the horse. His legs wrapped around the horses thighs, not comfortable for any ride, but necessary to stay on for the duration. Ten seconds went into fifteen, and finally the horse began to settle down. As soon as Matt felt the easiness of the horse's gait, he felt the lifting of his butt back into the air, almost causing him to lose his balance and fall off. He drew the reins tighter in his hands as he finally brought the animal under control.

The horse snorted and breathed hard for the moment and gave Matt a last buck before settling down. Once calmed down, the stallion felt the body of his master loosen up and relax.

Matt rode him around the corral to where the cowboys were sitting, still yelling and waving their hats. Matt had given them a good show. Better than they had expected. They were proud of their new boss.

Matt addressed the cowboys as he rode in the arena. "I'm taking off as soon as we can get fifteen hunnert heads together. Slick is gonna take half of you with him four days later and follow us. Reason is, we don't have time to wait. I need a thousand head to make it. I figure with fifteen hunert, I'll come out ahead. If something happens to me, in the meantime, Slick will bring up another fifteen hunnert or so. Knowing him, like I think I do, he'll catch up to me real fast. We need to get all the beef we can to Belle Fourche.

"When we get back, we'll have the biggest, damndest party you ever saw. And I'm leavin' it to Fong over there to catch a few turkeys on the way back.

"Now, I know, some of ya might have some mixed feelings riding with me. That's another reason I chose to split up the ride. Don't mind. I'd probably feel the same. I'm not a rancher. Fact is, I hate cows."

With that, the cowboys broke into laughter.

"I never wanted to be a rancher. It was kinda thrust onta me. Well, I'm here because it was my mother's last wishes. It's a challenge, not one I like, but one I have ta take on. I come back here to put my neck into a noose, or save this ranch. I hope I can keep out of the noose, and I'm thinking I can count on you men to help me save this ranch."

The men cheered in unison to show their new boss that they were behind him. Not one man showed any desire to do otherwise. Matt sensed this, and was pleased.

Dismounting, he gave the reins to Slick. "Walk him around."

Then, unbeknownst to anyone on the ranch, Deputy Bill Saunders had ridden up to the ranch. He stayed in the shadows of the hills just out of range of what was happening. Bill was a man in his middle thirties sporting a heavy crop of light brown hair. He seldom wore a hat, except when out on a trip like he was now. He was a six-footer. He had been a deputy for several years under Sheriff Wiseman and aspired to becoming the sheriff once Whitey retired which he hoped would be soon.

He was unable to hear distinctly, but he could make out that everyone's attention was being given to one cowboy. He heard the name Matt mentioned several times.

Word of a stranger arriving on a train in Virginia City, accompanying a coffin to the Double-O, made him decide to investigate. Seeing Beth Paterson, the female attorney from Virginia City, on this ranch made him even more curious. He had been infatuated with her ever since he laid eyes on her. Now, she had not returned to town for a few days, and he wondered why. He stayed and watched out of sight.

The next morning, he rode back to Bozeman and reported what he had seen to the sheriff, where little interest was expressed by him. But the deputy promised to return.

CHAPTER 29

HEADING FOR BELLE FOURCHE

For the next several days, Matt busied himself with preparations for the trail ride. It was like the Brazos all over again, except this time he was doing Steve's job. Every once in a while, Dan would see him looking towards the hill where his parents lay buried, alongside his brother, Lukas.

The weather promised rain in the hills the day they were ready to drive the cattle towards Belle Fourche. He thought to himself, "Why the hell did Pa have ta name this god-forsaken ranch, The Double-O. He named it after the cowboys' shifted balls. He remembered the good-looking man his father was, when he sat on his horse so many times, while looking after the cattle. Now, he thought, he was doing the thing he hated most. "All right, Pa. All right," he said to himself, feeling his spirited presence.

Dan rode up to Matt carrying a coat and a hat which once belonged to Wil. "Thought you might want to wear these."

Matt looked at the clothes, then at Dan. His eyes closed slightly, and his lips grew tight together. Russ rode up behind them.

He looked at the two men, and then towards the hill.

Dan offered the coat first.

After a moment of hesitation, when the two men thought that the world was going to come to an end, Matt slipped out of his Texas coat, gave it to Russ, and donned the coat of his father.

The hat was the kicker. It had seen harsh days and showed it. It was Wil's favorite. Dan held it out for Matt to take.

"Isn't the coat enough?"

A lone figure rode from the ranch house towards the trio. In a moment, Matt recognized Beth. "If Jean comes up here, the whole thing is off."

Beth rode up to Matt with a big smile on her face. "I was watching from a distance and swore not to interfere."

"With what?"

Matt turned and saw the other cowboys all around him on their horses encircling the trio. They were waiting for this moment.

He never saw Deputy Saunders, who had returned from town and was in hiding, watching everything going on at the Double-O Ranch. Still, the deputy remained out of sight, hearing what was being said. He could catch the name, "Matt" very clearly. His curiosity was burning inside him.

"Matt, they're your cowboys, now. Not your Pa's. And they've come to wish you all the luck in the world."

"Hell. I'm gonna need all the luck I can get. I also need this damn weather to hold back."

The deputy thought for sure he heard the word "Pa", and his face turned upwards with his ear to the wind. He could not make out the rest of what was said, but he watched as the metamorphosis continued.

"It's your Pa's lucky hat, Matt," Dan said. He wore it on every drive."

"Even the last one?" Matt asked.

He looked intently into the faces of each of the cowboys.

"We saved it when we buried your pa," Dan said.

Matt settled on the soft brown eyes of Beth as everyone held his breath and waited. His hand reached up to his brim and he took off his own worn and shaped Stetson and sailed it to the wind. He accepted his Pa's hat from Dan and proudly placed it on his head.

He sat back in his saddle and smiled at Beth. Looking at the cowboys he said, "I am not my dad. I am not a rancher -- yet."

Almost at the sound of his last word, lightning bolted from the sky, and a clatter of thunder followed. The cowboys resumed their positions for the drive, and as it began to sprinkle, Matt yelled out, "Head 'em out, Dan."

More thunder came out of the hills. Matt had been unaccustomed to this type of weather, having been away from Montana so long. He asked Slick, "You sure it's not gonna rain."

"Sun will be out all day. Might get some rain tonight though in Weatherby. See you in Belle Fourche, Matt."

"Or sooner."

Beth sidled her horse over to Matt's, leaned over and gave him a big kiss. He wrapped his huge arm around her shoulders and brought her in closer with a kiss that seemed like eternity to both. "You picked one hell of a time to start this."

"Never let a cowboy leave in anger."

"I'll be back."

"I know you will."

"Does this mean anything?"

"Maybe." Then she added, "Just get those cows sold and the money back in time."

"It's gonna be a long ride. See you before Thanksgiving." He rode out a little, looked back and whispered, "Save some more of those for me. I'm comin' back."

As he rode away, he could hear her faintly say, "As many as you want, cowboy."

He gave out his rebel yell and motioned for them to move out.

Deputy Saunders continued watching, becoming extremely jealous at a stranger kissing the girl he had a crush on. He figured it was Matt Andersen. What he could not understand was why he wasn't dead. More importantly, why had he returned.

Matt watched Beth ride back to the ranch, as he leaned forward a little to keep his horse gently walking towards Belle Fourche. The feeling was good. "Maybe I should be a rancher," he thought. Another high-in-the-sky lightning bolt struck out across the plains putting a quick end to his thought of being a rancher. The cows were in front of him, and he watched as the other cowboys moved them along. He thought again, "It's gonna be a long, hard ride. Well. Let's go Bear." He had given his horse its name.

CHAPTER 30

THE DEPUTY STIRS UP TROUBLE

It had been four days since Matt had left. In the meantime, the deputy had returned to Bozeman to report his findings to the sheriff. Sheriff Wiseman was a man with a lot of patience. He could understand that part of what the deputy was saying could be true; however, he also knew that the deputy was in love with Beth. He also knew that Beth was handling the estate for Mrs. Andersen since before she had passed away. Matt showing up on the Double-O Ranch was cause for alarm, if indeed it was Matt. After all, he was the sheriff when the freight office robbery incident took place. He would probably be able to recognize Matt, if he had a good enough look at him.

Trying to assure the deputy that he would investigate the matter was no consolation to the deputy who wanted swifter action. The sheriff said, "I'll ride out and talk with Beth in a coupla days and see what she has to say about all this."

"I already know what she's gonna say. I want ya ta go out there with me and talk with her now."

"Son, I've got a busy afternoon tomorrow that leaves me no time to run way out to the Double-O. If you want to, go ahead. But don't poke your nose in too far. You just might get it chopped off. Let me know what you find out."

"I'll do jest that thing."

"Right now, why don't you get yourself some sleep here while I make some rounds."

When Deputy Saunders rode up to the Double-O Ranch. lBeth was by the well, drawing water Slick was in the saddle behind the barn preparing to lead the second group of cowboys onto the trail, when he caught a glimpse of the deputy returning.

"Mornin', Beth." The deputy tipped his hat.

She had heard him ride up but waited for him to address her. Without turning, she said, "Mornin' Bill. What brings you out so early in the day?"

"You're looking beautiful as ever, Beth."

"And you're not seeing my face, Mr. Saunders. Else you would notice that I was not expecting company."

"Yes. I mean, no. I was admiring your beauty, Beth. I think you are the most handsomest woman I ever laid eyes on."

Turning, she picked up the bucket of water and poured some of it into a smaller pail to carry. "And I'll ask again, what brings you out this way, Deputy Saunders?"

"I'd certainly feel more easy if you'd call me, Bill."

"And what brings you out this way, Deputy Saunders?"

Dismounting, he took the pail from her and carried it as they walked towards the house. "You have a gentleman from Texas working on this ranch."

"Is that a question, or a statement?"

"I was told that he goes by the name of Matt Jorgenson."

She walked into the house as he opened the door for her. "Why are you concerned who works on this ranch, Deputy?"

"I am told that he might be Matt Andersen."

"Oh! And him being dead all these years. Now, Deputy, if that is all you have to talk about, I need to be finishing up for my bath, if you don't be a mindin', now."

"And that's another thing. Why are you staying way out here?"

Jean entered the kitchen from the far bedroom and joined in the conversation. "She's staying with me while my son is on a cattle drive, and I promised to help Fong on the ranch with the cooking for the men when they return."

Assuming that all the men had gone on the cattle drive, he asked, "But the men are not here? Are they, Jean?"

On that note, Slick rode over to the house, dismounted, and entered through the back door leading to the kitchen. Hearing the question as he approached, he answered, "We've fifteen men getting ready to meet with the others on the trail." Taking a drink from the pail, he asked, "What you doin' way out here, Deputy?"

"I heard the men were all gone."

"Well, we're not, Deputy. If you have any dealings with us, I would mind you to ask them of me, and not any of my guests." Slick opened the door of the kitchen and showed the deputy his way out.

Two ranch hands came and escorted the deputy to his horse.

"I just heard. That's all."

The deputy mounted up and began to ride back towards Bozeman. Nearing the cemetery, he stopped his horse, looked back and asked, "Looks like a new grave. Who died?"

Slick mounted his horse and rode up to the gravesite with the deputy following him. "Mrs. Andersen, a few days back."

The deputy looked once more at the new grave, then at Matt's head marker. "If I were to dig up that grave, would I find Matt's body?"

"Wasn't here when he was buried. 'Spect so. Wanna give it a try?"

"Hope I never have to."

Slick stared down at the deputy causing him to swallow hard and head his horse back to Bozeman. "If you come back to visit us bring a warrant or don't come at all." Certain the deputy would not return; he rode up the trail to join his cowboys.

On the road back, the deputy stopped by the Reverend George Riordan's house. It was an impressive house for a minister. It seemed that the townspeople built it better after his father was killed in the botched-up freight office robbery where Lukas and Jeff were also killed.

Seeing the carriage in the back, and the Riordan horse stabled, led him to believe the reverend was home.

The reverend came out and met the deputy on the front porch, where they sat and began talking.

"Looks to me, Brother Saunders, you got a lot on your mind."

The reverend's wife, Martha, came out with two glasses of lemonade which was the custom on a warm day when company arrived, and gave it to the gentlemen as they sat on chairs facing each other. "Want anything to eat, deputy?" she asked.

"No ma'am, thanks." Looking quizzically at the reverend, he asked, "Reverend Riordan, I got a question for you. What if I were to tell you that Matt Andersen was still alive and living right under your nose?"

"Well, Brother Saunders, I believe in the resurrection. I preach it."

"I don't mean from the dead."

"Brother Saunders. Matt was killed in a bank robbery. His body is buried on the Double-O Ranch."

"Yes sir. But remembering what people said about their being three people in the robbery and all."

"Proved to be two, Brother Saunders. Lukas and Matthew Andersen."

"I'm tellin' you that Matt is still alive."

The reverend put his glass of lemonade down which he had been sipping slowly while listening closely to every word the deputy was saying, and yet believing none of it. "Why are you telling me all this?"

"Ain't you even interested in gettin' back at the man who killed your pa?"

"We buried them, deputy. I saw the bodies, and read over their bodies myself, even though I strained to do so. Ain't nothin' goin' to bring back Pa, or anyone else, leastwise, Matt Andersen."

"No sir. If'n he were dead in the first place. I don't know, I jest don't know, but I heard them a talkin' and I saw a man who looked a heck of a lot like Wil Andersen calling himself Matt Jorgensen. Don't ya get it, Reverend? Matt Jorgensen. Matt Andersen."

The Reverend looked more puzzled than before and furrowed his eyebrows as if he was starting to believe some of what the deputy was saying. "How do you know what he looked like. You were a kid. Did Wil have a brother? A nephew?"

"I don't know. Never figured."

"Well, then that would kind of explain the similarities, both being Swedish. No, deputy. As much as I might like to believe you, I can't. I know who I buried."

"Something else I didn't tell ya."

The minister threw him a stern look as he sipped another drink.

"I heard them mention the word, 'Pa', as if talkin' about Mister Andersen. Just as clear as you talkin' to me right now."

"Sure the wind weren't playin' tricks with your hearin', deputy?"

"And he put on Wil's coat and hat and sat on the horse jest like Wil Andersen. No sir. That was Matt Andersen I saw. I oughta know. I growed up with him."

"Keep talking, son."

"Say it were, Matt. Say he weren't killed. Then, maybe there were three men in that holdup, and Matt was the third man, like we heard about. He got away."

"To where, deputy?"

"Don't know. But I'm sure as heck it's worth checkin' out. Now, don't it?"

Martha heard what was being said from inside the house and came out. "George. What does it mean?"

"Well, Martha, it might not mean anything, yet. We don't rightly know it is Matt."

"Don't know it ain't, either, if you excuse me, ma'am."

"We done buried the men responsible for it, George. Ain't we?"

"Sure, Martha. I'm a thinkin' however, that what the deputy here says kinda makes sense. Deputy, can you check with the McDougals at the general store and tell them what you told us. See if anything comes from all this presupposin'."

"That's been too many years now, George. He can't help us any now," Martha interrupted.

Standing up, the Reverend pointed his finger at the deputy and said, "If it is Matt Andersen, I wanta offer a five-hundred-dollar reward for his capture. You tell the people in town that." Then, turning to face Martha he added, "If there's any doubt about it being him, I'll retract that reward."

Then he looked at the deputy, and said, "You hear me, son. I don't want blood money for an innocent man's life."

The deputy finished his drink, looked at the Reverend embracing his wife, and stepped off the porch and onto his horse. The deputy rode off, leaving the Reverend and his wife in the house with their thoughts.

CHAPTER 31

THE RETURN OF WIL ANDERSEN

Deputy Saunders walked into the sheriff's office with a strut that denoted a positive attitude and arrogant pride. "Where's Whitey?"

Sheriff Wiseman walked out of the back cell into the front office with a broom in his hand. "Right here, Bill. Doin' some chores my deputy should be doing."

"It's him. It's Matt Andersen."

"What the hell you talking about? Why are you so dad burned sure about this? You hear rumors, and that's all they are, and you're sure you got a bead on a dead man."

"Cause, I saw him. All dressed up like his old man. It's either him, or Wil Andersen has come back from the grave. I heard them mentioning his name. And you can't tell me that's him buried on the hill, now neither. Cause I'm gonna talk with the McDougals and they're gonna tell me it's him."

"Damn, son. You better settle down right now. You've got a mean streak up your backside that's gotta come out."

"I ain't neither, sheriff. I'm doin' your job you should be doin', instead of all that paper stuff. Here we've got ourselves a real killer in town. And Reverend Riordan has offered a five-hundred-dollar reward for him, dead or alive."

"Whoa! Now just a damn minute, son. You're goin' faster than a locomotive outa Kansas. You told the Reverend about this?"

"Yes, and he agreed with me. Said I could tell you to tell everyone about the reward."

"What else did he say?"

"He told me to talk with the McDougals to confirm what they saw at the freight office robbery? That's all."

"Hell. The McDougals don't know anything. They're bragging, that's all. They were too damn scared to see what was going on, you oughta know that. And that doesn't sound like the Reverend to me. You put him up to all this."

"I didn't say anything that weren't the truth. You can ask him."

"And he thinks it could be Wil's son, too? Well, listen, you take the broom here and finish up where I left off. I'll hop over to the McDougals and talk with them just the same. Who knows? Maybe they can shed some light on this thing, I'm sure as hell certain it ain't Matt Andersen."

"No disrespect, sir, but he told me to talk to them."

"And you will, just after I visit with them first."

"Why don't I tag along with you?"

"All right son. But watch your mouth. I don't want you puttin' words into their mouths. They're fine people."

"You talk to them. I'll jest tell them what I saw and heard."

"What you think you saw and heard. Jest makes no sense all this with Matt comin' back from the grave."

The walk over to the McDougals' general store was short, being located next to the sheriff's office. Both Jim and Linda McDougal were in the store, it was the end of the month and inventory had to be counted. The store was empty, and the pair was taking advantage of it.

Whitey bade them good morning, and then told Jim about the deputy's thoughts. "Not having been there, Jim, I think you can understand my reluctance to all this. But my deputy here seems to think Matt Andersen is still alive."

"Matt Andersen? Wil's son who was killed in that freight office robbery?"

"Yes. I seem to recollect that you were one who said you saw a third person at that robbery. Still think the same?"

"Sure do. I think so. Yep. Zeb, too. Zeb fer sure saw him. 'Ceptin' he's dead, now."

"What did you see, Jim."

Linda came from around the counter and joined the conversation, asking, "Jim! What's going on?"

"Why? What're ya gonna do?" Jim asked.

"There's a five-hunert dollar reward for his capture, if it's Matt," the deputy spoke up.

"Matt? Matt, who?"

The sheriff looked chagrined at the deputy, smacking him with his hat. "Oh, Jim. Bill here thinks he's seen Matt Andersen. Now we know that can't be because he's dead. Still, because you said there was a third person involved, he seems to think it might be Matt."

"Matt Andersen? He's dead!" said Jim. "Ain't he?"

"Well, that's what we thought, now Bill stopped by the Reverend's house, and told him what he thought. Naturally, the Reverend went and offered a reward for his capture, thinkin' it might be Matt."

"Well, now, I didn't say I actually saw Matt. But come to think about it, yes, I might have at one time or other. Come to think of it, it did look like Matt."

"Jim. Did you or didn't you see a third person?"

"You know I did. I said afore I did, and I say it now, I did. Do that mean I get the reward if I tell ya what I saw?"

"You know better. First, we got to determine if who you saw was this here Matt fella."

"If'n it be him, then do I get it?"

"The real money would go to the person who captures him. If in fact it is Matt Andersen. Right now, we only know that he's a stranger at the Double-O and goes by the name of Matt Jorgensen. Might be a twist there somewhere. Dunno."

"Well, I seed him, as clear as I'm standin' here."

"You said you saw a third person. You never mention that it was Matt that got away."

"Sure, I did. Didn't I, Linda? I said it was Matt. I'm sure I did."

Linda attempted to say something but was urged by Jim to stay out of it. "No matter. I knowed it were. You got him down at the jail?"

"No. He's still up at the ranch."

"Then, you gotta protect me. I ain't gonna tell on someone lessen I get protection. That's the way it's gotta be. Now I gotta get back to work."

With that said, Jim turned to Linda and the couple continued taking inventory.

Whitey and the deputy began to leave. The sheriff said to his deputy, "Well, that's the same story all over again.

The deputy hesitated for the moment. "You go, Whitey. I just want to buy a can of peaches."

"Okay," Whitey said. "But come on back to the jail right away. There's still that matter of the broom."

Seeing the sheriff leave, the deputy turned to Jim and said, "If you're sure it's Matt, I'll see that you get protection.

Jim and Linda looked at the deputy with a curious stare, and Jim stuttered, "A hunnert dollars?"

Linda kept quiet but was disappointed in her husband.

In the deputy's mind, he began wondering how it would be to be married to Beth, if Matt was put in jail. "Get me a can of peaches."

Linda stared at Jim, and said, "Store's closed, Bill. Can't ya see we're takin' inventory?" She pulled a can of peaches from the shelf and told the deputy, "Pay me later. It'll mess up my count now."

Bill left the store hoping something substantial would come from Jim. Nothing ever did. As he left, he heard Linda reprimanding Jim.

"You never said that Matt was the other man. You thought like the rest of us that Matt was killed." She turned and took her pencil and tablet in hand and resumed the counting. She never said another word about it.

Jim thought about it, but never said anything else. Just thought about it.

Bill still believed that it was Matt Andersen he saw at the ranch. He was a good deputy, but also hot-headed. He was determined to prove he was right.

When he entered the office, Whitey handed him the broom, and walked out. "You stay here."

"Where you goin?"

Mounting his horse, the sheriff answered, "Cause of you, I'm riding out to find this Matt fella and have a talk with him. Anyone comes askin' for me, tell them so. I'll be stoppin' by the Reverend's first."

"Do I put a reward out for him?

Straddling his horse, Whitey said, "A reward is a reward. You know what will happen if you do. Keep quiet about this until I get back. Now, that's an order, Bill."

The deputy stood with the broom in his hand, and said, "If it ain't him, then he should prove it. If'n it is, the Reverend will be a payin' the reward. And we will have got ourselves a killer." Again, his mind was on getting rid of Matt and having Beth to himself.

CHAPTER 32

A LETTER

It's usually a two-hour ride to Reverend Riordan's, but Whitey took four, taking time out for a little fishing on the way out. This way, it gave the horse time to rest, and also to rest his own tired, old bones. Riding was no longer his strength. He would rather fish. His wife had been gone some three or four years, and now and he was alone. Fishing had always been his sport, and now it was his pastime.

He made sure he stopped by the Reverend Riordan's 'stead to talk with him and his wife about the reward before going on to the Double-O. After a cordial greeting at the Reverend's house, Whitey and the Reverend entered the house and sat down in the front room.

"What if this is an innocent man, Preacher?"

"Then there's nothin' to hide. And I don't have to pay the reward."

"But you're offerin' a five-hundred dollars reward for a man's head, that could get the man killed."

"If it is the man who killed my father, then vengeance will have been requited."

"'Vengeance is mine, saith the Lord.' Am I right?"

"Using the Good Book agin' me ain't gonna change my mind, Whitey. My father was shot in the back. Your deputy seems to think that this man, Matt, on the Double-O, is that same man. I don't know and, honestly, I hope to God it isn't."

"Then you could be sending an innocent man to his death."

"How?"

"Five hundred dollars will turn many a man's mind to larceny. Some will want to go after him and bring him back dead."

"The reward said nothing about bringing him back dead."

"The reward is for a killer, Preacher. If the killer is to be brought back, he's usually across his saddle. You still want to offer the reward?"

"What d'ya think, Whitey? What would you do if'n you were in my shoes?"

"I'd leave it in the hands of the law, and let me have a chance to bring him in. Alive."

"What if he gets you first?"

"Then you can offer your reward."

"Will you give me that chance, now?"

Martha Riordan walked into the room with her usual glasses of lemonade and offered the sheriff a glass.

"Thank you, ma'am."

"What brings you all the way out here?"

The Reverend addressed her. "He wants the chance to bring this Matt fella in himself. Claims the reward could do more harm than good."

"Will you bring him back, Sheriff?" she asked.

"I'll try. You haveta give me that chance."

"That's his job, as I see it, George. I told you, I never took stock in that story about a third man. And I don't now."

The Reverend looked at the sheriff and said, "You're probably right. Go ahead, Whitey. Check out his story. Forget the reward. It was done in anger anyway."

The sheriff drank his lemonade down without stopping, smiled, and said, "Thanks, Preacher. Ma'am. I've gotta stop my deputy from doing any more damage."

Bidding them adieu, he mounted his horse and began his ride to the Double-O Ranch. He had ridden a short distance when he was overtaken by his deputy.

"Bill. Where are you headed?"

"To join you."

"Why?"

"To capture this Matt Andersen. Figured you could use my help. Didn't see any harm in it."

The sheriff shifted in his saddle, he was tired of riding, and raised his Stetson back on his head. "Bill. There ain't no reward. The Reverend took it back."

"Why?"

"Cause I convinced him to let the law bring him in. I told the Reverend that I would find out who he is and what he's up to. And I don't need your help. Now git back to town and guard the jail."

Bill's face looked white for a moment and then he grew speechless.

"What's the matter, Bill. You look sick."

Bill regained his composure and said, "Might as well be."

"You wanna rest a while?"

"I saw . . . I saw some men gatherin' in town to ride out for that reward money, already."

"Goddamit. Did you tell them?"

"No, sir. They heard it from Jim. He went on down to the saloon and had a few drinks when he discussed the matter with the bartender. Some of the men there heard it. Some took off."

"Who?"

"For starters, Pokerface Jack and his brother Art. Another man by the name of Phil."

"Mean ones. Are they still in town?"

"Don't know. Don't think so."

"Well, you ride back to town, and get a hold of them. Let them know there is no reward. Right now!"

"I know I'm right."

"The hell you are, kid. That man is now a hunted outlaw. He's prey for any man's bullet. And it'll find him, if we don't find him first. Now beat it, fast."

"And you?"

"Git!"

Bill saw the most serious look he had ever seen in the sheriff's eyes. Knowing his job, he jerked the reins and galloped towards Bozeman.

The sheriff continued his ride to the Double-O. As he rode up to the porch of the Andersen house, Beth was waiting with a warm greeting.

"Good morning, Sheriff Wiseman. What brings you out this way so far from town?"

"You can call me Whitey, Miss Paterson. Everyone else does. Got any coffee?"

"Jean's in the kitchen. Light down and I'll get you a cup." She led the sheriff into the kitchen, and added, "You can call me Beth. Everyone else does."

Once around the kitchen table, the sheriff explained his reason for visiting the ranch. "Well, Beth, my deputy tells me you've got a new man on the ranch. Goes by the handle of 'Matt'."

"Came in from Texas with Dan. Helped bring back Shorty's body from Texas."

"Oh? What was Shorty doing in Texas?"

Jean answered while pouring fresh coffee into his big cup. "Three of the boys went to Texas just to get away for a while. Came back with exciting news about longhorns. Shorty got killed by an outlaw and was brought back here for buryin'."

"I see. Who were the other two boys?"

"My son, Dan, and Matt Jorgensen."

"Where they at now?

Jean continued, "Dan's with the herd. All the boys are gone on the trail drive."

Beth added to keep the sheriff from asking too many questions, "Except Slim Honeycutt, Whitey. He stayed behind in Texas. Found himself a girlfriend and plans on getting married."

"And this Matt fella. How come he left Texas to come up here?"

Jean answered, "To talk about bringing a herd of longhorns up here. Dan talked him into coming, thinking he'd do our ranch some good. Whatcha aiming at, Whitey?"

The sheriff sipped his coffee as he rose from the table and looked around at the ranch through the back door. "The ranch, the Double-O, I remember when Wil built this place."

Noticing his cup was empty, he held it up for Jean to fill.

"There was a five-hundred-dollar reward on that gentleman's head."

"A reward on Matt's head? What in tarnation for?"

"I said, 'was'. The Reverend Riordan put it there." He took a sip of his coffee and continued. "For the murder of his pa. I talked him into calling it off. Giving me a chance to talk to this Matt."

"Who murdered his pa?"

"Wil's sons, Matt and Lukas."

"The two buried on the hillside, Sheriff?" Beth asked.

"Supposedly."

"If he's buried on the hillside, how could there be a reward on another man's head?"

"Deputy of mine said he saw this Matt Jorgensen fella fittin' the description of Matt Andersen. Mighty curious of him. Said he watched and saw how he put on Wil's old clothes and looked jest like Wil did."

"Oh, that. He was riding trail and needed some duds. Nothing wrong with that, is there sheriff?"

"Not mine to argue. But I've got to talk to him. That is, before someone else does." He took another sip of his coffee. "So, who gets it?"

Beth asked, but with her mind concentrating on the reward for Matt. "Who gets what?"

"Gets the ranch?"

"That's why I'm here, Sheriff." Beth replied as she watched him look the spread over. "There's a clause in Annie's that will cause the ranch to stay operating the same as it has been."

"Oh? Then, like I said, who gets it?"

Beth stood up and walked over to the sheriff. Looking at him right in the eye without flinching, she said, "I'll be filing that claim in court when I finalize everything here."

"I understand. What concerns me now is this fella, Matt."

Jean said, "Sheriff, are you hard of hearing. Mrs. Andersen's attorney done said she's taking the matter to town. Anything wrong?"

"Don't know, Jean. Yet. But I need to speak to this here Matt fella. Guess I'll be riding out to join the herd. How long you say they been gone?"

Jean answered, "Didn't. Two groups. You'll find Matt in the first group. He took off over a week ago."

Beth added, "Still want to go after him?"

Lifting his Stetson off his head with his fingers, he scratched his forehead and answered her. "No. But I have ta. Damn deputy forced me into going."

Beth reminded the sheriff, as if he needed any reminding. "He's not in your jurisdiction anyway, if he crosses the county line, Sheriff."

He mounted and pulled his hat down tight over his eyes to keep out the glare of the sun. "I jest wanna talk with him, Beth. Marshal's same distance away in t'other direction. Guess I'll be goin'."

"Hold up, Sheriff. I do have something for you." Beth went back into the house and returned with an unopened envelope addressed to the sheriff. Giving it to him, she said, "Here. This belongs to you."

He looked at the sealed envelope and asked, "What is it?"

"I haven't read it. Supposed to remain sealed for you to open. It's a letter from Mrs. Andersen. She instructed me to turn it over to you. It was one of her last requests."

He immediately opened it. Taking his glasses from his inside coat pocket, he read the letter quietly to himself.

The two ladies looked on.

"Well?" Beth asked.

"You know what it says?"

Beth shook her head.

"Well, little lady, bless you. You know, you are the most stubbornness woman I have ever met, and I have met plenty, but you'll be pleased. Now, for sure I'm going to have to find Matt."

"Why?"

"Because he's Matt Andersen, for openers. And to save his cantankerous hide. This here letter is evidence of his innocence." Then, leaning down off his horse, he said, "Young ladies. I've known from day one that Matt wasn't killed, but I was hoping for his innocence. For these many years I had to live with this secret inside me."

"All these years?" Jean threw back.

He nodded and sat back up in his saddle.

"The guy who was killed jest didn't measure up to bein' Matt. Wil know'd it, too. Somethin' about a bracelet Wil gave Matt."

"Bracelet?" Jean asked.

"The dead man didn't have one. Wil gave Matt one that Matt swore he'd never take off."

"I saw Matt wearing a bracelet," Beth added.

"Well, now you know," Whitey said.

"Then why the pretense?" Beth asked.

"Because, if the townsfolk knew at any time, there woulda been a lynchin'. Wil and I kept it our secret. I didn't know Annie knew. 'Til now. And this letter is from an eyewitness. Good as gold."

Jean looked up at him and said, "I'll be dipped."

"If you see anyone coming out this way, tell 'em the reward won't be any good."

The ladies looked at one another, half smiled, and then watched the sheriff spur his horse into a gallop to follow the trail ride. "Like who?" Beth yelled out.

"Bounty hunters."

"Sheriff. The letter. I need it for the court."

"It'll be safe with me. See you in a week." The sheriff was out of sight in a few minutes leaving the ladies completely bewildered at the ranch. The letter was tightly concealed inside his coat pocket. He murmured to himself. "Matt Andersen. Still alive."

CHAPTER 33

BOUNTY HUNTERS

Later, that same day, Beth changed into her riding clothes. She and Jean talked as she dressed.

"What kind of man was Wil, Jean?"

"Oh. I don't rightly know. Proud, I suppose. Strong, good lookin', loved Annie. He also loved his sons."

"How'd he die?"

"Dan said that this guy with long hair baited him into an argument, and they started beating up on him. This guy with long hair, and all the others. Beat him 'til he was down, and continued beatin' him."

Beth winced. "What'd the cowboys do?"

"Are you sure you want to know?"

Beth agreed with a nod, biting down hard on her lip.

"Nothin'," Jean continued. "At first, as Dan tells it, they were glad Old Iron Nuts was gettin' his. Jest like he dished it out, but then the beatin' got brutal.

"When they let up on him, he rose, stood straight, and walked out on them. He said he didn't want any part of the cowboys. That's when the rustlers started shootin' him.

"They counted over fifteen bullet holes in him. Finally, a drover rode in, took his rifle out and shot him. That's when the cowboys vowed to get even."

Beth thought long and hard over the scene.

"Wish I hadn't told ya?"

"No. I'm glad you did. Just makes me see the harshness of this country, and how men can act so brutal at times."

Her horse was readied for her by one of the wranglers when she stepped outside. Taking the reins, she climbed into the saddle from the porch for her ride into Bozeman. "Got to get back to my job being an attorney, if we're ever going to get this will settled. I'll be at the Murphy's Boarding House if you need me."

She rode out towards Bozeman on a trail that wound by the foothills. It was not a straight road, but easier than cutting across the hills, and she could relax in the saddle for the long ride.

Pokerface Jack and his brother Art, along with three other worthless men had been riding towards the ranch when they ran into Beth.

Her fine figure of a woman in a saddle appealed to the men as they rode up after her. It seemed that a man's objective could sometimes be thwarted by the presence of a beautiful woman.

Seeing them coming, she spurred her horse off the road and up the hill to evade them. The men followed her with their horses panting from the long ride from town. Her fresh horse gave her the advantage.

Pokerface stopped his horse and removed his rifle from its boot and took aim at her. A shot from the rifle hit a tree and ricocheted off, missing her. A second shot came closer causing her horse to spook. She fell from her horse and rolled partly down the hill resting against a stump. She was hurt and unconscious.

Pokerface rode up with the other men, but he alone dismounted and ran to her side. Seeing that she was injured, he offered to help her but her limp body was too heavy for his grip.

Her eyes opened slightly to give her a glimpse of one of the ugliest men she had ever seen. His burly body reeking with body odor, alcohol, and bad breath, caused her to resist.

She fought as hard as she could to resist Pokerface's advancements. The harder she fought, the more he tore at her clothes, and the more she felt the pain in her sides from her injuries. Her blouse was torn from her body partially revealing her breasts banded by her corset. Her fingernails caught hold of his face and dug in, bringing blood which quickly covered his cheek and heavy beard.

His hand slapped her across her face and knocked her back to the ground. She lay motionless as he began unbuckling his pants.

Art dismounted with the other men to join in as they saw this as a moment of fantasy. Their thinking was that she was too much woman for one man.

But Pokerface did not want their company. He drew down on them with his forty-four and told them, "Keep away. She's mine. Git yur own goddam woman."

Art responded with a wild-faced grin, "I spotted her first. By rights, she should be mine."

"You come any closer and you won't have any need for a woman anymore. Hear me?"

Knowing his brother was bluffing, and that he had the height of the hill in his favor, Art lunged at Pokerface with his full body, knocking him down the hill. The two began fighting, and the more they fought, the further down the hill they rolled.

The other men rode down the hill after them with their horses kicking up dirt and leaves in all directions.

Beth's eyes opened, and when she saw what was happening, she raised herself up with as much strength that she could muster and mounted her horse. She had great difficulty swinging her leg over the saddle, but with grit, she did it. With her spurs digging into the horse's ribcage, she rode further up the hill to a trail and galloped away. The men never knew she left until the fight was over.

From a far distance away and out of sight, she watched the men as they mounted and rode towards the Double-O.

She rode easy for a while. Still a distance from the ranch, she brought her mount to a halt, slid out of the saddle, and lay down on the leaf-strewn ground.

Arriving at the ranch, the bounty hunters were coldly greeted by Jean and her two ranch hands, but they knew from the looks of the ranch that the round-up was on and Belle Fourche was the destination.

All they had to do was follow the tracks. They also learned from Jean what the sheriff had said about the reward being "no good". They paid no attention to her and knowing that the sheriff was hours ahead of them, they left and followed his tracks.

Beth's horse had left its place beside her and wandered down the slope. She was too weak to go after it and watched it gallop towards the barn.

The ranch hands who were cleaning the barn watched the riderless horse come across the meadows and towards them. One of them immediately alerted Jean, while the other caught it, and brought it around.

Knowing the danger that she was in; Jean ordered her buggy to be brought around. She headed towards Bozeman while the ranch hands mounted up and rode out, following her. One ranch hand took the main road with Jean following close behind. The other, riding Beth's horse, began combing the hills.

Darkness seeped into the hills and began covering her cold, shivering body. Being unconscious kept her from feeling the cold, and the pain of broken ribs, and a banged-up head.

As the ranch hand rode into the hills, he heard no sound from her to attract him. Finally, sighting her, the ranch hand gave a whistle to his friend to join him. Soon, the other ranch hand rode to meet up with him.

Jean brought her buggy up to a halt, waiting for the men. She cried, "Oh, my God!"

One of the men carried Beth to the buggy and, with Jean's help, placed her carefully in the back.

Raising herself up, she tried to yell. Her voice was silent. Jean cupped her mouth with her hand assuring her she was going to be all right, now. "Easy, Beth," she said. "Easy. We've got ya now, honey."

"She's almost dead, Jean." One of the ranch hands observed as he picked up a blanket from inside the buggy.

"Careful, Johnny. Easy with her." Jean took the blanket and wrapped her body with it. Seeing her bruises, and feeling her weak body, she cried out, "Johnny, get in. We've got to get her to a doctor."

She whipped the horses and drove the team to the river. Once there, she brought the team to a halt. She bathed and cleaned Beth's body where the skin was torn and bloody and examined her body for signs of broken bones and bruises. She found the broken ribs where Beth winced at the slightest touch. Washing down the worst wounds, she was careful not to cause any more bleeding.

Johnny brought some tree moss and gave it to her to apply to the wounds. "This'll heal her 'til we get her to the Doc."

She noticed that Beth had fallen asleep. "Thank the good Lord we found her in time. It'll be good for her to sleep now."

Jean cradled her in her arms and held onto her carefully in the buggy, while Johnny drove them towards Bozeman.

CHAPTER 34

A SHERIFF GONE FISHING

On the next evening, the bounty hunters caught sight of the campfire Whitey had made. He had just begun frying the fish he caught in the stream near by. The scent of fresh fish caught the men's attention as they rode into the camp.

"Evenin', Sheriff," was Pokerface Jack's greeting as he began to dismount.

"Didn't know I asked you in, Pokerface."

"Oh, you know'd us, Sheriff. We won't do you no harm. We're all from Bozeman."

"Hi, Art. And I know you, Phil from Bar X. And you're, Jerome, and, my stars, it's little Skinny Henry. All from separate ranches. What brings you fellas way out here on the Bozeman Trail?"

"Oh, you know, Sheriff. Same as you. We're out lookin' for this here Matt fella," Pokerface answered.

"What makes you think I'd be lookin' for him?"

"Cause you're out of your territory," Art replied, bending down by the fire to take a closer look at the fish that were frying.

"I'm just fishin'. Found the fishin' to be good up here. Always come to this spot."

"Maybe," Pokerface added.

"This here, Matt fella. What if he isn't the one, you know, you're lookin' for?" Whitey asked, nonchalantly.

"Whatcha drivin' at, Sheriff?" Art asked.

"Grab a plate and help yourself, Art. There's enough fish to fill all your gullets. Told ya I was fishin'."

"Answer him, Sheriff," commanded Pokerface.

"Well. If he's not the fella he's supposed to be, then there will be no reward. Catch my drift?"

The men stood up straight with a tin in their hands and looked at one another. Phil surmised, "Then we don't get nothin'."

"You lookin' to catch up with this here Matt fella?" Whitey asked.

"Yes sirree. Five hunnert smackers. A lot more than we make in a year," Art answered.

"Go ahead. Sit yourselves, I've got enough fish for all of ye." Whitey's hand attended a pan that was frying the fish over a low lit fire, while sprinkling a little salt on them with his other fingers. "Coffee's hot, if'n you got a cup."

"Now, that's right neighborly of ya, Sheriff," Pokerface said.

"Well, it's a cold night, and a fella kinda likes sharing a cup around the fire with someone he knows," Whitey added.

"Yep. Ain't that the truth, Sheriff."

The sheriff had an uneasy feeling in his bones while he watched the men lift their saddles from their horses and made themselves comfortable around his campfire. Not that this was anything out of the ordinary, but being a sheriff, he had knack for sensing trouble in his thirty years as a sheriff; this was one of those nights.

"How'd you fellas ever decide to go in together to become bounty hunters?"

Art leaned back against a log and took out some makings for a cigarette. "We were playing poker in town when we heard about this heah ree-ward. Five hunnert smackers. Whoowee, that sure is a lot of money."

Skinny Henry said rather excitedly, showing his poorly kept teeth, "Yeah. If'n I get my hands on that much money, I can buy Ma somethin' new from the catalog. Somethin' she's always wanted."

Pokerface added, "What we mean to say, Sheriff, is that thar money is gonna make us rich."

"Five hundred dollars? Split amongst five men."

"Four men and a kid, Sheriff. Skinny don't get a full split like the rest of us 'cause he ain't big enough." Jerome's huge voice bellowed out into the night followed by a rumble of laughter that shook the campsite.

Skinny rebounded with pouted lips but was shoved to the ground by Jerome as he got up to attack him. "Settle down, Skinny. Whacha get is half what I get. Ain't that enough, seein' I'm bigger'n you?"

The rest of the evening saw the men get more rambunctious as they drank hard liquor to wash their fish down, and smoked heavy, dirty cigars. The sheriff slept near the fire with one eye open the rest of the night.

Seemed the men never slept come morning. Jerome spent much of the night throwing his sticker at the log where Skinny lay drunk. Once he missed and stuck it in Skinny's boot causing Skinny to cuss and throw dirt. All Jerome did was laugh.

However, the rising of the sun found the bounty hunters fast asleep and the sheriff riding out of the camp. Away from the camp, he never looked back but gave a sigh of relief to be out of their company.

An hour later he met up with them again waiting for him in the middle of the trail.

Sitting drunk on his horse, Pokerface addressed him in a slurred speech. "Where ya goin', Sheriff? Ya forgot to tell us last night."

"Don't know what you mean, Pokerface."

"Don't know what I mean. Ya heah that fellas? Now, Sheriff, we didn't get a chance to politely thank you for all that fish ya cooked up for us last night. Ain't proper we let it go without thankin' ya."

"Thanks, Sheriff," Art said.

Jerome rode his horse around to the back of the sheriff and eyed him carefully.

Realizing all the men were still suffering from their night of drinking, he began to speak to them softly and without trying to anger them any more than what they appeared to be now.

"Gentlemen, I hate to tell ya, but there ain't no reward."

Pokerface looked angry with grit teeth. "No reward? What you mean, Sheriff?"

"Reverend Riordan, who offered the reward, retracted it. There is no reward."

"You don't have any intentions of trying to get the reward yourself, are ya Sheriff?" Art jeered.

"No, son. A sheriff don't get a reward. He sees that it's given."

"You said there's no reward. What you mean?" Pokerface retorted.

The sheriff knew that these men were in this for keeps. He knew also that what he said was not pleasant to their ears.

Pokerface drew his .44 and pointed it at the sheriff. "Mighty pretty words, Whitey. But I don't believe ya. My boys and I are thinkin' you're riding out here to warn this heah Matt fella about our comin'. Ain't that right, boys?"

The men showed assent with Pokerface by pulling out their weapons, pointing them at the sheriff.

More sweat than he ever knew flowed from every pore in his body. Whitey ran out of stories to tell and thought of the letter buried deep inside his coat pocket; the one that could free Matt, but it was evidence. Evidence he did not want to share with anyone at this time. He also had a letter from his sister in another pocket. Knowing the men and knowing that this was his only piece of evidence, he gambled on using his sister's letter. That was, if they would let him.

Seeing him reach inside his coat, thinking he was going for a gun, the men cocked their pistols, Jerome cocked his shotgun.

"I have a letter inside my coat. If I'm allowed to get it, I think this whole silly thing can come to an end right now."

"Silly thing? You call this a silly thing. I'm about to blow your head off with this here shotgun," Jerome growled.

"Hold it, Jerome," came the command from Pokerface as he sidled up to the sheriff's horse and retrieved the letter. "Let's see what it has to say."

The sheriff held tightly to the letter, hoping beyond hope that Pokerface would let him read it. Pokerface wanted to read it himself. As luck would have it, Pokerface could not read.

Staring at the letter for awhile, he looked up at the men, and then back at the sheriff. Knowing he never learned to read, but ashamed to tell it, he had to ask the sheriff, "What's it say, Sheriff?"

With a sigh of relief, and almost with a laugh, the sheriff answered him. "It says that this here Matt you fellas are set out to get is Matt Andersen."

Art's face smiled as he yelled out, "We're rich. Didn't I tell ye?"

"That's enough for us, Sheriff," Pokerface said.

"Well, it's really a letter written to Mrs. Andersen from a gambler who was playing cards with Matt and his brother the day the minister was killed. And, well, it says, Matt didn't kill the minister."

"Well, what's that mean to us?" Art asked.

"You dumb turd, it mean we ain't rich, like ya been crowin' about all this time," Pokerface answered, slapping Art with the back of his hand. "That right, Sheriff?"

"Yes, Pokerface. Sorry, but it just means that. Of course, it's for the judge to decide. But I must admit, this is strong evidence."

Pokerface brought his .44 up to the sheriff's chin and cocked it. "Give me that letter back." He grabbed the letter from the sheriff and crumpled it in his hands. "Now, loosen your gun belt and give it to me."

The sheriff took his gun belt off and handed it to Pokerface, while watching the looks on the other men's faces. He realized he was about to meet his Maker, and he wanted to see the faces of the men who were about to put him there. "You gonna kill me?"

"No, Sheriff. That'd be too damn foolish. We ain't killers. No sirree. We jest want you to go along with us, see. When we find this heah Matt fella, we want you to recognize us as the rightful inheritors of that reward money."

"I done told you, there won't be any reward."

"Now we heard you. Ain't we boys? But we jest want to make sure. We don't want you to stop us from getting the reward by doing something foolish."

Art asked, "Like what, Pokerface."

"Like telling him about a certain letter." He took a match from his hat band and after striking it on the butt of his pistol, he lit the letter on fire. After it was consumed in flames, he threw it to the wind. As it landed on the ground, the ashes revealed partial words that could still be read on the outside of the envelope by the sheriff as he looked down upon it.

"Mrs. Dorothy Phillips

Route I

Virginia City, Montana

The ashes of Dorothy's letter blew away.

The sheriff looked at Pokerface again with his .44 dangling in his hand.

"Now ain't that sweet," Pokerface said sarcastically.

"What we need with the sheriff, now? The letter's gone. Send him on his way, Pokerface," Skinny said.

Pokerface thought for a second while eyeing the sheriff.

"You're right, Skinny. For once in your life, you're right. You the only one who knows about the letter. Right, Sheriff?"

"No. There are others." He almost mentioned Beth's name, but quickly figured that he would be endangering her life had he done so. Then he thought about Jean possibly knowing about it, too.

"Like who?"

"What ya thinkin', Pokerface?" Art asked.

"I'm a thinkin' that's what Mrs. Wrisley meant when she told us the reward was no good. Well, Sheriff. You've done us a big favor. Now that we know it ain't no good, we gonna let you go, Sheriff. Now, knowin' we ain't harmed you, none and we ain't done nothin' wrong, but burnt a little piece of paper." He continued his tirade, "When we bring Matt in, you can remember this and give us our reward. Right, Sheriff?"

The sheriff knew it was no use to try to reason with them, but he blurted it out anyway. That was his style.

"Mister, there's no possibility of any kind of reward. You understand that? And if you don't let me go now, you will be charged with kidnapping, threatening an officer of the law, willful destruction of evidence, and more that I'll think of later."

"We ain't done all those things. Pokerface, tell him," Art retorted. "Let's go and let him be."

"That's the most sensible thing any of you have said all morning," the sheriff said, as he continued to look at Pokerface. He felt it was now or never to firmly and without showing any fear say, "I'll have my gun belt back."

Still holding the gun belt in one hand, and his .44 in his other, he said, "No, no, that's more'n a year's wages we got comin'." He thought some more, and said, "No one knows about that letter, and about us knowin' 'ceptin the sheriff here."

Whitey said stiffly one more time, "My gun belt, Pokerface."

Pokerface wrestled with it in his hand, as his other hand quivered, holding onto his revolver. Then he said, "Here. It's all yours." And he dropped it to the ground.

The sheriff dismounted, and with his back to Pokerface, knelt to pick it up.

Pokerface leveled his revolver at the sheriff's back and discharged two quick blasts from it. He watched as the sheriff fell face down into the dirt.

The other men were stunned. "You stupid fool! What fer you kilt the sheriff like that? Now we're never goin' to get that money," Art cried out.

"I dunno. I dunno. I had to do it; he was gettin' at me. He asked for it, tellin' me we ain't goin' to get the reward."

"He's right, Pokerface. We ain't, now," Art yelled.

"Hush, up. Nobody knows but us." He turned to the other four and said, "And nobody here is gonna tell. Right?"

There was an uneasy feeling among the men, but they knew they had to show a sign of agreeing with him. They gave him their assented nod.

"What we gonna do now? Tell me that," Skinny asked, twisting his hat in his hands.

"Same as before. Nothin' changes. We're gonna capture ourselves a Matt Andersen. Then we're gonna ride back and collect our reward money."

"You bastard! How we gonna collect our reward when we jest kilt the sheriff? Answer me that," Art asked.

"Cause, you shit-head. The stupid deputy is gonna act in his place and give us the damn reward money. If there be no sheriff, he's gotta take his place and give it to us'n."

"We'll be hung. That's the law," Skinny added real fast and nervously.

"We'll be blamed for his death. They'll lynch us," Art yelled out.

"Thought of that, too. When we come back this way, we pick his body up, take it back to town. In the meantime, we shoot Matt, and blame him for the sheriff's demise. Our word about what happened, and we're law-abidin' people."

"We're gonna keep killin'," Skinny quickly said.

"If need be. You scared?" Pokerface asked.

Skinny turned his horse and galloped away as fast as he could. Pokerface went after him, firing his '44. A bullet had Skinny's name on it, and he fell, his horse ran away.

Pokerface returned to the others and replaced his revolver. "I'm sorry. Hell, I liked him, but let me tell you, we're in this for keeps, we done kilt a sheriff, and now Skinny. I'll kill the whole lot of you for five-hunnert dollars. I ain't never had that much money in my life. Split up four ways gives us each over a hunnert dollars."

Skinny's brother, Phil rode to the place where he lay. He dismounted and knelt down by his brother's body. Picking his head up, he placed it in his lap. He knew Pokerface was mad. His blood was boiling inside, but he knew that to fight him now would be his demise, also.

He and Jerome, a tall man and heavy built, buried him beneath some timber and rocks to keep him safe from the animals. Then they said a few words over him, and the group moved on. Phil kept a tight lip.

The night wind howled through the mountains.

CHAPTER 35

A SHOOT-OUT INSIDE MATT'S CAMP

It took them three more days in the saddle before the bounty hunters, turned killers, found Matt and his men. From a vantage point, the men sized up the group. Four men against twenty or more. The odds were too great for Pokerface's group.

"Which one is this here Matt fella?" Pokerface asked himself aloud. "Wil Andersen. Yeah. He's gotta look like his Pa, big and mean looking. I remember him real good. Gotta look like him."

The men dismounted and waited. They began talking among themselves. Phil said, "What we need is a surprise move on the camp. We got a full moon tonight, why not wait til then?"

"Yeah," Pokerface agreed. "When they camp."

That night, the cattle were restless and the moon was shining at its fullest. It was a night made for a stampede, and it was their plan to cause one. The men moved slowly towards the cattle. They could see the flickering light of the campsite just ahead.

Voices were low around the camp, as not to stir up any unnecessary noise. The drovers rode easy around the cattle. Some hummed a tune, it seemed to calm them down.

Pokerface looked back at the men, took out his blanket, held it high, and snapped it. The other men did the same with their blankets while Pokerface spoke softly as not to be heard by others, "Chase them! Chase them!"

The cattle moved feverishly. The drovers, attempting to gain control once more, moved quickly to steer them back towards the camp. Most of the men in the camp moved to their horses and joined them. It was going to be a long time before they would bring them under control.

Matt and a few men stayed behind. Matt knew someone outside the camp was to blame; it was a strong hunch he had learned in the cavalry. He elected to wait and see.

Carefully, the men took up positions inside the camp. Only Matt, Fong, Fong's helper, and two cowboys stood in the light of the fire.

Pokerface Jack and his group felt their plan had worked. Now the task was to move in quickly, find Matt, and take him. They would kill him if necessary, as the reward was for him dead or alive. The problem of course was the fact that they still did not know which one was Matt.

"You in the camp," Pokerface yelled out. "Can we come in?"

"With your hands above your heads," Matt answered.

Only Pokerface and Art moved into the light to meet Matt. The others stayed outside the camp for a quick ambush. "Hell, mister, we came to help you. We were jest ridin' here from Bozeman."

"Hands over your heads, or we'll be forced to kill ya."

Pokerface and Art rode in with their hands over their heads. "We'd be damn fools to try to spook your cattle and then come ridin' in like this, now, wouldn't we, mister?"

"Why didn't ya ride out after them?"

"Wanted to let you know we're here to help. Bein' out there in the night, your men might 'av shot us for bein' cattle thieves. Which we ain't."

"What about the rest of your men out there?"

"We're all by ourselves, mister. Honest."

"He tellin' the truth, Dan?"

Dan, and a few of the wranglers brought in the other two bounty hunters from outside the camp. "I've got two others."

"Wanna change your story, friend?"

Pokerface swallowed real hard, and said, "Well, ya got us. We wanted to find out who you were before we rode all the way in. Now, that's a fact. Now, seein' how you look like you got control of this cattle company, well, we feel better already."

"Not hardly. Drop down!" Matt ordered.

Pokerface and Art stopped short of spurring their horses as Matt cocked his gun.

The other drovers let the killers know that they meant business thrusting their guns closer to their faces. Dan remembered the night he saw Long Hair and the others shoot Wil in the back. It was a similar night like this. He told one of the wranglers near him, "Watch Matt's gun. Draw and fire when you see it move. Don't wait."

"Now, why'd you spook our cattle?" Matt asked the bounty hunters angrily, biting his lower lip to keep him from losing his temper.

Matt's group stayed on their horses, waiting for Matt to make the next move.

"You Matt Andersen?" Pokerface asked, pushing his Stetson up over his eyes.

"Who's askin'?"

"Name's Pokerface. "You look like you could be him." Pokerface kept his hands high as he stared around the camp. "There's a reward out for you, if you are."

"A reward?"

"Couple hunnert dollars. Dead or alive."

"Still aimin' to collect?"

"Nope. Jest thought you'd like to know."

"Then you won't mind steppin' down and givin' up your guns."

"Well, now, if'n we did that, what would you'n do to us?"

"Good question. For spookin' our cattle, that caused us a day's wages for all my men, I suppose your horses and guns would help make up for it."

Phil spoke up, saying, "You'd do that, yet for us?" As if he was well pleased with not being shot.

Art stammered, "It's more'n fifty miles back to Bozeman, at least."

"Nearer a hunnert. Kinda make a man think twice about becoming a bounty hunter, wouldn't you say?"

Matt watched as Art began to bring his hands down.

"Don't any of you make so much as a twitch. Take their guns, Dan."

Instead, Pokerface spurred his horse. Turning, he galloped to freedom into the night. The rest of the killers, knowing their fate about killing the sheriff, pulled their guns, and began shooting. Their thoughts were about safety. Only Pokerface found a hole in which to ride.

Matt drew and cocked his revolver but froze. His finger still could not pull the trigger.

Dan's gun was out of his holster at about the same time, firing. Fanning it, he brought Art down.

The rest of Matt's men followed instinctively and fired at the remaining two. Their shots were accurate. Two would-be bounty hunters lay dead on the hard ground, another was wounded, but played possum. It was Phil.

Pokerface had his horse running swift and fast, as he escaped into the night. Only his shadow against the light of the moon kept him in sight for a while.

"Matt! He's getting away," Dan yelled out.

"Let him. Anybody hurt?"

Seeing that none of his men were injured in the fracas, Matt ordered the men, "Move their carcasses outside of camp. The rest of you help the others bring the cattle in."

Pokerface escaped the barrage of gunfire and headed back for Bozeman.

Matt stood watching him as he disappeared into the night. "That's one son-of-a-bitch I wanta catch up with."

Looking at Matt with his gun back in its holster, Dan asked, "Why?"

Matt heard the question, but pretended he did not. He knew the men's eyes were on him, and the question gnawed at his guts as well as theirs. "Why? Why couldn't I pull the goddam trigger?"

The early mist that next morning made things seem fresh and new, as if nothing catastrophic had happened the night before. The drovers had brought the cattle under control a few extra miles, fortunately towards Belle Fourche, and still caught a couple hours of sleep. Once the chow was grubbed down, the cowboys cleaned the campsite and mounted up.

The sun was barely up and shining when the men were all in their saddles and riding out. They left the dead for the animals of the woods. Unseen, Phil crawled away seriously wounded but his anger at Pokerface kept him moving.

CHAPTER 36

TWO HERDS JOIN UP

Russ and his group met up with Matt's company three days later. It was mid-morning, and he sighted Matt just over a ridge. He told his men, "Keep 'em moving. I'm riding out to meet Matt."

On seeing Russ coming, Matt turned and rode towards him. When he caught up with him, he was pleased at seeing the cattle following, now it was looking like a full herd.

"Lose any?" Russ was quick to ask.

"A few. Had a stampede three days back. How about you?"

"A couple, maybe. Good hands."

"Yeah."

"What happened out here?"

"You mean at our camp site three days back?"

"Well, that, and the sheriff."

"The sheriff?" Matt asked, looking more surprised.

"Found him shot up in the meadow. Two bullet wounds in the back."

"Dead?"

"Almost. We got to him just in time."

"Did he say what happened?"

"Nope. Hadn't come to. Couple of the fellas made a litter and took him back to a house we saw on the way up. Don't know if he'll make it, though. Shot up real good." Russ took his hat off and wiped the inside with a handkerchief he took from his back pocket. "Found another one out there in the meadow by the sheriff in a make-shift grave. Skinny Henry, wrangler from one of the other ranches."

"Did the sheriff kill him?"

"Could be. Three more at your camp site."

"Three? Should 'ave been four."

"Nope. Only three."

"One must have been playin' possum," Dan suggested. "One of our guys missed."

"With all that shootin', couldn't see how?" one of the drovers said.

Another retorted sharply, "I noticed Matt didn't shoot his iron."

Matt stood up in his saddle, looked at the man, slapped his holster with the palm of his hand, and rode past him.

"Four dead bounty hunters. What happened to Skinny? Did the sheriff shoot him?" Dan continued.

"Not likely. Shot in the back just like him," Russ answered.

"His own men shot him?"

"Appeared so."

Matt stopped and turned back to the group. "They're after my hide. Puzzling how they know'd where to find me," he said.

"Probably my dumb fault," Russ said, apologetically. "They rode past us a day into the ride, and being friendly, asked about you. I knew a couple of them from town. That Skinny, the one in the meadow. Meek as they come. Gambling chums, ya might say. Said they were told by Mrs. Wrisley that he was out this way. I told them about your group being four days ahead. Didn't think anything was wrong seeing they had talked with Mrs. Wrisley."

"Trust your neighbors, but don't tear down the fences."

"Huh?"

"Old Chinese proverb, Russ. Anyway. One got away, before the shootin' began. Mean-looking cuss. See him?"

"That'd be Pokerface. Ain't seen him since he rode by."

"Pokerface is a mean lookin' codger. Have a feelin' I'm gonna meet up with him again someday."

Russ's men brought the rest of the cattle to meet up with Matt's herd, as the two men joined their group. All of the men relaxed again seeing reinforcements with friendly faces. Russ designated himself to ride point, knowing where they were headed, and the best way to get there.

"I see you've made good time. Stampede moved them this way, I take it.

Matt answered, "Dumb luck."

Talk went around camp about Matt not shooting his gun. One drover said, "He drew it fast, and cocked it. Hell, I thought he'd take them all on. But he froze. Dan was the one who shot the first one. I knowed I kilt one, cause he fell."

"Hell, they all fell. I emptied my gun, but don't mean I hit anything," another drover said,

"But I tell ya, he stood there frozen. When it was all over, he still stood there with his gun in his hand. His hand was quivering. He was scared shitless."

Dan walked over to the man who made the last remark and ran his fist into his stomach. The man folded up. Dan brought his fist across his face, breaking a tooth.

Two of the men pulled Dan away from him.

Freeing himself, he stood over the man.

The man was bleeding and looked afraid at what Dan was about to do next.

Dan reached down and picked him up.

"Matt accidentally killed a boy in Texas that was barely fifteen. He hasn't shot his gun since, probably never will, but let me tell you somethin'. You ain't ever gonna see any man faster'n him." He walked away and left the men to regroup themselves.

They doubted Matt's ability to lead from that moment on, relying more on Russ and Dan for their leadership.

The cattle brought a good price in Belle Fourche overall, it was a good drive. They lost very few head on the drive, which meant a good profit. What really made them happy was the fact that they had made the drive and would get back to the Double-O in time to save the ranch.

Everyone assumed that Matt would be staying, although at this point they did not want him for their boss. Even though their feelings were against him, no one let Matt know. Dan sensed it though.

The men were liquored-up real good when it came time to ride home, but ride they did. The morning was crisp with the cold Montana air, but by now Matt was used to it. It was not a wet cold, but it was cold just the same. The cold helped keep Matt's eyes open and helped him stay on the ride. The effects from the drinks took its time to wear off.

It was many days when they returned by the place of ambush. The sun set high in the azure blue sky speckled with a few clouds. The wind had a chill to it, but not enough for any one to need a jacket.

Some of the men who had known the sheriff for years, talked at times about his fishing in the woods this time of season.

Dan and Matt rode ahead to the house where the sheriff was taken.

Bob and Shirley Miller were dirt farmers, who had taken the sheriff in. When they were asked about him, Bob said, "We couldn't do anything for him, so we took our buckboard, and drove him to ol' Doc Shellenberg's down the road."

Matt asked, "Where might that be?"

"He's not there anymore," Shirley answered politely. "We checked back with him a week later and found out that the marshal dropped by and took him away. Said there was a good doc in Virginia City that he knew."

Russ asked, "Then he's in Virginia City?"

Bob said, "Spec so. Doc said he's got a sister living there."

CHAPTER 37

THE REWARD

It was noontime in Bozeman. Deputy Bill Saunders was in the sheriff's office having his lunch when Pokerface entered. Pokerface was well known, but not well liked in Bozeman. One man who had a very distinct hate for him was the deputy. His dislike for him was for no other reason than that he was a dirty, smelly vagrant, who used more cuss words than were in the dictionary and looked like he had been raised in an outhouse.

"Afternoon, Deputy," he said, grinning, and out of breath.

"You see something funny?" asked the deputy.

"No sir."

The deputy rose and walked over to Pokerface. Pulling his revolver, he said, "You're under arrest, Pokerface."

"Huh? What'd I do? I didn't kill no one. Honest."

"You almost did. You son-of-a-bitch." He took his gun belt from Pokerface's waist and pushed him into an opened cell, and locked it. "Had she died, you'd be in hell right now, mister."

Pokerface had forgotten about his ordeal with Beth, and how he attempted to rape her. "Oh, hell," he thought.

"You'll stand trial. I hope they hang you by your balls."

Then he protested. "What is it I was supposed to have done, Deputy?"

"You bastard. You know what you did."

"If I did, I wouldn't be askin' ya now, would I?"

"You tried to rape a woman, and almost beat her to death."

"I did? When was I doin' this?"

Bill went back to his eating, knowing it was futile to argue with a man like Pokerface Jack.

"You done got the wrong man, Deputy."

After awhile, Pokerface began to remember why he came to the jail in the first place. He went over the story in his mind which he had made up on the way to Bozeman. He started it out, saying, "You want this Matt fella in a big way, don't ya?"

"Has nothing to do with you."

"Nothin' ceptin' he kilt four of my friends."

Now the deputy had ears to listen. Putting his lunch aside, he went to the cell and asked, "What killin'?"

"You askin' a reward for this here Matt Andersen fella? Right?"

"I'm listenin'," the deputy said, becoming real interested.

"It's him, I know's it. He done shot and kilt Skinny. And all my friends."

"How?"

"Is there still a reward?"

The deputy's patience was being tried, but he would not give in. Walking over to the cell, he grabbed Pokerface by his filthy shirt and said, "You stinkin' vermin'." He let go and stood facing him. "Tell me what you know, Pokerface."

"There a ree-ward?"

"It'll go easier on ya."

"Alls I know is, we went to get him, and he ups and shoots us instead. I got out by my teeth. I hightailed it straight here." Pokerface watched the change of expressions which came and went on the deputy's face. "You goin' after him?"

"No. 'Spect the sheriff will when he returns."

Pokerface's grin changed to a quick frown. "Sheriff? Do I git out, now?" Pokerface asked.

"The lawyer will be around. You'll have your say. Then the judge will decide your fate."

"You got me a lawyer?"

"No. But the woman you tried to rape. She's a lawyer."

Pokerface sat down and put his face in his lap. "She's a lawyer?" he asked, regretfully.

"Relax, Pokerface," Bill said with a little sarcasm in his voice. "Your lawyer is a man. He'll be in first thing in the morning."

The next morning, Attorney Richard Aldergate appeared at the jail with a release for Pokerface.

"Mornin', Deputy," Aldergate said as he walked into the jail. "You're holding one Pokerface Jack Smythe on a charge of rape," he said as he laid his briefcase on Bill's desk.

"That's him in the cell, Mr. Aldergate," Bill replied.

"I have a release for him from Leonard W. Stanford, our circuit judge. Please see that he is released."

Bill received the papers from Aldergate, and said, "He's a rapist."

"Where are your witnesses?" Aldergate asked, closing his briefcase.

"We have none," Bill replied again.

"You have your job to do, Deputy. I have mine. Please release him."

Bill took the keys from his desk drawer, and with some reluctance, he opened Pokerface's cell and released him.

"Thank you," said Aldergate.

Pokerface didn't spend any time asking questions, he simply looked at Aldergate, then at Bill, smiled and headed for the street.

Aldergate left immediately after him, saying, "Good day, Deputy."

Bill stood at the empty cell and looked down at the papers in his hand. Throwing them hard on his desk, he exclaimed, "Damn!" Walking to the door, he stood for a moment until Aldergate had disappeared, and he watched Pokerface head for the Golden Eagle Saloon. Bill slammed the door, walked over to his desk, and sat down.

CHAPTER 38

THE LADY LAWYER

Although Matt still felt resentment from his men, it was a pleasant ride back to the Double-O Ranch. The cowboys made it to Belle Fourche and back with two days to spare before Thanksgiving, 1882.

Matt felt good about the drive and made it as planned per his mother's request. He knew she would be pleased. If for no other reason, he did it for her. Now, after learning from Dan and Russ how the men felt, he would be turning the ranch over to the cowboys, and heading back for Waco.

When they reached the ranch, Jean and the two ranch hands that had stayed behind went out to meet them. It was not a happy reunion. Matt sensed heaviness in the air about them.

Jean stepped forward to greet them. "The sheriff was here, Matt, looking for you. He knows who you are."

Dismounting, he eyed the other wranglers as he addressed Jean, "He found me."

Russ added, "The sheriff got shot out in the meadow."

"Oh, m'lord."

"He's all right, I suppose. Marshal has him in Virginia City at his sister's. We got four of his would-be killers."

"Bounty hunters?"

"More like greeders. They jest wanted a quick way to make money. Not fighters." Matt stopped for a moment and asked, "You saw them?"

"Briefly. They stopped by. I told them nothing. But they saw by the tracks that you men had gone on a drive. They followed your tracks."

"I know. Russ told them where to find me."

Matt saw a look in Jean's eyes that sent chills down his back. "Where's Beth?" he asked.

"Oh, Matt. Something awful happened."

"Is she hurt?" He could tell something happened by the tears in her eyes. "What?"

"She was ambushed, and we found out it was the same men. They beat her and tried to rape her. She was hurt pretty bad when we found her. She's at Lucy's Boarding House in town."

"She's at the other end of town," Russ added.

Eyeing the older ranch hand, Matt told him, "Git me a fresh horse."

"You've been in the saddle for weeks," Dan quickly reminded him.

The words flew past Matt as he dismounted. He walked over to the horse trough and threw his head fully into it and doused himself with plenty of water, refreshing himself.

Fong ran to prepare some food for his trip. Within minutes Matt and Dan were on the road towards Bozeman.

The other riders had made their outhouse stops, came out, and just watched.

Matt was fast to say to them, "Bed yourselves down for the night. This ain't your concern." He knew they were not interested in helping him.

The men walked to their bunkhouse, not looking at Matt.

All except Russ.

"I'm comin' too," he said.

"You're needed here with the men, Russ. We'll be back in a coupla days."

Before Matt's command could be obeyed, Russ was riding with the two cowboys towards Bozeman. "I have a feelin' you're gonna need me."

Jean waved her apron in the breeze as she saw them ride. "Beth's gonna be all right."

It was almost night by the time the trio reached Bozeman. Lucy's Boarding House was the only one in town good enough for a lady. But like Russ said, it was on the other side of town, which meant they would ride through Bozeman where they would be seen.

They rode easy, as not to attract attention.

However, riding past the saloon afforded the one Pokerface a good glimpse of them. He had anticipated their riding in, and he still wanted to get the reward. He stepped outside and watched as to where they were headed.

They turned into the boarding house and, tying their steeds to the hitching post, they made inquiry at the front desk. They were told that her room was one with a back door as the entrance. They slipped around the backside of the house.

Pokerface walked in the shadows down the street towards the house and watched them. He figured Bill was going to need help in arresting them, but he did not want to be a part of it.

A dim light let Matt and Dan know that someone was home. Matt's knock on the door was soft but rapid.

On the other side was a lady frightened by the noise of the knock. "Who is it?" she asked.

"Me, Beth. Matt. I've got Dan and Russ with me. Are you all right?"

"Just a minute, Matt."

She eased herself out of her bed and turned up the kerosene lantern beside her. The light flickered, then glimmered, and revealed her beautiful, fine figured body.

Lingerie draped her breasts, hips, and thighs as she slipped her thin sheer robe around her shoulders and tied it at the top. She was a complete lady.

Her look in her vanity mirror revealed some healing scars across her face. She still had the blackness that prevailed under her eyes, and across her nose.

She opened the door and greeted the trio with sleepy, teary eyes. For the moment, between opening the door and saying "Hi", Matt could see her silhouetted figure through her gown and quickly turned away. Taking his hat in his hand, he ushered the other two to stay in the hallway, covering Dan's eyes who was about to enter the room.

"Hi," was all he could muster.

She threw her arms around him with a welcomed hug and a kiss, and shrugged a little from the pain she felt in her side. "Oh, Matt. It's good to see you. You too, Dan. Russ." Then realizing the lateness of the evening, she asked, "But why so late. You could have waited until morning."

"Put something on. We gotta talk."

He gently ushered her back into the room, closed the door, then stood on the outside with the other two.

A few moments passed, and she reopened the door, inviting the three inside. She was dressed in her jeans and a shirt, which clung tight to her breasts.

Pokerface ran as fast as his short legs would carry him to get Bill at the jail. Convinced of what was happening, Bill rounded up some men to be deputized.

Pokerface's mouth kept flapping while this was going on. "We got the sheriff's killer. And I get my reward."

His whinny of a laughter drove Bill into a slow anger. "Shut up, Pokerface." But the damage had been done. Most of the townspeople knew the sheriff and liked him. Over the past thirty some years, they came to know him well.

Pokerface's flapping lips also led them to know that this was possibly the same Matt who was in that robbery. "He's the same fella who helped rob that freight office twenty-four year ago. Our sheriff killed his brother then."

Bill got two men and walked back over to the jail. There he administered the oath to each of them as deputies under his jurisdiction.

The crowd of men gathered. It was becoming a mob.

Once inside Beth's room, Matt said, "Jean told us about how you were attacked, and almost raped."

"Oh, Matt. I'm okay."

Gently putting his arms around her, he said, "Beth."

"Jean tell you about the bounty hunters?"

Pushing her gently away, he blurted out, "Bounty hunters?"

Beth turned her back to the men, unbuttoned a few of the top buttons of her blouse, and slid her shirt from her shoulders. The black-and-blue wounds from the fall showed much hurt along with bite and fingernail wounds from her attacker. The killer's teeth and fingernail marks were pretty much healed.

But Matt could see the soreness they left. The marks made him wince inside.

She rebuttoned her blouse and turned back towards them. "A lot of my pain comes around my ribs, which the doc has taped."

"Did they . . . ."

"They tried, but their lust got the better of them. When they were fighting over me, I got back on my horse and rode away. By the time they settled the fight, I was gone. They rode towards the Double-O."

"Those bounty hunters caught up to us. Three or four of them are dead. We killed 'em," Dan said.

"Why, Matt?"

Twisting his old hat in his hand, Dan answered, "They came into the camp and tried to kill us. That's why."

Beth shrugged at the thought and closed her eyes

"Guess they thought they would take Matt in for the reward," Dan continued. "We thought we killed four of them. Think one might have just been wounded. When Russ rode by later, he only found three." He looked at Beth, took a deep breath and continued, "It was hard, 'cause we knew some of 'em."

"One of the men fled," Matt added. "Slipped away into the darkness, leaving the others behind. Real coward. Got the others to fight, and he left."

"Which one was it. Do you know?" she asked.

"Pokerface Jack," Dan answered. "Real mean lookin', but a coward. Always a cheat at cards, and anythin'."

Beth gasped, realizing it was the same man who almost raped her. "Oh, Matt." After composing herself, she said, "The deputy, Bill, has been by every day seeing that I'm doing all right. Then, one day, Pokerface rode in hard and fast, and wanted the reward for your capture. That's when he got arrested. I had filed charges against him for attempted rape, and assault and battery."

Matt started for the door.

"Where you goin?"

"To the jail. I've got a score to settle."

"And to your grave. Stay here Matt. They've been waiting for you. Besides, they let him go days ago."

"Why?"

"The judge said it was his word against mine. No witnesses. Same old thing. A victimless crime."

"He did that to you, and they let him go."

Dan asked, "So why do they want Matt?"

"Said you killed the sheriff, and the rest."

"Didn't the sheriff make it?" Matt began to look bewildered.

"He died, Matt. Without gaining consciousness."

"Oh, hell." Matt hit his fist against the door jam, looking outside the window. "We didn't even see the sheriff. Russ found his body."

"As to shooting Skinny, his own men did it," Dan added.

"He said you shot Skinny in the back."

"He was shot in the back. But one of the others did it, before they came into our camp."

"Jest speculatin'," Russ suggested. "We came up two days after Matt's drive and found both the sheriff and Skinny shot up in the meadow. Skinny was dead and partially buried. The sheriff was still alive. Seems they had no need to bury him. Skinny's grave looked like they were in a hurry. Two of my men made a litter and carried the sheriff to the nearest house for help.

Dan assured her, "He was alive. Shot up pretty bad. Two holes in the back. Same size as the one that got Skinny. Same person did it, I 'spect."

"Same coward," Matt said. "The marshal took the sheriff to Virginia City."

"You men met the marshal then?"

"No. Some people we met on the trail took the sheriff in. Tended to him. Later, when the marshal dropped by, he took him to Virginia City to get patched up."

"All over some damn reward money," Matt said. "Who did it? And why?"

"The Reverend Riordan," Beth affirmed. "The minister who was killed in the robbery. Well, his son put up a five-hundred-dollar reward on you, Matt. Dead or alive."

"All bullshit. He didn't know it was me." Turning back to Beth, he said, "But why would the Sheriff come after me, when he knew I had to come back?"

"Maybe he wasn't after you. Maybe he was after the bounty hunters, to stop them from getting you," Dan again suggested.

Beth's eyes opened wide, and she said, "The letter. Matt. There was a letter. Your mother gave me a letter and made me promise to give it to the sheriff. I gave it to the Sheriff when he came out to see you.

"What'd it say?"

"Didn't read it. The sheriff rode away with it without telling me what it said. But he claimed that it cleared you. He knew who you were all along, and that you were not dead."

"He did?"

"He knew that the body he brought back to your dad was not you because of a leather bracelet that was missing on the right wrist. The one your dad gave you on your sixteenth birthday. That leather bracelet you're wearing now. He confided that to your dad."

"That means I stood a chance of being cleared."

"No. The Sheriff said you probably would have been killed. Lynched. That's how mad the townsfolk were. They wouldn't have listened to reason."

"The hell they wouldn't have."

"What, Matt? That you were mixed up in the robbery as much as Lukas? You were in town with your brother. Remember? You couldn't be found when Sheriff Wiseman brought back the body."

CHAPTER 39

THE ARREST

Crowd noise began to be heard outside. Matt watched out the window as the deputy came walking to the door with the men he had just deputized.

Dan fanned the kerosene lantern out with his hat, while Russ ran to the door and looked outside.

A mob of men had gathered outside with lit torches. One of the citizens yelled out, "Send the killer out!"

Bill demanded, "Send him out, Beth! We know he's in there!"

"Oh, my lord. It's Bill. And he's got the rest of the town up in arms." Beth said, as she looked out the window.

Matt fell to the floor and pulled her down with him. "Get down. All of you."

Russ said, "Let me see what I can do, Matt. They don't have a quarrel with me."

"You didn't come along to do my fightin' for me," Matt said. "I'll go out."

Before Matt could stop him, Russ moved towards the door and yelled out the window. "Hold it. This is Russ Thompson. Foreman of the Double-O. I'm comin' out."

Bill barked back, "We want Matt Andersen, Russ. Not you."

"Hell, Bill. I know that. I jest figured you oughta know somethin' before someone gets hurt."

"Send Matt out. You stay."

Matt said to Russ, "They're not in a listenin' mood, Russ. Stay out of it, I'm tellin' ya." Looking around in the darkness he asked Beth, "Is there any other way out?"

"Afraid not, Matt. You'll have to give yourself up."

Looking at her beautiful face as she expressed concern for him, Matt yelled, "I'm comin' out."

"Throw your guns out. All of you."

Dan watched Matt unbuckle his gun belt. It was the first time he ever saw Matt take off his gun. "Matt."

"I don't want anyone hurt, Dan. Beth, you stay here and stay down. I'm goin' out alone, and when it's safe, you can come out. Agreed?"

Beth stood up and yelled out, "Deputy. This is Miss Paterson."

"Don't want you, Beth. Just Matt," Bill called back.

"I'm his counselor, Deputy. If you take Matt, then you take me." She began walking towards the door.

Matt moved between her and the door, keeping it shut with his body.

"Since when, lady?"

"Since right now, Mister Andersen. You're in deep trouble." Beth's words were those of warning. "They've come to arrest you, Matt. They know who you are. You go out there without me, and they'll think they have a license to shoot you and ask questions afterwards."

"Makes sense, Matt. Russ and I will go with her," Dan agreed.

Matt dropped his chin and moved away from the door. He watched as Dan and Russ slid out the door with her, and then he closed it. He watched them from the closed door, but could not make out what they were saying.

Soon, Beth came back to get Matt. She opened the door and said, "They seem ready to listen, Matt. Come out with me."

Matt eased his body out the door with his gun belt in his right hand held above his head.

The deputy held his shotgun aimed at Matt with both hammers cocked. His eyes gave Matt all the warning that was needed.

"Drop your gun belt. Now!"

Reluctantly, Matt threw his gun belt down. Looking at Russ and Dan, he said, "He's the law. Let's see what the law wants."

Two of the men took Matt violently, and tied his hands behind his back, wrapping the rope around his arms.

"Now, I'm going in with you," Matt cried out. "Cause I favor the law, I'd jest as soon fight 'ya What you got is hate and vengeance. God only knows why you're throwing it all at me, but you are."

"He killed our minister. Hang him!" someone in the crowed cried out loudly.

"Move it. We got a rope for ya," a citizen said, pushing him off the porch.

Matt looked towards Dan and Russ and saw some men ushering them over to the jail. The streetlamps gave little light for him to see what was happening to them. The bigger light came from their torches. He was accustomed to little light in the army. Now his trained eyes gave him the edge on the mob.

The same man that pushed him knocked the Stetson from Matt's head, while a noose dropped over his head.

With his arms tied behind his back, Matt was led to a tree that, ironically, stood outside the Golden Eagle Saloon across from the freight office where he saw his brother gunned down twenty-four years earlier.

Matt's mind went quickly back to the shot that killed Reverend Riordan. The town was smaller then. Now the freight company was a little larger. But it was the same freight company that his brother and Jeff had set out to rob.

Matt was taken from the deputy's hold, pushed and shoved to the front of the saloon where the tree stood. Its limb looked as if it had hung other men at other times.

Matt tried to see who was yelling, but because of the tugging of his rope, it was impossible to catch even a glimpse. It was a man's voice though.

Another familiar voice cried out, "He killed Skinny." It was that of Pokerface Jack. "He shot the sheriff, too." The deputy tried to recapture control of the mob, which, because of Pokerface's yelling, he had lost. He fired off one chamber from his shotgun, which bought their attention for a moment.

"He'll hang for it, but not this way. Now all of you go home. I'm the actin' sheriff, now."

"They were good men," the man with a shotgun yelled.

He was a stout man with red hair and a red beard. He acted more pious than anyone, and wanted blood spilled for any sin. He believed Matt to be a killer and needed to die. He yelled out, referring to the bounty hunters. "Hard, honest working ranch hands." He walked up to the front of the crowd, spit on Matt, and said, "He killed our sheriff. You heard Pokerface."

Matt tried to say loud enough for them to hear. "He also said that he and four others rode out after us, too? Bounty hunters." But the words were just drowned out in the jeers and cries from the crowd.

Beth walked up to Matt and reached for his right hand. She clasped her hand inside his letting Matt feel her warmth and love. Pointing at Pokerface, she addressed the crowd, even though she sensed the futility of it. "Will you believe it when I tell you that that man tried to rape me?" She pointed to Pokerface.

Matt's eyes saw steel again in anger as he envisioned what had happened to Beth, and that Pokerface was in the crowd cheering the mob to kill him. His teeth grit hard as he held his anger in. Thinking to himself, he wished he had known about Beth when he met up with Pokerface the first time. It would have salved his conscience of having to take their lives. Now, he was feeling justified that the others were killed. He continued to look hard into the crowd for Pokerface.

One of the ranchers cried out, "Shut up, woman."

As they drug his body away, she followed them, talking along the way. "Know this. I was riding to town and they chased me up into the hills and spooked my horse out from under me. Then they tore my clothes off and fought over who was going to get me first. They rode off and left me for dead. I've got busted ribs and teeth marks across my body. Want to see them?" Her words went into thin air.

In shaking anger, mostly from fear, the rest from rage, the red-bearded man swung his shotgun at Matt, aiming to knock him down.

The barrel hit Matt's arm hard, but he remained standing. Matt felt great pain as he said, "Mister. You use that on me again and it'll be the last thing you'll ever do."

"You heard him. Let's hang him, now," the red-bearded man yelled out.

The mob pushed him harder towards the tree.

Bill fired the other chamber and brought the mob to a halt, again. "Now, I'm ordering you to disperse."

"That was his last charge. Take him!" a voice yelled out.

Beth watched in horror as the mob knocked Bill down, and took Matt to the tree. As she tried to go to his rescue, she was turned around by two men who told her, "Keep out of it, woman."

Another woman from the sidelines took her back upon the sidewalk.

Pokerface took charge now, grasping a good hold of Matt's arm and pulling him towards the tree. "You see. You're gonna hang for killin' Skinny."

A buckboard was brought over to the tree, and Matt was forced into it. As one of the men threw the rope over the branch, two other men kept Matt from falling. The noose tightened around his neck.

Pokerface looked uglier than sin in the sight of Matt as he asked him, "Got any last words, killer?"

With his strength almost gone, Matt said, "Go to hell!"

Bill regained himself, and seeing Matt in the buckboard with the noose around his neck, he felt a sense of responsibility he had never felt before. He was the sheriff, now. As sheriff, he was the law. If he was going to represent the law, he had to do it now.

It was that strong sense of sudden responsibility that made him push through the crowd with his revolver in the face of the first man who tried to stop him. "Break it up. I said, break it up!" He grabbed the shotgun from the red-bearded man and shoved it at the mob. Then, pointing the barrel skyward, he pulled both triggers, and threw the shotgun back at the man. "Now get home." Reaching the buckboard, he jumped up, knocked Pokerface off, and stood facing the two men who were holding Matt.

"I'm the law." He drew his revolver and fired at the feet of two men from the crowd who started towards him.

Another man started at him and was brought down by a burst from Bill's '44 which struck him in the shoulder.

"I said, I'm the law. I'll kill the next man who even breathes a dirty look at me. And that includes you two." He looked at the men holding Matt. He took one of their guns from its holster, and pointed it at them.

They released Matt's arms and jumped down from the buckboard. The wounded man was taken from the crowd by two men for treatment.

Pokerface lay on the ground looking up. He was not about to draw on Bill while his gun was out, but he continued to yell, "He killed the sheriff, and Skinny."

"And the law will see that he hangs. The law, Pokerface. Not you." Breathing hard, he took in a deep breath and said, "Now, all of you, get home.

"We'll let you lock him up, now, but if you don't hang him, we will," the red-bearded man yelled out.

Bill then freed Matt from the noose, shoved him off the end of the buckboard, and led him to jail.

Matt looked back at Bill as he began his walk towards the jail, and said, "Thanks, Deputy."

Bill looked angrily at Matt, still holding a lot of energy inside, said, "You'll hang. Now git."

The crowd began to slowly disperse, each man and woman looking carefully at Bill. This was the first time that they had ever seen his anger. They were not sure what he would do next.

Once inside the jail, he locked Matt in a cell. Turning to Russ and Dan who were waiting for him, he said, "You're both under arrest.

I'm convinced you're involved in this whole thing, too. Git in there." He gave them the second of two cells.

The two men gave up their empty gun belts and entered their cell.

"Well," Dan said, "Can anything else go wrong?"

Beth walked into the jail, and over to the cell, turned and asked the deputy. "That was some show, Bill."

Bill smiled back and hung up the shotgun he had confiscated from the red-bearded man.

"Circuit Judge still in town?" she asked.

"He is."

"He's the one who turned down my charge against Pokerface," she said. "He goes strictly by the book. So, gentlemen, my advice to you is to get a good night's rest, you're gonna need it for the trial." She gave Matt a smile and a wink. He knew she was now his attorney, as well.

As she walked out, she turned to Bill. "Thanks for saving them, Bill."

He felt the warmth in her voice he had yearned for so long. He knew now that he was earning her respect, any more than that would be wishful thinking on his part.

She left the jail and went back to her room.

Later, a figure approached the jail. He poked his head inside, and when he saw that Matt, Dan, and Russ were locked up, he straightened up and walked in. It was Pokerface Jack.

"Evenin', Sheriff." He smiled, showing his ugly teeth. "New sheriff, that is."

"Mister," Bill said angrily as he rose from his chair and walked around to the front of the desk where he confronted Pokerface. "You're one foot away from being stepped on."

"Hold it, now Sheriff. New sheriff." He tried to smile again to calm Bill's temper. "That man is Matt Andersen. Ain't he?"

"We'll find out in a court of law. No sooner," Bill answered.

345

"And there's a reward on him. Where's the reward money, Sheriff? New sheriff?"

Bill walked back around his desk and opened the drawer. Taking a wad of money out, he said, 'Right here. And it's going back to the Reverend. He took the reward off."

"Right there? In that thar drawer? No safe?" Straightening himself upright, he shouted in a shocking manner, "He did what?"

"There's no reward. Now clear out of my office before I jail you for vagrancy."

Bill took Pokerface by his collar and began to lead him outside.

"What's gonna happen to him?"

"He'll be tried for murder, and that could take a long, long time. Of course, he could get exonerated."

"Exon . . . You're using big words on me, new sheriff. What's that mean?"

Taking Pokerface by his dirty shirt, Bill threw him bodily out in the street. "It means, he might come after you. Now git home."

Pokerface picked up his body and placed his hat squarely back on his head as he watched Bill slam the door.

The jail was a dark and lonely place at night, with light shining through the shutters, and creeping under the door.

Down the street came the sounds of people laughing and drinking inside the saloon. A few men wandered along the middle of the street, while less than a few roamed the sidewalks. The dispersed crowd became ordinary men and women. For a Montana town, the scene was of serenity.

Pokerface went and joined the drinking at the saloon. Throughout the night, he drank by himself, no one came near him. Perhaps it was because of the stench of his body. Perhaps it was because of his boisterous attitude and loud voice.

"He killed the sheriff. Hang him," he kept saying. Perhaps it was because he had been beaten by the new sheriff. "He killed Skinny. Hang him."

He left the saloon in a drunken state of mind, but able to walk straight. Instead of going home, he sat down on the sidewalk across from the sheriff's office, thinking to himself. "The reward's in there. And I'm out here." The tedious job of thinking put him to sleep, and he slumbered on the deck of the sidewalk.

The sun broke the spell of night and brought a light mist across the town of Bozeman. The lonely figure of a man on a horse came into town.

At the sound of his horse traveling down the street, Pokerface's eyes opened slightly and saw the man riding slowly towards the jail. Pokerface turned and faced him. He could tell from the way he sat in the saddle, that he was Phil Jacobs, Skinny's brother, the man Pokerface had believed to have been shot and killed in the showdown in the meadows.

Pokerface squinted to get a better look as the figure approached closer to Pokerface. He stood up, started to smile, then grinned. "That you, Phil?"

Phil never said a word, but kept walking his horse. He was nervously happy to see the man he had come to kill for having killed his brother. He drew his revolver and held it in his right hand as he let it hang down by his side.

Looking intently at Phil, Pokerface could make out that Phil was leaning to his side which meant he was favoring a wound. He could make out a revolver in his hand. He reached for his six shooter and drew it. He held it pointed at Phil.

Phil had always been a patient man; one who seldom lost his temper. It was ingrained in him with his Jewish upbringing as a child. But now he had held his vendetta inside too long. He was taught, and he believed in the *lex talionis*, the biblical teaching of "an eye for an eye, a tooth for a tooth". He was his brother's keeper.

"This is for Skinny." He pulled the trigger of his revolver which sent a bullet past Pokerface's body, hitting the jail door.

At the sound of the shot, the jail door swung open, and Bill quickly ran out. He watched as Pokerface fired into Phil's body, bringing him down to the ground.

Frightened, Pokerface exclaimed, "Self defense, Sheriff. It was self defense. You saw it. He shot at me. He was gonna kill me."

The deputy went to Phil to examine him and found him still alive. Some of the town folks were awakened by the gun firing and were on the street. Bill said to them, "Quick. Get the Doc."

Phil was hanging on with hardly a breath. Yet he said in a determined voice, while pointing to Pokerface, "He killed my brother, Skinny."

"He's a liar. Don't listen to him," Pokerface yelled back.

Phil continued in broken sentences,

"He killed . . . the sheriff . . . shot him . . . in the back while . . . was on the ground," Phil continued in broken sentences.

Hearing these words, Pokerface grabbed Phil's horse and lit out of town.

Bill laid Phil's body down, drew his revolver and fired at Pokerface. His bullets passed into the air, and Pokerface, armed again with luck, disappeared.

Bill's deputies came around the jail in time for Bill to order them to follow Pokerface. Mounting their steeds, they took out after him.

Phil was barely holding on when Doc Phillips arrived with his black bag. Beth followed the doctor to see what was happening. While being treated in the street for a wound to his side, and another in his left leg, Phil repeated, "He killed my brother . . . and . . . and he shot the sheriff. Git him . . . please."

"Looks like you have to release your prisoners, Sheriff," Beth said.

"Don't tell me my job, Miss Paterson." Pointing to some of the men in the crowd which had gathered, he asked them to move Phil inside the jail.

"No need, Sheriff." Doc said. "He's dead."

The undertaker took over, and with the help of a few of the men, Phil was placed in a buggy and taken to the funeral parlor at the end of town.

Bill and Beth watched as the crowd began to disperse. It was mostly the same people who had been there a few hours before.

"Ironic, isn't it," Beth said, with her arms folded and still watching the crowd disperse.

"The crowd?" He nodded and agreed. "Yeah. One moment they have hate in their hearts and want to lash out at the first person in their way; the next moment, they're satisfied, and looking forward to having a plate of bacon and eggs."

"You gonna let your prisoners go?" Beth asked.

Bill turned and walked into the jail office where the three men were perched upon the bars waiting for the next move. "I still have to keep Matt, find out if he's Andersen or not."

"What's going on?" Dan asked.

"You're free to go," Bill answered, as he opened the cell for Russ and Dan, releasing them.

"You're staying," he said, looking at Matt.

Beth watched Matt's bewildered look.

"Skinny's brother just told us who killed his brother and the sheriff," she told him.

"Who'd he say it was?" Russ asked.

"Pokerface," Bill answered. "That frees you and Dan."

"And me?" Matt asked. "What about me?"

"I have enough circumstantial evidence to hold you for the murder of Reverend Riordan twenty-four years ago. If you're Matt Andersen, and I think you are, you will hang."

Beth swirled around at Bill and with a stern voice asked, "Why this personal vendetta, Bill?"

Bill sat on the edge of his desk and eyed both Beth, and then Matt. "It's not personal, Beth, jest that I am the law now."

"A damn good sheriff, but also a damn fool," she retorted.

"Maybe, but if he is Matt Andersen," seeing Beth's eyes ready to cut him off, he quickly asserted, "if he is, then he must stand trial for the killing of Reverend Riordan. And, I gotta tell ya, Beth, when this goes to trial, those townspeople are gonna want blood. They loved the Reverend."

The deputies returned empty handed, Pokerface got away. It had been a long hard night, and now the day had been spent in vain looking for a killer. Dan and Russ were set free, but Matt's life hung on Beth's professionalism and the acceptance of her by one judge of the court.

CHAPTER 40

THE HEARING

Judge Leonard W. Stanford was the circuit judge out of Virginia City for the citizens of Bozeman. He was a graduate student of William and Mary. The "W" in his name was for "Waldo" after the great writer and counselor, Ralph Waldo Emerson, for whom he was named. He was certainly a learned man of the law, even though he appeared to be too young to have this much knowledge. He was long and lanky, and awkwardly clumsy looking as well. He used his large pipe as a way of looking older, and he enjoyed puffing on it.

Sheriff Bill Saunders was summoned to the judge's temporary chambers, which was his hotel suite, early the next morning.

Bill described the shooting of Phil by Pokerface as self defense. But was quick to add that, "Phil Jacobs sought revenge because Pokerface killed his brother."

"Dammit, Sheriff. I am not interested in that case at this time. Your notes on that shooting substantiate a release of your prisoners. I want to know about this Matthew Andersen. I seem to have some papers filed earlier this morning by a Miss Beth Paterson, attorney for the defendant."

Bill looked astonished at hearing that Beth had already prepared her report to be filed with the court, vis-à-vis, Judge Leonard, the presiding circuit judge.

"Yes sir. I have him in jail," he replied.

"Is the prosecuting attorney present?"

"I don't know, sir. I'll have to check."

"I want to see the three of you in my office as soon as possible. Please see to it."

Bill stopped a moment before going. "Beth, or Miss Paterson, is a woman," he said.

"Yes. I surmised her to be a woman by virtue of her name. What is your point, man?"

"You are going to let her try a case here in Montana?"

"Sheriff. You are stepping on the very foundations of my court," the judge warned.

"Sorry, sir." Bill was unnerved at the tone of the judge's voice.

"You seem to think that a woman has no place in the courtroom."

"Yes, sir. I mean, I have never seen a woman lawyer before, sir."

"And just what did you think she was when you first met her?"

"Beggin' your pardon, your honor. I thought of her as a lady. One which I would want as a wife."

"And not as an attorney-at-law?"

"No sir. I don't believe a woman has any place in the courtroom. Your Honor."

"Why are we having this discussion, Sheriff?"

"Your Honor. It has to do with the killer, Matt Andersen."

"You have already identified him, and you have already convicted him?"

"I am convinced, sir, beyond all reasonable doubt that he and Matt Andersen are one and the same, and that he killed the Reverend Riordan."

"Why?"

"What do you mean?"

"Sheriff. I am a lenient man. Up 'til now, I have seen no cause to lose my temper, but you are trying me. Now, before I do something violent, get out of my chambers, immediately, and bring back the parties in question. Do I make myself perfectly clear, Sheriff?"

With that reprimand, Bill turned and left the judge's hotel suite, and temporary chambers, and had his two deputies look for Richard Aldergate, the Prosecuting Attorney.

He went to Beth's room, and not finding her there, went back to his office to retrieve Matt. Beth was there talking with Matt.

"Beth. I'm glad I found you. The judge wants you and Matt in his chambers, his hotel room. My deputies are getting Richard Aldergate."

By mid morning, Matt stood before Judge Stanford, who was still smoking his pipe with great enjoyment. Richard Aldergate, the prosecuting attorney, and Beth, the attorney for the defense were all present. The sheriff stood by the door.

The Judge began the questioning.

"Mr. Jorgensen. This is a preliminary hearing, and not a trial, as some appear to deem it so. The court has only circumstantial evidence about this case, but perhaps enough to bring it to trial. I want to hear all sides of the case before I decide whether or not this case warrants a trial."

Bill grit his teeth as he listened to the judge's seemingly whimsical excuse for wanting to get out of trying the case. He began to speculate in his mind that the judge had more important matters elsewhere and wanted to leave to attend them. He kept silent though.

Beth knew she had a strong case for Matt. She was not certain as to how Aldergate was going to come across with his argument.

"Mr. Aldergate," the judge summoned from his desk. "Are you prepared to argue your case against the defendant?"

"Yes sir, I am."

"May I ask, on what grounds you stand this man before me?"

"It's all in the papers I filed with you, your Honor."

"I know what you have written. I want you to tell me, yourself in your own words right now. How say you?"

"Your Honor. It has been brought to my attention that the defendant had been asked by the deceased Mrs. Annie Andersen to return to the Double-O Ranch to take over as the sole heir to her estate on condition that he prove himself to be a worthy rancher."

"And, Mr. Aldergate, will you address the court as to how this defendant would become the sole heir to the estate?"

"By virtue of the fact that he is her only surviving son."

"I object, your Honor," Beth said, raising her voice slightly.

"This is not a trial, Miss Paterson. You need not object. I will listen to both sides and decide if we should go to trial or not. Please continue, Mr. Aldergate."

Beth settled down and kept her face towards the judge. She listened carefully.

"Now, Mr. Aldergate. You know for a fact that this defendant is the late Mrs. Andersen's only surviving son? Or is it mere speculation?"

"Your Honor. Why else would he return from Texas to take over a ranch?"

"Did anyone say he returned from Texas? I don't think so."

Bill was beginning to think that the judge had some bias intention on his part for discussing the case in this manner.

Aldergate continued, "If it pleases the court, your Honor, may I offer my findings as I have filed them in my petition?"

"I know what you have filed, Mister Aldergate. I am interested in facts, not speculation. I am fed up with speculation. You're through for now." He looked into Beth's petition and read awhile. He knew at this point he was buying time. After a few moments, he said, "Miss Paterson. I'd like to hear your arguments if I may."

Beth snapped to attention at hearing this, and almost spread her lips into a smile.

"Your Honor. In the interest of a fair and expedient hearing, I would like to ask the court to rule a dismissal based on the mere circumstantial evidence offered by the prosecuting attorney concerning my client. It is all hearsay and contains no element of fact whatever."

"No, sir. Your Honor, please," Aldergate retorted. "What about the fact that he inherits the ranch on the merits of his capability to do so. And this to a stranger, and not a rightful heir, would be ludicrous in the eyes of justice."

The judge looked at Aldergate, and then pursing his lips, he said to Beth, "Miss Paterson, what say you in this matter?"

Perkily, she returned, still looking at the judge and not at Aldergate.

"Your Honor. It is correct that he is the lawful heir. The question is, your Honor, does not the testator have the right to leave real property to whomever he or she desires, be it to a legal heir, or a perfect stranger. No consideration is necessary in leaving an estate. If Mrs. Andersen chose Mr. Jorgensen to be the heir to her estate, then she and she alone had this right to so choose. And, your Honor, since there are no other contesting witnesses to the inheritance of this estate, I am sure the court can find no reason why the estate should not go to Mr. Jorgensen. Again, I ask for a dismissal."

"She has a good and valid point, prosecutor." The judge looked at Aldergate and waited for his response. After a quiet moment, the judge added, "Do you not have an argument against this, prosecutor?"

Twitching with his notes, he answered, "No sir, your honor. I do not."

"Nor I, prosecutor. And since you have no witnesses to attest to the identity of this person, other than his being Matt Jorgensen, I can not find any reason for holding a trial just because he inherited a ranch." Then, looking at Beth he added, "He did inherit the ranch, did he not, Miss Paterson?"

"That, your Honor, is another petition which I filed in your office for your review at your next earliest convenience. We will await your decision on that, hopefully soon, your Honor."

"I'm afraid I won't be here in the morning, Attorney. I will be leaving for Virginia City on the early morning stage. It's not far from here. You can set up a date soon and visit me there."

"Yes sir, your Honor," Beth smiled.

The door to his chambers was suddenly opened and a lady dressed in black entered. With the deputy's permission, she sat down. Once seated, she opened her purse, and gave an envelope to the deputy to give to Beth.

After giving it to Beth, Bill walked up towards the bench. He had stood all that he could while listening to the arguments. He asked permission to approach the judge, "Your Honor. May I be heard?"

"Certainly, Sheriff. But this hearing is over. Is it about another matter?"

"Now I don't know courtroom stuff, but I do know gun law. I am a lawman. What makes me a lawman is that I can recognize a killer and I ain't afraid to take him on. That man there is Matt Andersen, a killer."

"Sheriff, I appreciate your position as a lawman. Do you have any proof? Any evidence to substantiate your accusation?"

"No sir. Jest my gut reaction to this whole cock-eyed thing. I know this is Matt Andersen, the Andersen brothers were bad. They drank, they gambled, they ran around with every two-bit whore and prostitute in town. They're no good, and my job is to put them behind bars. He was just like his brother, all bad. Remember the Minister."

He walked around Matt and looked fixedly upon him with his eyes. "He was a killer in Texas. He just killed four men here. I'm the law. My job is to put killers in jail."

"And that is all you do. I'm the judge, Sheriff. I will make the decision concerning this case in the legal and proper manner for which I deem fit. Therefore, it is my findings, that under these circumstances, and in the best interest of Mister Jorgensen and the best interest of the State of Montana, I find there to be insufficient evidence to hold a trial to determine the identity of one Matt Jorgensen or Matt Andersen, however the case may be. By doing so, I hereby declare this hearing complete."

"Thank you, your Honor," Beth replied. Then reaching into her files, she continued, saying, "If it pleases the court, I would like to bring forth some evidence which will help clear up the good name of the Andersens. May I, your Honor?"

Judge Stanford looked bewildered at Beth for a moment. He then said, "Attorney, you have already won your client's case for him. To go any further, you could jeopardize it, and yourself." Then he looked at the prosecutor and asked him, "Since this does not concern the hearing, I am assured that you have no objections to her reading a letter?"

The prosecutor shrugged his shoulders and stepped away from the bench.

"Are you saying you have been withholding evidence?" the judge continued questioning Beth.

"Evidence, Judge Stanford?" Beth asked. "For which case? Certainly not this one where we are merely ascertaining a person's identity. However, where there is room for doubt, I see no reason why we can not clear up a person's past record and good name."

She brought out an envelope and gave it to the judge.

After reading it, he gave it back to her. "Where did you get this?" the Judge asked.

"It was brought to me by Sheriff Wiseman's sister, Mrs. Dorothy Phillips. She found it among his things when he died. Knowing that I was handling her estate, she brought it to me."

"You're just now presenting it as evidence, Miss Paterson?"

"She just gave this to me," Beth asserted.

"Will you please have this woman, Mrs. . . . ?"

"Mrs. Dorothy Phillips," Beth interrupted.

"Yes," the Judge said. "Please have Mrs. Dorothy Phillips step up here." He pointed to his desk.

Beth went to Dorothy, a woman in her fifties, pretty and well kept, and asked her to accompany her to the judge's bench.

"Are you Mrs. Dorothy Phillips?" the judge asked, as he watched her walk up to his desk.

"Yes, your Honor," she replied. "I am Sheriff Wiseman's sister."

"I see. And did you give this envelope containing this letter to Attorney Paterson?" the Judge queried.

"I did, your Honor," she again replied. "I found it in his coat pocket that he was wearing when they brought his body back."

"I'm sorry," the judge apologized, recognizing Dorothy was still grieving for her brother's loss. He looked back at Beth.

"May I read it, now your Honor?" Beth asked. Gaining his approval, Beth explained, "I gave this to Sheriff Wiseman, unopened. It was at Mrs. Andersen's request, Judge Stanford. In event of her death, I was to give it to him. She wanted to present it to him in event, as you say, a trial should ever take place concerning her son."

He looked at Dorothy, and said, "You may return to your seat, Mrs. Phillips. Thank you."

After Dorothy sat back down, Beth began to read the letter.

"26 September 1877"

The Judge stopped her and said rhetorically, "It's been five years? Please continue."

Beth read on,

"Dear Mrs. Andersen.

I take pen in hand to write you now because I want to clear my conscience of my sin. My wife died a few days ago and told me that I must confess. I promised her I would. But I never knew who to confess to.

So, here I am now. I am making my confession to you. I was gambling inside the saloon when your two sons were involved in a freight office holdup. Not Matt. But your son Lucas and another fella.

Your sons were playing poker with me. They lost. Matt stayed after Lukas went outside. He played another hand with me. I saw Matt walk up to Lucas to try and stop him. That's when the other man came out of the freight office. Matt tried to get him on the ground when the man's gun went off and killed the Reverend Riordan. Then shots rang out and Lucas went down, and the other man was shot right in front of us. I knew it was not Matt, because Matt was across the street on the ground.

I heard the sheriff and others looking for Matt. They never found him. Later I learn that Matt was killed. It was not Matt. It was another fella. I never heard about Matt since. But I know he was not killed.

My wife and I have since moved to San Antonio.

If this makes you feel better, I am a happy man. I look forward to meeting my Georgetta soon.

Yours truly,

Jan Olafsen, Storekeeper, San Antonio, Texas"

"Well, Sheriff," the judge said. "Looks like there won't be need of a trial for that Matt, either. In the event he should ever show up. Not with this kind of evidence. For right now, then, if there are no further arguments, I find no just cause for a trial, and I ask the Sheriff to release this man back to society where he rightfully belongs."

He looked at the sheriff and added, "If you ever need me, Sheriff, you know where I can be reached. Court adjourned. Thank you."

With that, he hit his gavel on the desk, leaned back in his chair, and relit his pipe.

After the hearing was dismissed, Aldergate gathered his papers and left the judge's room.

Beth left with Matt, and Bill followed, walking down the stairs of the hotel together. No words were exchanged with Bill, but Beth had loads of smiles for Matt.

Once out the door of the hotel, Bill saw Pokerface leaving his office with a fist full of money. He drew his Colt and fired at him, causing him to freeze in his tracks.

"Stop right where you are, Pokerface!"

Pokerface threw his hands up filled with the five-hundred dollars he had just taken from the sheriff's desk.

"It's mine, sheriff. I earned all of it."

"You jest stay put, Pokerface. Unbuckle your gunbelt nice and easy like, and drop it to the ground."

Pokerface had no intention of going anywhere while the sheriff had his Colt pointed in his direction, and he did as the Sheriff ordered.

Matt and Beth watched as Bill drew near to Pokerface.

What Bill did not count on was Pokerface's sudden release of the money to the wind.

As Bill's eyes watched the money blow in the wind, Pokerface drew a dagger from his boot and slid the blade into Bill's stomach.

Bill dropped his Colt and fell against Pokerface, bleeding.

Matt dove for Bill's colt, rolled over on the ground and was ready to shoot, but Bill's body came between him and Pokerface.

Matt watched Pokerface reach down with his free hand and pick up his gun belt, using Bill's body as a shield.

Pokerface removed his gun and brought it to firing level at Matt and began to squeeze the trigger.

Matt knew the test was still whether or not he could kill a man again. He felt his fingers begin to freeze around the trigger. His hand shook. He was feeling that moment all over again.

Dan and Russ had been standing at the hotel watching. They had their guns leveled at Pokerface but did not fire for fear of hitting the sheriff.

The sound of a pistol rang through the noontime air and dissipated into the sky. The .45 in Matt's hand was smoking. Pokerface hit the dirt with a bullet between his eyes. Matt's aim was sure and true as he stood there, the victor.

CHAPTER 41

A FREE MAN

The door to Beth's room was slightly ajar; now her hand pushed it open slightly to let it swing open.

Her body entered the room and filled it with her beauty. She paused in the center of the room, looked back and asked, "You coming in?"

Matt had a masculine grin on his face that betrayed his humor in this type of situation. He entered her room and closed the door behind him.

Beth pulled the curtains closed, turned, and looked at Matt standing in the middle of the room. "If you'll give me one moment, I'll change, and we'll ride out to the ranch."

"Take your time," was his reply.

She was quick to change and was back inside the room, fully clothed and ready for the ride to the ranch.

"Ready?" she asked.

"I suppose," he replied.

She noticed him favoring his left arm.

"Your arm. Oh, my gosh. I forgot all about it. Here, let's have a look."

With her help, he removed his shirt. She took the water pitcher, poured some water into the basin and began to wash his arm down with cool water. The touch was pleasing to her. "Your arm is swollen. How's it feel?"

"Better."

His eyes undressed her as she caressed his arm and stroked it with a cool damp rag.

She felt his breath on the back of her neck and began to enjoy it. Her thoughts were towards him at the moment, wishing they had more time to spend together before the ride to the ranch. She took her time tending to his arm.

He could move it with little pain. His right hand began rubbing her ribs. "Soreness gone away?" he asked.

"Mostly. That feels good." She turned inward towards him more, still holding his arm.

He pressed into her ribs slightly, bringing her body into his, finding no resistance from her.

She turned more into his arms and found his warm blue eyes staring into hers. Their lips touched gently. Parting them, each found the warmth of the other as their hearts pounded in unison.

A slight break gave her a chance to look into his eyes once more, and she whispered, "We've never really kissed until now."

"Did on the prairie."

"When?"

"When I took the cattle to Belle Fourche."

"Not like this." She resumed kissing him passionately as they fell to the floor.

"I have a bed."

"It'd be softer."

They laughed together, and in a moment of ecstasy, she whispered once more, "I heard you were the fastest."

He smiled, and looked into her eyes once more and said, "With guns, my dear."

EPILOGUE

THE RANCH GETS A NEW NAME

Once again, Matt had found favor in the eyes of the men at the Double-O Ranch, for word of what happened in town had reached the ranch before Matt and Beth arrived.

The ranch hands had prepared them a welcome.

Matt brought the team to a halt outside the main house where the ranchhands had proudly gathered.

Dan and Russ rode over to the buggy. "The men want to express their appreciation for you, Matt. And you, too, Beth," Dan said. "We knew you were the best. We jest wanted to see you in action."

Beth and Matt eyed each other and smiled. A hidden meaning inside that statement made them laugh out loud.

"What's so damn funny?" Dan asked.

"Nothing, Dan. We're just too damn tired to do anything but laugh."

"And, what about the ranch?" Russ asked.

"Well, Beth," Matt asked. "What about the ranch?"

"You did it, Matt." She looked at him, and then at Russ and Dan, and the other men. "Tomorrow, we're going to Virginia City to make it all legal. You men should be proud of Matt."

Some of the men mounted their steeds, while others busted open some kegs of rotgut whiskey and began drinking out of tin. All of them took their hog-irons out and began shooting them in the air, yelling at the top of their lungs. The horses and riders reacted to the excitement and enthusiasm that filled the air.

Dan exclaimed, "And, when you get back, Thursday's Thanksgiving."

Russ threw a bottle at Matt. "Pull a cork on that old busthead, Matt, and join us. You, too, Miss Paterson."

"Would you like it if I stayed?" Matt asked Beth.

"You proposing? I don't know if I want to get married. I sacrificed a married life and children for a law career."

He offered her the bottle and tilted it up for her, making sure some of it would spill and run down her blouse. Then he kissed her. "Not here, not now, but when the time is right."

"Can you live in this town? Bozeman?" Dan asked, as his horse reared on him.

"The Double-O? Pa named the spread, 'The Double-O'. Means 'shifted balls'. I remember as a kid, Pa said, 'you have to have shifted balls to run a spread'. Well, I guess I earned mine."

"I'm gonna change her name to 'The Double-R Spread'. The Ruby River will be my Brazos River."

"That mean you're gonna stay?" Dan asked.

"Well, Dan, can I bring in some longhorns?"

Dan gave out a yell that would have been the envy of any rebel as he shot off his .45.

Beth looked towards the new Double-R in the distance, and said, "Shorty would've liked that, and Mrs. Bickerdyke will be plumb tickled."

Matt held Beth close and looked around. He was finally home.

An excerpt from the next thrilling story in the Brazos series

THE MAN FROM THE BRAZ

PROLOGUE

THE DESTINY OF A FAST GUN

February 2, 1871

A perperson's destiny is next to impossible to see at the beginning of one's life, for certainly no one can ascertain what he will become as it is not a person's privilege to see. A "fastgun" was a euphemism that had not yet been established. To become a fast gun would certainly be a turning point in Matt Andersen's career, a career he had not chosen and for which he had not prepared himself, and as a man on the run, he called himself, Matt Jorgensen.

He would find out that his destiny was determined by a set of circumstances, none of which were under his control. But once he had attained the mastery of his calling, his destiny was sealed, and his life took on a totally new meaning.

For two men to come together under the umbrella of similar circumstances and forge a relationship together in time and space would be an act of God no one could understand or envision. Such was the case with Matt who became famously known as "The Brazos Kid", and Rod Best, Marshal of Abilene. How they met and became the best of friends, in spite of their fierce competitiveness in a business that called for guts and glory, would plum the depths of their exciting and romantic adven-tures which they shared together as two of the bravest gunfighters in the history of America's West.

One of the most infamous of days in the annals of Western folklore happened February 1, '71. Matt Jorgensen and his friend Steve Andrews rode into Waco, Texas where they were bent on spending the night earning some extra spending money playing that famous game of fortune, poker. Matt grew up in Montana and, with his brother Lukas, learned the game well enough to make some spending money.

Matt was now a professional hired gunman who, with Steve, his Civil War friend and companion, ran the Brazos Bar M Ranch south of Waco across the Brazos River. Both men were in their thirties. Matt stood six feet four inches, with broad shoulders. His eyes were steely blue, and he had a gentle smile, which befriended him to the ladies. He wore denim pants, a dark blue woolen shirt and a tanned leather vest. A loose bandanna covered his throat, and a gray Stetson fit his head real nice. Tonight, he just wanted to play cards.

Steve was a good-looking man with a bushy moustache and a full head of light brown hair hidden under his well-worn Stetson. His dimples let people around him know that he was also a gentle man like Matt, but firm. He was six-foot two straight up and down. He, too, wore a leather vest, but he wore his bandanna a lot looser than Matt, and his Stetson was black.

The men found themselves an active table towards the rear of the Green Slipper Saloon and offered to join in as soon as a certain chair became vacant. The chair the dealer was sitting in was Matt's favorite seat. He chose never to sit anywhere else, as an early acquaintance warned him to beware of card cheats and killers who walk behind unsuspecting players. Besides, he enjoyed having the wall to lean on from time to time.

"You can sit in right now, men," the dealer offered as he shuffled the cards. "Sit down."

"No rush," Matt replied, standing at the bar instead. "Two whiskeys!" he ordered.

"Suit yourself," the dealer continued. "Might not get another chance with all the cowpokes pouring in this time of night."

"The Red Garter's down the street," Matt replied. "They can go there."

"That one's filled up already. What are you two waitin' for, if I might ask?" The dealer started dealing the cards to the other two gentlemen.

"You're sittin' in my chair."

"Your chair? Your name's on it?"

"Nope," Matt answered as he paid for the drinks. "Thanks."

"Then why d'ya say it's your chair?"

"I never sit in any other."

"Never seen you in town before."

"I come in once or twice a month," Matt answered, swigging down his drink. "You're new in town."

"Been here a few weeks," the dealer replied, filling out the hands of his two players. "You won't play unless you sit in my chair, right?"

Matt turned and stood with his back to the dealer but watched his actions through the long mirror that hung behind the bar. Steve sipped his drink as he walked around the table watching the men play.

"You're superstitious, I'll bet," the dealer suggested, watching his two counterparts throwing down cards for a draw. "All right, mister," the dealer continued. "After this hand, I'll take the other chair."

The dealer gathered his winnings from the two gentlemen players and moved to the other side of the table, taking his money and cards with him.

"I've never heard anyone being so superstitious in my life," a player said as he watched Matt walk over to the table.

Steve sat in the chair next to him. "He's superstitious."

"I have," a tenor voice came from the far end of the bar. "I met a man up in Abilene that did. A marshal. Always sat with his back to the wall. Nothing superstitious about it. Just didn't want anyone to take advantage of him behind his back."

"That it?" the dealer asked, tossing a double eagle into the pot for the ante.

Without a reply, Matt sat down, threw in his ante, and then took a cigar from his leather vest.

"You don't say much," the dealer said as he began dealing out the cards. "What about your friend?"

"Let's play," Matt said, lighting his cigar.

"Sure, mister," the dealer replied, finishing up the deal. "Mind telling us your names?"

"Steve Andrews," Steve answered, peeking at his cards.

"Matt Jorgensen."

"Matt Jor . . ." the man at the far end of the bar said, almost spilling his drink. He was short, rather stout, sported a thin moustache and a goatee, and wore a black derby that suggested he wasn't a cowboy.

"The Brazos Kid?" he asked, looking at Matt.

"Sometimes called in my younger days," Matt responded with his eyes leveled to the man's hands dangling at his sides. He could see he didn't wear any guns. "Brazos to most, now."

"I hear you're one of the fastest guns alive."

"I'm a mite slower," Steve mused and titled his hat forward.

"My name's Kelly Williams, reporter for the *Waco Gazette*," the man said as he started to walk over to Matt's table.

"Who's faster?" the dealer asked.

"The marshal this man met in Abilene," Matt answered, letting out a ring of cigar smoke while he examined his cards.

"Not anymore, " Kelly said.

Matt took out his cigar, tilted back his hat, and looked straight into the little man's eyes.

"What do you mean, Mr. Williams?" the dealer asked, holding the deck of cards in both hands.

"He was killed in a saloon a few days ago. News just came in from the *Abilene Journal*, ready for the morning edition."

"Who was killed?" the dealer asked again.

Kelly watched Matt's face grow in anger. He shut up fast and walked back to his seat at the bar.

Matt threw his hand down on the table, rose and walked over to the little man. "What's his name?"

"You know who I'm talking about," Kelly said, taking a nervous sip of his beer.

"Who?" Matt demanded.

"Rod Best! The Marshal in Abilene."

"The hell he did!" Matt yelled at the little man, turning him around and picking him up by his lapels, almost hiding Kelly's face inside his coat.

"Here," Kelly said, "I've got my notes right here."

Matt turned loose of Kelly's coat and allowed him to reach into his pocket. His hand came out with a note pad, which he quickly handed to Matt.

The notes were scribbled in Kelly's own shorthand, so he had to read them for Matt. Putting on his spectacles, he took the pad back, and read aloud, "1 February '71, about 10 o'clock p.m., Rod Best entered Jason's Saloon … Abilene, Kansas … became drunk … involved with man's wife … husband shot Best before he could draw."

Matt stood silent.

"I know you were good friends; everyone knows, I suppose. What are you going to do, Brazos?"

The Waco and Northwestern Railroad left early the next morning from Waco, and Matt was on it heading for Abilene, Kansas to pay his respects to his old friend.

As the heavy black engine chugged along, leaving a plume of smoke and ashes strewn across the land abutting the tracks, his mind raced back to the time he had to leave his home in Bozeman, Montana just thirteen years earlier. It was the same year he met Rod Best.

It was a cold February evening, 1858, as chilled winds whipped through the Montana hills.

Matt turned from just having a serious conversation with his father, walked over to his mother, Annie and said, "I love ya, Ma."

His mother knew he had made his decision to leave.

Matt walked into the house for a last look at his brother, Lukas' body, which was draped on the floor with that of another man, Jeff Daniels, a killer.

Matt's father Wil, and Anse Peterson followed him in. Anse was the bartender at the Golden Eagle Saloon in town, and Wil's best friend. Having known Wil for many years, he watched the wild antics of Matt and Lukas as they grew up and often visited the saloon.

Matt knelt down and touched his brother's uncovered hand, and asked, "Can I help bury my brother?"

Anse answered him. "Best not, Matt. Sooner you leave, the better."

"He's right, son," Wil concurred.

His mother sobbed.

"Wish I hadn't shot that horse, now," Anse said.

"Where's the carcass?" Wil asked.

"I pulled it off to the side, and partially buried it with some weeds. Jeff said he'd finish it. Guess he never did."

Jeff was the no-good varmint who had talked Lukas into joining him in robbing the local freight company in town. The scheme failed, and Jeff and Lukas were killed. The town minister, riding by in his carriage at the wrong time, was also killed. Because Jeff was dressed in Matt's clothes at the time, the town folk mistook his shot-up carcass to be Matt.

Anse had shot Jeff's horse earlier because of a broken leg, and in town, Jeff took Matt's horse. This added to the evidence that it must have been Matt who was the second man killed in the robbery. If the horse's carcass was seen, it would have given rise that a third man was involved, and an investigation into who that third man was could have led to Matt, who was still alive and hiding.

"Damn," Wil said. "Can't take a chance. At light, you and Matt backtrack, and make sure it's buried deep."

"Yes, sir."

"And you, Son. When that's done, you're gonna head out South."

Matt stood up and felt Annie's warm embrace.

Annie looked over her son's shoulders towards Wil. "Why?" she asked quietly.

Wil put his big hand on Matt's shoulders and wrapped his other arm around Annie. "Cause, I love ya, Matt. That mean anything to you? One son's dead. I don't want both my sons killed."

Tears fell from Annie's cheeks.

Matt's tired body finally felt the pangs of weariness from running scared, the drink, and the beating from Wil's fists earlier when he first found out Lukas was dead. Wil's quick temper led to a beating. Wil forgot for the moment that Matt had nothing to do with the botched-up robbery, and that he could be implicated in it as well if he were caught. Matt was in town only to stop Lukas, but failed, and in all the excitement and gunfire, escaped unseen.

Still sobbing, Matt collapsed in his father's arms as Anse helped keep him from falling.

Anse helped Wil carry Matt to the back of the house and put him down on the bed where he slipped into a deep sleep.

Wil lingered over him for a while to assure his safety, and then he returned to the arms of Annie. Together, they kept awake. Anse sat on the porch and kept watch through the night.

Daylight was slow to come to the ranch that day, but before the winter sun had peaked its head over the nearest rise, Wil was on a hill digging the graves.

Matt and Anse rode down the road that led to town, as the sun had just broken the sheet of night.

Annie, dressed heavily with a long brown coat and scarf around her head, climbed the hill to join her husband. Looking out, she watched the shadowy figures of Matt and Anse ride away.

"He'll be back, Annie. Soon."

"I know."

Annie watched Wil. They were burying one son, and watching another ride away, and she never before felt that much pain in her heart.

"The cowhands shoulda gotten up by now. They can help you."

"I'd rather do it myself."

Annie stood there, watching Matt and Anse as they disappeared down the road. Wil stopped digging, grabbed her cold hand and held it tight as they watched the two men ride away.

A hard rancher, Wil bred and raised cattle as well as horses that earned him a decent living. His desire was for his sons to follow suit. He felt somehow now that he had failed them.

The first of the wranglers crawled out of the bunkhouse. Seeing Wil and Annie on the hillside, they quickly dressed and joined up with them. They had heard about the botched-up robbery before while putting the bodies in the front room. They were not aware of Matt's return, or of his having left. They believed that the two bodies being buried were those of Matt and Lucas.

Now, they carried the draped bodies in a buggy to the northern slope of the hill. The men helped finish the digging, in spite of Wil's resistance. Once the holes were deep enough, the men lowered the bodies gently into each of them, one at a time.

"They were shooting at Matt, too," Wil said softly to Annie as he held his arm around her. "If we tell the townsfolk, it was Matt, they'd lynch him. This way, two graves, two crosses. Matt and Lukas.

No one will know the better." He paused on the hillside and looked down the road one last time. "He tried to stop Lukas. That's good enough for me."

With the last clump of dirt on the graves, he whispered to himself, "I wish he could have stayed." Then he cried loudly, "Hell!" and threw the spade as far as he could.

Annie grasped Wil's hand and squeezed hard. "Ready, Wil?"

"Yeah." Wil nodded and returned to the freshly dug mounds. Taking off his hat and bowing his head, he said slowly, "Lord, bless our children. And forgive them their deeds. Both are in Your hands, now. Amen." One son rested there in the grave, and the other was riding away. The couple left the wranglers and walked down the hill together. At the bottom, they stopped, turned, and looked back at the hill. "They'll always be with us, Annie, Wil said hoarsely, "sharing a cup of coffee with us in the morning. And we'll still see them ridin' the range. They'll always be with us."

Annie leaned against Wil, wiped her face with her apron, and looked into the morning sunlight.

"I know that Wil."

Wil caressed her gently. "You can bet on it."

He looked again at the hill where two crosses stood, and thought, "If there was only another way."

The snow began to fall gently to the ground.

www.ingramcontent.com/pod-product-compliance
Lightning Source LLC
LaVergne TN
LVHW091528060526
838200LV00036B/522